THE SHADES OF
TIME AND MEMORY

THE SHADES OF TIME AND MEMORY

The Second Book of the Wraeththu Histories

STORM CONSTANTINE

TOR®

A TOM DOHERTY ASSOCIATES BOOK
NEW YORK

THE SHADES OF TIME AND MEMORY: THE SECOND BOOK OF THE WRAETHTHU HISTORIES

Copyright © 2004 by Storm Constantine

This book is printed on acid-free paper.

Map by Ellisa Mitchell

A Tor Book
Published by Tom Doherty Associates, LLC
175 Fifth Avenue
New York, NY 10010

www.tor.com

Tor® is a registered trademark of Tom Doherty Associates, LLC.

Library of Congress Cataloging-in-Publication Data

Constantine, Storm.
    The shades of time and memory / Storm Constantine.—1st ed.
        p. cm.—(The second book of the Wraeththu histories)
    ISBN 0-765-30347-7
    EAN 978-0765-30347-9
    1. Wraeththu (Fictitious characters)—Fiction. I. Title.

    PR6053.O5134S53 2004
    813'.54—dc22

                                                                    2004048044

First Edition: October 2004

Printed in the United States of America

0 9 8 7 6 5 4 3 2 1

This book is dedicated to Mischa Laurent,
highfather of Wraeththu fandom.

HADASS.

Camp

Caraway

Jasminia

ELHMEN

(SAHALE)

Lemarath

WRAKE

TAM

Kar Tatang

GIMRAH

Shappa

Strabaloth

THAINE

Ardith

Kapre

Clereness

Jael

Se.

FERIKE

Saphrax

FLORINADA

1993
Ellisa Mitchell

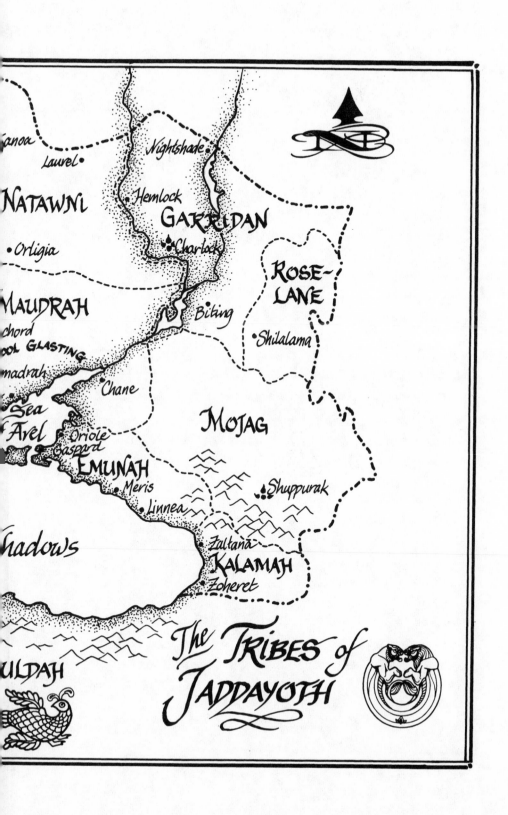

The Tribes of Jaddayoth

ACKNOWLEDGMENTS

I would like to acknowledge all those who have been with me on the journey through writing and producing this book, and whose help has been invaluable. First, thanks to Gabriel Strange and Lydia Wood, who have done so much to help me in various projects and Web sites; to Wendy Darling, for her immense and priceless input with my writing, the Inception online magazine; to Wendy again, and to Bridgette Parker, for creating the har Lisia, (protagonist of their Wraeththu Mythos novel, *Breeding Discontent*), and helping me incorporate his character into a couple of scenes in this book; to all the other writers who have contributed, and continue to do so, terms, scenarios, and characters to the Mythos; to my editors at Tor, Beth Meacham and Anna Genoese; to my agents Robert Kirby (UK) and Howard Morhaim (USA); to my husband, Jim Hibbert, for the zillion and one things he does continually to support and assist me; to Ruby, for her visionary artwork; to Taylor Ellwood, Paul Kesterton, and Ellen Nicholson, for their contributions to the dehara of Wraeththu (the "Invent-a-God" crew!); to Paul Cashman, for his long-term support and input; to my friends Mark Hewkin, Deb Howlett, Gill and Darren Pearce, Linda Price, Jon Sessions, Paula Wakefield, and Freda Warrington. Finally, a big thanks to everyone not named above who is part of Wraeththu fandom. There really are too many to thank by name, but you all know who you are.

The Official Storm Constantine Web Site:
http://www.stormconstantine.com

Inception, an online information service and fanzine:
http://www.inception-magazine.com

Forever, the Wraeththu fan-fiction archive:
http://www.angelfire.com/ca6/forever/

The prophet Athanorax of the Sulh was once asked: Are we now all that we shall be? He did not reply, but merely drew a line in the sand with the toe-nails of one foot. With the other foot, he stamped upon the line, until it could be seen no more, and then he walked away.

It is a fact that history is but a line in the sand, muddled by many feet, until the line itself can no longer be seen. There are those who remember it, and tell of what they saw. They say the line went this way or that. They say a scorpion ran along it, or perhaps a lizard. Others might say that the line it-self was in the shape of a lizard, but who can tell? There are some who profit by this state of affairs and become the shining stars of our race, and there are some who are doomed to be forgotten. Certain names are pur-posefully erased from the line, while others are remembered, when perhaps they should have vanished into oblivion. One thing is certain: Wraeththu will never be all that it can be, for the harlings of tomorrow will either look back upon the past with fond remembrance for a lost Golden Age, or believe that the times they now shape are far superior to all that went before. In each view lies striving and dissatisfaction.

Did Athanorax know the truth of it all? Was this why he made his faith-fully recorded statement about it? Again, who can tell? If he knew, he did not say. He climbed a mountain and stared at the clouds, or went to an inn and got drunk. All that remains is the question, and it is not the right one. Answers, in some ways, are easy. It is the question that eludes and slips away. The right spell, the right magic. All in the words.

—Wraeththu: the Dream, *by Ferminfex Jael*

The story of the Aralisian dynasty is the mythology of Wraeththu. Each character blazes from it like a comet. How much is truth? How much is fiction? Are gods made this way? That Thiede brought his Tigron, Pellaz Cevarro—later Pellaz har Aralis—to Immanion, to rule in his name over the united tribes is true. It is also true that in the year ai-cara 30, Thiede trans-formed and left this world. What is not so certain is whether he was actually murdered by the one who came to rule at the Tigron's side: Calanthe.

Never has a name been so loaded with meaning. When he came to Im-manion, the entire world cried out in fear and ecstasy. An idea, more than an individual. He was like a god, in that wherever he laid his feet he created change, and not all of it was good.

—The Aralisians, *by Ishtir har Parasiel*

INTRODUCTION

In the early times, two events specifically shook the world of Wraeththu from its innermost core to its outermost etheric body. The first was when Pellaz har Aralis, who eventually became Tigron of Immanion, died and was reborn into new flesh. Only the most insensitive hara remained unaffected by that, and even they were no doubt plagued for several days afterward by strange dreams and unaccountable bad tempers.

The second event was, in some ways, more dramatic and devastating than the first, and this was when Calanthe, erstwhile chesnari of Pellaz, stalked like a dark angel into Immanion and faced Thiede, progenitor of all Wraeththu, in his inner sanctum.

Some say they fought for possession of Pellaz, others that they warred for power, and yet more claimed that it was a symbolic preordained ritual, in which Thiede transcended the boundaries of earthly existence and fulfilled his ultimate potential. Around the world, different tribes cling to different versions of the myth, and you can be sure their particular preferences flavor greatly the context of their spiritual beliefs.

What is known for certain is that Calanthe went to Immanion, the city of the Gelaming, and claimed what he believed was his. Pellaz was left without Thiede, his mentor and creator. With Thiede gone, who knew what would happen? At that time, Wraeththu knew so little about themselves and Thiede had left them without sharing any of the knowledge he had. Had Cal liberated Wraeththu from a harsh dictator, or left them vulnerable and ignorant with no greater power to protect them? Only time would tell.

For most hara, when the phoenix of Wraeththu was newly hatched from an egg of flame and still in danger of falling from the nest, the only way to receive information from halfway across the world was through the subtle ethers, and much of what is channeled from this puzzling realm is subject to personal interpretation, error, and bias.

Immanion lies in the heart of Almagabra, a warm country whose landscape seethes with ancient spirits and capricious gods. An implacable ocean lies between this land and Megalithica to the west. News, as it was carried across the waves, was often changed or forgotten completely. Sometimes, when a snippet of information reached some cold forgotten corner in the north of Megalithica, it was nothing more than a worn-out thread, a ghost of a whisper or a lie. When information such as this became intertwined with a har's psychic vision, you could almost guarantee the conclusion he reached about what really happened bore no resemblance whatsoever to the truth. In such ways were new myths made, expanded upon, and believed. Pellaz and Calanthe became a legend, to be feared or adored according to your beliefs and where you lived.

Many hara had good reason to fear the Gelaming, the tribe who believed themselves to be the greatest of all. For, in Gelaming eyes, if you did not ascribe to their beliefs, you were an enemy of all Wraeththukind. Sometimes, the Gelaming were right in this assumption, but sometimes not. If your history was suspect, it was best to hide it and flee to a far location, like the City of Ghosts in Northern Megalithica. Best to forget the name of your previous tribe and pray that nohar came looking for you. Better still: keep your secrets to yourself.

CHAPTER ONE

In the early mornings, just after dawn, when the sky was salmon pink and mists curled across the water, and birds flew like the last of dark dreams escaping the shattered towers of the old human city, Moon Jaguar would walk to the edge of the world and stare out to the place where the phantoms lived.

The creatures that lived within the Sea of Ghosts would often come to land and wrap themselves around the broken towers on the shore. The mist beings could make parts of the world disappear and reappear, and they moved quickly. It was best to pay them respect.

Seven Wraeththu clans lived in the ruins of the city, and at one time they had been Uigenna, though prudence had forced them to change their name and their customs, following the Gelaming invasion of Megalithica. Now, they had no tribal name, and in time, no doubt, the clans themselves would become separate tribes, but for now they existed in tenuous alliance.

Moon's father, Snake Jaguar, had come from a land far to the south, but he would never speak of it, no matter how much Moon begged or pleaded for old stories that all harlings loved. Snake was the shaman of the Jaguar clan and held in great esteem by their ruler, Great Jaguar Paw. Moon lived with his father, and his father's protector, Raven Jaguar, in the House of Relics, situated very close to the shore of the Sea of Ghosts. Humans had filled the Reliquary with artifacts that recorded moments of their history, but most of the artifacts had been destroyed during the conflict that had brought the city to her knees some thirty or so years before.

Moon liked the Reliquary: its cavernous dark rooms, its shattered display cases, the bones spilling amid the glass shards. His own room, high in the building, had probably once been an office, although over time he had adorned it with various items he'd filched from the lower galleries. His father lived in the far side of the building, and Raven lived in a storeroom nearby, his senses forever on high alert in case Snake should need him. Moon presumed Raven had gotten to know Snake long before the fragmented Uigenna tribe had had to flee to the north, pursued by Gelaming patrols that were intent on rehabilitating any hara whose beliefs did not emulate their own. Raven lived in ascetic simplicity, in what was hardly more than a broom closet. It was obvious something very bad had happened to him in the past and that it had affected his mind. Now, Raven's dedication to Snake was his entire reason for being. They were not chesna, nor did they ever take aruna together, which in Wraeththu terms was most unusual, if not freakish. They shared secrets and pain, and this, more than physical or emotional expressions of affection, bound them close. Snake too was damaged. Even though Moon lived far from his father, sometimes at night he could hear him limping around his room, never weeping, never sighing—just pacing slowly.

Moon was seven years old, nearly adult, and by then he had realized that other harlings of the clan avoided him, because his father was strange. Even Great Jaguar Paw feared Snake, because his temperament was inclined to prophesy doom rather than joy. The privacy-loving Jaguar clan skulked around the shore of the Sea of Ghosts and interacted with other clans only for trade. Snake, so the other clans said, made sure the rest of the Jaguars were as grim as he was.

A week or so after his seventh birthday, which he'd celebrated alone, Moon went as usual to the shore. Looking back at the Reliquary, Moon realized for the first time that his father, Raven, and himself, although occupying in some regard the same space, lived in isolation from each other. There were not even ghosts for company. Since Snake's chesnari had died, not long after Moon's birth, the idea of family had shattered in the same way the relics had. Moon did not feel lonely—he never did—but today he felt different: an echo of some early childhood warning traveled across the great sea.

The dawn was pink and gray, stealing through brooding cloud and there was a metallic taint to the air. A ship sailed through the mist toward the docks, some distance to the east. Somehar in the rigging blew a mournful salute upon a windhorn. Birds looped drunkenly around the black mast. Moon squatted on the cracked concrete walkway above the water and stared at the ship with his hands funneled around his eyes. He thought about strolling over to the docks to see who or what might have arrived, but then the vague aches that had plagued his belly for some weeks intensified into a cramping pain and he had to lean forward to vomit into the water.

Moon, like all hara, was rarely ill, so this particular seizure, which could not be ignored, filled him with panic. In some places the land was poisoned, and those poisons were strong enough even to kill a har. Moon rarely left his immediate environment, so he couldn't imagine how he could have come into contact with such danger, but now, when he stared out over the water, his whole vision was tinged with red and he had a pain in the back of his neck. He was afraid that if he moved too quickly, some part of himself might fall out of his body. He was poisoned and he was too far away from the Reliquary to call for help.

Moon curled up into a ball on the ground and lay that way for a long time. By the time the sun had hauled itself out of the mist, he realized he had slept and now felt better. But when he got to his feet, he had to hold his stomach with both hands, because it felt loose and unsafe. His skin was crawling as if ants were marching all over it. Slowly, and with great care, he made his way to his father's domain, because despite the fact they rarely spent time to-gether, Snake was the one har Moon trusted in the world.

Raven had already been to Snake's room to deliver breakfast, which the shaman was now eating in a slow and dignified manner. Snake Jaguar's name derived mainly from the appearance of his eyes. One was very dark, almost black, while the other, on his damaged side, was bright gold. This was his snake eye, his seeing eye, and with it he could see into anyhar's soul, so he was required to keep it covered, out of politeness, for most of the time. His face was very beautiful, unmarked, and so was the right side of his body, but the left side was maimed. A chemical fire, so strong that not even a harish frame could recover from its cruel breath, had ruined him, created his golden eye, and had consumed entirely the har named Silken whom Snake had loved and who had been Moon's hostling. It had been an accident: no rogue hara or humans had done it. Evil had come out of the ground, evil that had waited so long for release, it had become impatient with anticipating human or harish detonation. It had erupted from the ground on its own, to burn out in a mo-ment of glory, which had unfortunately incinerated seven hara of the clans and injured a further three. Two of those had later died, but Snake had sur-vived. To a normal har, to be less than perfect was anathema. Snake, however, appeared barely to care about such things. He lived, for the most part, inside his own head.

Now, Moon went to his father and knelt before him. He said, "Tiahaar, am I to die?"

Snake raised his head. Ropes of black hair hung over his face, down to the floor, and from between these ophidian coils the golden eye glowed, while the black eye contemplated the darkest reaches of the universe. "What is this?" Snake asked.

Moon explained, as best he could.

Snake continued to eat his breakfast, listening intently. Then, when his son finished speaking, he said, "Moon, you are becoming adult, that is all. Go to Raven. He will instruct you in these matters." His expression was distant. He did not look Moon in the eye.

Moon had expected something more dramatic than this. "A ship came," he said. "A black ship."

"Unneah from the south," Snake said. "They bring little of value, but later you might go over to the docks and barter for tobacco for me."

"How far south?"

"Not far enough," Snake said. He reached for his staff and began to struggle to his feet. Moon jumped up to help him.

"Will we ever go home?" he asked.

"I doubt it," Snake said, for a moment allowing himself to lean upon the shoulder of his son. "Why do you ask now?"

"I don't know. I wonder what it was like."

"Go to Raven now," Snake said, pulling away. "Tell him that I have sent you."

Moon rarely communicated with Raven, even though Raven was supposed to have raised him after his hostling's death. Raven was always so taciturn and preoccupied with his dedication to guarding Snake that Moon had raised himself without realizing he had done so. Why Snake should send him to Raven now, Moon was unsure. He doubted that Raven could teach him anything, because he was as wrapped up in his private world as Snake was.

Raven's eyes were discomfortingly entirely black, so you could never be sure what he was thinking, if indeed he thought at all. His skin was very dark, like that of a panther and his face looked like the sculpture of a mythical king. He, more than any other har of the clan, was most like the big cat from which they'd taken their name. He could sit motionless for hours, staring at a single thing. Then he could strike, and take a bird from the air so quickly, nohar could really see it. Moon didn't like him very much, although he wasn't consciously aware of that. He interacted with too few hara to understand the concepts of like and dislike.

Moon found Raven on the Reliquary grounds, tending their vegetable patch. He moved with precise gracefulness, in what to Moon that day seemed an annoying manner. His thick black braids, which hung to his thighs, were bound at his neck by a single braid, to keep them from dangling over his work.

"Snake says you are to instruct me," Moon said.

Raven fixed his attention upon Moon and said, "In what regard?"

"He says I am becoming adult and that I should come to you. He said to tell you he'd sent me."

Raven stared at him in his usual impenetrable manner for some seconds, then snapped, "He said this?"

"Yes. What must I learn?"

Raven turned away. He seemed troubled. "I am not a good teacher," he said. "There is too much I have forgotten."

"Perhaps we should go to the docks instead. A ship has come. Snake wants tobacco."

Raven said nothing. He stood with his back to Moon for what seemed like an hour, but was probably less than a minute. Then he began carefully to put away his tools and tidy up his work area. Moon waited impatiently. He was thinking of the docks and the aroma of cooking sugar-dough from the food stalls that lined its perimeter. He had not yet eaten.

Raven had finished his work. "Come," he said, and beckoned for Moon to follow him.

"I'm hungry," Moon said, trailing behind.

They went into the small orchard, near to the run where the hens scampered about. When they saw Raven approaching, they all rushed to the netting, squawking and flattening their wings against the ground in devotion.

"I felt ill," Moon said. "This morning I was sick." They were in a circle of trees and the air felt very different there, still and close.

"It is feybraiha that you are going through," Raven said.

"What's that?"

"The advent of sexual maturity. You will be able to create harlings of your own now."

"Why would I want to do that?" Years ago, when Snake had been somewhat more communicative, he had taught his son about his own kind. He had told him about aruna and how it could be used for spiritual growth, for creating harlings, or simply for pleasure. Moon hadn't thought about it much since, mainly because it was not something that figured in their routine domestic life. Snake and Raven were not like normal hara in that respect. Now, feeling as if iced water was filling up his veins, Moon began to remember what he'd been told, that one day his body would be ready for aruna and when that time came he must see to its desires. He faced this har he did not even particularly like and asked, "What must I do?"

"Nothing," said Raven. "You must be aware of what this will do to you. It will wake you up. You will never be able to sleep again."

"I don't believe you," Moon said.

Raven almost smiled. "I'm trying to tell you about a new responsibility you will have. Your body will wake up, and you must look after its needs."

"What about *your* body?"

Raven didn't answer. He simply began to take off his clothes, so that Moon could see the pale scars against his dark brown skin, scores of them, down his back and along his right flank. It looked like he'd been whipped or attacked by a savage beast, but other than that he was perfect. The scars, in some ways, only emphasized this perfection. "You are like one of the statues," Moon said, "the ones in the Reliquary."

"Get undressed," Raven said.

Moon had no preconceptions whatsoever, and did not feel shy about what must happen. He was nervous, because it might hurt, but other than that was quite content to do as he was asked. He lay down on the damp grass, which was still cold because the sun had not touched it. Overhead, the tree branches swayed and rustled and birds hopped from limb to limb. Moon could see clouds racing across the sky.

Raven lay down beside him and the warmth of skin against skin was pleasant. Raven stroked his back in a way Moon thought somehar had done to him before, presumably his hostling, many years ago. Sometimes, Raven's breath drifted across Moon's face and when it did so, he received impressions of vague fleeting pictures, as if they'd been painted in faint watercolors. Moon had a strong impulse to put his mouth against Raven's own and really taste those images, but Raven carefully avoided such contact. Moon guessed he didn't want to share what was inside him. The stroking and tantalizing breath kindled desire in Moon's body. He had never felt such a thing before and was startled by its power and the control it had over him. What was the purpose of it? Raven's caresses became more invasive and Moon saw a picture in his mind of a great door. He knew that behind it was some kind of treasury and that the treasure would not be what he expected. He gasped and arched his body a little and Raven slid on top of him. He put one hand on Moon's face and murmured, "Relax."

"I can't." Moon kept his legs clamped close together, knowing he shouldn't, but feeling that once he allowed Raven to do what had to be done, it would change everything forever. He wasn't ready for that change. He hadn't thought about it. This was all too quick. He couldn't stop the tears. Should it be like this?

Raven put his mouth against Moon's lips and gently exhaled. He gave to Moon images of Silken, images of Moon himself as a harling, laughing and playing in sunlight: the two of them together. He gave to Moon images that must have come from Snake, long ago, of dusty red lands and soaring mountains. Moon saw his father as he'd once been: whole and vigorous. These images were not painful, nor did they make Moon sad. He felt a wistful longing for things he'd never had, but it was a sweet longing. He understood, for a brief moment, what living truly was, and how magical it was that hara could come together this way, mingling their beings, sharing all that is deep and passionate. He was sinking into an ocean of soft feathers, the most comfortable place in the world, where pain and sorrow could not exist. This was like entering the otherworld, walking the spirit paths in a place far better than cold reality. He curled his legs around Raven's lean back and Raven pushed inside him.

"This is so strange," Moon said.

"Hush."

"But it is. It's so weird that a piece of you is inside me. It's such a strange thing to do. Whoever thought of it?"

"Stop thinking," Raven said.

But Moon couldn't stop. His body responded fully to physical sensation, but the more it did so, the more his mind raced. He was chattering to himself like a maniac, full of questions. What had made Snake cut himself off from other hara? What had happened to Raven to make him so dour? Where had they come from? Where was the red dusty land? Who had they left behind? He saw a shining web stretching across infinity, and it was studded with points of light. He knew that each of these points represented others who were connected to him and surely now, at this moment, they must be aware of him too. Who were these hara? Where were they?

Raven's movements had become more urgent and deep, his breathing fast and ragged. It was like a storm hurtling across the Sea of Ghosts in a boil of dark cloud to break over the shore. The ground was shaking. The trees were shaking.

Moon opened his eyes, which had been shut tight and saw the branches overhead vibrating wildly. Leaves and twigs were raining down and the hens were screeching in terror. This wasn't aruna: this was real. Moon cried out and tried to pull away from Raven, but the climax of aruna crashed over them and snatched Moon's senses in its flow. Wave after wave of indescribably delicious sensation coursed through his body while around them the world shattered. They would be buried in the debris. They would be killed, and they were so helpless, imprisoned by animal instinct that didn't care if everything around them was exploding. Moon screamed in ecstasy and terror. Clear thoughts came to him in the eye of the storm: aruna is selfish, it doesn't give a damn what happens to us. It has a mind of its own.

A deafening crash came from the direction of the Reliquary, and everything went black. In the darkness, pinned beneath Raven's heavy, panting body, Moon waited for the sky to fall in. Everything had ended. The dark had come.

Moon opened his eyes, fully expecting to find himself in some kind of spirit realm, but was surprised and relieved to find that he was still lying on the ground in the orchard, which was indeed covered in debris as if a terrible storm had hit it. Raven was nearby, pulling on his clothes.

"What was that?" Moon asked.

"I don't know," Raven said. "Earthquake, maybe."

"Did we do that?"

Raven smiled, something he did so rarely, but which made him look truly beautiful. "No, we didn't," he said dryly, but not without humor. "Don't worry. It's not bad."

"How do you know?"

Raven tied up his braids again, which had come loose during aruna. "I should check on Snake."

It was at this point that Moon realized his whole body was throbbing and aching in a not altogether unpleasant manner. He didn't want to move and yet he did. "I'll come with you," he said and sat up. The world swayed, and for some moments he had to sit with his head between his knees.

"You should really stay here," Raven said. "You should rest."

"I want to see if he's okay."

Raven didn't say anything else, but simply headed in the direction of the Reliquary. Moon quickly pulled on his clothes and scrambled after him. He didn't feel remotely in control of his limbs, but at least they seemed willing to propel him in the right direction.

The door to Snake's room was stuck, because something heavy on the other side was wedged against it. Both Raven and Moon leaned upon it, pushing with all their strength. Moon nearly passed out with the effort. By the time they'd managed to force the door open a few inches, his vision was totally occluded by darting spots of light.

Raven squeezed through the gap and ran into the room. Moon had to follow more slowly. He felt utterly nauseous now, not least because hot fluid had fallen out of him in an unexpected gush and had soaked his trousers. The room was a mess. An ornamental pillar had fallen, which was what had wedged the door shut. A lot of the ceiling ornaments had come down and covered the floor and furniture. Snake was lying facedown in the middle of the room, his arms and legs spread out. He was wearing a long robe, but his feet were bare: the sight of his upturned soles was heartbreaking, because they looked so vulnerable. One of the feet was twisted and withered, and Moon so rarely saw that. Snake always kept himself covered. It brought new tears to Moon's eyes.

Raven was squatting down beside Snake and now turned over his body.

Moon stood over them, both hands pressed against his mouth, sure that his father was dead. But Snake groaned and his eyelids flickered. Raven stroked dust and flakes of plaster from Snake's face. "Look at me," he said.

Snake drew in a long breath and struggled to sit up, his arms flailing upon the air. Moon went to assist Raven lift his father. "Are you all right, Snake?" Moon asked, at least three times.

Snake did not seem to be aware Moon was there. He got to his feet and shrugged off his helpers. Slowly, he limped across the room and went to a cupboard where he kept some rough wine they'd bartered for some months before. This, he swigged from the flagon, then wiped his mouth with the back of his good hand. He came back to his companions and handed the flagon to Raven, who gave it directly to Moon, saying, "You need this more."

Moon took a drink, knowing that both he and Raven were waiting for Snake's pronouncement, because it was clear he had one. His golden eye glowed with its own light in the gloom of the room, where swirls of dust eddied in a beam of sunshine that came in through a high skylight. "It is not unconnected," he said at last.

Moon and Raven said nothing.

Snake nodded to himself and limped to his chair, where he sat down heavily. He looked down at his withered foot, staring at it in surprise and contempt as if he'd never seen it before. Intuitively, Moon fetched his father's boots and knelt to put them on for him. He was surprised when Snake reached out and placed a hand on the top of his head. "How are you, Moon?"

Moon looked up. "Fine."

"You shouldn't have come here. You should rest." He stroked his son's hair and Moon saw in Snake's eyes an expression he'd never seen before: intimate and caring. "It shouldn't have been like this," Snake said. "You should have had a feast and many friends around you. Silken should have been here to wind your hair with flowers." He glanced briefly at Raven. "We let you down. We made no preparations. We could have done, even just the three of us. I'm sorry, Moon."

"It was fine," Moon said. "Really. I liked it." He felt like crying again, but this time with happiness. Perhaps aruna had confounded his senses, and perhaps it had changed everything, as he'd suspected it might. Snake had never spoken to him like this before. Raven was a silent presence behind him, but even though Moon couldn't see him, he felt connected to him. This was some kind of miracle. "Was there an earthquake?" he asked his father.

"Yes, it was that." Snake flexed his shoulders. "Give me the wine, Moon. I need another drink."

Raven brought the flagon over, but let Moon hand it to his father. Snake took a long drink, his throat working rhythmically as he swallowed. Then he said, "It is time to talk."

Moon and Raven sat at Snake's feet, and even though they weren't touching, Moon felt as if Raven was holding him in his arms. It must be a dream: they had died in the earthquake after all. This could only be Paradise. How strange that he'd not known about this intimacy, had never missed it.

"They will come looking for me," Snake said. "It is only a matter of time."

"Who?" Moon asked.

"My family," Snake replied. "Your family, Moon. The end of one story is only the beginning of another. Years ago, I made a decision and I intended to keep to it. I know now that it is beyond my control."

Moon waited, holding his breath. He hardly dared breathe in case the sound of it took this miracle of communication away.

"Your hostling," Snake said, and then for some moments was silent. "There are some who will tell you he was a vicious killer, Moon."

Moon uttered a choked laugh, because he had to make some kind of sound.

Snake's right hand lashed out and clamped over Moon's mouth. "We were the same, he and I. We were together from the beginning. We were Uigenna. The memories you have of love and nurture are not false, but they are not the whole picture. I made a choice to accept the Uigenna way of life, and I never regretted it, even though I knew my brothers had taken different paths. I am what I am."

Moon struggled a little, but his father's hand gripped his jaw firmly. Moon could barely breathe.

"I have killed hara," said Snake, "and I have killed humans, and if things were different I might still be doing that." He took his hand away from Moon's mouth and leaned back in his chair.

Moon was panting. He felt stunned.

"Survival of the fittest, the best," Snake said. "That was our way, until the Gelaming took away our power. We are hiding now, beaten and cowering. This is not life, it is mere existence. We are not jaguars, we are ghosts." He thumped an arm of his chair with his best hand. "So, he cries out to me in his pain! So, I can never hide or forget. This is the way of it. He will want me for my gold eye."

"Who?" Moon managed to ask.

"The one who was my brother," said Snake. "The beloved. We were kin when I was human. He is already hunting us, and he is our enemy."

Raven made an anguished noise. "I am at your side," he said, his voice little more than a growl. "None shall harm you."

Snake didn't take his eyes from Moon. "When your mind walked the shining path," he said, "when your body sang the song of the universe, it was heard. It was inevitable, and was always destined to happen. A powerful seer has heard it and he smelled your ecstasy. He recognized the essence within that smell. I saw this as the ground shook. Soon, he will tell of what he's seen, but not yet. The darkness has come to the city of angels and he who dreamed is awake. He is more awake than all the powers that seek to contain the truth could ever have imagined, and once he has rubbed the sleep from his eyes, he will begin to think. And that is even more dangerous."

"I don't know of what you speak," Moon said.

Snake leaned down and cupped Moon's chin in his good hand, this time with gentleness. "The moment you came into yourself, so great events took place elsewhere. You were not a catalyst. It was preordained."

"I will kill him," Raven said. "I will kill any of them."

Snake glanced up at him and spoke archly. "Any?"

"Even *him*," Raven said. "He has become one with those who ruined me."

"It will not be enough," Snake said. "They are too powerful."

"What do you speak of?" Moon asked in a shrill, desperate voice. "Tell me!"

"The Gelaming," Snake said. "Raven speaks of them. He has his own story, which is only his to tell. All you need to know is that my brother rules the Gelaming. He is Pellaz. You will remember this name."

CHAPTER TWO

⊱┈⊰⊱⊸⊷⊙⊶⊹⊰┈⊱

Is this it?" Caeru har Aralis, Tigrina of Immanion, was taking lunch with his best friend, Velaxis Shiraz. Velaxis had the beautiful yet watchful face of a spiteful pedigree cat and platinum-colored hair that hung to his waist, currently tightly plaited and bound with black pearls. Caeru, a slight, willowy creature, had a constantly startled appearance. His hair was the color of ripe corn and his skin smelled of summer. He and Velaxis were Gelaming, from the cream of Wraeththu tribes, and they had recently suffered a cataclysm.

Now, they sat upon the wide terrace outside Caeru's royal apartments that overlooked the hanging gardens of the palace Phaonica. The terrace had been repaired, the shattered furniture replaced, but there were still signs of damage in the gardens, despite the fact that landscapers had been hard at work on repairs for weeks. Caeru's favorite tree had come down: perhaps the thing he resented most of all. He could no longer look at it while he took his breakfast.

"What do you mean?" Velaxis asked, in his usual drawl, which held more than a hint of poison. "Is what *it*?"

Caeru gestured expressively with both arms. "You know. Is this it? The great change. The divine Cal comes into the city like an angel of death, dragging magical destruction in his wake. He confronts Thiede—presumably they had some kind of fight—and as far as we can see, Cal won. This was supposed to be the dawn of a New Age, and what do we have? A few buildings have fallen over and now I get an unwanted visitor to dinner most evenings, but what else is different?"

Velaxis turned his eyes to the sky. "Well, apart from the obvious, i.e., no Thiede around and a hell of a lot of rubble in the streets, there are some other things to consider." He began to make a list, marking each point on his fingers. "One. You sit in the Hegalion more than you used to, which means you have true political power for the first time. Two. I do believe Pellaz actually looked at you the other day. Three. You are now regarded as something other than a simple celebrity for the mindless masses to adore . . ."

"I always had power," Caeru interrupted. "I worked for it."

"You had land, true, and a place in Thiede's heart. But Thiede isn't here anymore, and Cal is attempting to give you *real* power. He is your champion, much as you must hate the fact."

Caeru laughed. "I don't believe it! You're his advocate."

Velaxis picked up a glass of cold greenish wine. He took a drink. "He treats you better than Pellaz, your so-called consort, ever has. Why knock it?"

"I don't need anyhar to 'treat me' one way or another. Things were fine before. I've lost Thiede, my guide. He was effectively murdered. And I should be happy about this?"

"Thiede isn't dead. You know it. The changes were needed."

"Thanks, Vel. You're so supportive."

Velaxis shrugged. "In your position, I'd be making the most of it. I'd be doing more to shape things to my liking."

"Meaning?"

"Whatever has been said of Calanthe, our esteemed new Tigron, and however dreadful he may really be, one thing is obvious: he feels guilty about you. To my eyes, that speaks of advantage."

"He doesn't feel guilty about me. Why should he?"

Velaxis tilted his head to one side. "You don't need me to spell it out. He comes here every day, just to check you're not cutting your own throat or scheming his annihilation. He doesn't come here for the cuisine, Rue. Haven't you ever asked yourself why he visits you so often? You're never anything but frosty. Think about it."

Caeru stretched in his chair. "He comes here, I think, because he is confused about Pellaz. He has been reunited with the har he has loved for many years, but now he finds that our sweet Pell is not the same. He's nothing like the har Cal fell in love with, and perhaps if he were honest, Cal might admit he's been chasing a dream. Now, he's trapped in it. That's confusing. So, he comes here to study me, to see if he can learn anything about how to handle the situation. That's all. I won't help him. He can lie on this bed of thorns he's made for himself."

"What can *you* teach him about Pell? The pair of you have barely spoken for years."

"Maybe I could teach him how to survive Immanion and the Gelaming. But I won't."

Velaxis put down his empty wineglass. "Then you are stupid."

"Why say that? You know I'm not, otherwise you wouldn't be sitting here. Say what you mean."

"If I were you," said Velaxis, drawing a circle in a puddle of spilled wine on the table, "I would consider getting closer to this new, second Tigron that we have. Pellaz is unassailable, but Cal is not. He's vulnerable, raw, and unsure of himself. Hara are divided over whether he is a good or a bad force. He needs allies, as you need allies. Swallow your pride and give him what he wants: on your terms."

"He'd never go against Pell."

"I'm not suggesting he should, or even that you should encourage that. All I'm saying is that Pellaz shouldn't be allowed to have Cal all to himself, because if you don't do anything that's what will happen. At one time, Cal was the dominant force in their partnership. He was the one who brought Pell into the Wraeththu fold and then initiated him into the ways of aruna. But, whatever romantic memories he clings to, he has no power over Pell now. He'll end up being a cat's paw, like most of Pell's close friends. I think it's about time our esteemed first Tigron woke up to reality. He's treated you abysmally since the day you came here."

"Well, I shouldn't have come . . ."

"Oh, don't start that again! I can't bear it when you try to have a conscience. Tell me you don't like having this fabulous home and all the land Thiede gave you. And don't pretend you're all grief-stricken about Thiede's disappearance. You're not. You're famous in your own right. Tell me you don't like hara virtually dropping to their knees in the street when they catch sight of you. You love it. You wouldn't give any of it up, even if Pellaz threw himself at your feet and declared his undying love."

"Is that what you think of me?"

"It's what everyhar thinks of you. Don't be like Pellaz. Don't blind yourself to the truth. Use it to your advantage. Wallow in it."

Caeru refilled their wineglasses. "You are a harsh vizier, Vel."

"Somehar has to be. It's beneath you to be kind." Velaxis picked up his wineglass again, stared into its depths. "It has not escaped me that you haven't forbidden Cal to call. You could have done so, at any time. You enjoy playing with him, don't you?"

Caeru was silent for a moment, then he said, "I heard something recently."

Velaxis glanced at him in inquiry, but said nothing.

"It came originally from Cal himself, on the very first day after he came here and everything was in chaos. I didn't think about it much, but then it was confirmed through the grapevine of the Tigron's staff. A conversation overheard."

"Oh, gossip! I can't wait."

Caeru pulled a sour face. "Pellaz said that everything he owns belongs also to Cal. That includes me."

Velaxis gestured languidly with one hand. "Well, of course, Pellaz believes that."

"But does Cal? He said it to me once, but I think it was just to get a reaction, or to shut me up or something."

"Why not find out?"

"I don't belong to anyhar. The idea is absurd."

"But the fact that it was said . . ." Velaxis shrugged. "Changes were—and are—needed, Rue. Cal came here and overturned the old order. The Hegemony is alone now and so are the Aralisians. Thiede has withdrawn from the field. That's the biggest change to Wraeththu since it all began. If you are Cal's, then he is yours, and perhaps not before time. Pellaz cannot be allowed to function in the way he used to. It's my belief it's partly up to you to make sure this happens, and you have to do it quickly, while the winds of change are still strong. Don't let the dust settle."

"And what do you get out of it?"

"Now, you are being harsh. You know I'm fond of you."

"Fondness aside, you work for the Hegemony. Is this what they want too?"

"We all want what is best for Wraeththu."

Caeru didn't even bother responding to that. Velaxis, for all his good qualities, was ambitious and self-serving. His words could mean only one thing. Pellaz had hidden enemies within the Hegemony. Caeru had hardly dared to believe such a thing. Even though he'd worked hard to be popular, the perfect Tigrina, adored—as Velaxis had pointed out—by hara in the street, he knew that Pell's indifference to his apparently spotless Tigrina was regarded unfavorably by nearly everyhar in Immanion, if not farther afield. Still, Caeru had always believed the Hegemony regarded him as nothing more than a useful trinket to dangle before the masses, to keep them sweet. He was the hostling of Pell's heir, Abrimel, and appealed to those parts of the harish psyche that cherished the idea of motherhood. If he had been human, he would have been a gracious queen, beautiful and dignified, forever at the side of the king. As it was, Pellaz had spent their entire life together trying to keep Caeru at a distance. Thiede had arranged their union, against Pell's wishes, and the Tigron had never let Caeru forget that. The Tigrina had got used to the situation. He wasn't blind to his privileges in life. If he could go back in time, he would still make the same decision about coming to Immanion. For years, he'd drifted along, doing what was expected of him and reaping the benefits. He had trained himself not to be wounded by Pell's behavior. Sometimes, though, Caeru still dreamed of when he and Pell had first met, when they had conceived a pearl in passion and what Caeru had thought was lasting feeling. Waking up to reality after such dreams was never pleasant. It kept something alive in Caeru's heart he would rather let wither and die. The truth of why he allowed Cal to visit him was because he was curious about the ghost that had haunted and blighted his relationship with Pellaz. Fascination and envy were uneasy companions. But Velaxis had spoken wisely. It was time, perhaps, to make an offering.

Caeru worked himself up into such a state of tension that by the time Cal presented himself at the doors to the apartment, at the usual time just before dinner, Caeru felt giddy with nerves. He'd asked his kitchen staff to prepare a more sumptuous meal than usual and had changed his mind about which wines should accompany it several times. He dressed himself with care, teased out his startling pale hair into a lion's mane, and darkened his eyes with heavy kohl. He wasn't sure what he was going to say or do, and this in itself was disorientating. He only knew a nexus point had arrived, complete with potential vortex.

Cal himself appeared oblivious to any undercurrents in the atmosphere. He came in like a stray cat, lissome and alert, as if pondering where best to make his home. It was clear he didn't yet feel comfortable in Immanion. His hair, like Caeru's, was the palest gold, although he kept it fairly short for convenience's sake. Cal, in Rue's opinion, was not a har to spend much time looking after himself. He often looked as if he'd just got out of bed. He was a gypsy creature, disorientated because he was no longer on the move.

Caeru received him on the terrace and at first maintained the somewhat steely demeanor he reserved for his dealings with the new Tigron. "How are you managing alone?" he asked icily, referring to the fact that Pellaz was out of the city, visiting friends in Galhea, no doubt in an attempt to smooth certain feathers that had been extremely ruffled over recent developments.

Cal threw himself into a chair, with the easy languorous grace that Caeru both envied and despised. "I have kept my pining to a minimum," he said.

"I'm glad. It would distress me so to see physical evidence of it."

"Your claws appear to be particularly sharp tonight."

Caeru shrugged, as if Cal was barely worthy of his notice, and signaled to a member of his staff to bring out the first wine. As the serving har fussed with the bottle, the Tigrina leaned back in his chair, smiled sweetly at Cal, and said, "Will Pellaz be carrying fond messages from you to your son in Galhea?"

Cal grimaced. "Congratulations, you hit bone! No. Not yet." He narrowed his eyes. "What's going on?"

"I have no idea what you mean."

"Okay. Fine." Cal took the wine that was offered to him. He sipped. "Mmm. As dry as your tongue, though just as fine."

Caeru smiled fiercely, but inwardly he felt himself slump. Cal was magnificent. He could not be anything but Tigron, or Pell's consort. It was almost surreal to be sitting here talking with him, a har who had been a threatening idea for so long. Caeru had hated Cal from the moment he'd first heard about him and only later discovered this hatred was, in some respects, justified. But looking at him now, no matter what he might have done or been in the past, it was no surprise Pellaz had always adored Cal. Haunted by memories of this exquisite being, how could Pellaz ever have been expected to care for anyhar else? No wonder he'd loathed the fact that Caeru had ended up at his side instead.

What am I doing? Caeru thought. *This is pointless.*

"I'm putting a program together," Cal said as the first course of meal was brought out. "I think it's important that victims of the atrocities in Megalithica should receive firsthand Gelaming care. They've been neglected too long. What do you think?"

"I don't care. I just appear at state functions and look pretty."

"You could help me. It's a big job."

"I don't want to. You can't make a difference, so why bother trying?"

"I have the kind of nature that has to keep trying. You might have noticed."

"You do have a trying nature, that is true."

Cal laughed. "I'm so pleased you enjoy our meals together. It's a kind of blood sport, isn't it?"

"So I'm told. You don't have to come, so I assume you enjoy it too. Is it the same with Pell? Are you into being dominated? Perhaps you still remember the young boy you had incepted into Wraeththu. It must be quite a shock to see how he's turned out. And now he has you, bound hand and foot. Was it worth the trouble?"

Cal didn't say anything, and Caeru realized he had hit a nerve, perhaps several. Not good. That wasn't supposed to be the purpose of this meeting, even if it was almost impossible to rein in the bitterness. "Tell me your plans," he said. "I don't want to help you, but it might pass the time to hear about them." He knew Cal would recognize a peace offering when it was given to him. Apology would be going too far.

Cal spoke of his dreams, those he had cherished for years. Caeru realized that Pellaz was perhaps not the only reason Cal was here in Immanion. He spoke with greater and greater passion as the meal progressed, of how he wanted to help all those hara who had been incepted into violent tribes and who were still hunted as criminals now that the Gelaming had mostly established control in Megalithica. "It is all about choice," he said, "and how some hara never had it. If I'm going to be a Tigron I might as well try to do some good. Looking pretty is not enough for me."

"You never had to go through what I did," Caeru said. "Don't judge me."

"I know what you went through. We all went through *something*. Remember: I was Uigenna. I have blood on my hands. You don't. Pell doesn't expect anything of you, Rue. In that, you are lucky."

"Are you confiding in me?"

"I wouldn't be so stupid. It's just a fact, and everyhar knows it."

"Calanthe: champion of the underdog. It's a good image; as good as mine, I suppose, though just as rhetorical."

Cal sighed through his nose. "You are exhausting." He pushed his plate away from him. "Dinner was good. We eat like kings, while in other places . . ."

"Shut up. I don't want to hear it."

"I know. Not many do."

"I'll give you five years at most before you get totally disillusioned and just sit back to enjoy the good food. Don't you realize what Tigron and Tigrina are? Carnival attractions. We're not supposed to have opinions or *do* anything."

"That's not true. Pell does a lot."

"Five years, that's all," Caeru said.

"I'll prove you wrong." Cal stood up. "Thanks for dinner."

"Don't thank me. I didn't invite you."

Cal began to leave the terrace, and for several seconds, Caeru debated what to do next. It might be better just to let Cal go, but then there would be Velaxis's scorn to deal with.

"Wait a moment," Caeru said.

Cal paused. "Yes?"

Caeru took a deep breath, and hoped it didn't show. "Where are you going?"

"Back to my apartment to gloat over my useless plans."

"You don't have to leave."

Cal frowned. "But I thought . . ."

Caeru stood up. "Look, if you really want us to be friends, we could go out tonight. I'm bored. I want to visit the high waterfront. There's a club there, called 'Serpent Sapphire.' It's a rich har's playpen. Had good reports. I want to see it."

Cal hesitated. "Hmm. Why do you want to go with me?"

Caeru made a careless gesture with one arm. "I enjoy our fights. I'm in the mood to socialize. Do I need another reason?"

"I'm not sure."

"How brave are you? Will you do it?"

"I don't know . . ." Cal rubbed the back of his neck. What would it take to persuade him?

"Of course, it might embarrass you to be seen in public with me."

"It's not that."

"Then what?"

"I can't help suspecting this might just be a ploy to get at Pell, but then I'm unusually paranoid."

Caeru laughed. "Why should he care? I'm less than dirt to him. He knows I can't affect his life, or anything in it, one little bit. This is nothing to do with him. I just want to go out. Be Tigron in this sense: escort me."

Cal nodded, a little distractedly. "All right."

"Sit here. Wait. I'll get ready."

Caeru rushed to his dressing room and spent a frantic ten minutes deciding what to wear. He eventually settled on an understated appearance: simple trousers and shirt of matt-black silk. He smoothed down his hair and cleaned his face of any cosmetics. Tonight, he did not want to be a pretty bauble. He wanted Cal to see him differently.

When he finally reappeared on the terrace, Cal said, "I see. We are incognito. Now who's embarrassed to be seen with whom?"

"Sometimes, there is power in being natural," Caeru said. "Tonight I am me rather than Tigrina. Don't you know about that yet?"

"I know about masks," Cal said.

They walked through the palace to the covered stable yard, which was surrounded on all sides by high-columned galleries. Fortunately, these had not been too damaged by the earthquakes that had shaken the city when Cal had first arrived. Caeru asked that an open carriage be made ready for them. A ride through the balmy evening air would be pleasant. They would hear the purr of the sea and smell the flowers that hung heavily from the trees along the Processional Way. They could survey what was left of the ruins caused by Cal's elemental fight with Thiede.

From the moment they sat down in the carriage, Caeru knew that a different kind of tension had arisen between them. Cal wasn't stupid. He knew all the games. He might be wondering which one Caeru was playing.

Serpent Sapphire was situated on that part of the harbor frequented by the high-ranking families who lived on Immanion's fabled hills. It was surrounded by exclusive bazaars, which stayed open into the night and sold unusual items from around the world. The club itself was fronted by floor-to-ceiling window doors, which were all thrown wide, so that patrons could sit there to smell the sea and listen to the waves. An awning, from which ornamental serpents dangled, extended over the walkway outside. Beyond the first bar was a series of dim-lit rooms, with different snaky themes. There was no sign of damage to the building, so repairs must have been undertaken very quickly. Although it was relatively early in the evening, several parties were already sitting at the tables in the bar, presumably having dined there on snake meat.

This was a club where the high society of Immanion met to dance, get drunk, and behave disgracefully in relative privacy. Exotic hara from the most obscure tribes around the world acted as valets and escorts. The club's proprietors had delved deep into the darkest corners to find the most unusual hara, whose skins and hair were strange colors, or who were physically abnormal to some degree. In the wake of the initial great inception, many isolated tribes had developed in peculiar ways, which were often influenced by questionable magical practices that had soaked them in strange subtle energies. Such energies caused interesting mutations.

The first group of socializing hara Caeru noticed included the general of the Gelaming military forces, Ashmael Aldebaran, who was also a member of the Hegemony and a close confidant of Pellaz. Caeru knew that Ashmael had already accepted Cal completely, which Caeru had taken personally and found extremely insulting. Never once had General Aldebaran shown any support for the Tigrina. He'd made no public statement, but everyhar knew he shared Pell's view that Caeru was a scheming and manipulative adventurer. Therefore, it was hardly surprising that when Ashmael caught sight of Caeru and Cal together, his expression was eloquent in the extreme. He appeared shocked and puzzled but also intrigued.

"Oh, look, a friend of yours," Caeru said. "Would you like to join him?"

Cal groaned in what Caeru supposed was a kind of mild despair and said, "Do we have a choice? Won't it look odd if we don't?"

"Let's see," Caeru replied. "What would appear worse? Should we sit alone at a table, with the obvious implications, or join a party who are eager to discover why you, Pell's soul mate, are out on the town with me, the dark stain in Pell's life?"

"Did you plan this?"

"No. I would never plan to be in the same room as Ashmael Aldebaran."

Even as they were speaking, Ashmael beckoned them over. He would be considering the fact that it could be no coincidence Cal and Caeru were out together while Pellaz was away from the city. This would not be happening otherwise. Caeru could sense Cal's discomfort. He knew Cal felt he was being disloyal to Pellaz and also that he couldn't understand why he should feel that way. A small part of him resented it too. Caeru moved to take hold of Cal's arm, but Cal jerked away before he could make contact.

"Relax," Caeru said to Cal. "You have to get used to this. I'm Tigrina, remember, and you are Tigron. We are supposed to be seen together."

"I remember," Cal muttered. This had never been part of his vision of reunion with Pellaz.

A har with pearly-scaled skin swooped to Caeru's side, clearly having recognized him immediately. He stared at Cal askance and asked how he might be of service. Caeru said they would like to be conducted to General Aldebaran's party, and then ordered the most expensive liquor the premises could offer. No mention of currency was made, but Caeru knew that later an outrageous bill would be sent to Phaonica, to be handled by the Tigron's office.

As they approached Ashmael's table, the general stood up, but this could hardly have been a gesture of respect. There was a hard edge to his voice as he uttered a greeting. He gave Caeru a particularly chilling glance. "It isn't often we see the Tigrina out in the city at night," he said.

"It isn't often I get the chance," Caeru responded, more from instinct than sense. He generally avoided Pell's friends, who all frequented establishments of this type.

"Now you have an escort," Ashmael said. "How charming and convenient. You must be delighted. Are you fulfilling the role adequately, Cal?"

Cal directed a single dark glance at Ashmael and sat down. Caeru realized that if Ashmael continued to snipe in this manner, Cal would be lost to him by the end of the evening. "I thought Cal should see more of what his colleagues get up to when they're playing," Caeru said. "If I hadn't persuaded him to come here, he'd have been working on his own all night."

"Can't have that," Ashmael said, raising his glass.

Cal ducked his head. "I was forced into it."

"You don't say!" Ashmael said, grinning.

Everyhar in the club was discreetly observing Ashmael's table. By morning, the scandal of Cal daring to escort the Tigrina to a club would be all over Immanion.

Music pulsed out into the perfect Almagabran evening, spilling out of the open shutters along with sensual perfume that had been scalded by the hot dancing bodies. Cal appeared to enter into the spirit of the evening. He drank, though not to excess, and danced a few times, but Caeru could feel his wariness, an animal instinct that was teetering toward the imperative to flee. He hadn't come this far, nor gone through so much, to risk offending Pellaz.

In a way, we are married, Caeru thought, and that is bizarre. He thinks so too. I know he does.

After midnight, more hara came to the club, expanding its clientele to the point where it was no longer comfortable. It was impossible to talk, because the music was so loud. Caeru realized he could achieve nothing more in this place. He yelled into Cal's ear: "I want to leave now. Do you want to stay or will you come back to Phaonica with me?"

"I'll come with you," Cal said, on his feet before he'd finished speaking.

They sat in silence in the carriage, while Caeru paid more attention than was necessary to the passing sights. This hadn't quite worked out how he'd planned, but then, how had he planned it anyway? He sighed. "This hasn't worked, has it?"

Cal stared at him unflinchingly. "What were you expecting?"

"I don't know. Something new. Is he always going to be at your shoulder? If so, that's a shame. I dared to think we might be friends, given all the effort you've put into charming me. It was an act, wasn't it? You never thought you'd reach me. Now I'm being nice and you're running scared."

Cal raised his hands. "Your feud with Pell is big and it had been going on for a long time before I got here. Don't try to involve me in it."

"But you *are* involved. You're here. Didn't you take magical training or something to transform yourself into a good har? If you want the job of Tigron, you have to take all of it on. You have to take me on, because I won't let you do otherwise."

Cal rubbed at his face. "Back off, Rue. You've had your fun."

Caeru relented. "I'm sorry. I really am. I wanted this to be different, but I can't help going for the jugular. I hope you understand why."

"Yeah."

The carriage ascended the curving driveway to the palace. Mellow lights gleamed out from a hundred windows. "Your home," Caeru said. "Isn't it beautiful?"

"You are astounding," Cal said. "You could have just said, 'Don't set foot in my apartment again.' Believe it or not, that would have worked. You didn't need to go to all this bother."

"Strangely enough, that was not my intention."

Cal grimaced. "Pell's not wrong about you."

Caeru laughed. "Thanks. I said I was sorry. Come and have a nightcap."

"No."

"Please." Caeru stared into Cal's eyes, searching for some spark, some glimmer of complicity. "I took your place. You took mine. Somehow, we have to let that go. Both of us."

Cal sighed deeply. "All right. We'll talk. But the minute you start yapping like a bitch, I'm out of there."

Caeru's staff had thoughtfully lit a fire in his sitting room, because the evening warmth had slipped away to chill. A decanter of brandy and two glasses stood waiting on a table. Caeru detected Velaxis's hand in that. He poured himself a glass and drank it quickly while Cal was still padding around trying to find a comfortable place to sit.

"Brandy?" Caeru asked, offering Cal a glass. "The best, imported from Thaine."

Cal shifted in his seat, took the glass, and sniffed it. "Reminds me of Saltrock."

"Once the home of your erstwhile friend, Seel, of course," Caeru said. "Another of my great admirers. And yours too, now, from what I've heard."

Cal cast him a glance and Caeru raised a hand, "Sorry, I promised, I know. I'll not say anything."

"It's in your blood."

"No it's not. It's in my mouth. I can't stop myself."

Cal laughed, an unexpected sound. "This is insane."

Caeru walked behind Cal's chair and watched the back of his head as he drank. "I'm not always like this. It's you. It's fear, maybe, or something . . ."

Cal glanced around at him. "I'm not always like this either. Usually, I could take you out with a single well-aimed word."

"So, here we are, tongue-tied, spitting out inappropriate knots."

"Too much alike, maybe . . ."

"They say Pell seduced me initially because I looked a little like you. Not that I do, of course. It's just the hair, but, who knows?"

Cal grinned. "You will never be as wondrous as me, Rue."

"I know that."

"Aha, a concession! One point to me."

Caeru smiled, and leaned forward. He didn't mean to do it, but somehow he was compelled to put his mouth against Cal's own. He felt the sudden sigh of breath, saw a vague flurry of images. He could feel how Cal's neck pained him, twisted as it was, and saw how he had been waiting for this to happen all night, from the moment he'd agreed to go to the club. Underneath the sparring, all the time, had been this. Cal didn't pull away for a good half minute.

"Rue, no . . ."

Caeru ran his fingers through Cal's hair. "Why not?"

"It's not a good idea. You know it isn't."

"What are you afraid of? Didn't Pell once say to you that all he owned was yours? He did say that, didn't he?"

"He didn't mean this. He didn't mean you scheming to get me while he was away, so you could act out your own private vengeance plan. If you are mine and I am yours, then Pell should be part of it too."

"I cannot imagine a greater abomination."

"I'm sure you can."

Caeru leaned on the back of the chair. Cal's neck was still twisted. He must be in agony by now. "It's not anything like vengeance," Caeru said. "The truth is that I want to know why I've suffered all these years. I want to find out for myself. And you are curious too, because I am the har with whom Pell conceived a child. You never did that together, and you know how powerful aruna has to be to achieve such a thing, because you've been a hostling yourself. You want me too, Cal. Admit it."

"Yes, I want you. Who wouldn't? You know your assets, I'm sure. We should talk about this, and then I should talk with Pell."

Caeru laughed. "You must still be insane after all, Calanthe. Pellaz can't stand the sight of me. I was supposed to be nothing more than a one-night stand. He abused me. He made me trust him enough to let him do that unspeakable thing to me. Then he left me. When are you going to wake up? Pellaz is not the fantasy you have in your head. He is brutal and vicious and he is Tigron. He can do what he wants to you, as he thought he could with me. Perhaps we need each other more than you think. Pellaz died. He never came back. Can't you understand that? The har who lives now is something other than the human boy you stole away from home. You can never have him back."

It was clear that Cal had now heard more than enough. He uttered a growl, leapt to his feet, and wheeled around, so swiftly and aggressively that Caeru instinctively took a few steps back. "I could justify wringing your scrawny neck, if I thought about it long enough," Cal said in a chilling tone. "You know I'm capable."

"Get out," Caeru said. His voice was calm, but inside he was terrified. He knew exactly how capable of murder Cal was. He could almost see himself lying dead and broken on the carpet.

"Why?" Cal laughed. "This is wonderful. Can't you take what you dish out? You want truth? You came here with your son—an eminently suitable excuse—because you craved some of what Pell had got. And oh, how much of that you've greedily taken. Did you really expect him to welcome you with open arms? Would he have left you in Ferelithia if he hadn't bitterly regretted what he'd done in ignorance? You are no innocent, Rue. Inside, you are still a singer in a two-bit band with a lust for power and possessions. You always will be, whatever jewels you drape on your body and however well you playact at being royalty. What a performer! Your son must be proud."

"I said get out," Caeru said.

"Why? We've only just started. We haven't even reached the interesting stage yet. Let's share breath again. Let's really show each other the truth inside."

"Do I have to call somehar to throw you out?"

"Can't cope with what you invoked?" Cal inquired. "How disappointing."

"Go," Caeru said. "This is finished."

"No, it hasn't. Don't you understand? You've won. But maybe it doesn't feel like victory now."

"Victory?"

"Here I am," Cal said coldly, opening his arms. "Come, drink, taste. Sate yourself. We are the rulers of all Wraeththu: flawed, magnificent, and vain. We deserve each other."

Cal was only a few steps away, yet it seemed like a vast distance. He was in pain. Caeru could see that so clearly. He mustered all of his courage and crossed the distance between them. He took Cal's face in his hands. "The hatred has to stop," he said. "It has to."

Cal's breath tasted of brandy and incense and burning candles. His hands were hot on Caeru's skin, sizzling with energy. He was hungry for contact, drawing the breath from Caeru's chest, from the depths of his belly. Aruna with Pellaz must be terrifying for him. He needed this. He needed grounding.

They sank to their knees on the carpet, struggling with clothes, clawing flesh. There was a sound like the ocean in Caeru's head and it was the seething of hot blood. This savage union was a vortex of chaos, of insatiable need, a desire to end all pain. Frustration, bitterness, fear, and resentment: they were all there—site guardians of Phaonica. Caeru fell back and hit his head sharply against the floor. Cal was on top of him. Caeru could feel Cal's heart banging against his ribs. Then, in the midst of madness, Cal became still. It was as if time itself had stopped. Caeru became aware of a gentle but insistent pressure between his legs, where it felt as if his soume-lam was gasping for breath. Aruna with Cal was going to happen. It really was. They had both just realized what they were doing.

"This was what Pell felt, the first time ever," Caeru murmured. "He felt you, like this."

"And this is what he saw," Cal said, "that night in Ferelithia. He saw what I'm seeing now."

"In this way, we are one."

Cal uttered a cry that was almost grief, and Caeru's body arched in pain. It was like fighting with history.

CHAPTER THREE

Velaxis came calling very early next morning, almost as if his psychic sight had picked up on the events of the previous night. Caeru was still in bed, lying facedown in a nest of pillows and covered partially by a sheet. Velaxis stalked into the room and threw wide the curtains. Sunlight streamed in harshly.

"Oh, dear," Velaxis said, examining Caeru's body. He pulled at the sheet. "You appear to be stuck."

"What?" Caeru rolled over, blinking.

"With blood. How barbaric."

"Stop pulling that. It hurts."

Velaxis sat down on the bed and folded his arms. "I demand a mission report."

"Mission accomplished," Caeru said, yawning. "At least I think so."

"Well done. What state is our beloved Tigron in?"

"The marks will still be there by the time Pellaz gets home."

"Hmm, perhaps not the best plan."

Caeru dragged himself from the bed, wrapped in the sheet. His back was very sore. It wasn't that Cal had scratched him. They'd taken the brandy to bed with them and somehow the bottle had broken. At some point during the proceedings, they had rolled on the pieces. At the time, they had both been too high on aruna to deal with the wounds. Caeru had barely felt it. Now, he realized he felt nauseous. "It should have been different," he said. "I didn't handle it very well." He went to the door and called for his dresser. His back needed attention.

"Details," Velaxis said. "It's your duty to tell me."

"Cal's not happy. He hardly knows where he is. The dream of Immanion has become something of a nightmare."

"And destined to get worse once Pellaz returns," Velaxis said. "You shouldn't have left marks, Rue. That was cruel."

"I didn't mean to. We broke some glass by accident. Cal will tell Pell what happened, anyway. I know he will."

"Was this a one-off roonfest?"

"I don't think so. He comes to me nearly every day. He'll be back."

"I wonder how Pellaz will react."

"He probably won't care. You know what he's like. He's never jealous of me. He wouldn't let himself be."

Caeru's dresser came into the room and uttered a shocked cry when he noticed the wounds.

Velaxis laughed in delight. "Over breakfast, you must tell me every detail. I'm not squeamish. Tell me everything. Then I shall wait in nervous anticipation for the next installment, which I presume will be tomorrow."

Caeru could barely get through the day. Now, he wanted to talk to Cal. They had to establish some kind of order. Last night had been vicious. It mustn't happen again. Caeru planned everything he intended to say. He would show Cal his tender side and build up his trust. The time for snarling was over. Pellaz was due to return to Immanion in a couple of days.

But Cal did not turn up at the usual time. Caeru couldn't eat anything. He sat on the terrace, wrapped in bewildered numbness, considering that Cal was going to treat him in exactly the same way Pellaz had. The only positive aspect was that this time there had been no conception.

At nine o'clock, Caeru sent one of his staff to Cal's apartments, but the Tigron was not in residence. Caeru drank himself into a stupor because it was the only way he could sleep and he could no longer stand to be awake. His back hurt so much the pain invaded all his dreams, most of which were hideous.

The following morning, Velaxis appeared, brimming with disgusting eagerness to hear more lurid stories. Caeru told him what had happened, or rather what hadn't happened.

"Go to his apartment today," Velaxis said. "Go yourself."

"I can't do that. It's too humiliating."

"I think you should. Cal's confused. He's probably frightened."

"I don't think he's ever that."

"Clean yourself up and go. Pride is pointless now and only an impediment to progress."

Caeru sighed. "All right. But I'll never forgive you if he throws me out."

"The Hegemony is due to meet this afternoon. You should both be there. Sort this out before that."

It took ten minutes to reach Cal's apartment: to Caeru it felt like over an hour and yet mere seconds. He had no idea what reception he'd get. A member of the Tigron's staff let him in and, without any apparent hesitation or disapproval, conducted him into Cal's presence. Caeru was disappointed to find that Cal was not in any kind of emotional agony, but was poring over immense piles of paper in his office. After Caeru had been announced, he said, "I was going to come and see you later."

"You didn't come last night," Caeru said, staring meaningfully at the attendant until he went away.

"No, I went to see Ashmael."

"Right. And what did *he* have to say?"

"You don't want to hear. We were stupid, Rue. Really stupid."

"I know. I'll be lucky if I'm not scarred for life."

Cal laughed uncertainly. "There are particular images that will stay with me for the rest of mine."

"So, what's your decision?"

"What do you mean?"

"You know. Well? Did Ashmael help you make it?"

Cal sighed. "Sit down. We have to talk."

"No. I just want an answer. Are you going to repeat history and turn your back on me?"

Cal put his hands on Caeru's arms. "No. It's just . . . Oh, hell, I don't know what it is."

Caeru pulled away from him. "I think I do. You want permission first. Isn't that it?"

"I want to talk to Pell, yes."

Sometimes, Caeru considered, the female side of being har manifested itself at the most inappropriate times. A small part of him, that seemed to be hovering somewhere near the light fitting, looked on in horror as he sank down on a chair and began to weep. He couldn't stop himself. It was decades of disappointment and heartbreak spilling out in one long stream. Even as he abandoned himself to misery, he realized that Cal must be thinking this was a deliberate ploy to get attention and sympathy. That only made it worse. *Get out!* A rational part of his mind advised. *Get out now before you make more of a fool of yourself.*

Blindly, he got to his feet and made in what he hoped was the direction of the door. All of Cal's staff would see him like this. It was vile.

Cal grabbed hold of him before he could leave the room. "Rue," Cal said lamely. "Don't."

Caeru pulled away. "You don't get it, do you?" he yelled and thumped his own chest. "It's in here. All of it. It's called love. It's like a magic spell or a curse."

Cal frowned in what appeared to be genuine perplexity. "You *love* me?"

"No! Not you, you idiot!" Caeru yanked open the door and ran down the corridor outside. He was dimly aware of curious hara observing him from various doorways.

Cal came after him, of course, and dragged him into another room. He slammed the door and leaned upon it, so that Caeru couldn't get out. "Calm down," he said. "It's not that bad."

"Fuck you!"

"I won't have this. You understand? I'm sick and tired of being this chaotic force that fucks up everyhar's life. Don't do this to me. Let me be."

Caeru laughed bitterly through his tears. "*Now* we're ourselves, aren't we?"

"I've taken you on. You asked me to and I have. If I can heal the rift between you and Pell, I will, but us being together before I've talked to him won't help. He'll read it all wrong."

"He won't. You don't know him. He expends universal energy into maintaining the belief I don't exist. Everyhar knows it. It'll go down in history."

"Not in my version of events it won't."

"Rewrite history, then. It'll do nothing to help me." Caeru rubbed his face. The tears had stopped. "How I wish I hadn't come here."

"It's a bit late for that, isn't it?"

"I meant *today*," Caeru snapped.

Cal laughed, so infectiously that Caeru found himself smiling, even though he didn't want to. "I promise you: I'll make Pell see sense."

Caeru reached out and touched Cal's face. "You're sweet, really, aren't you?

Your optimism is just so sweet." He withdrew his hand. "But totally improbable. Come to me tonight, Cal, or never come at all. For once, I want things to be on my terms."

He pushed Cal aside and left the room, considering that was probably the best parting shot he'd ever delivered.

CHAPTER FOUR

Many times, Pellaz broke his journey through the otherlanes to ride upon the back of the world, to feel the road beneath his *sedu*'s hooves, to watch the season flow past. Over the years since he'd become Tigron in Immanion, he had been prey to depression at regular intervals but what he felt now was deeper and more profound. He needed to escape the otherlanes to assure himself the world was real and that he wasn't just dreaming it. He realized he was afraid: the fabric of reality might break apart at any moment and he would be sucked into the place where his spirit had fled a long time ago. This might all be a dream. He might still be dying, somewhere.

Usually, Pellaz could find solace at the House of Parasiel in Galhea, where several of his closest friends lived. But the news he'd had to take them—or rather the truth after the variety of wild rumors and speculations they'd heard—had not been entirely welcome. Seel thought he'd gone mad even to entertain the idea of having Cal back in his life and was incandescent with fury over what had happened to Thiede; Cobweb had been mightily offended be-cause Cal had refused to accompany Pell there; Swift had been outraged they hadn't been informed of the details sooner, as he regarded Cal as family, and Tyson—well, it was difficult to read Tyson's reaction because he was Cal's son, and so like his hostling. His sullenness could hide excitement at the prospect of reunion with his parent or—given his blood—murderous impulses.

But perhaps more unsettling than any of the Parasilians' reactions to news of Thiede's fall and Cal's instatement were the private words Cobweb had had with Pellaz the previous night. They had walked in the gardens of We Dwell in Forever, a house now as famous as the family who lived within it. Cobweb was a creature of magic and mystery, more feminine than any har had a right to be, and he possessed the second sight.

As they passed beneath the weeping willows that cast their sorrowful locks upon the surface of the quiet, moon-kissed lake, Cobweb said, "Cal is always somehar else's sword." He reached up to bend a pliable twig around his fingers, twisting and twisting it, although it did not break.

"Tell me what you mean," Pellaz said. "Whose sword is he now?"

"That of the one who wished Thiede dead."

"Are you speaking of the Kamagrian parage, Opalexian?"

Cobweb said nothing. He went to squat beside the water and gazed down into it. Pellaz joined him, wondering if Cobweb could conjure pictures on the silvery surface.

"Thiede isn't dead," Pellaz said, "not in the normal sense."

"He is strong," Cobweb said, "and he passed from flesh with his inner eyes open. That is all. He might place his feet in many worlds, but he did not want this, Pell. Don't deceive yourself otherwise."

"The Kamagrian did not wish Thiede dead. Opalexian is a recluse."

Cobweb looked Pellaz directly in the eye. "When Cal went to speak in the Hegalion that first time, he spoke of the Kamagrian. He told the Hegemony about them, these strange offshoots of Wraeththu who refer to themselves as female. They had healed and trained him in the mystic arts. Why did Opalexian take it upon herself to do that? In sending Cal to Immanion, she changed the world. It was great shock, was it not . . . ? For some . . ."

Pellaz sighed. "I won't try to deceive you. I have known of the Kamagrian's existence since Flick and Ulaume went to live in Roselane. I visited Shilalama often. You know that."

"I have seen your visits there," Cobweb said, "and what you learned."

Pellaz wasn't completely sure whether Cobweb was telling the truth or how much he really knew. "Opalexian asked me to keep quiet, and I did," Pell said. "It was not yet time for Wraeththu to know about the Kamagrian. It was safer for everyhar to believe those who lived in Roselane were Wraeththu ascetics, a community of misfits. Opalexian feared persecution."

"I wonder why? She is as powerful as Thiede was."

"I respected her wishes. It did no harm. And since Thiede's disappearance, she hasn't come charging into Almagabra with a horde of Kamagrian Amazons, so we can only presume she still intends to keep a low profile. I asked her to come to Immanion and speak to the Hegemony, but she declined the invitation."

Cobweb ignored these comments. "Hara do not know the truth about your relationship with Shilalama, do they? You still keep your silence."

Pell looked away, sure that Cobweb would interpret correctly the lies in his gaze. "It is irrelevant. My visits there were social, and primarily concerned Flick and Ulaume."

"Do not look for Thiede in the parage, Opalexian," Cobweb said. "Along that path lies delusion and danger."

"I have no intention of replacing Thiede, if that's what you're implying."

Cobweb stood up and took a deep breath through his nose. "Be careful, Pell. The winds of change are, in reality, a hurricane of transformation. It is all far bigger than you know and it has yet to begin."

"What can you see? Tell me."

"Shadows," Cobweb said, "and somewhere a leaking truth."

"That's *very* helpful."

"It's all I can say. You will soon know. Seek your brother."

"Terez is in Immanion. What can he tell me?"

"Not Terez," Cobweb said. "He is *your* sword, Pell, and he is sharp. Use him wisely. Use him as your scout to find the one you really need."

"Then, are you speaking of Dorado? Is he still alive? What do you know? Tell me!"

"Very little. A hunch. When Cal went to Immanion, the reverberations of what happened opened portals that are usually closed. I saw many things that night. And one of the things I saw, or felt, was your kin. He has greater strengths than you, in some respects, as all the Cevarros have their own particular strengths."

"We are no longer Cevarros," Pellaz said, "we are har Aralis. But not Dorado. He went with the Uigenna. He cannot be part of what we are. He can only be part of our lingering problems in Megalithica."

"Listen to yourself. What scorn! And from which tribe does your beloved Cal derive? Who incepted Terez?"

"That is different."

Cobweb laughed. "Of course. When you finally start using your brain, Pell, come and see me."

"And what's that supposed to mean?"

"You'll know."

Cobweb would say no more on the matter, but the conversation had a profound effect upon Pellaz. He had slept badly that night and his dreams had been disturbing, even though he could barely remember the details when he woke up. Now, as he rode through north Almagabra toward home, he contemplated the delights of running away into the wilderness and shunning all responsibility. He was tired. He needed a holiday, not the simmering cauldron of intrigue that comprised the Phaonican court. In his mind, he spoke to Thiede: *Have we come to this? No wonder you opted out.*

There was, as he expected, no response.

Pellaz directed a command to his *sedu*: "Open a portal, Peridot. Let's go home."

The *sedu* shuddered with power and around them space and time became unstable. Peridot leapt into the spaces between the worlds. Pellaz thought he knew the otherlanes well. He knew their dangers and their delights. In some ways, they were the back alleys of creation, for in these places lost and desperate spirits gathered and lurked, their clawed and icy fingers ready to pinch a healthy living soul to grab some of its essence. Pellaz did not fear these sad entities: they were no more threat to him than tiny insects. But what he did fear was the yawning black hole that opened up unexpectedly in front of Peridot, like a bandit in their path.

It was a portal, but it was also an entity. Pell sensed Peridot's panic as the *sedu* struggled to veer past the manifestation. Pellaz could feel a strong force emanating from it that sought to suck them from their path. It was malign and it possessed intention. It had come for them specifically.

Pellaz thrust his hands deep into Peridot's astral being, reaching for his organs of energy. He fed the *sedu* with as much strength as he could muster. Their combined power was just enough to allow them to scrape past the danger. As they passed it, dark tendrils whipped out from it, like stinging vines.

"Out!" Pellaz directed the *sedu*. "Now."

Peridot needed no further encouragement. He burst from the otherlanes into earthly reality, transforming as he did so, back into a white horse. Pellaz saw that Peridot's neck was streaked with blood. Something had gouged him in the otherlanes. His own cheeks were stinging and the backs of his hands looked burned.

Once Pellaz reached his apartment in Phaonica, he went to his bathroom and immersed himself in scented water to soothe his hurts away. There was no longer any sign of injury on his body, but he ached inside as if his entire being were frozen. The journey home had unsettled him greatly, although now, back in the real world, he did not think the manifestation in the otherlanes could have been a deliberate attack. The otherlanes were infinite and Pellaz realized that even with his experience he really knew so little of them. It was probably an isolated incident, but in future, he'd take precautions before traveling. He saw no reason to confide in anyhar else about this.

Relaxing in a bath the size of a swimming pool, he watched the green light come down through the windows in the ceiling. He studied the marble columns around the room, the glint of brass and gold among the fixtures. How can this be? he wondered. Where did all this come from?

Phaonica appeared as if it had stood for thousands of years, yet it was comparatively new, as was most of Immanion.

We take so much for granted, Pell thought, *but how did Thiede do this, really?*

He didn't believe Thiede had built Immanion through the use of magic, which was a popular myth, but neither had it been built from scratch the hard way. So much of the Wraeththu world had arrived complete and developed, in little pockets around the globe. It didn't make sense, and to think about it was like trying to imagine the infinity of space. It was as if the mind shied away from it.

Ever since Cal had come to the city and endured his world-shaking fight with Thiede, Pellaz had felt unsafe. He missed Thiede: his mordant humor, his wry affection, but most of all the way he'd somehow kept the world glued together. Without him, it was in danger of falling apart. Pellaz did not think the Aralisians and the Hegemony were enough to keep it together. They were all so uninformed about what Wraeththu really was and how it had come to happen. One thing was certain: Pellaz har Aralis, Tigron of Immanion, felt more insecure and in doubt than he'd ever felt in his life. And where did the Kamagrian fit into the picture? They had found, trained, and healed Cal, because Pell had asked their leader, Opalexian, to do it, but nohar knew that. He'd begged the universe to grant a wish, and it had, with the help of the Kamagrian, but there had been a high price attached to it. In retrospect, even Pellaz wondered whether he'd done right in asking for it.

He rose from the bath and wrapped himself in towels, leaving wet footprints as he padded back into his bedroom. He found Cal there, sitting on the bed. He did not look happy.

"Thanks for coming here so quickly," Pell said. "Galhea was . . . difficult. Ground me."

Cal smiled. "Welcome back. Come here. I've missed you."

Pell sat beside him and laid his head on Cal's shoulder. "Help," he said. "I feel strange."

Cal embraced him and sighed deeply. "You're not alone. Can we escape?"

"No."

"I'm sorry."

"Don't apologize. We knew we'd have to deal with . . . fallout."

"Is it worth it to you?"

Pellaz kissed Cal on the mouth. "It'll all work out." He lay against Cal's side and for some time they were silent. Pellaz sensed Cal had something to say. He watched the flies circling high in the room and listened to the gentle clink of wind chimes on the terrace outside. This should be perfect.

"Pell," Cal said. "There's something you should know. I've spent some time with Rue."

"Has he upset you?"

"Yes and no. It got out of hand."

"I see. That doesn't surprise me."

"I need to talk to you about it. We've been together several times and I don't know what I feel about it. Am I being disloyal?"

Pellaz sat up. "I'm not going to be angry or hurt, Cal. It was obvious to me that Rue would want a piece of you. I won't give him the satisfaction of resenting it. I can't afford to give anyhar that power."

"Can you stop hating him?"

"I meant what I said to you. Rue is your Tigrina as much as mine. Do as you see fit, but don't involve me."

Cal laughed sadly. "That's ironic. I said that to him too."

"You might be a binding over a wound. In that, you will be doing me a service."

"You know he still loves you, don't you? It shocks me how much."

"He will say that to you, because to say otherwise would show him in a bad light."

"You're wrong. I think you've misjudged him. When I first came here, the three of us stood together in the Hegalion, united. I thought that would be the beginning of strength. We need it. All of us. And love is strength."

"In the Hegalion, I got carried away with the moment," Pell said. "I wish I could maintain it, Cal, but I can't. Too much has happened. It is difficult to misjudge somehar for over twenty odd years. You forget that life went on for me while we were apart."

"Please think about it."

"You be for Rue what I cannot. I'm generous enough to concede that."

"It means nothing without you."

Pellaz rose from the bed and went to his wardrobe, discarding towels along the way. "Perhaps you should be more concerned about your son. I've spoken with Swift and Cobweb about him." He pulled out some clothes and dressed himself. "We think Tyson should come to Immanion, but I predict it won't be easy for you."

Cal put his hands behind his head, stared at the ceiling. "I haven't seen him since he was a tiny harling. It doesn't feel real. I remember going through it all, but now . . ."

"Difficult to imagine he sprang from you. The thought of you and Terzian together hurts more than anything Rue could do. You were making pearls with the Varr while I was almost senseless with grief over losing you. That's bizarre."

Cal's tone was defensive. "I can barely remember what Terzian looks like. I thought you were dead."

Pell laughed awkwardly, in an attempt to lift the atmosphere. "We don't have to discuss this. It's history. After all, I did the same thing with Rue. Let's drop it."

Cal, clearly, didn't want to drop it. "Grief over you did terrible things to me too. I was out of my mind. Tyson sprang from that, if anything. I'm not sure I want to go back to that dark place. Do I really have to see him?"

"He's yours, Cal, and none of what happened was his fault. I have an abysmal relationship with my own son, and it's not something I'd recommend. Build bridges."

"Then you do the same."

Pell closed the wardrobe doors carefully. "What's on the agenda for today? I doubt I'm allowed the luxury of rest after my journey."

"Later this afternoon, an audience in the Hegalion with delegates from various tribes, all wanting Gelaming aid. It's not essential you're present for that, as both Vaysh and I have been vague about your return time from Galhea. This evening, you're booked for the caste ascension of some high-ranking young har in the High Nayati. You offered to officiate last week, when you were drunk at that party, remember? The parents have requested, most humbly, that the Aralisians turn out in force."

"Damn. Oh, well. Let the unholy trinity of Tigrons and Tigrina do their worst. I'll pass on the delegates, though. Will you handle it?"

Cal jumped up from the bed and wrapped Pell in his arms. "It's part of what I'm here for, isn't it? To take on some of the burden."

Pellaz was assailed by a poignant image of Thiede that was accompanied by a pang of loss. He pushed both image and feeling away and held Cal close. "Eat with me now. I'll tell you the horrors of Galhea."

Pellaz usually enjoyed conducting caste ascensions, but that night his mind was elsewhere. He noticed that Caeru seemed to be aware of his distraction, because the Tigrina took over most of the officiating. Pellaz was so accustomed not to feeling grateful for anything Caeru did, he was quite shocked to discover this had changed. More than that had changed. Pellaz no longer sensed the hungry, desperate, and often vicious need that normally oozed from Caeru like the essence of disease. He even smelled different. Caeru raised his arms to channel energy, and thereby raise the initiate from Neoma to Brynie level. For a moment he transformed into a skinny young har with ragged yellow hair and artfully ripped clothes. Pellaz could almost smell the perfume of a Ferelithian night, thirty years ago. Was Cal working some subtle magic? But there were more disorientating things to consider. As the ceremony progressed, Pell's mind kept flashing back to the otherlanes journey, and the black entity that had accosted him there. Sometimes, it felt as if that presence was still with him, tainting the sacred atmosphere of the High Nayati. Shadows pressed close and the vaulted ceiling was lost in darkness. Unearthly creatures might cluster there, whispering together.

Cal and Caeru intoned the words of the ceremony and the young har they initiated knelt before them, while Pellaz fought a battle with the demons of his imagination. He remembered the words that Cobweb had said to him, the mention of Dorado. Cobweb had implied Pellaz needed help: as usual, he'd concealed more than he'd revealed, but that was the way of seers. For the first time in years, Pellaz felt young and powerless. He did not have enough information, certainly not enough to feel secure, and had no wise har to go to for advice and assurance. Despite Cobweb's warning, he found himself thinking of Opalexian. He wanted to speak to her.

The ceremony concluded, and the newly elevated har went home to celebrate with his proud parents. Tentatively, Caeru asked Cal and Pellaz if they'd like to come back to his apartment for supper. Cal did not answer, but directed his attention to Pellaz, who found himself consenting, simply because the thought of being alone was too unsettling. The unseen world was pressing close upon the membrane of reality. All of Pell's senses were heightened.

Before they left the High Nayati, Pellaz went alone to the shrine of the Aghama, Wraeththu's prime deity. Here, a bronze image of Thiede was lit by the soft glow of candlelight. Pellaz cast some grains of incense over the flame that eternally burned there. The perfumed smoke rolled over him. He prayed to Thiede for guidance, and perhaps there was a sense of a tall presence behind him, the ghost of a hand on his shoulder.

You are Tigron, said a voice in his head. *Take control.*

"I need you. There are cracks in the world."

Fight darkness with light. Fight light with darkness.

Pellaz sighed deeply. For so long, everyhar had believed Thiede had influenced everything that happened to Wraeththu. He was their progenitor and their god. But he had also been a har of flesh and blood, and Pellaz could not believe one individual could have controlled so much. Had he forced Pellaz to create a pearl with Caeru against his better judgment? Had he influenced all that had happened to Cal? If it were true, then surely Pellaz would have sensed it in some way. He saw his own life as a pageant, parading across his mind's eye. Historic events, deep passions, betrayals, victories. If Thiede was not the greater power, then what was?

A candle hissed in its own wax on the altar and Pellaz opened his eyes.

Now you begin to see . . .

"Speak to me."

A pearl of light, the star of all stars . . . unexpected.

Pellaz held his breath. Dare he believe the words he heard in his mind came from anywhere but his own dreams and desires?

Do what is not expected of you . . .

"How can I find you?"

In the star . . .

On his terrace in Phaonica, Caeru's behavior was cool but cordial. He clearly made a point of not sitting too close to Cal, and asked Pellaz for news of Galhea. Pellaz found it fairly easy to play the game and offer up the gossip, but he did not tell his companions anything about the things that concerned him. He felt like an outsider, but strangely, this did not distress him. He could see plainly how disorientated Cal felt being in Immanion and how Caeru could ground him in a way that Pellaz could not. There was really only one Tigron. Pellaz smiled, drank a little wine, and heard himself chatting amicably, but inside he was saying to himself: *We were mad to think we could ever have it back, Cal. I died, and what we had died with me. What we have now is a revenant; lurching, damaged, and undead. How could we have been so stupid to cling to a dream for so long?*

He realized he loved Cal more now than he ever had, but it was not the consuming passion of youth that had sustained his dreams over the years. It was not as hot and urgent; it was deeper, more real.

The time came when Pellaz knew he could leave without giving offense. They had gone indoors because the air on the terrace had cooled. He could leave, because it was expected of him. He had made a concession in visiting the Tigrina's apartment and this would be regarded as a first step. He would return to his own rooms, either with Cal or alone, and he would become resentful of being manipulated. He would remember everything that made him angry, and the cycle would begin again. He could see himself walking out of the door, inclining his head in a formal farewell. It would be so easy, and he yearned for it.

"I could do with another drink," he said. "Have we exhausted your stocks, Rue?"

"No . . . I'll see to it." Caeru left the room in a hurry, clearly surprised.

Pellaz sat down in a chair. He felt light-headed, as if he'd summoned up strong and capricious energy.

"What are you up to?" Cal asked.

"I'm tired," Pellaz said, "very tired. I love you and I want what's best for you."

"What's the matter?" Cal squatted beside Pell's chair. "You look . . . odd, and what you just said sounded worryingly final."

"I'm not going anywhere," Pellaz said. He reached out and stroked Cal's face. It was still difficult to believe Cal was here in Immanion. It didn't feel real, after so many years of longing and fantasy. But it was one of only two possible conclusions to their passion: reunion or death. Who or what had decided upon the happier resolution?

Stop thinking this way, Pellaz told himself.

Caeru came back into the room with wine and paused when he caught sight of Cal by Pell's chair.

"Something's not right with Pell," Cal said, standing up.

Pellaz said nothing. It was pointless to lie.

"It's me," Caeru said. "Isn't it?"

Pellaz closed his eyes briefly. "No, it isn't. Come here. Stand before me."

Caeru put down the wine on a table and approached Pellaz warily.

"I want to look at you," Pellaz said, "and remember a night in Ferelithia, a long time ago."

"Don't," Caeru said, shaking his head.

"I know, it will be difficult. We are so entrenched in our beliefs. Do you really still love me, Rue?"

"You are different tonight. Cal has spoken to you, hasn't he?"

"You know he has. You know what he wants. But it's our decision, Rue. The truth. No masks. You know why I feel the way I do about you?"

"Yes."

"Has it ever been justified?"

"It just *is*." Caeru picked up the wine again and swigged from the bottle. "Despite that, seeing as you asked, and you never have before, I *do* still love you."

Pellaz steepled his fingers beneath his chin, conscious it was a gesture Thiede often used to make. "You think you do. You're supposed to. It's all part of the Aralisian myth. But only a mad har would still care for me after all I've said and done. Are you mad, Rue?"

"Pell, let's not do this," Caeru said, "it's too painful."

"Is it because of the way I look? Are you simply infatuated with that? It's an explanation, isn't it?"

"Maybe I just have a good memory."

"How reliable is that? Can you really remember what we said to one another, or what I was like?"

"Yes," Caeru said. "I can. You changed my life. I didn't want you to be Tigron. I wanted you to be a normal har. When I found out what you were, it gutted me, made me physically ill. It was a presentiment, because I knew what would follow, yet still I came to find you."

"Romantic," Pellaz said, "tragic. A good story."

Caeru uttered an angry sound, took another drink. "Why am I bothering with this? You're just being you, as always."

"No," Pellaz said. "I'm beginning to see, really see."

"You sound drunk. Go home. Take Cal with you."

Pellaz stood up and Caeru backed away. "No," Pellaz said, "I want to go back there, to that night in Ferelithia. I have to understand why it happened, why everything after it happened. We have to go back."

"It's impossible."

"No, it isn't." Pellaz turned to Cal. "Help me here. You understand what I'm saying, don't you?"

"I think we should go further back, to the moment I saw you die," he said. "*That* is impossible."

Pellaz began to pace around the room. "I don't know," he said. He did feel drunk, which was odd because he'd only had a couple of glasses of wine. He felt he was very close to seeing through an illusion, that at any moment everything around him would shatter and a different place would be revealed. "I think I'm onto something." He stopped pacing. "Cal, you want the three of us to be together, don't you?"

Cal shrugged awkwardly. "It would be . . ." He paused and shook his head. "No, not at the moment. You are being too weird."

"Well, I think we're supposed to be together," Pellaz said, "but we're supposed to go into it blind, without awareness. I'm supposed to regret being with Rue again, as I have all the other times."

"Other times?" Cal said.

"Yes," Pellaz replied. "He's not told you about that, then. It's a sordid little cycle we have, and one that could so easily continue. The whole situation could implode, destroy us, move us on to the next tragedy. But if we approach this union with our eyes open, it might be different. I have to recapture a feeling, change what is."

"I have no idea what you're talking about," Caeru said. "You're not making sense."

"It doesn't matter." Pellaz paused.

There it was: the threshold. He could see it. He had the power to make a choice and he'd stepped outside of himself to do it. Perhaps Thiede had helped, perhaps not. But one thing Pellaz was sure of: for this moment, he was in control. Beyond the threshold might lie madness or danger, self-loathing in the morning, or nothing at all, but at least he could see the possibilities and it was his choice whether to step over that threshold or not. He took a deep breath. "I'm going to your bedroom, Rue. Join me in a few minutes. Don't say anything. Just be Tigrina, as I will be Tigron. Cal, come to us a short while after that."

Pellaz didn't wait to hear Caeru's protests, but left the room. He knew the way to the bedchamber because, on many occasions over the years, driven by drink and maudlin sentiment, he had visited his consort there and had cruelly taken aruna with him, only to ignore him for weeks afterward. He remembered well the bleak bitter mornings of self-recrimination and disgust. He had believed his motive had been to wound and damage, to make sure Caeru never got too comfortable or too happy, but now he realized there had been true desire, released by wine: a secret, unacknowledged yearning to seek the essence of that night when Abrimel had been conceived.

Pellaz paused at the door and had to lean upon the frame for a moment. He never drank alcohol now when he was alone, because when he did, the risk was there. When that happened, and he was drawn to Caeru's door, did it reflect his true feelings or simply an unwise delusion conjured by drink? Whatever the reason, these revelations were shocking. Pellaz felt physically sick, which was almost enough to send him fleeing for his private rooms, but he strengthened his resolve. He had to find out the truth.

The room was decorated in dark crimson and gold, a sensual nest, but Pellaz knew that Caeru invited few hara there. An air of desolation hung amid the motionless drapes and in the aura of the lamps. Pellaz undressed and lay on his back on the bed, staring up at the shadows. He felt driven and sure, mainly because he sensed this wasn't supposed to happen, not in the way he intended it would. He closed his eyes and summoned the past, smelled it, let it envelop his being.

He sensed Caeru come into the room, but did not open his eyes. Perhaps that pressure on the bed wasn't Caeru at all, but an unseen creature that had seeped through from the otherlanes and had followed him home. He focused his thoughts: Ferelithia. Music. The smell of the sea. An open window on the night. He remembered the darkness of Rue's room, the aroma of anticipation and desire on the air. What had soured that?

Caeru squatted over Pellaz, ran a hand down his chest. Pellaz could feel his gaze as warm energy. This was Caeru's own moment of choice and decision. He could take some small revenge very easily now, but instead, he uttered a soft sound and lowered himself slowly onto Pell's ouana-lim. They began to move together, Pell's hands on Rue's hips. "Lie down on me," Pellaz said.

A jewel that hung around Caeru's neck on a silver chain pressed coldly against Pell's chest. *I could have had this at any time,* Pellaz thought. *There was never any point to anything: how I felt, what I did. It was all worthless. It wasn't even mine.* He opened his eyes. "We were controlled, do you understand?"

"Ssh," Caeru murmured and kissed Pell's mouth. "It's all right."

He didn't understand. All he wanted was the contact, acceptance, harmony. At this moment, he must hardly dare to believe this was happening. "You feel good, Rue. You always did."

Caeru stopped moving and buried his face in Pell's hair. His body trembled and presently Pellaz felt Caeru's tears trickling down his neck. This couldn't be cruel. Pellaz couldn't allow that to happen. He saw Cal come into the room, and move to the side of the bed, his head tilted to one side. He appeared amused, if somewhat puzzled.

"We are going to create something bigger than all of us," Pellaz said softly. "It might be our strongest defense."

"Against what?"

"I don't know yet, but I will."

Cal sat down on the bed, put a hand on the back of Caeru's head, which he had not raised. "Are you talking of a pearl, a harling?"

"Yes, born of our three beings."

"Is that possible?"

"We won't know until we try."

Caeru had gone utterly still.

"Will you do this, Rue?" Pellaz asked. "Will you host this pearl?"

Caeru's voice was muffled by Pell's hair. "I see darkness," he said. "I see fear, and it has a face."

"I will protect you. Trust me."

Caeru raised his head. "I will do this thing," he said, "but not to create whatever it is you wish to create. Understand why I will do this thing."

"I do," Pellaz said, "but I can make you no promises. Live fully in this moment. It is real, whatever happens."

CHAPTER FIVE

$\rightarrowtail\!\leftarrow\!\!\Longrightarrow\!\!\bullet\!\!-\!\!\bigcirc\!\!-\!\!\bullet\!\!\Longleftarrow\!\rightarrow\!\!\leftarrowtail$

The Gelaming enclave of Imbrilim in Megalithica had begun its life as a camp for refugees fleeing Varrish and Uigenna atrocities. Now, it was an expanding town in its own right, the center of Gelaming power in that country. Following Cal's arrival in Almagabra, Abrimel har Aralis, son of the Tigron, had applied for a position in Imbrilim. Pellaz had granted this request, no doubt without pausing even for a moment to reflect upon his son's possible motives in wanting to leave Immanion. Abrimel wished he didn't care about it, but even after so long, his father's indifference to him still possessed the power to wound deeply. All his life, he had suffered on his hostling's behalf, perhaps the only har alive who knew the extent of Caeru's pain, which he hid beneath the brittle, sniping exterior that prowled the intrigue-soaked salons of Immanion, armed with a razor tongue and a shield of cold disdain. Abrimel had hated the idea of Calanthe with the same ferocity that Caeru had, and steadfastly refused to accept Cal as part of the family. It was obscene, and Abrimel was astounded that the Hegemony had been so accommodating and had passively accepted Thiede's murder, because that was what Abrimel believed had happened. Everyhar knew Cal's history. It was a joke that he had become joint Tigron in Immanion. As for Caeru, Abrimel was disappointed that his hostling had not been more hostile to Cal. Caeru might utter bitchy remarks about the new Tigron, but the fact was they took dinner together nearly every evening, and Abrimel had noticed how Caeru perked up near the hour when Cal was due. The possible scenarios that could blossom from these meetings were too nauseating to consider. Thinking about the whole sorry situation made Abrimel so furious he had to break things around him. There was no way he could remain in Immanion, because, if he did, he knew he'd do something he'd bitterly regret and which would ruin his life.

Now, he had found a kind of peace in Megalithica. In Imbrilim, he had status. He was the representative of the Aralisians on Megalithican soil. He had a job, supervising the collection of data about the various tribes that had established themselves in the country. He saw himself as a historian: facts were calm, beautiful things. He enjoyed writing them down in a neat hand upon clean white pages.

The news came in the evening, at the hour when neither day nor night holds sway, but the soft gray twilight of the veil between the worlds. Abrimel, working alone in his office, accompanied only by his two cats and an especially fine wine from the West Coast, felt the shiver in his flesh when an otherlanes portal opened up beyond the town. He did not raise his head from his work, because arrivals of Almagabran hara were a regular occurrence. It was rare their visits concerned him. But that night, a knock came upon his door and Abrimel had to put down his pen. He lifted a cat from his lap and went to answer the door himself, because none of his staff were at home. He found Velaxis at the threshold and for a moment, his heart was stilled. "What is it?" he demanded, afraid something had happened to Caeru.

"May I come in, tiahaar?" Velaxis inquired delicately.

Abrimel stood aside. "Yes, yes, of course. Why are you here?"

"I bring news," Velaxis answered, stepping into the house. "Where are your manners, Abrimel? Aren't you at least going to conduct me to a comfortable room and ply me with fine liquor?"

"What news?" Abrimel asked. Velaxis had not visited him in Imbrilim before.

"Caeru carries a pearl. You are to have a brother."

Abrimel stared at Velaxis for some moments. "What?"

"You must be pleased. After all, this is a most unlikely event."

"Who is the father?"

Velaxis laughed. "Pellaz, of course. Oh, and I believe Calanthe also."

Abrimel slammed the front door. "That is not possible."

"The Aralisians work miracles. I have pondered minutely the mechanics of how they achieved it. It makes me feel quite breathless."

Abrimel leaned upon the door and closed his eyes for a few seconds. He visualized his hostling and saw him as a young, stupid, gullible, starstruck har, who deserved everything he got. Abrimel, by contrast, felt a thousand years old, a sagacious hermit weighed down by the knowledge of the universe. "How could you let this happen?" he asked Velaxis. "You influence him more than any other. How did this happen?"

Velaxis sauntered up the hall. He opened a door, looked in, found a cold dark dining room, and closed the door. "The usual way, I imagine," he said. "Where is your sitting room, Bree? Do I have to find it myself?"

Abrimel took Velaxis into his office and grudgingly shared the wine. His mind was a whirl. He could not believe what he'd heard. "Are you sure about this?" he asked, more than once.

"Absolutely," Velaxis replied. "There is no doubt. Rue has been shattered by the experience—but not, it has to be said, in an undesirable way. He has suffered a few unpleasant side effects. The details, really, are too gross to relate."

"One unpleasant side effect being that he and my father are reconciled."

Velaxis gave him a measured stare. "There has, inevitably, been some degree of reconciliation. I would have thought you'd be pleased for him."

"This is Calanthe's doing."

"Naturally. He has been doing quite a lot. Now a har of his blood will be part of the Aralisian dynasty. It is fortunate you are the firstborn."

"It is all irrelevant. I will never be Tigron. Our life spans will see to that. Or if I am, it will be in some far distant time, and I too shall be very old. I expect one of my great highchildren can look forward to the honor of inheriting Pell's crown, such as it is. A young har should take it."

"You've been thinking about this, haven't you?"

Abrimel shrugged. "I thought about it a lot once. It has little meaning to me now."

Velaxis swirled his wine around in its glass. He stared into it. "Perhaps you should think some more."

"Keep me out of it."

"If something should happen to Pellaz, to his consorts . . ." Velaxis raised his shoulders eloquently. "Well, as it stands, a harling of the triumvirate's combined essence might well be seen as the obvious heir."

"Nothing will happen to Pellaz. He is too strong. He can outwit any foes."

"Some said that of Thiede."

Abrimel stared at Velaxis, speechless.

Velaxis put down his glass, and leaned forward in his seat to take Abrimel's hands in his own. "I am very fond of Rue," he said. "I helped raise you, and you are like a son to me. All I ask is that you remain aware, that's all. There are different factions. No matter how much you might want to hide away in exile, Bree, you are important to some hara. You might have no choice about becoming involved."

"Tell me what you know."

Velaxis released Abrimel's hands. "There is nothing to tell, as yet. But there are changes afoot. It does not involve the Hegemony. I don't know who or what it involves, but I can sense it in my blood."

"You're lying."

"I suggested to Rue he should become close to Cal. He took my advice, and now this has happened. That, for some reason, I did not foresee."

"Are you an enemy of my father's?"

"No, no. I am no har's enemy, but neither am I their ally. I am loyal only to myself, and in that I am the most honest har alive. I'm not asking you to trust me, Bree. That is not necessary. Just remain alert and aware. Keep informed. Don't make any bad decisions."

Abrimel uttered a sound like a growl. "Rue is a fool. He's learned nothing. He's still in Ferelithia with stars in his eyes."

"That might well be true," Velaxis said. "Aren't you going to send him a message of congratulations? I could deliver it for you."

"I could wring his neck."

"A short message will do. I can dictate it for you. I think that politically you would be wise to send it."

"Do as you see fit. I don't care."

Velaxis sighed. "Bree, you are Aralisian, and Pell's son, no matter how much either of you try to forget that fact. You isolate yourself deliberately, when you could be one of the Gelaming's brightest stars. Skulking over here in Imbrilim is probably not your best course of action."

"I cannot be part of a travesty. I will not accept that Uigenna lickspit as Tigron."

"He is not that bad. It could have been far worse."

Abrimel laughed harshly. "Could it? If I think about what's happened, I fill with black dread. It was just a beginning, and no matter how many of you in Immanion try to delude yourselves to the contrary, it will end badly. Wraeththu is headless without Thiede. Headless and sightless."

Velaxis helped himself to more of the wine. "But perhaps also free." He smiled. "The wine is good here. That alone might convince a har to stay. Get paper and a pen. You will now write to your hostling."

CHAPTER SIX

Diablo was so mean, it wasn't a joke he was named for the old devil. If you came across him in the dark, you'd be forgiven for thinking he was made entirely of black sticks, the remains of charred cooking embers or a forest fire, even though his skin was the mottled faded yellow of old leaves. He saw the spirits of the trees, those who were part of nature and those who weren't. He could move quickly, like a black whip or a tongue of smoke. Up close, his eyes were too big and his chin too pointed, a legacy of the weird subtle energies that coursed through the landscape of his birth. This was the Forest of Gebaddon, quite some distance south of the territory of Galhea, in Megalithica. Weirdness soaked the soil, rising up as mist sometimes, warping plants and animals alike, and also the hara who were condemned to live there. Diablo was both young and old: young in that he had lived the equivalent of only twenty years on this earth (although, where he came from, time was not quite the tick-tock discipline it was in other areas); and old because he had never been young. From the moment he'd poked his twiggy fingers through the cracked shell of his pearl, followed by his head on its too long neck, he had been as ancient as time itself. He was an outsider in a community of outsiders, where the drudgery of existence held no charm and it was mandatory to hold every other living being in contempt.

The elders of his tribe spoke of dispossession, of exile and torment. They railed against invisible oppressors that existed beyond the pulsating membrane that comprised the edge of their world. If they spoke of a time to come when they would claw back all that had been taken from them, it was not in a spirit of hope. All they wanted was revenge and if anything existed beyond that, it wasn't worth thinking about. Given the chance, they'd rid the world of Wraeththu and humans alike. In their time, they'd already done quite a lot to further that aim.

Diablo had not been conceived in love. He did not know who his hostling or his father was, as he'd hatched in a bed of pearls, far from warm harish bodies, smothered in damp autumn leaves. An older har, whose job was to supervise hatchings, had taken care of his physical needs, told him where to forage for food and so on, but Diablo had never been held close in another's arms, never heard the soft whisperings of affection with which hostlings normally shower their offspring. When other harlings had hatched beside him, they'd fought among themselves fiercely for possession of particular feeding and resting areas. It was not unknown for harlings to kill one another in these battles over territory. They were, in fact, regarded as hardly more than dangerous animals by the older hara of the tribe, who would beat them off with sticks if they dared to approach an inviting campfire at night. When they were ready for feybraiha, the harlings would sit and howl like young wolves on the tall gray rocks outside the rough settlements of adults. Hearing this call, hara would come to them, shut them up with the contact they craved so desperately, and if the essence of their physical exchanges did not inspire spiritual passion, awareness, and insight, it at least dampened their ferocity. The harlings, tamed by what could hardly be called aruna, could now be taken into the main body of the tribe and soon most of them even forgot where the hatching grounds were.

Many years before, a coalition of Gelaming and what eventually had become Parasiel had stormed the Varr citadel of Fulminir in the cold north of Megalithica. Here, the Varr leader, Ponclast, had made his stand against the forces that opposed him. Ponclast's right-hand har, Terzian of Galhea, had not been quite dead then, but certainly in Gelaming captivity. One of those who had led the assault on Fulminir was Terzian's son, Swift. Perhaps the Fulminiric Varrs, when they'd realized this, thought Swift had been seduced by power and wealth, or else by the har who the Gelaming had given to him as consort, Seel Griselming. Perhaps they thought Swift was more like his father than Swift would ever have dared to think. Others might not even have believed their eyes. But whatever the Fulminiric Varrs had thought, the Gelaming and the Parsics, who had confined the conquered hara to their strange hell in

Gebaddon, had no idea what the consequences of this exile would be. They were no longer Varrs, but Teraghasts, a forgotten tribe, sealed away, disposed of without actually having had to be killed. Nohar had really considered what would happen to them after the magical seals had been set across their boundaries, and not even the most paranoid ever believed they would start breeding. Although enlightened hara might talk of how harlings could be conceived only in love, this was not true. They could be conceived in very different emotions, if the intention and determination was strong enough.

Thiede had once said that the remnants of Ponclast's tribe might find enlightenment in the Forest of Gebaddon, but he'd never really cared about it. He'd known he was strong enough to confine them and that was all that mattered. If he ever thought about them in the years after the rout of Fulminir, it was only to consider briefly whether he should have had them slaughtered after all. To be fair, he and his allies had had to witness firsthand the atrocities these hara had been capable of, and the only thing the victors had cared about in the aftermath of that trauma was ridding the world of such a degenerate strain immediately. The defeated Varrs were beyond rehabilitation and couldn't even be domesticated.

Because Swift had led the forces that conquered them, and because the typical Teraghast memory was very long and accurate, the name of Parasiel was a curse. Even though the name had not even been imagined by the time the last incantation had been uttered at the edge of Gebaddon, it had somehow found its way in through chinks and cracks, carried on the wind, in seeds, in dreams. If you spat and hissed the word, it could have a very strong power of its own. It was chanted often, in the hope that all the spite, hatred, and resentment would somehow filter through the barrier that the Gelaming had constructed, fly across the landscape, and reach into the heart of We Dwell in Forever like the black spores of disease. Fortunately, the Parasilians had long forgotten their abandoned brothers, and as the best part of a curse is the victim knowing about it, the worst hexes simply slid off the barrier, or if they found their way through had transformed into nothing more than the whisper of a whining ghost by the time they reached Galhea.

Ponclast, the erstwhile lord of Fulminir, had changed very much. Perhaps some of those changes would have pleased Thiede, because Ponclast was no longer a har masquerading as a man. He had slid into the darkest corners of his feminine aspects while maintaining the steely resolve of his masculine traits. His body was long and thin, the skin very white. His black hair hung down his back in a strangely glistening flag, as if it was wet, yet it rarely was. He dressed in tattered robes of darkest crimson, but kept his fingernails very short and neat. It was important to him, in spite of everything, to have clean hands. Because he was har, he possessed a freakish kind of beauty, but it would never inspire poetry in another's heart, even though it might arouse some exceedingly dark prayers. He concealed himself, for the most part, in an underground lair that was his hive. In this place, hara of the tribe came to him and learned about how harlings did not have to be conceived in love. Ponclast, like a monstrous queen bee, was fecund. Most harlings of the tribe came from his body. There were very few moments when he was not with pearl and because he was so long and thin, the sight of him in this condition was not pleasant. His children were like the bursting boils of his hatred. They tumbled from him twisted up and snarling in their pearls, sustained, as was their hostling, by feelings of injustice and bitterness, which in Ponclast's case were very focused indeed.

On the night when Calanthe had locked in psychic combat with Thiede, something had happened to the magical barrier surrounding Gebaddon. It didn't break or fade; it remained as strong as ever, and in some areas became even stronger, but something leaked through it and slithered through the warped undergrowth of the forest. It found its way to Ponclast, brooding as usual in a deep cave, where tree roots were like stalactites around him. It came to him like a little bird and landed on his outstretched hand. It was the ability to see through the veil. It was Thiede's destruction and because Thiede had put so much of himself into Gebaddon to keep the exiles at bay, when he transcended the earthly realm part of his essence went looking for a place to rest, a place called home, where it would feel comfortable. It was unfortunate that Gebaddon was the nearest it could find.

Ponclast felt knowledge enter him like a blade to the throat. For some moments, he was held in stasis, in pain. He witnessed and experienced firsthand some of Thiede's torment, fear, and confusion, and didn't know what it was. It could just have been another miserable torture conjured up by the poisoned soil of Gebaddon. But when the sensations subsided and Ponclast lay heaving upon his throne of damp dark boughs, he knew. Thiede was gone. The barrier still stood, but the Teraghasts were somehow changed. Ponclast knew that he might now find a way for a part of them, if only a small insubstantial part, to squeeze through the boundary.

For weeks Ponclast worked in secret upon his plans, trying many, discarding all. Some of his hara, lured in ignorance into his subterranean hive, died during the experiments. He toyed with sending hara into trance, so that they believed they could pass like smoke through the barrier. He performed dark rituals of grissecon to invoke unmentionable forces into hara's bodies, which might find the barrier no more obstructive than mist. None of these trials worked. He needed something bigger, more daring. And yet he knew he must be subtle. If he acted too quickly or too rashly, the Gelaming would no doubt pick up psychically on his activities. They would be alerted to his newfound freedom, albeit small, and would squash it swiftly. Sometimes Ponclast wondered whether he was dreaming a cruel dream, and that the possibility of justice at last was an illusion. He dreamed often of Terzian, had always done so. In death, Terzian had transformed in Ponclast's mind into a shining angel. Their past disagreements had been forgotten. Terzian was a martyr, a dark saint. He must be avenged. And vengeance could not be taken in prison.

During his experiments, with the smell of blood and singed flesh around him as he meditated, Ponclast prayed so hard to the image of Terzian, he conjured a living thought that appeared to him as a flickering outline of radiance. The tragedy of betrayal poured from this image, the treachery of sons. Ponclast's son, Gahrazel, whom he had fathered in the days when he'd led the Varrs, was long dead. Ponclast himself had ordered Gahrazel to be executed for treason. It was not unreasonable to suppose that Terzian's son, equally traitorous, should suffer in a similar way. When Ponclast, deep in trance, saw Terzian's beautiful image hanging before him in darkness, it seemed that Swift's name was upon his lips. The House of Parasiel must be razed to the ground, its hara expunged without trace. But how could Ponclast achieve this? He was not mad, so under no delusion he had the power to affect outside reality in such a shattering way. Not with the resources at his disposal. Not yet.

"Help me, beloved," he said to the phantom of Terzian. "Bring me aid." He cut his wrist and offered blood into a bowl of fire, then he sealed the wound. "Bring it quickly." He worried that the Gelaming would somehow curb him before he could act.

One night, weeks later, Terzian came to Ponclast in a dream. He carried between his hands a window into the world beyond and through this window Ponclast perceived an astounding thing. The reverberations of the event he witnessed were so strong they made the entire barrier around Gebaddon vibrate and resonate a thousand tones like the strings of untuned harps. They made the barrier glow a deep reddish purple and any Teraghast hara unfortunate enough to be within fifty feet of it were thrown into convulsions. Some of them choked on their own tongues. Ponclast, however, writhing in sleep, saw a different kind of light. He saw a soul comprised of colors the harish eye could not normally perceive. He saw it streak like a comet through the layers of the universe until it splashed into the body of Caeru har Aralis and took possession of the newly formed pearl it found there.

The image of Terzian said nothing, but Ponclast knew regardless that he was being shown this event for a reason. This was no ordinary har that had been conceived. It was, in some ways, an abomination, created too soon and in ignorance. Ponclast thought that if Thiede had been in this plane, his etheric servitors would have blocked the soul before it got within twenty layers of earthly reality. They would have sent it back to the center of creation, and Caeru would have woken the next morning with only a sore body and consuming nausea. He would not have been with pearl. But Thiede was gone, and his protégé, Pellaz, had acted imprudently. He had called into being a kind of demon he lacked the strength or wisdom to control. When it hatched, this demon would want to take into itself all that was Thiede. It would surpass in power any that had come before. Gebaddon, to this being, would be a morsel to consume with relish.

Now the image of Terzian spoke. It said, "If you would take for yourself the power of the Aghama, destroy this pearl. Have it brought to you and devour it. Then will the House of Parasiel be given into your hands and your kingdom shall spread across the earth."

Ponclast awoke with this prophecy ringing in his head. He sat upright in his cold bed and stared into the darkness, where no shining spirit hung. Even to a har such as Ponclast, who made the Kakkahaar Lianvis appear only as a benign trickster, the idea of ripping a pearl from its hostling and then devouring it was hardly a prospect to relish. His mouth was rank with the taste of blood. He cared nothing for the Aralisians, and in fact one of his dearest fantasies was to impale the entire family upon poles outside Phaonica, but he also knew that if he concurred with the suggestion that had seeped through to this world, he would be crossing a boundary he had never dared to cross before. He would deliver himself to forces that previously even he had shunned. He knew in his heart that he was being offered a calling card from entities he had sensed, but never seen. These beings, ancient and incomprehensible, lurked in the shadows of the ethers. Their creatures fed on the basest of emotional energy. Their concept of creation was destruction, and no living thing, of any plane of existence, possessed the knowledge to control them. But if the correct offerings and compromises were made, these beings might well reward a lesser entity for service.

"Yes," he said aloud, his breath steaming on the air.

At once, it felt as if his throat were gripped by a giant invisible hand. *Do you know us?*

The touch was icy, yet as hot as the core of the earth. It reached inside him like an army of imps, examining every thought in his head. "Help me," Ponclast gasped, "and I will serve you."

We do not obey summons. You did not call us, wretched hermaphroditus. We summon you.

"Yes," Ponclast wheezed. His life was draining away, his body lifted up from the bed.

You will work for us, for it is time. You have been chosen. Work well, and there will be rewards.

Ponclast felt he had nothing to lose. He and his hara were living a half-life, in suffering. They were no longer magnificent or powerful, but mean little phantoms grubbing away at toxic earth. Given the right nourishment, the Teraghasts could become greater than the Varrs had ever been. And if Ponclast had virtually to sell his soul to achieve it, then so be it. "I will do as you ask, willingly and of my own volition."

The unseen hand withdrew and Ponclast slumped back upon the bed. He could perceive a small sphere of deepest black before him, which was visible even within the darkness of the cave. *Choose one of your children to be your champion. Bring him to you and mingle your essence with his. Through this, he will be given the gift of flight, the ability to travel the spirit paths between the worlds. This is the first gift and will enable you to realize your first duty. Destroy the child of light.*

"I will do this."

Once he had spoken, the sphere of black light shot toward his body and entered it through the solar plexus. There was a dull thud, a sense of being punched, like a stab wound, but nothing more. The invisible presence vanished. Ponclast was sweating from every pore. His body shook as from the throes of deadly fever. He crawled from his bed and drank water from a pool beneath the roots of a tree. He lit some misshapen candles that lay in puddles of ancient gray wax. Then he composed himself for trance.

Ponclast extended his inner sight and cast it like a lurid beam over all of his children. It swung this way and that, pausing to consider, to examine, before eventually moving on. Ultimately, it came to rest upon a particular har, who had just killed a comrade in a moment of pure despair. Ponclast's sight lingered over the har for some moments, then he sent forth a messenger, the hiss and scratch of his inner voice, and he called this son to him.

So Diablo came to the lair of his hostling, whom he had never met. He followed a call that was almost like a scent. He paused often to smell the air as he followed it. He came slinking along the damp noisome passageways, his body stooped close to the ground with wariness. His eyes glowed yellow in the darkness and his hot breath created clouds around his head. Very soon, he crouched before Ponclast in the central chamber.

Ponclast observed this feral imp with interest. He considered that Diablo was a living expression of his own desires. He beckoned with a clean white finger, "Come to me, my son."

He could tell that Diablo's first instinct was to attack, but that he was clever enough to realize such action would be pointless. He could also tell that Diablo was not afraid. Cautiously, Diablo came forward until Ponclast could rest a hand upon his son's head. "I have a job for you," he said. "You were born of my body. You are part of me."

Diablo stared at Ponclast with what appeared to be suspicion or disbelief.

"I am your hostling, and we must take aruna together, because I have a gift for you, and that is the only way for me to pass it to you."

Diablo cocked his head to one side and grinned.

To Ponclast, the kindling of arunic energy had nothing to do with desire or feeling. He willed it to manifest and it did. Diablo became soume in the same spirit. It meant nothing greater than if Ponclast had offered him some food or water.

Ponclast could feel an alien energy deep inside him. It flickered like a black flame in his belly, in the place where normally his personal life force glowed white. At the climax of aruna, it poured from him into Diablo, and Diablo growled and shuddered beneath him.

"You have learned something," Ponclast said. "And now you must work to master it."

Diablo whimpered and curled up his body. Black sweat ran over his damp skin. Ponclast gazed upon him, and for a moment remembered Gahrazel, so beautiful and whole. Diablo was hardly of the same caliber, but he would have to suffice. Ponclast extended a hand and laid it on Diablo's shoulder. "Rest," he said. "Tomorrow we shall explore wondrous new territory."

CHAPTER SEVEN

Banners of gold were hung in the streets, an air of festival filled the city. The new era had dawned. The Aralisians had put aside all rancor and had conceived an extraordinary and magical pearl. The harling who must eventually come from it would be superior to all others, even to his parents. Surely this meant that all that had happened had been for the greater good. Cal had brought harmony to Phaonica.

Caeru was not so easily convinced. Over the ensuing weeks, he allowed himself to be seen regularly in public as evidence of his condition became noticeable to others. He knew that Pellaz had suggested the idea, then manipulated and coerced his consorts, not because he sought harmony in his domestic sphere, but because he felt threatened. He would reveal to his consorts nothing of his fears, but it was Caeru's belief that Pellaz thought Thiede would come back to them in the child.

The conception itself had not been an easy process for Caeru. He remembered how he'd felt that night in Ferelithia when Pellaz—or rather their mutual desire—had opened up a deep part of himself that was normally sealed shut. It was the cauldron of creation, the secret organ where seed and egg combined, and because—for the Gelaming—harish conception could be achieved only by spiritually elevated aruna, it did not take place entirely in the earthly realm.

Caeru had allowed two hara into that secret place; it had torn him apart, and not just in a physical sense. The organ itself had felt as if it had been beaten into submission and it did not close up again as quickly as it should have done. Caeru had felt this inside, and it had been a hideous feeling: not pain exactly, but as if a black hole into another universe had been spiraling inside him and he could have been sucked inside out, right into it. Now, his body had more or less found its balance again, and the pearl was developing as normal, but Caeru felt very different to how he'd felt carrying Abrimel's pearl. This harling seemed to gnaw at his being, to suck out his life: he felt tired and drained. The bizarre aruna that had created the pearl had hurt him greatly and the dull, deep ache never went away. He carried it with him always, along with a sense of heaviness, of being dragged down. He felt no connection with what grew inside him, which was the complete opposite of how he'd felt before. As the weeks passed, he became more anxious, afraid that, between them, they had created some kind of abomination. He could confide nothing of this to Pellaz because, not really to his surprise, the Tigron had not returned to the Tigrina's apartments. Caeru had not seen him alone since that night. Pellaz was occupied with secret plans and had spent many hours in private discussion with his brother, Terez. Cal visited Caeru regularly, as had become usual, but he too seemed distracted and uneasy. Something was approaching and it seemed that none of them dared speak of it, as if the words alone would conjure up a storm.

Caeru could not even open up to Velaxis, whose only reaction to the conception had been to praise Caeru for his enterprise. Caeru did not enlighten him. He was isolated from everyhar, both emotionally and physically. Cal appeared afraid to touch him again.

The situation had not been helped by the cool reaction to the news by Abrimel. Perhaps it was only to be expected. A formal message of congratulations had come from Imbrilim, which sounded as if it had been put together by a clerical assistant. Abrimel made no mention of visiting home. Caeru missed him badly, perhaps as much as Pellaz missed Thiede. He sent a message himself, asking his son to visit, hoping Abrimel would read between the lines and understand how much his hostling needed his support, but so far Abrimel had not even replied. He was angry because Caeru had accepted Cal. He was angry because he felt he was being pushed out. Abrimel was a grown har, and the Tigron's son, but the difficulties of his childhood meant he could never feel close to Pellaz. Now, a new son had been conceived, this time in different circumstances. Pellaz, if not the whole of Gelamingkind, would embrace the new harling far more readily than the forgotten embarrassment, who'd turned up on the doorstep of Phaonica with his hostling, and who had not been welcome.

One afternoon, as yet another party of dignitaries from a far country was entertained in Phaonica's court, Caeru said quietly to Cal, "What have we done? I need to talk to you. I feel strange."

It was a totally inappropriate moment to say such a thing, as they were surrounded by visitors. Pellaz was not present, a situation that had offended some of the dignitaries who felt the Tigron ought to be giving them his attention.

Cal cast Caeru a quick, startled glance and murmured, "I will speak to you later."

Caeru could tell it was the last thing that Cal wanted to do. Perhaps it was so difficult because what they'd shared that night had been a mutual invasion of mind, body, and spirit, far deeper than any har had a right to explore. Caeru now knew things about Cal and Pellaz that he really wished he didn't: the gibbering terrors and insecurities that lurked in the farthest reaches of the mind, the hidden corners where demons were buried. Had Cal really wanted to discover how deeply Pellaz had loved Thiede, and how much he missed him and how he resented Cal for his banishing? Had Pellaz wanted to know the minutiae of Cal's exploits over the past thirty years? Cal had claimed that Terzian the Varr, for example, had meant little to him. Well, that wasn't true for a start. Many times that night, Caeru had received images of Cal's thoughts of Terzian, as he remembered their time together, when Tyson had been conceived. Cal had felt sad that Terzian was dead. These recollections must have washed over Pellaz like a caustic bath. Of course, the intensity of the experience had dredged old feelings from their graves, but they were like words spoken in anger. They could never be taken back.

Caeru thought: *We are the progenitors of the Aralis dynasty. We are powerful. We can do things that most hara cannot, but perhaps we are not wise to do so.*

That afternoon, amid the social small talk and ingratiating behavior, Caeru knew that he had to talk to somehar about it, otherwise he might burst apart, and the only possible candidates were Pellaz and Cal. Pellaz had withdrawn again, not in cold hostility, but merely because his mind was occupied by other things. Caeru didn't think Cal had seen much of him since that night either. So Cal would have to be Caeru's confidant, whether he wanted to be or not.

The afternoon seemed endless. Caeru's face ached from smiling so insincerely for so long and his stomach convulsed regularly with vicious cramps. He sought to hide the pain and drank too much wine, which he knew was a bad idea, not least because it was inconsiderate to the pearl. Hara came up to him and said, "You look radiant" or "You look marvelous," and Caeru had to grit his teeth and utter a polite and pleased response. He felt far from either state.

"Will you come to me for dinner?" he asked Cal, during a merciful lull in the social maelstrom.

"I can't," Cal replied. "I have a prior arrangement. I'll come later. Okay?"

Caeru nodded without speaking. He looked at Cal, and for a moment was assailed by a strong conviction that Cal was ready to flee Immanion. As to why this should be, Caeru could only guess. He wondered who Cal was having dinner with that evening.

Caeru ate alone on his terrace, all the time feeling nauseous. He would be glad when this experience was over and he could hand the pearl to members of the palace staff, who would care for it. If, when it hatched, it had bright red hair, he thought he'd lose his mind. It wasn't that he didn't want Thiede back again, but not in this way. It was unnatural and horrifying. He put a hand over his belly and pressed against the taut skin. It would not be an easy delivery either, he was sure.

The dinner dishes had been cleared away, and from the direction of the harbor, Caeru could hear the throb of distant music. He felt cold, yet his face was hot. He leaned back in his chair, trying to find a comfortable position. Perhaps Cal would not come.

Why did I agree to hosting this pearl? Caeru wondered. *Was it just for love, for Pell? We should have talked. We should have proceeded slowly. Pell was afraid. He felt he had to do this thing.*

Caeru rubbed his stomach. It would not be long now, maybe a week or two. Afterward, perhaps he might feel something like normal again.

He heard a door open inside his apartment, just a brief creaking sound. That would be Cal at last. Caeru was feverish with the desire to unburden himself. Cal would reassure him. He was always so down to earth. But nohar came out onto the terrace.

After a few minutes, Caeru got carefully to his feet and went inside. The apartment was in darkness, which was odd, because his staff usually made sure every room was softly lit after sundown. Barefooted, Caeru padded through the empty rooms, which vibrated with a tense, breathless atmosphere. He called out, "Cal, are you here?"

Silence: too silent.

Caeru now felt unnerved. He turned on some lights, but that did nothing to improve the atmosphere. There was nohar around. He must go to his staff's quarters, just to assure himself he wasn't completely alone.

As he made his way along the corridor beyond his personal rooms, the lights went off again. Caeru tensed, held his breath. He had the feeling somehar was following him, soft-footedly trailing him from room to room.

Get a grip! he hissed to himself in a low voice.

He ran to the door at the far end of the corridor. There was enough light coming in through the windows to his left, which looked out over the city. But when he got to the door, he couldn't open it. It felt as if something heavy lay against it on the other side, something that gave a little, but which he couldn't shift. It felt like a rolled-up carpet. Caeru pushed with all his strength, and his stomach complained with a thousand needling hurts. An arrow of sharp pain shot through his soume-lam, up through his belly and into his spine. He had to double over, gasping, hugging his own body. He shouldn't be doing this. He'd damage himself. He should go back to his rooms, turn on the lights, go to bed, and stop being so ridiculously paranoid.

But he couldn't dispel the impression of something unseen behind him, breathing in the darkness. Something watching him, preparing to strike. He made one last effort and mercifully the door opened enough for him to squeeze through it. He stumbled over what lay beyond and arrested his fall with his hands. They made contact with something soft and wet.

Caeru backed away, stood up, closed the door, and leaned on it. He stared for long seconds at what lay on the floor: the body of one of his house staff, a young har who had only been appointed a couple of months before. His eyes were open, as was his belly and chest. The blood was black in the moonlight: the har lay in an inky pool.

Caeru swallowed bile, yet felt strangely calm and detached. *Only a door between me and whoever did that,* he thought.

He ran across the room, which was the reception hall of the staff quarters. Beyond were living chambers, kitchens, and a laundry. They were deserted. Caeru could no longer feel any pain in his body. He just kept running, swiftly, and as silently as he could, keeping to the shadows, away from the moonlight that came in through the windows. He intended to make for the rear entrance that led to a series of courtyards and other areas of the palace. He intended to run through the back warrens of Phaonica to Pell's rooms, because now there was nohar else he could consider turning to. Part of him, he realized, suspected that Cal had come visiting after all. This was irrational and unfair, yet he could not dispel the impression. He would consider its implications once he was safe.

The main back door was locked. Caeru looked out of the windows in its upper half, down at the courtyard beyond. He paused only a moment, then went to one of the other doors, some corridors away. This was locked also. He would have to break a window, next to one of the stairways, and climb to the ground. Being in the latter stages of pearl-bearing was not the most convenient condition for such activity.

Caeru went into one of the kitchens, whose windows were close to the main door. He picked up a wooden chair and hurled it at the glass. He saw it shatter, as if in slow motion, saw the glass burst outward. He lunged toward it. But then strong arms grabbed him from behind, pinned his limbs to his body. A hand went over his mouth, forced back his head. He could not see who held him, but his nostrils filled with a stench of rot. He struggled and kicked, writhed in his captor's hold, but they were too strong. They dragged him backward into a small dark pantry and he felt then that he was about to die.

In the heat of the moment Caeru didn't think of who or why, he merely fought to survive. He couldn't see the face of who attacked him, because their head was completely covered with a scarf. They beat him about the head with something hard and heavy, until he could not move. They thought he was un-conscious, perhaps, but a small part of his mind remained alert. He seemed to hover above himself and he could see the attacker's arm rising and falling. He could hear the dull thuds of a weapon in flesh and the muffled grunts his own body was making. He could smell a foul, terrible stink. He saw the attacker throw something away that landed with a metallic clatter on the stone floor. Then they plunged their hands into his body, and his consciousness shot back into his flesh. He felt fingers inside him, pulling and tearing. It was beyond pain. It was worse than that. He felt something give way, the most sickening thing he could imagine. It was the last conscious thought he had.

Pellaz stood in a shrine of the High Nayati, at the feet of a statue of Aruhani, dehar of aruna, life and death. He was about to utter the litany of the Sacred Offering. With him were several other members of the Hegemony, and some visitors from Maudrah in Jaddayoth. It was the first public engagement he'd conducted since the night he'd spent with Caeru and Cal. This ritual was for no purpose other than to entertain and perhaps impress the visitors from Maudrah.

Pellaz had only agreed to officiate because Cal had claimed to be busy elsewhere. Caeru was in no state to be out, apparently, although Pellaz had avoided seeing him alone for weeks. He hadn't experienced the nauseating re-gret and self-disgust that usually followed being intimate with Caeru, but the circumstances, after all, had been very different. Still, he felt uneasy, as if he was waiting for the negative feelings to manifest. He shrank from visiting the Tigrina in case those dark passions were rekindled in force. He still didn't trust himself around Caeru.

Also, emotional issues aside, Pell's time had mainly been occupied with in-vestigating the otherlanes. He and his brother Terez had been trying to replicate the event that had taken place on Pell's way home from Galhea. So far, they had been unsuccessful, but Pellaz knew of no other way to gather any information about what might be threatening him. It was all too vague and nebulous, yet it ate away at his mind. Something wasn't right. An intangible presence loomed over him, loomed over all of Immanion. He had told only Terez about it, because Terez had spent time in another world: he had a sense for these things.

Pellaz spoke the words of the ritual, in a clear ringing voice, and a priest of Aruhani handed him a plate of ripe red fruit, which he laid on the dais in front of the statue. He bowed his head and began to back away: the ritual was finished.

The statue moaned.

Pell's head jerked up in surprise. The candlelight in the Nayati had gone red, and sinister shadows wriggled over the features of the dehar. It looked as if Aruhani was in pain. Before Pellaz could turn to any of his companions to find out whether they could perceive this phenomenon themselves, the statue exploded. Pellaz was hit by a storm of flying stone and hot liquid. The impact threw him backward to the floor. He saw a jet of what looked like dark blood spewing out of Aruhani's ruined belly and it rained down upon him.

Pellaz cried out and rolled to the side, and then hands were upon him. He heard many voices, low with concern, but couldn't make out the words. His mind was filled with red. He fought off those who sought to assist him and leapt to his feet. The candlelight had returned to normal. The impassive countenance of Aruhani stared down at him, perfect and serene. The statue was intact.

"What is it?" somehar asked. "Tiahaar . . . ?"

Pellaz stared about him wildly, disorientated. The vision had been so real. He glanced back at Aruhani, and then pushed his way through the anxious crowd about him, clawing his way to the exit. His personal guards called out to him, but he ignored them. When he reached the main doors, he heard the cry from Phaonica: a scream, high and keening. He saw a flock of black birds circling the highest towers. He saw red lightning in the distant sky, above the softly swelling Almagabran hills beyond the city. He didn't even pause to visit the stable yard and find Peridot. He ran home alone, through the empty streets, and all the time that terrible cry echoed in his ears.

By the time Pellaz reached Phaonica, the palace was a blaze of lights and even as he ran up the steep driveway to the main entrance, he could tell something had happened to incur a great deal of activity. Before he reached the door, a messenger on horseback, galloping out of the main yard, nearly knocked him over. He recognized Pellaz instantly, and said, "Tiahaar, the Tigrina has been attacked. I was coming to find you."

Pellaz said nothing but ran into the palace, making directly for Caeru's apartments. He could not think, could barely draw breath. He could only remember the vision he'd had in the Nayati: the blood, the ruin.

Every lamp was now lit in Caeru's rooms, and the place was filled with security staff. Pellaz went into the main salon and recognized the har standing in the middle of the room, issuing orders to a collection of minions. This was Davitri Bilasso, a native Almagabran, and he was head of palace security. Pellaz went straight to him. "Report, Davitri. How bad?"

"Quite bad," Davitri said in his usual dour manner. "But he is alive. Just."

"Who did this?"

"We have yet to ascertain that fact."

"Well, do so. How could you let this happen? Our security is your domain. We will need to speak on this matter very soon."

Davitri inclined his head respectfully, and Pellaz left him to ponder this chastisement. He went to the Tigrina's bedchamber. It was empty but for one of Caeru's staff, whose bare arms were red to the elbow and who was carrying out a bowl of stained water and some towels.

"Where is he?" Pellaz demanded.

"They have taken him to the Infirmary, tiahaar."

"His condition?"

The har ducked his head. "Poor, tiahaar." He then spoke fiercely, somewhat beyond normal protocol. "Some monster came. Some monster did this."

"What did they do?"

The har lowered his eyes. "His belly was cut, tiahaar."

Pellaz went back to the main salon, where Davitri Bilasso was still engaged in briefing his hara. "Take me to the Infirmary," Pellaz ordered. "Now."

They rode in a carriage so that Pellaz could ask questions along the way. It appeared that—ironically—all of Caeru's staff had received a summons to a bogus emergency security meeting elsewhere in the palace. Only one har had missed the message and had paid for that with his life. Fortunately, the Tigrina's steward was not totally gullible and even before he and his hara reached the venue of the meeting, had felt compelled to return home. If he had not done so, then Caeru might already be dead. As it was, the physicians' primary diagnosis was not too optimistic. The pearl had been slashed from Caeru's body. It had not been found at the scene of the crime, although the weapon used to perpetrate the atrocity had been recovered. It was one of the cook's knives from the kitchen.

Listening to all this, Pellaz sensed his flesh freezing over, as if it were turning to ice. Through numb lips, he asked crisply, "Has Tigron Calanthe been informed of what's happened?"

Davitri Bilasso held Pell's gaze. "He is missing from his apartments, tia-haar. We presume he is out in the city somewhere. I have sent agents to look for him, both physically and through the ethers."

Pellaz nodded. "Good." He was in no state to attempt telepathic communication with Cal himself.

The Infirmary of Immanion was renowned throughout the Wraeththu world. It did not look like a hospital, nor did it feel like one. Its entire structure was designed to promote healing on all levels of being. Its ambience was calm and restful and the staff moved with serene purpose. Voices were soft in that place and the lighting subtle.

Pellaz was asked to wait because the Tigrina was in surgery. Bilasso offered to wait with him, but Pellaz dismissed him. The officer's task was to find whoever had committed the assault. The Tigron waited alone, his mind empty. When he did think, it was of trivial things, adjustments he should make to the Aruhani litany, a different mix of incense for the ritual. Where was Cal?

A har dressed in a white robe of soft silk brought him some water and murmured, "Tiahaar, if it's any help, you should know the Tigrina is in the best hands."

No, it was not much help.

After a couple of hours, Pellaz was conducted to a room on the third floor, where a group of healers sat cross-legged in a ring around a low bed. Each chest emanated a low, soothing tone. A dark-skinned surgeon stood beyond their circle, dressed head to toe in theater garb of deep blue that did not show the blood. His hair was wound tight upon his head and his expression was not encouraging. When Pellaz entered the room, he bowed and indicated they should speak in private.

"I want to see him first," Pellaz said.

Taking care not to disturb the circle of healers, Pellaz peered over their heads. Caeru's body was covered in a flaking film of dried blood. His belly was obscured by a sheet, which was draped over a cage of some kind. Black snaking tubes emanated from beneath the sheet, their open ends disappearing into large black glass jars arranged upon the floor. Caeru's eyes were closed, his hair dark and matted and wet. He had been badly beaten about the head.

Pellaz stared for some moments, then turned to the surgeon.

"My office, tiahaar," murmured the surgeon in a strongly accented, musical voice. He gestured toward the door.

The surgeon was named Sheeva, and he, like most citizens of Immanion, was not a native Almagabran. A member of his staff brought Pellaz hot coffee spiced with cinnamon, and Sheeva produced from a drawer in his desk a bottle of strong herbal liqueur, with which he suggested the Tigron fortify his drink.

Pellaz did this. He noticed that his left hand was shaking, while the right hand was still. He could taste blood in the back of his throat.

"I will tell you straight," said Sheeva. "If the Tigrina makes it through tonight, he has a good chance of survival. The worst element, despite appearances, is shock. The head injuries look worse than they actually are. There is no fracture to the skull. However, I'm afraid the pearl he was carrying was excised during the attack. Certain internal organs, and not just those associated with reproduction, have been badly damaged, but not beyond my skills of reconstruction. However, Caeru will have to face adjustments. Fortunately, the conception chamber—the cauldron of creation—is relatively intact, for which we should be thankful. I have never treated a har who has lost this organ, and the psychological effects of that could be—unpredictable."

Pellaz nodded. "It might sound strange, but I know little about these things." He grimaced. "I don't know how my body works. Why the hell is that?"

Sheeva smiled gently. "Don't worry, few hara do know—yet."

Pellaz frowned. "Why not? Isn't it the most important thing?"

Sheeva leaned back in his chair, tapped the desk in front of him. Perhaps he didn't want to be giving this lesson. Pellaz didn't blame him, but he wanted his question answered. "Wraeththu had a lot of growing up to do, you know that," Sheeva said. "For a long time, we were all children, whatever our ages in physical terms. Only now are we rediscovering abandoned yet essential skills and discovering new ones. We are no longer playing in the ruins, tiahaar. The dust has settled, and we are standing around, blinking in the sunlight. Now, we must rebuild. We do not need the kind of medicine that humans had, because our bodies are more efficient at healing themselves. But sometimes, as in Caeru's case, intervention is unavoidable, because so much physical damage has been done. We are learning about our bodies, and how they function. This learning cannot simply be academic, because it is impossible to explain in academic terms exactly how we reproduce. All you need to know for now is that the conception chamber is the main aspect that sets our reproductive method apart from that of human females, whose fetuses were, of course, conceived in the womb that bore them. I, and many others, suspect that this organ has functions beyond mere reproduction, but ultimately there is much we have yet to understand about such matters."

"Thank you," Pellaz said. "I appreciate your time in telling me this."

"You're welcome."

"How badly is Rue damaged? How is this going to affect him?"

Sheeva breathed in deeply through his nose. "The area in the Tigrina's body that corresponds to an actual womb has suffered great trauma. At some point in the future, he will need further reconstructive surgery. I will do what I can in respect of repairs, but it's doubtful he'll be able to host a pearl again. He should, however, be capable of normal aruna in a soume sense."

"Do whatever it takes," Pellaz said.

"Mostly, it is up to him," said Sheeva. "Caeru has the power to heal himself on mental and emotional levels, which of course affects the physical body. I am simply the mechanic. I repair physical breakdowns."

"I have been told you are the best."

Sheeva inclined his head. "I was appointed here because of my reputation, and I will do all in my power to uphold it."

"Is there anything I can do?"

"Stay with him tonight, tiahaar. Give him your strength. It is the best medicine."

Pellaz returned to the room where Caeru lay motionless on his low bed. The healers were still chanting softly, their palms upraised to direct energy into their patient's body. Pellaz stepped inside their circle and knelt on the floor. The chanting trailed off and one of the healers said, "Tiahaar, we respectfully request you allow us to work in peace."

"Go," Pellaz said.

"What?"

"Leave this room. All of you. Go."

The healers were silent, watching him.

"I am Tigron," Pellaz said. "This is my consort. I will heal him." He dismissed the other occupants in the room from his attention and sat cross-legged beside the bed. He drew back the sheet that covered the cage over Caeru's belly. All the time, a mantra churned in his mind: *Don't think of Orien, don't think of Orien.*

He removed the cage. The chief healer made a protest, but Pellaz only snarled at him. "Get out."

Pellaz placed his hands, palms down, the tiniest distance above Caeru's savaged flesh. Sheeva had done an exemplary job in patching him up, but it was still a foul mess. Pellaz summoned the power from the center of creation to flow through him. He directed it into Caeru's body. For a while, he remembered the time, so long ago, when he'd tried to heal a terrible wound on his friend Cobweb's leg. He remembered the feeling of the energy then and how weak and sporadic it had felt in comparison to what he could achieve now. Images of the past flickered across his mind's eye, but gradually, the flow of the energy took him deep into trance and then he did not think at all.

Late the following morning, Vaysh, the Tigron's aide, came to Caeru's room in the Infirmary, because the staff were concerned that Pellaz would not leave the Tigrina's side. They had summoned Vaysh to reason with Pellaz, who ignored anyhar else who tried to speak to him.

Vaysh's voice, harsh and commanding, at least permeated the fog of trance in Pell's mind. He heard somehar say, "Pellaz, wake up. Come back to Phaonica. Let the hara here do their job. You're in the way."

Pellaz raised his head and saw Vaysh standing at the door. His red hair looked shocking against the pale colors of the room.

"Pell," Vaysh said. "Get up."

Pellaz could no longer feel his hands and arms, although he could sense that the healing energy still coursed through them strongly. At some point during the night, he had actually allowed his fingers to rest on Caeru's wounds. Pellaz remembered, vaguely, that he had been involved in a battle: a fight with Caeru's will, because he had only wanted to die. Pellaz hadn't allowed that to happen. He'd had to work healing on several levels, but it wasn't over yet. Caeru himself was still unconscious. Pellaz dismissed Vaysh from his attention and closed his eyes, concentrating once more on the task in hand.

"Pell."

He heard Vaysh cross the room, felt a hand upon his shoulder. Pellaz was fizzing with power: it took hardly any effort to use some of it to hurl Vaysh back toward the door. He landed in an undignified heap.

Vaysh scrambled to his feet and spat, "Why are you doing this? Don't tell me you care!"

"Get out," Pellaz said in a low voice. To emphasize his displeasure, he hissed like a furious cat.

Vaysh stared at him for some moments, then left the room without another word.

Some time later, Ashmael Aldebaran arrived. Pellaz had lost the capacity to speak, but locked gazes with Ashmael for what felt like a long time. After this, the general said laconically to somehar unseen behind him, "Leave him. Scoop him up when he passes out."

This occurred some time in the early evening. Pellaz didn't know what happened, only that he woke up around thirty-six hours later in another room in the Infirmary. He was instantly alert, full of energy. A healer came to his side, offered water.

"Does he live?" Pellaz asked.

The healer nodded. "He is awake, tiahaar."

Pellaz drank the water in one gulp, then got out of bed.

Long gauzy drapes blew softly in the breeze that came in through the open windows. Wooden chimes tocked rhythmically in the draft. Caeru's eyes were open: he stared at the sky. Pellaz sat on the edge of the bed. They had covered Caeru with a sheet again, and his hands rested on the cage. His fingernails were still crusted with dried blood, as was his hair. The bruises on his face were already fading, because a har heals quickly, but tubes still emanated from beneath the cage, draining out fluid. Some wounds, being fundamental, were slower to heal.

Caeru turned his head slowly on the pillow. "I saw you," he said. "I saw you with me in the darkness. You were shining."

Pellaz reached out and touched Caeru's face. "How do you feel?"

Caeru grimaced. "I don't feel anything. I don't hurt. I just *am*. They gave me something to drink. It was bitter. It took all feeling away."

"Do you want anything?"

"Yes. The truth. They won't tell me. How bad is it?"

"Bad," Pellaz said softly.

Caeru swallowed. "No more harlings for me, not inside me. That's it, isn't it?"

Pellaz nodded his head slightly. "It seems that way."

"Has it all gone? I don't know. Tell me. What else won't I ever be able to do again?"

"The surgeon has repaired most of the damage. It will heal, in time. You are still har, Rue."

"I lost our child."

"You didn't lose it. Somehar took it from you."

Caeru pressed the fingers of one hand into his eye sockets. There was a thin streak of dried blood on his arm too. "I didn't want the pearl," he said. "Don't you understand? I did it for you, but not for myself. Have I made this happen?"

"No," Pellaz said. He took Caeru's hand in his own, pulled it down from his face. "Did you see who did this to you?"

Caeru shook his head. "No. Who would want to do anything like this?"

"Are you sure you didn't see?"

"Yes."

"No suspicions?"

"No! Don't even think it."

"Has Cal been to see you?"

Caeru looked away. "I asked for him. They told me he is not in Immanion anymore."

Pellaz closed his eyes. "Thiede," he said, a prayer, a plea, or a curse: he could not tell.

"Cal didn't do this to me, Pell," Caeru murmured. "You don't have to worry about that."

Pellaz uttered a low growl. "I will find who did, I promise you. And when I do, I'll rip their guts from them. I promise you that, as well."

"We weren't meant to create that pearl," Caeru said. "Somehar stopped us."

"I know," Pellaz said, "which means it was more important than even I thought."

"Who, though? Who would hate us that much?"

"I'm not sure it's hate," Pellaz said. He let go of Caeru's hand and stood up. "They should clean you up. It's not right. They should clean your hands and your hair."

"Show me the damage," Caeru said. "I have to see. I had to wait for you to come before I could bear to look at it."

Pellaz paused for a few moments, then leaned down and drew back the sheet. Caeru raised himself up on his elbows and looked down at his belly. Through the narrow bars of the protective cage, the wounds looked better than they had: a strange map of stitches and black crusts. His stomach appeared sunken, as if a great part of himself had been hacked away.

Caeru lay down again. "If you had not been here, I would have left this life," he said.

"I know," Pellaz said. "I wouldn't let you go."

"Why? You don't love me. We are not chesna. You could have been free."

"I will go to Galhea," Pellaz said, "and I'll take Terez with me. There is work to do. When I return, I will visit you. Be home by then, Rue. I hope to bring you news at that time."

"Why?" Caeru insisted, ignoring all that Pellaz had just said.

"I didn't want you to die," Pellaz said. "Make of that what you will. I can offer no more."

"Thank you," Caeru said. "I will help you, Pell, whatever happens."

Pellaz nodded thoughtfully. "I'll have them clean you up," he said. "I'll send Vaysh to you. He can sit with you."

"Vaysh," Caeru said dully. "Is that because I'm like him now? Barren? Is he going to talk to me about that, try and make me adjust?" He laughed bleakly.

"No," Pellaz replied. "It's because Vaysh is trained to protect a har, which is more than can be said for our so-called security staff. But that is not your concern. Just get well again."

CHAPTER EIGHT

$\succ\!\!+\!\!\leftrightarrow\!\!\cdot\!\!\ominus\!\!\cdot\!\!\leftrightarrow\!\!+\!\!\prec$

Calanthe har Aralis came to his senses in darkness. He sat up. He could hear his own breath, and from the way it echoed sensed he was in an enormous building or cave. He could see nothing. Puzzling thoughts flashed through his mind. *They will travel to the city of winds and ghosts. There are jewels there, amid the rubbish.*

Before he'd woken, he'd seen his son Tyson, so like himself. He had seen Pellaz, too bright to look upon, like a white-hot flame.

Where am I?

He almost laughed aloud at the clichéd question. What could he remember? A meal in a restaurant in Immanion. Low tide, the reek of seaweed, the smell of fish simmering in spices, tart wine. He could not see the face of the one who sat opposite him. He could hear a voice, but not the words. He could remember a feeling of relief, of unburdening himself, feeling he'd been understood. He remembered things making sense, like a door opening on a room he thought he'd never find. After that, a blank. He must have been drugged, knocked out, but there was no pain in his head, no sense of sluggishness. He had no idea what had happened to him and yet felt emotionally numb. He could not be afraid. It was like a dream.

And then, a pinprick of light in the immense darkness ahead of him. It zoomed toward him, growing in size, until it bobbed in front of him, a sphere of radiance the size of his head.

"Am I dreaming?" Cal said to this phenomenon.

The sphere pulsed a little, as if it were breathing. Cal heard a voice in his head. *No more than any other har, Calanthe.*

"What is this place? Why am I here?"

It is a hidden palace, at the end of a lonely back road of the otherlanes. You are here to be of use to your kind, for there is none other like you. You will re-member soon the conversation that took place in Immanion, and the agent who persuaded you to come here. The journey was made without sedim. *It has disorientated you, but this will fade.*

"Who or what are you?"

I am Perdu.

Cal thought this name should be familiar, but couldn't remember why. "What are you?"

Living essence, as you are.

"Then manifest. I will not talk to a ball of light."

The sphere contracted until it was a blazing mote of brilliance, then exploded with a dazzling display of sparks. Cal shielded his eyes for a moment, sure that sizzling particles had burned his face. He could smell cordite. Light had come into the space he occupied, light that illumined rather than concealed. He saw an almost unimaginably huge chamber, like a temple, its domed roof veined with organic struts and beams. He saw a floor of what looked like polished obsidian. Standing upon it in rows were bowls of radiance on tripods seven feet tall. Be-yond them, ranks of tall pillars disappearing into the distance, like the reflec-tions in multiple mirrors. At last, his reluctant consciousness focused on the tall figure before him. He was wary now, knowing what he'd see: the slanting cat-like eyes, the mane of bloodred hair. Thiede. "Am I dead?" Cal said. "Is this your revenge?"

Thiede concealed his hands in the wide sleeves of his indigo-colored robe. "We cannot die that easily. You already know that, I believe."

Cal got to his feet. "I have sensed you, Thiede. Often. What I mean is, now I'm here, can I ever go back?"

Thiede smiled. "Yes. I do not seek revenge. There is nothing to warrant it."

"Then why have you brought me here? To get me away from Pell again? I suppose that's it."

Thiede shook his head. "Not at all. You are here to finish what was started, what the Kamagrian started for you."

"Which is?"

"To become Tigron, worthy of the title."

"Is Opalexian part of this?"

"In some regard. We were so wrong, Opalexian and I. But we are learning, as you will. I needed to bring you here because I cannot manifest in your realm. This is not just because you banished me, Cal. It was expedient for others that I was removed. Part of a greater plan, of which I was entirely ignorant. If I return to Immanion, there is a strong chance that my presence would be sensed and I would be destroyed, utterly, my essence erased from space and time. Opalexian knows this now too. She hides, she fears. They could come for her also, in the guise of an assassin or a liberator. Who knows?"

"What are you talking about? Be clear with me."

"Wraeththu is under threat," Thiede said. "Grave threat."

"From what?"

"From the enemies of those who made us."

"Who made us?"

Thiede smiled again. "The gods," he said. "As everyhar believes."

"I don't. I think the answer is more prosaic than that."

"We have much to discuss," Thiede said. "I will show you my realm, my humble home. You are safe here, as your son will be."

"Tyson, I saw him. Is he in danger?"

"Not Tyson, Cal. The one as yet in pearl. I want you to go into the other-lanes and save him. You must do this very soon, almost at once."

"What!"

"An enemy has cut the child from Caeru's belly. It intends to deliver the harling to a foul master, who will devour it. You must intercept this agent very soon, and it will be difficult for you, because I cannot provide you with a *sedu*."

"That is impossible, not difficult."

"Not at all. I can teach you how to do this, now. But there are dangers."

"Why can't you do it?"

"Because I cannot risk making my presence felt in the ethers. I need you, Cal, we all need you. I know you have an inkling of what might have been. You were sent to Immanion before you were ready. We did not need to fight. I never needed to fight you."

"It was torture, not fighting."

"Yes. I tortured you. I saw in you the thing I feared, but now I realize you are the sword to combat the source of that fear. It was inevitable you should share its taste and flavor. When I chose Pellaz, a higher power chose you to be his protector. My mistake was that I did not see it. I should have brought you to Immanion the moment Pellaz died. You should have been there from the beginning with Seel and the others. Imagine a world where that happened, Cal. Imagine it carefully."

Cal grimaced. "I don't want to. Because it didn't happen. You can't change the past."

"No, none of us can do that. You have been through fire, Cal. You are the strongest blade, forged in madness and hatred, refined through trial and experience. You walked through the fire, and emerged from it, relatively intact. Hara do not realize what you are, what you've achieved." Thiede paused. "Enough of this flattery. There is work to do. Your son . . ."

"What of Caeru?"

"He lives," Thiede said. "If I'd acted more swiftly, I could have prevented what happened to him, but the information came too late. You cannot concern yourself with him. Devote yourself entirely to taking the pearl from the one who stole it. Remember how you felt as you came to my inner sanctum on the night we fought in Immanion. That is how you must be now."

"Does Pell know I'm here?"

"No, for the time being his safest course is to remain in ignorance."

"He will think . . ."

"We both know what he will think. Do not dwell upon it. Focus upon what must be done now."

"And if I succeed in this task, what next?"

Thiede gestured languidly. "You finish the training Opalexian started for you. You learn how to be of use when the time comes and mighty forces reveal themselves in the realm of earth. Wraeththu have always believed themselves to be the stuff of angels, haven't they? Well, consider this. The fall from heaven never ended, Cal. The battle continues. But what we have to consider, as lowly beings, is whether light is good and dark is evil. Always a puzzle, eh?"

"The war of angels." Cal laughed. "What are you saying?"

"That sometimes truth can be wrapped up in a myth or a fairy story. You will learn."

Cal considered. "This feels right," he said, certain. "I am right to be here."

Thiede smiled. "I am glad to hear it. It is strange, but of all hara you probably have the most reason to loathe me, yet you do not. I have never sensed hate in you, not like in Seel Griselming, for example."

"I'm happy to adore whatever Seel hates," Cal said.

Thiede regarded him wryly. "You should get over that. It could be used against you."

Cal gestured emphatically with both hands. "All the time I've been in

Immanion, I've yearned for something, felt there was something I should be doing. Is this it?"

"I hope so."

"I thought you'd be sure."

"We should never be that. I made that mistake once too often."

"I am ready," Cal said. "Show me."

Calanthe har Aralis had disappeared from Immanion and nearly everyhar in the city had their own thoughts on that. Phaonica had tried to keep private the details of the attack on Caeru, but they leaked out anyway. Some thought that Cal had been killed, his body hidden. Others believed he had reverted to type and had attacked Caeru in a moment of insanity, before fleeing the city, in the same way he'd once fled Saltrock after murdering the shaman, Orien Farnell. The ability to kill was in his blood, after all: tainted Uigenna blood.

Nohar had thought the Aralisians could be so vulnerable in their own home, which was why security had been relatively lax. This was amended immediately, and investigations ensued into who or what had perpetrated the attack. There were no clues. Nothing unusual had been noticed that night and nohar knew from where the message summoning Caeru's staff to a fake meeting had come, other than that it had been composed on Security Office stationery. It all pointed to an inside job, and every member of the palace staff was subjected to rigorous interrogation.

While this was being conducted, Davitri Bilasso directed his best psychic agents to search for Cal's signature in the otherlanes, but there was no trail to follow. Trackers scoured the countryside, and spies slid like oil through the back streets of surrounding towns and villages, seeking clues. Nohar found anything. It was as if Cal had disappeared completely, as if he'd never been in Immanion. Did this signify guilt or something else?

Pellaz didn't know what he thought. As far as the issue of Cal was concerned, he was emotionally numb and could think in terms only of solving the mystery, of revealing the threat that hung over his family. He mourned the loss of the pearl, far more deeply than he thought was possible. It had represented so much, and its conception was an event that could never be replicated. The dream had shattered. He told himself he'd been right all along. His relationship with Cal had ended in a soup of mud and blood somewhere in Megalithica over thirty years ago. Everything since had been a fantasy, a wish, a delusion. They were not meant to find happiness together. Several times, Pellaz had attempted to establish mind contact with Cal, but there was no hint of his presence in the world. It was as if he had never even existed.

Pellaz summoned his brother Terez and together they rode out of Phaonica's stable yard on powerful white *sedim*. Halfway down the palace drive, they opened a portal to the otherlanes and flashed out of earthly reality, leaving behind them only a lingering rumble of thunder and a smell of ozone. Nohar who witnessed that departure was in any doubt that the Tigron was in the mood for a fight.

CHAPTER NINE

It was evening in Galhea when the *sedim* leapt back into the world, out of a thundercloud and a ring of lightning. They crashed down onto a road outside the town and without pause galloped directly toward the house called We Dwell in Forever, with ice flying from their manes and steam purling from their necks.

Prior to this arrival, and ignorant of its advent, Tyson Parasiel had experienced a presentiment. Tyson was not a har naturally given to psychic episodes. He, like his hostling before him, had mostly neglected spiritual training and lived very much in the world of the empirical senses. He'd gone to lie down on his bed, late in the afternoon, because he'd spent most of the previous night getting drunk with friends, and Swift, his half brother, had made him work all day. He'd anticipated being able to get an early night to recover but Cobweb had told him there would be guests for dinner and that he must be present. Tyson, stiff-necked with dread, knew he'd have to catch a few hours' sleep before enduring the company of others. He rarely felt comfortable with any hara but those who were his friends among the Parsic military and the staff who worked on the family estate. Cobweb would not reveal who the guests would be, but Tyson supposed they would be Gelaming and probably from Immanion.

News of the attack on Caeru and of Cal's disappearance had already been

sent to Galhea. No doubt the Gelaming believed Cal would flee back to Forever, as he had done many years before, after his murder of Orien Farnell in
Saltrock. Cynically, Tyson knew this was most unlikely. However much Cal
might be redeemed and repaired, Tyson knew his hostling wanted to avoid him.
As a harling, he'd harbored romantic notions about Cal, and had envied his ad-
venturous life, but as an adult, he guessed that Cal was mostly like himself and
somewhat scornful of cozy domestic arrangements. He wasn't resentful that
his hostling ignored him. He had no interest in meeting Cal now, because in
some ways he didn't want to shatter the illusions of childhood and he was wise
enough to realize his early fantasies could not have been based on reality.

He'd once dreamed of roaming the world with Cal, having all sorts of wild
and improbable experiences, and sometimes, even now, that old restlessness
stole over him, but for the most part he was content to feed off Swift's generosity and live the life of a rich har in luxury. He had a chesnari of sorts, a har
called Ferany, who lived in the town. Tyson knew that Ferany believed that one
day he and Tyson would take the bond of blood and then Ferany would move
into Forever and a series of harlings would follow. Tyson allowed Ferany to per-
sist with this dream unmolested. He still wasn't sure himself whether it would
ever come to pass or not. What else was there to do? There had been talk recently of Tyson going to Immanion, but he'd not been enthusiastic about the
idea. If he'd been younger, then maybe. All he'd been able to envision was being a rustic har from the sticks who wouldn't fit in, and whose reluctant hostling
would regard him with distant expressions of pain.

However, recent developments had effectively closed that avenue of possibility, so a life with Ferany appeared ever more likely, however mundane. Ferany was an exotic har, who was unusual because he veered neither toward
masculine or feminine aspect, as most Galhean hara tended to do, however
good their intentions to be utterly balanced. This was undoubtedly a remnant
of being Varrs, as the Parsics had been known when Tyson's father Terzian
was alive and intent on conquest. Terzian had actively suppressed his feminine side, yet had encouraged it in others, such as Cobweb, who had hosted
harlings. It might also be because Galhea had a human community, onetime
slaves, now free citizens, who lived in their own areas, but whose separate
genders perhaps subtly influenced the way hara lived. Ferany, a more modern
creature, was truly androgynous and Tyson knew that some of the human residents of Galhea found him creepy because of that. It was perhaps what all
hara were supposed to be like and what the Galheans considered to be freakish might simply be a vision of the future. Ferany did not approve of some of
Tyson's excesses, but held his tongue, probably because he cherished being

close to the highest-ranking family in the community and—who knows—he might have harbored ambitions to move to Immanion one day, where the hara were much more like him. He got on very well with Cobweb, which sometimes unsettled Tyson greatly. Tyson loved Cobweb as a hostling, because he'd brought Tyson up when Cal couldn't be bothered with the responsibility of parenting, but Tyson was still wary of Cobweb's inner sight.

As he slept, Tyson dreamed of leaving home. He sailed on a great red ship, over an ocean comprised entirely of shifting black sand. The sand moved like waves, and sprays of granules blew up over the side of the ship, stinging Tyson's hands and face. He gazed toward a distant horizon, where a city of gold hung in the sky. The dream was pleasant, somehow soothing, and Tyson was sorry to be woken from it. Somehar stood at the end of his bed and leaned over to shake one of his feet. "Tyson, it's time to wake up."

Tyson didn't open his eyes at first, but pressed the fingers of one hand against them. He could still taste sour liquor in his throat. He groaned. "In a minute."

Again, the har shook his foot and said, "Tyson, it's time to wake up."

Tyson opened his eyes, raised his upper body, and supported himself on his elbows. A wave of cold shock coursed through him because he saw himself standing at the end of the bed. A tall har with white-gold hair and dark violet eyes. He said, "What?"

The har leaned over the end of the bed, shook his foot, and said, "Tyson, it's time to wake up."

It was then that Tyson realized he wasn't looking at himself at all, but at his hostling. Cal had returned to Galhea after all. "What are you doing here?" Tyson demanded.

Once again, the har at the end of the bed shook his foot and repeated the words he'd spoken before. At that point, Tyson knew the har before him wasn't real. The shock of this caused him to draw up his feet and hug his knees. He couldn't speak. At once, the vision of Cal expanded, grew huge, until his head was pressed against the ceiling, his arms splayed out around his head like the branches of trees. "Wake up!" he said, and vanished.

At that moment, the door to the room opened and Cobweb put his head around it to say, "Ty, have a bath, clean yourself up. Downstairs in half an hour."

Tyson opened his eyes. He'd been asleep. He'd been dreaming. He called Cobweb's name to stop him from leaving.

"What is it?" Cobweb asked.

"I dreamed of Cal," Tyson said. "He was here."

"Hardly surprising," Cobweb said dryly. "Get ready, Ty. You must be present tonight."

No message had been sent from Immanion to warn the House of Parasiel that the Tigron would be visiting them, but Cobweb rarely needed advance warning of anything, in any case. He always just *knew*. Tyson could tell that Pellaz har Aralis was disappointed that Cobweb had foreseen his visit. He had hoped to storm in by surprise. As it was, he found that a sumptuous dinner had been prepared for him and rooms made ready. Cobweb had made sure the entire family was present: Swift and Seel, their son Azriel and his chesnari Aleeme, who was the son of Flick and Ulaume Sarestes in Shilalama, and had moved to Galhea some years before. The head housekeeper, a Kamagrian parage named Bryony, who had once been a human servant of the Parasilians, was also present, to supervise with a steely Cobweb-trained eye the serving of dinner, so that Cobweb was free to pay full attention to any subtle nuances in conversation around him. It was clear that, for whatever reason, Cobweb wanted the House of Parasiel to present a united front to the Tigron.

Tyson was relieved to see that Pellaz had brought Terez with him, because of all Gelaming he had met, Tyson liked Terez best. He was not as arrogant as most of them were. In appearance, Terez was very similar to his brother— olive-skinned and black-haired—although Terez was taller and his features were more severe. He seemed older than Pellaz, although he was a couple of years younger. He wore his long hair in a braid down his back, plaited so tightly it was almost savage, whereas Pellaz affected a less rigid appearance, at least with friends. His hair fell in unruly bangs over his forehead, while the rest of it tumbled over his shoulders and down to his waist. It got in the way constantly while he was eating. Over drinks before dinner, the Tigron recounted in detail all that had happened in Immanion.

"We can only suppose Cal has been abducted," he said. "Or perhaps he was also attacked." He shook his head. "We are frustrated. There are no clues. Not even our most clear-sighted seers can find anything."

"Perhaps Cal was the one who attacked the Tigrina," Tyson offered, anticipating the icy response.

Pellaz fixed him with a stare. "Rue is most emphatic that is not the case."

For a moment, Tyson fantasized about being in Immanion, feeling utterly disenchanted, disorientated, and fed up, surrounded by haughty, preening Gelaming. He could imagine very easily it could drive a har to murder.

"Cal didn't attack Rue," Pellaz said, perhaps prying into Tyson's mind. He turned away and resumed his conversation with the others present.

Cast, as usual, to the sidelines of the social gathering, Tyson reflected that Pellaz felt uncomfortable around him, for the same reason Seel always had. Both Pellaz and Seel had been jealous of Terzian, because he'd had a relationship with Cal that neither of them had ever had. Simple as that. Not that they'd ever admit it. When they looked at Tyson, they saw Cal taking aruna with Terzian. He was living proof of it. All through his childhood, when Seel had looked at him in a certain sour way, Tyson had imagined being a spark of life in the cauldron of creation, being made by two hara lost in bliss. Even a har who hadn't trained very much could project a thought like that. It was the psychic equivalent of throwing stones and had helped to assuage the bitterness Tyson had sometimes felt when Azriel had received better treatment than he had. It wasn't Azriel's fault. He was aware of it and embarrassed about it, but from the moment of Azriel's birth, Seel had made sure his and Swift's son supplanted Tyson in the family hierarchy. If Tyson had been older at the time, that wouldn't have happened, but those years had been chaotic, with so many changes. Cobweb, usually the power in the house, had been stretched out of shape by it all and Seel had breezed in to mold things to his liking.

Now, Tyson wondered how soon he could make an escape from the party. It was clear that Pellaz wanted to speak to Cobweb alone, because the actual point of his visit was not revealed before or during dinner. There was much to discuss, of course, as everyhar present had their own theory as to the motive for the attack on Caeru. Uigenna assassins. Human rebels. Shadowy unknown hara from unknown tribes who resented the way the Gelaming extended their empire. Tyson could tell that Pellaz was holding on to his feelings, if not his entire being, with the greatest of effort. He almost felt sorry for the Tigron, for the first time ever. Everyhar would consider that Cal had done this terrible thing, and perhaps Pellaz feared it too, but was straining to deny it, to find alternative answers. And that must be why he was here in Galhea: to question Cobweb the seer in the hope that Cobweb would provide him with an explanation he could bear.

After the last course had been served and Bryony was organizing the staff to clear the table, Cobweb put Pellaz out of his misery and suggested they go for a walk together in the gardens. Pellaz virtually vaulted over his chair to escape the room. Swift talked about going down to Galhea, proposing that Terez might want to sample the town's night life, but Terez declined. As he stood up from the table, he caught Tyson's eye with a piercing glance, and by that Tyson guessed the har had something to say to him privately. He closed his eyes briefly to acknowledge the unspoken request and Terez left the room.

"He can be dour, that one," Seel remarked, and Swift made a soft sound of agreement. Terez was not very popular, mainly because he *was* dour, and he kept his silence. He had had an awkward start to his Wraeththu life and it had marked him. Pellaz kept him very close, which meant he had to meet a lot of hara, some of whom disliked his manner, while others resented his relationship to the Tigron. Terez did not go out of his way to accommodate or charm hara. He went his own way, like a stray cat. He might live among the rooftops of Immanion, never going indoors, and rarely seen. Pellaz might leave food out for him.

"What do you think?" Swift said to Tyson, interrupting his reverie.

"Of what?" Tyson finished his wine. He must remember to secure a bottle from the kitchens before going to Terez's room.

"About this whole business. Pell is here to pick Cobweb's brains, that's for sure."

Tyson shrugged. "I think Cal went mad and did it." He stood up.

Seel grimaced. "Speak your mind, why don't you?"

"It's what *you* think, isn't it?" Tyson said sweetly. He didn't wait for a response but left the room.

After he'd crept into the kitchens and raided the wine store, Tyson went directly to the room that Cobweb had had prepared for the Tigron's brother. Fresh flowers filled the air with a tart lemony scent and a jug of Bryony's elderflower cordial stood on the nightstand. Terez sat on the end of the bed, looking out of place and uncomfortable. When he wasn't close to Pellaz, it was as if he were missing a limb.

"What did you want to see me about?" Tyson asked, closing the door. He knew Terez responded best to direct approaches.

"Are you ready for a journey?"

"What?"

"Sit down," Terez said.

Tyson sat on the window seat and began to open the wine. "Well?"

"Pellaz wants me to find our brother, Dorado. Cobweb mentioned him a short while ago. Now this business in Immanion has happened and it's clear that Cal is implicated in some way. Pell will find out tonight what Cobweb knows about Dorado and why he is significant. Pell and I think you should come with me to track Dorado down."

"This is a surprise."

"It's not an order, but an offer. You were to be brought to Immanion, but now is not a good time for that."

"I didn't want to go, in any case. I'm curious as to why the Tigron wants me out of the way now."

"That is not how it is. If you come with me, you will learn many things. You cannot escape your heritage, Tyson. It will catch up with you. Pell is extending a hand to you. You would be wise to take it."

Tyson pulled out the cork from the bottle he carried. "I see." He went to the cupboard where glasses were kept and poured out two measures. One glass he handed to Terez, the other he drank himself very quickly. He could barely take in what had been said. "Where will you travel to?"

Terez shrugged. "Dorado was incepted into the Uigenna. It's most likely he will be in hiding. We hope Cobweb will help us find him. We anticipate he will still be in Megalithica. If not, I'll go wherever I have to go."

Tyson laughed and shook his head. "This is most unexpected. For years, I dreamed of travel . . ." He sat down again. "I have no desire to be part of Phaonica's court."

Terez smiled tightly. "No. I can see you would not fit well there."

"Did Cal?"

"No," Terez said. "He was itching to work, to help hara, to make a difference. If he hadn't disappeared, he would have done great things, I'm sure."

"I'm surprised to hear you speak of him warmly. I don't know why, but I thought you'd resent him."

"No," Terez said. "The only thing I could resent him for has no meaning now."

"Which was?"

"Stealing my older brother away from home, away from me, taking his humanity from him. What meaning has that now? I am Wraeththu too. All that went before is a past life. Irrelevant."

Tyson hesitated a moment before speaking. "Shouldn't you be looking for Cal now rather than Dorado?"

"I will find Dorado first. One thing at a time. Many hara are looking for Cal."

"He came to me today," Tyson said.

Terez glanced at him sharply. "What?"

"In a vision or a dream. I think he was trying to tell me about this. He said it was time for me to wake up."

"This is good," Terez said. "You have a link. What is your answer to my proposal?"

It took only seconds to make a decision. Tyson saw himself in years to come, still working for Swift on mundane tasks about the estate, the father or hostling of a couple of harlings: a predictable life, devoid of adventure. "Count me in," Tyson said.

"Can you remember," Pellaz asked, "when we first met?"

Cobweb took his arm. He had been silent since they'd left the house. "Yes, how could I forget? I was a wreck of a har, lying in my own filth, prisoner of the Irraka, and slowly dying of blood poisoning. You were the one who began the healing process. I remember you, Pell. Your innocence, your strength, and your passion for life."

"Am I still that har?"

Cobweb stopped walking, pulling Pellaz to a halt beside him. "Is this the gist of the interrogation you were planning? I was expecting something else."

"If it wasn't for me, you'd be dead," Pellaz said. "Cal and I rescued you from the Irraka and brought you back home. Never once in all the years of our friendship have I reminded you of that. But there is a debt between us. I'm sorry, Cobweb, but I have to call that in. You have to speak plainly to me. No more riddles or enigmatic mystical remarks. Did Cal attack Rue? I know you know the answer."

Cobweb sighed deeply, his expression sorrowful. "To answer your first question: no, you are clearly not the har I first met. To answer the second, which you have so bluntly and indelicately demanded, it is also no."

Pellaz exhaled long and deep, his eyes closed. "Thank Aru!"

"You didn't have to call the debt in. I would have told you that, in any case."

"I'm sorry. These are desperate times. I don't have the time for vague clues. I need clear information."

"Thanks. I don't deliberately try to confound you. A lot of what I perceive is muddled and confusing. I never play a game with you, Pell. I'm hurt you should think that."

"I didn't intend to hurt you. Understand my position. I don't know which way to turn. What else can you tell me?"

Cobweb took Pell's arm again. "Let's sit down." They had come to the side of the lake, a haunted and beautiful spot in the tangled gardens of Forever. Some of the ancient yews had wooden benches fixed around their trunks, and now Cobweb sat down on one of them, gesturing for Pellaz to sit beside him. "So much happened here," he said. "Cal and I shared a traumatic moment in this place."

"I know," Pellaz said rather impatiently. "You told me about it a long time ago."

"He always would have come back here," Cobweb said. "He loved this house, and I think he loved Swift and me too. But he will never return as long as Seel is here. He has lost his refuge, and that is sad."

"Where is he?" Pellaz asked. "Why did he run from Immanion? Was it connected to what happened to Rue, or did he run simply because he realized he'd done the wrong thing in coming to me at all?"

"Pell, I can't give you precise answers. I wish I could, but I can't. Some things I am sure about. I know he didn't attack Rue, and I think he left the city for both of the reasons you just suggested. I think also he had no choice in leaving. It was a complicated issue."

"Who did attack Rue? Any tiny sliver of information you can give me will be worth your weight in diamonds."

Cobweb closed his eyes. "It is too dark in the inner world. I can't see. I don't think Rue was the target."

"They had come for me? They were looking in the wrong place, then!"

"No, not you, Pell. The pearl. It was the pearl they were after."

"We have already considered that. The attacker took the pearl, or at least disposed of it away from the scene of the crime. It's sick."

Cobweb lowered his head and rubbed at his temples. "Rue was simply in the way, his flesh a barrier. There was no murderous intent, only a sense of driven purpose, a job to be done. And that is really all I can tell you."

"Have you any impression of the attacker?"

"No, they disguised themselves well. I have no idea of what they looked like, who they were, or where they came from. I don't even know whether they were har or not."

Pell nodded thoughtfully, his mind trying to make some kind of sense of what Cobweb had told him. "Who would want to harm the pearl?" he murmured, thinking aloud. He glanced at Cobweb. "Cal met somehar for dinner that night. We still don't know who."

"I can't help you with that," Cobweb said. "I'm sorry."

Pellaz sighed deeply. "What is going on? And where the hell do I begin to try and find out?"

"I have been feeling very strange recently," Cobweb said. "It's as if powerful forces are on the move in the world. Nothing is certain. The fact that Thiede is no longer incarnate in this plane is the cause of it, I'm sure. Whether that is a good or a bad thing, I don't know yet. Now I want you to be honest with me. Did Opalexian want to get rid of Thiede?"

Pellaz took a deep breath. "The truth? Okay. This is all I know. Some time ago, when Lileem and Terez disappeared into the otherworld, I learned the truth about Kamagrian. I met with Opalexian in Shilalama. She was far from happy about me being there. I had to trade. I wanted to win her confidence. Basically, I asked her to find Cal and to heal him, to bring him to me, and she agreed to do so. She knew then that I trusted her. She has that over me. I'm not sure how hara would react if they knew my selfish desires were primarily the cause for Thiede's dismissal from this plane. As long as Thiede was with us, he'd never have allowed Cal and I to be together." He shrugged. "I wonder now whether Opalexian had her own agenda and used Cal to get rid of Thiede. It seems increasingly likely, but in that case, why hasn't she taken advantage of the situation? She is as reclusive as she ever was."

"She might be preparing to play a long game," Cobweb said. "It isn't that long ago that Cal came to Immanion and did her work—if that was what he was doing. In her position, I'd continue to lie low for a while. Wouldn't you?"

"I will go and see her, I think."

"I wonder how much good that would do, or how much truth she'd give you."

"She is fanatical about one thing, and that is that Kamagrian and Wraeththu must never come together. We know that aruna between a har and a parage can open up portals to other worlds. The question I want answered is whether Opalexian wishes to prevent such events because she fears for her parazha's safety, or whether because, if we ever did learn how to control our combined force, it would teach us things she'd rather we didn't know. And if so, why?"

"They are weighty questions," Cobweb said. "I don't think Opalexian will answer them. My impression is that she believes Kamagrian to be superior to Wraeththu, and that she has used you, and thinks she continues to do so. She thinks you are easy to control."

"The danger could lie in her belief in her superiority. Perhaps that was the issue between her and Thiede all along. But Kamagrian need Wraeththu to exist. Parazha cannot reproduce—or have not yet learned how to. They are only born when they occasionally form within harish pearls."

"It's feasible Opalexian wishes to create a ruling elite, a shadowy cabal of Kamagrian Illuminati sustained by the ignorant populace."

"It's feasible, yes," Pellaz said, "but if you met her, I think you'd find it as hard to believe as I do. She might have wanted to get rid of Thiede, but I really don't think that was because she craved his power over Wraeththu. I think she feared what he might do."

Cobweb was silent for a moment, then said, "I could come with you to Shilalama. My sight might be of use to you there."

"Thank you," Pellaz said. "I think it might." He paused, then said, "Would Opalexian wish to harm our pearl? Is she capable of that?"

"All I think is that in conceiving that pearl, you created something more powerful than you knew. The child was in danger from the moment of its creation. It is a great tragedy that nohar foresaw that, including myself. As for whether Opalexian ordered its murder—consider this. The harling that might have hatched from the pearl needn't necessarily have been Wraeththu."

"She wouldn't have killed such a child."

"No, I agree. But she might well have considered abducting it, especially before anyhar saw its condition."

"You are suggesting her as a candidate then, and think the harling might have survived excision from Rue's body?"

"I'm not suggesting Opalexian ordered it, no, because it would have been more practical for her to wait until the pearl had been born before attempting an abduction. The pearl protects its secret until it hatches. But I do think there is a distinct possibility the child might not be dead. Rue was very close to term."

"These are interesting things to consider," Pellaz said. "Now I want to know how Dorado fits into this picture."

Cobweb fixed Pellaz with a luminous stare. "I am a powerful psychic, Pell. You know that. But I believe the power your brother has makes my ability look like a tiny candle flame. He is the sun. His light can shine into the darkest spaces."

"How do you know this?"

"I don't. I just believe it to be so. On the night of Cal's arrival in Immanion, many doors opened. I have already told you that. It felt as if the whole of history were rushing through my mind. I saw so many things it nearly killed me. I saw Dorado. And he saw me too. He knows I am speaking to you now, telling you what I can. He is resentful, Uigenna to the core. That is why you must send Terez to find him. He will have no dealings with you."

"Where is he?"

"Somewhere here in Megalithica. I see a ruined human city, close to a great body of water. It could be the ocean, but something advises me it's not. I see a northern landscape. I see mist driven by powerful winds. He is in this place, watching me, as I watch him."

"He will hide from Terez, then. He must know everything we're planning."

Cobweb shook his head. "He is waiting, that is all. His focus is upon you and he is damaged, both physically and mentally. I believe this means he has not considered Terez. He fears the power of the Tigron, nothing more."

"And what do I do with him if Terez finds him? Rehabilitation? How?"

"It would require a political solution. The Gelaming could stop oppressing Uigenna hara in this country . . ."

"Cobweb, it is not oppression! If they refuse to abandon their violent ways, then . . ."

"Hush," Cobweb said. "You asked me and I told you what I thought. Everyhar has the right to be free."

"Free to murder, plunder, use up, and move on? You know how the Uigenna are, Cobweb. They were the closest allies of the Varrs! You know how your own tribe used to be, your own consort—or should I say *master*? What were you in those days? Hardly more than breeding stock! If you want to talk about oppression, remember your own life when Terzian held the keys to it!"

"Parasiel evolved from the Varrs," Cobweb said, his voice steady. "Stop shouting, and just think about that for a moment."

"It could only happen when Terzian had died. Thank all the gods that happened!"

"I loved him very much," Cobweb said. "Don't say any more."

"He was . . ."

"So did Cal," Cobweb continued. "If you say any more, Pell, we're going to fall out—badly. Just stand back for a moment and watch yourself."

Pellaz uttered an angry sound and put his head in his hands. He was consumed by furious emotion. Cal had loved Terzian: he knew that was the truth. "Cal should have stayed here in Galhea when he first had the chance," he said at last, "before we realized what we felt for one another. How much that would have changed things."

Cobweb put a hand on Pell's shoulder. "He didn't stay because he loved you more. You know that. He only came back here when he thought you were dead. Let go of the past, Pell. You must."

"I wanted so badly for it to work," Pellaz said. "I thought it could have done. I was wrong. And now Thiede is gone and the whole world is falling apart."

"It's not over yet," Cobweb said, stroking Pell's hair. "Be strong, my beautiful friend. But be wise also. Send Terez to look for Dorado, and we will go to Shilalama together. I am interested in meeting Opalexian, very interested."

Pellaz raised his head and breathed deep, banishing the unwelcome feelings. He must not become their prey. He could betray no weakness. "I have told Terez to ask Tyson to accompany him on his search."

Cobweb was silent for a moment, then said, "Ty will appreciate that. He pulls at the bit here. An adventure will do him good. He needs to find his own place in the world."

"But you do not wholly approve of my idea. I can tell."

"It's not because of me," Cobweb said, "it's because of the one who will be left behind. Tyson has a chesnari, a har I like very much. He will be devastated."

"Tyson will return," Pellaz said. "Terez will look out for him."

"I know. I'm not concerned for Ty's safety. I just worry that once he's had a taste of the world, he won't come back here. He is Cal's son, after all, even if it does feel like he's mine. He needs a bigger life than any that Galhea can offer him."

"Then he deserves to have one."

Cobweb nodded. "I know. Thank you for giving him a chance, Pell. I know it's not easy for you to accept him."

"Let's go back to the house. I'd like to talk to Tyson before we sleep tonight. Terez and he can leave first thing in the morning. Perhaps you could give them some idea about where to start looking. Tell them what you told me."

Cobweb stood up. "Okay. I could do with a drink now. A large one."

Pell looked up at him. "I'm sorry for what I said. Take it as a compliment. I can be myself with you."

Cobweb smiled. "Apology accepted. Let's go."

Cobweb and Pellaz joined Tyson and Terez, in the bedroom where they were still talking. They discussed between them where Terez should first search for Dorado, and it seemed fairly conclusive to all of them that Terez and Tyson should head north. Pellaz decided that they should not ride *sedim*, not just— he said—because Tyson wasn't trained to control a *sedu*, but also because more clues could be picked up from the countryside along the way. Tyson knew the Gelaming were reluctant to let outsiders own or even ride the *sedim*, and suspected that was Pell's prime motive in suggesting they use more a conventional mode of travel.

Pellaz, clearly picking up on this thought, said, "One day, you will come to Immanion, Tyson. At that time, I will see to it that you are trained how to control a *sedu*."

The message—to Tyson—was clear: behave and prove yourself, and I will be more inclined to be generous.

The discussion was brief, because Terez wanted to make an early start in the morning. They would ride north and investigate ruined human communities beside lakes. Cobweb was fairly sure it would not be a coastal town. Megalithica was a big country. The search could take months, if not years. In the meantime, Cobweb would continue to seek psychic information, which would be relayed to them through Pellaz's close telepathic link with Terez.

Tyson did not want to go to bed, because he no longer felt tired. He'd have been quite happy to start traveling immediately. Cobweb said he'd go to the library to find a good map for Terez, and Tyson trailed along behind him. He thought he might as well study the map for a while and perhaps make some notes about which locations they should visit. *Sedim* would make the job so much easier, he thought. Pellaz didn't trust him with one. Perhaps the Tigron wasn't as keen to find Dorado as he seemed. Surely, if he had any sense of urgency, he'd have made sure his trackers used the most efficient method of transport available.

"Where do you think you're going?" Cobweb asked as they reached the doors to the library.

"With you," Tyson answered. "I thought . . ."

"No, there is somewhere else you should go," Cobweb said. "Go now."

Tyson held Cobweb's gaze for some moments, then glanced away. "All right. If I must."

Cobweb made a sound of displeasure. "I cannot believe you even contemplated leaving here without doing so."

"To be honest, it slipped my mind. This has been a big surprise."

"Don't lie to me, Tyson. You will never get away with it."

Tyson sighed heavily and trudged to the stables. The one thing he would not miss about home was the fact that Cobweb always knew everything. As for the other thing, he wasn't sure whether he'd miss it or not. At the moment, he had no feelings about it, other than a mild discomfort about the possibility of an emotional scene. He rode swiftly into town, directly to the house where Ferany lived.

Tyson didn't want to advise Ferany's parents he was there, so trusted Ferany had gone to bed and threw stones at his window. Eventually, a light came on and Ferany opened the window. *He is beautiful,* Tyson thought, *but that is not enough.*

"What's wrong?" Ferany asked.

"Come down. We have to talk."

"Why the secrecy?"

"Just come down here."

It was not that difficult to tell Ferany about how he was leaving Galhea. Of course, he could not divulge the true nature of the job he'd been given, but said that he was working for the Tigron and would be traveling with Terez. Ferany appeared to accept the news well. "Will you be gone for a long time?" he asked.

"I expect so," Tyson replied, and now came the difficult part. "Ferany, I have to say this: don't wait for me."

Ferany frowned a little. "I'm not sure I understand you. I live here, so . . . Did you think I'd be celibate while you were away? What do you mean?"

Tyson took Ferany's hands in his own. "I mean . . . I might not come back."

"Are you involved in something dangerous?"

"No." Tyson took a deep breath. "This isn't what I want, Fer. I don't want *us,* you moving into Forever, blood bond, harlings, or whatever. I'm sorry. I think this has happened for the best."

Ferany removed his hands from Tyson's hold. "I see." He laughed, raggedly. "Strange, I thought we were chesna. I thought we both felt the same."

"When I got this offer, I knew," Tyson said. "I just felt this . . . I don't know . . . huge sense of relief. Oh, hell, that sounds bad. I didn't mean it how it sounds. It's just . . ."

"Cobweb spoke to me some days ago. We talked about the future and he told me he was looking forward to me becoming part of the family."

"Oh. Well, it's taken us all by surprise, this offer of a job."

"Only a couple of days ago, you were rejoicing that you wouldn't have to go to Immanion. You were moaning about the Gelaming. Now this. I can't take it in." Ferany gazed up at the sky and Tyson could see the glitter of unshed tears in the moonlight. "I can't believe this," Ferany said. "I really can't. How can you just *change* so much so quickly?"

Tyson rubbed his face. "It's not that I'm not fond of you, Fer. I am. You're beautiful and great company. Aruna with you is like . . ."

"Oh, shut up!" Ferany interrupted. Without further words, he punched Tyson in the face, which sent him reeling. "You shit," he said and walked back into the house, slamming the door behind him.

Tyson continued to see stars for several moments longer. That had not been quite the reaction he'd anticipated.

CHAPTER TEN

The moment Abrimel har Aralis let in the darkness was the moment he heard the news from Immanion about his hostling. Anyhar would be forgiven for assuming he must have been filled with a cold focused rage, directed particularly against not only the assailant responsible for the attack, but the hara who had been instrumental in getting Caeru with pearl. But this was not the case. The darkness in Abrimel's heart was a kind of quiet self-justified glee.

This time it was not Velaxis who brought the news. It was an official from Caeru's office, who obviously, and kindheartedly, had felt it was important for the Tigrina's son to be made aware of circumstances when everyhar else had forgotten him in the chaos. The message had not come directly to Abrimel, who'd been out in the field at the time, but had been received by one of his staff, who had the unenviable task of relaying the information to his employer once he returned to Imbrilim. In a daze, Abrimel asked the right questions in a clipped and strained tone, nodded curtly to the answers, and everyhar who witnessed his strangely blank response imagined he was stunned by what he'd heard. Abrimel was known as a private kind of har. Nohar expected him to confide in them or demonstrate his feelings.

Left alone, Abrimel nursed the gratifying thought: *Serves you right,* and was amazed to discover he didn't feel the least bit guilty about it. Caeru had brought his misfortunes on himself. He'd learned nothing during all the years he'd lived in Immanion. The irritating coziness of newfound harmony among the Aralisians must surely now be shattered. Abrimel could not even bring himself to send a message home, offering condolences or support. In a deep hidden corner of his heart, he thought that perhaps Caeru might come to him now, full of tears and regret, seeking his one true son. In this fantasy, Abrimel and Caeru ran away from everything Gelaming and forged a new life together, more to Abrimel's liking. But no message came from the Tigrina and certainly no personal visit. Abrimel, enmeshed in his own feelings, did not for one moment consider that Caeru was actually lying in an infirmary bed taking far too long to heal. He imagined that his hostling was drooping and weeping around Phaonica, mourning the loss of a son who Pellaz would have not only accepted but also loved. As the days passed, this thought became more real in Abrimel's mind and heart. He and Caeru should never have gone to Immanion in the first place. If Caeru hadn't been so stupid and besotted, they would have had a different, wonderful life together. Furious, Abrimel decided that he no longer had a hostling or a father. He cast the pair of them off like dead skin.

The power of coincidence is very powerful indeed. It slips like oil through the dense, multilayered fabric of reality and wherever it finds a chink, it slithers through. The slithering, in this instance, belonged to Diablo of Gebaddon, who flopped out of the otherlanes, covered in a dark viscous fluid and barely in possession of his sanity, into the tall grasses at the edge of a spinney in a field near Imbrilim. The higher powers of the universe, which are perhaps often bored or have a dark sense of humor, made it happen that Abrimel was walking in the fields, lost in gloomy thoughts, at the very moment this event occurred. He felt a shiver in his flesh that jolted him out of his reverie and glanced up from his study of the ground, expecting to see an otherlanes portal closing above him. There was an eerie shimmer to the reddening evening sky, but nothing more. It faded so quickly, Abrimel wondered whether he'd imagined it. For some moments, he continued his walk, tearing dead seed heads from the grass around him, wondering what he should do with his life and whether he had the motivation or stamina to change things. The darkness of the trees ahead appeared inviting and he had a desire to walk into it. Peace could be found in the landscape. It was so empty, yet even as he thought this, he knew that behind him Imbrilim was expanding outward like a disease, as human conurbations had done in earlier times, and would no doubt eventually smother all that was beautiful and free in nature. Abrimel's momentary disgust with his own kind was pure and fierce. He saw all hara as posturing effete fools, animated dolls that acted out lives in the manner that humankind had once lived. But they were not real. They were an aberration. This kind of thinking was common in the most damaged of first-generation hara, but less so in pure born Wraeththu. Perhaps it was these pessimistic thoughts that drew Diablo, beaten and robbed of his spoils, to be expelled from the otherlanes in that spot, at that time.

Entering among the trees, Abrimel heard rustling, which at first he took to be the early scurryings of a nocturnal creature, but this was followed by a pitiful sound that did not sound animal at all. The light amid the tall somber trunks was dim: beyond them the sky was a deep red. It was moments before the sun sank beneath the horizon. Abrimel picked up a stout fallen branch and began to poke around among the yellow grasses and bare brambles that leaned this way and that in a tangle about him. Eventually, he came upon Diablo, who was lying in a shuddering heap beneath a tree, where he'd managed to crawl before collapsing.

Abrimel observed this quivering mass for some moments, unsure whether it was an animal or a human refugee. It didn't appear harish to him, because he'd never beheld a har in such a state. He poked it with the branch and it jerked and moaned. He saw limbs moving feebly, a flash of pale face through a cage of protective fingers.

Abrimel pulled aside the grasses and brambles, scratching his hands quite badly in the process. Acting on instinct rather than through compassion, he dragged the body out into the field by its feet and then stood over it to examine what he'd unearthed. He saw an emaciated creature, clad in dark clothes that appeared to be rags tied around its body in complicated knots. He could tell at once it wasn't human, but neither did it appear completely har. It was a goblin of a creature, one moment moaning in apparent pain, the next hissing in a clearly defensive manner. It was pathetic, utterly repellent, but also intriguing, simply because Abrimel was perplexed as to what it was. It was his job, after all, to catalogue Wraeththu tribes in Megalithica, where some extremely interesting permutations had already been discovered. Abrimel had never seen a har like this, if indeed it was a har, and not some elemental creature that had somehow been trapped in a corporeal form. Whatever miserable thoughts had previously occupied his mind, he was in truth fanatical about his work; the sight of this strange being shouldered aside his gloom and kindled his professional curiosity. It looked as if it might die soon, so Abrimel was eager to transport it back to Imbrilim in order to study it properly. It weighed very little, so he was able to hoist it over his shoulder quite easily. It smelled bad, like old musty hay.

Most inhabitants of Imbrilim were in their dwellings, eating their evening meals, as Abrimel crept along a newly paved street to his house. He passed one or two hara, who paid him little attention, as they were absorbed in their own conversations. He looked as if he was carrying a sack over his shoulder, so it was hardly a sight worth investigating. He entered his home through the rear entrance and went directly to his study, where he dropped his burden onto a couch. The creature opened its eyes, which were unnervingly large and dark, indeed quite beautiful. It growled at Abrimel. Abrimel was not afraid. He was strong and had interviewed some particularly intransigent Uigenna during his work. He had learned long ago how to defend himself. "What are you?" he asked. He did not expect a response and went to pour a measure of fiery sheh into a glass, which he then offered to the creature on the couch. It snatched the glass from Abrimel's hands, drank the contents noisily, then crushed the glass in its long twiggy fingers, discarding the bits onto the carpet with an oddly flamboyant gesture. Abrimel wondered whether it was, in fact, dying after all.

"Are you har?" Abrimel asked. "Can you speak?"

The creature maintained a low throaty growl, much as a frightened feral cat might utter.

"I will not harm you," Abrimel said. "You are safe here."

The creature appeared mindless. Abrimel thought he might have to have it locked up, because there was no way he'd allow it to remain unsupervised in his house throughout the night.

"I will give you one last chance," he said in a clear slow voice. "If you can communicate, then do so now, otherwise I shall have to have you taken away by the town guards. Do you understand? If you cooperate I will feed you and give you a place to stay for the night. You have nothing to gain by being difficult." It was a wild hope. He didn't really think he'd get a positive response, and was therefore surprised when the impish har on the couch stopped growling and nodded its head once.

"More," it said, holding out its hands, which were not at all cut from breaking the glass.

At this point, the creature became "he" rather than "it" in Abrimel's view. He saw in those huge eyes a terrible suffering and empathized with it. "I am Abrimel," he said. "Tell me your name and I'll give you another drink."

"Diablo." The har said it in a sibilant, earthy way, drawing out the word, so it sounded like an invocation rather than a name.

"Interesting," said Abrimel. "Don't break the next glass I give you."

For over an hour, Abrimel watched Diablo devour vast amounts of food. He ate with surprising neatness, his movements economical yet constant, like a machine. He also appeared to have a limitless appetite and Abrimel guessed

Diablo had not eaten much for a long time. Abrimel allowed his strange guest to attend to his body's needs in silence and busied himself with writing some preliminary notes on his find. He only raised his head when he became aware of being scrutinized and he physically jumped when his gaze collided with the wide-eyed stare of Diablo. Perhaps, if he was cleaned up, he wouldn't look so unnerving. His body was trembling so that the snakes of lank hair hanging over his face vibrated like wires. He might be suffering from shock.

Abrimel laid down his pen and forced himself to return the stare in silence. It was a mistake to let anyhar know you might be afraid of them.

"Is this Galhea?" Diablo asked, his voice strangely accented.

"No," said Abrimel. "This is Imbrilim. Galhea is some distance north."

Diablo stared at his hands, flexing his long fingers in a disturbingly determined manner. Abrimel could not help but be relieved this was not Galhea. "Do you have a tribe?" he asked.

Diablo nodded, then got up from the couch, from where he hadn't moved since he'd arrived, and began to prowl around the room, examining everything he came across.

"Where are they?" Abrimel persisted.

"Not here," Diablo answered.

"Were you abandoned? What happened to you?"

"I fell from the spirit path," Diablo said, "but I had to. I was lost. I had to fall where I could."

Abrimel remembered the feeling he'd had before he'd found Diablo. He stood up. "You mean the otherlanes?"

Diablo glanced at him blankly, then removed a book from a shelf. He opened the book, sniffed it, and then returned it carefully to its place. He did this with several volumes.

"Who are your tribe, Diablo? Where do they live? How do you travel the otherlanes, the spirit path?" Abrimel knew these were too many questions at once, but couldn't help himself. If Diablo had really fallen from the otherlanes it was astounding, because he'd clearly been traveling without a *sedu* to guide him. As far as Abrimel knew, no har could open an otherlanes portal without such help.

"Why?" Diablo asked. "Why do you want to know?" He appeared to be genuinely perplexed by the questions.

"To understand you," Abrimel said. "It's my job. I study all the different Wraeththu tribes, but I've never met anyhar like you before."

Diablo merely shrugged. "You can't meet us. We are in Gebaddon."

Abrimel had to sit down again. "Gebaddon? Are you sure?"

Diablo grinned at that. "Yes."

"Your tribe can travel outside the forest?"

"I do," Diablo said. "Soon, I will go back."

It occurred to Abrimel then that his peculiar guest might very well disappear without a moment's warning. "Don't leave yet," he said. "Talk to me first. I want to know about you."

"I cannot talk to you," Diablo said. "We are enemies, whoever you are."

He was unafraid because now he was fed and had recovered from whatever had happened to him. He had the means to escape whenever he wanted to: that much was obvious. "Why am I an enemy?" Abrimel asked carefully.

"All hara outside Gebaddon are enemies."

"Do you understand what your being here means to those outside the forest?"

"Yes. It means I must kill you before I leave."

"Why? Haven't I helped you?"

"My hostling would kill me if I didn't. I would be punished. Nohar must know of us yet."

It was extremely discomforting to realize that Diablo meant every word he said. He had no doubt he could kill Abrimel whenever he wanted to, and that certainty lent credibility to his threat. Abrimel swallowed with difficulty, because his mouth had gone dry. The urge to fight or flee strained nervously at the threshold of his being. He must not betray fear. "I am not your enemy, Diablo. I am a scholar. Your tribe was imprisoned in Gebaddon. Perhaps that was not a good thing. Perhaps the world should know the truth. You can tell it to me."

Diablo laughed. "Nohar must know," he said again. "Didn't you hear me?" He took a few steps toward Abrimel.

"Perhaps your enemies are my enemies also," Abrimel said, his voice deceptively level. He did not flinch away.

Diablo paused. "What do you mean?"

Abrimel didn't really know. He'd said it as an act of self-preservation, but then he realized that maybe it wasn't a lie. "I am outcast too," he said. "I am the son of Pellaz har Aralis, Tigron of Immanion, whose tribe condemned you to exile. I am cast out, as you are; forgotten, as you are. No har shall hear from me that the Varrs have found a tunnel from their prison."

Diablo stared at Abrimel inscrutably, but Abrimel was sure that beyond the grimy and somewhat imbecilic appearance a sharp mind was busy at work. Eventually, Diablo said, "If what you say is true and you wish to live, there is one thing you can do."

"Yes?" said Abrimel.

"Return with me to Gebaddon. Speak to my hostling, for he might have a use for you. If you lie, you'll die, or maybe my hostling will have no use for you at all, and you'll still die, but it is your choice. I will kill you here if you prefer."

Abrimel knew he was being offered something unique. The Varrs had been left to rot in Gebaddon, but it seemed that something quite different had occurred. The scholar in him yearned to probe these secrets. The angry child within him yearned to ally with Pellaz's enemies. But how far did he want to go? If he took this step, there might be no turning back. Did he wish his father, and all that he stood for, dead? But maybe he had no choice. Maybe, if he refused this offer, Diablo *would* kill him, moving quicker than the eye could see. This har before him was nothing like any har he'd ever seen, and appeared to be second generation like himself, but perhaps in Gebaddon some of the original Varrs survived, individuals more harish than Diablo, with whom it might be possible to communicate properly. He had to ask. "Does Ponclast still live?"

"He is my hostling," Diablo answered.

"Take me to him," Abrimel said.

Diablo held out a hand. "Hold on to me," he said. "Don't let go."

Abrimel took the offered hand. He looked into Diablo's eyes and saw strange lights in their depths. The portal came from within Diablo, from within his eyes. Abrimel was sucked into a vortex of energy. For a brief moment, he feared he would never see the realm of earth again. Then the capacity for thought was smacked from his mind.

The experience of traveling the otherlanes without *sedim* was not pleasant. To Abrimel it felt as if his skin were scraped from his body, that his bones were crushed. It seemed to last for an eternity, but then with a great clap of thunder and what felt like a dozen blows to the body with iron bars, Abrimel found himself once again on firm ground, covered in a crust of ice that was already breaking away from him, evaporating like snowflakes on a hot plate. He collapsed against Diablo, still gripping the strange har's long-fingered hand. He couldn't understand how Diablo had managed to open a portal, nor how he could have dragged somehar with him into that vast confusing network of nonreality. How did he find the paths? How did he know where he was going?

For a short time, Diablo allowed Abrimel to lean against him, fighting for breath, then pushed him away. "This is Gebaddon," he said.

Abrimel looked around himself, saw the dark twisted trees, the huge growths of pale fungi, the flash of eyes through the undergrowth. They were standing at the mouth of a cave, which was mostly hidden by a thick curtain of tattered ivy, whose leaves were all of different shapes and sizes, few of which resembled a normal ivy leaf.

"Come," Diablo said, lifting aside the foliage. He had not let go of Abrimel's hand, perhaps as a security measure.

Abrimel had heard all the stories of Ponclast, as nearly every second-generation har had done. He had imagined the Varr leader as a huge, overtly masculine, barrel-chested sort of har, with a great booming voice and a deep aversion for the feminine side of his being. Therefore, when Abrimel entered the inner chamber of the cave and saw Ponclast for the first time, he was shocked. Ponclast was not a bulky har, but attenuated and pale, almost sylphlike. His hair was a mass of dark rags and tendrils, blending with the rags and tendrils of his crimson robe. He was abnormally thin, his eyes sunk deep in his face. The overall effect, though somewhat unusual, was also strangely aesthetic. Ponclast and his environment were like a painting to illustrate a dark and mysterious tale. There was a tragic and romantic element to his appearance. Engaged in some business with toxic-looking liquids in a row of wooden bowls, he stared at Abrimel long and hard. "What has taken you so long?" he asked, presumably of Diablo. "I expected you back days ago."

"A problem," Diablo said.

"And what is this?" Ponclast demanded, indicating Abrimel. "Don't tell me the harling hatched and matured in the otherlanes."

"No pearl," Diablo said, bowing to his hostling. "Taken."

Abrimel was suffused by an icy chill: he presaged what was to come.

"What?" Ponclast snapped. "Explain."

"I did as you asked," Diablo said. "Cut the har, and the pearl was mine. On the spirit path, he jumped on me. Took the pearl. Filled me with fire. He threw me off the path, and I was lost for a long time."

Ponclast's mouth was a grim line. "That makes no sense," he said. "Come here. I'll see for myself."

Diablo went to Ponclast and before Abrimel's astonished gaze, shared breath with his hostling. The sight was grotesque, not least because of the appearance of the participants. Abrimel swallowed with difficulty. What was he doing here? He must be insane. These hara must be the ones who had attacked Caeru.

After what seemed far too long, Ponclast pushed Diablo from him. "Whatever attacked you concealed itself as well as you can. I can only assume parties other than our allies have an interest in the Tigron's spawn. This is unexpected, but no fault of mine or yours." He stared directly into Abrimel's eyes. "I have no pearl, yet another son of the Tigron stands before me." He glanced at Diablo. "You have done well, under the circumstances."

"I am not your enemy," Abrimel said, although he was no longer sure about that. What he'd heard didn't sound real, but he knew it must be. Somehar had attacked Caeru, and what better candidate than a har with the greatest grudge against the Gelaming?

Ponclast laughed, although his eyes remained cold. "No." He made an expansive gesture with both arms. "Well, tiahaar, I wish I had lavish accommodations in which to entertain you. As you can see, conditions here are rather less than you are no doubt used to. How can you be of use to me? How can you convince me I can trust you?"

"The pearl you spoke of—it was the one my hostling carried."

"Yes. It should have been destroyed. Does that bother you?"

"No, it should have been destroyed. I always felt the pearl was wrong. But my hostling . . . ?"

Ponclast did not answer this half-formed question. "Unfortunately, something intervened while Diablo was at work. Somehar, or something, else now has the pearl."

"Did you mean to kill Caeru?"

"No, he was irrelevant," Ponclast said, "but if the thought of his death distresses you, you have no right to be standing here."

Abrimel closed his eyes briefly, felt as if a cloak he had worn since childhood had fallen from his body. It had been heavy, warm, and comforting, but restrictive too. "I cast off my parents," he said. "As they cast me off."

"What is your function?"

"I work in Imbrilim, the Gelaming enclave. I collect data about the tribes."

"Not very glamorous," said Ponclast. "However, I expect you still have many contacts in Immanion."

"Some."

Ponclast came toward Abrimel, seeming to glide just above the floor, his robe rustling over dead leaves. He extended a thin white hand and Abrimel saw how clean and perfect it was: the hand of a torturer, perhaps. His touch, on Abrimel's cheek, was cool and dry. "We could have an alliance, you and I," Ponclast said, "but first you must let me put a seed in you, a seed that, should you betray me, would burst into poison bloom and destroy you."

"I am in no position to argue," Abrimel said. "You will not let me leave here without this insurance."

Ponclast smiled. "You are bright," he said. "Look upon me, Gelaming. I am not a creature to be desired, to dote on, to worship. I am wrung out, dried and bloodless. I have been drained of life. But I intend to get it all back. Perhaps you will help me."

He took a few steps away, turned his back. "There is an old human legend," he said, "that concerned a rite of initiation for warriors and kings. To acquire divine strength, they had to make love to the great goddess of creation. Hardly a tiresome task, you might say. But she manifested to them as a hideous hag. If they could steel themselves to kiss her with passion, to adore her as the most comely of maidens, she would grant them immeasurable powers. I know what I am, tiahaar. The harish equivalent of hag, but lie with me, and perhaps great powers shall also be yours." He turned back to Abrimel, his expression unfathomable.

Abrimel could not imagine being able to take aruna with this creature. He was interesting to observe, like an exotic and dangerous animal, but certainly no object of desire. Abrimel thought that if he now had to be ouana to save his life, then he must be about to die. Ponclast, however, appeared to pick up on his panicked thoughts.

"Submit to me," he said in a dry, toneless voice. "It is the way my influence is transferred to you. The story of the hag was a joke. I do not expect passion from you."

But just for a moment, Abrimel thought, *you hoped for it. Easy to dismiss it as a joke after you looked into my eyes.*

In such revelations lay advantage.

CHAPTER ELEVEN

Many times, Moon considered that Raven had made a big sacrifice in taking aruna with him. There was no doubt that Raven's behavior changed thereafter. Something had woken up within him too, but it was not a good thing. He seemed tortured. Moon's awakening involved a new awareness of his own body and those of others around him. He would never have believed it possible, but he actually yearned for further contact with Raven. It was obvious this would not happen. Raven avoided him now and even Snake had commented on his strange behavior.

"I have done this to him," Moon said.

Snake shook his head. "No, it was done to him a long time ago."

"What was?"

Snake stared at his son for a few moments, then said, "I cannot tell you his private troubles. But I will say this: the Gelaming were involved."

For a few days after Snake's first pronouncement that the Tigron of Immanion would come looking for them, Moon had lived in fear. But nothing had happened, and the feelings had faded away. He didn't believe now that they were in any kind of danger. "I feel bad," Moon said. "I feel I need something."

Snake continued to stare. "Go to where others gather," he said. "It is time you should do that."

For some days, Moon shrank from the idea, for he knew what his father meant. He should forge friendships with other hara. Moon had spent so much time alone, and he knew how the clans regarded Snake and his household, that the prospect of trying to be sociable, never mind anything else, filled him with icy dread. But he could not deny the sensations that raged within him, demanding release and satisfaction. He realized he wasn't like Snake and Raven. He wasn't dead inside.

One evening, he found himself walking toward the harbor and knew he was about to take an irrevocable step. He could hear music playing and the sounds of voices and laughter. It was a different world, one he had never entered. He was not sure how he'd be received by it. He visited the harbor during the day to barter for provisions, but its nighttime face was something else. It didn't look the same.

Open-fronted bars faced the water, their awnings hung with lamps. Food vendors cooked their wares in the open air, currency brokers sat in their kiosks, and visitors from farther south, mainly traders and trappers, thronged there noisily. Groups of hara sat around fires, some beating out hypnotic rhythms on drums, while others danced, uttering strange cries, their long hair swinging. No-har took much notice of Moon as he skulked through the crowds, but occasionally a har of the clans would recognize him and stare, or else nudge their companions and point. Moon knew he should perhaps nod in greeting and smile, and that such behavior might break the ice, but lacked the will to do so. He felt awkward and vulnerable. Eventually, he approached a broker and swapped a few artifacts he'd brought with him from the Reliquary for a handful of rough iron coins. This was enough to buy him drinks for the evening, in fact enough for him to drink himself senseless.

As the broker handed over the coins, he narrowed his eyes and said, "You're Snake Jaguar's harling."

Moon nodded.

The har continued to inspect him for some moments, then said, "Try the South Wind Inn. Young ones go there."

"Thanks," Moon said.

The broker gestured behind him. "That way."

Moon stumbled off, his face crimson. He knew it was obvious why he was there and the broker's helpful advice only made it worse. He couldn't do this. He should go home.

The South Wind was only a short distance from the broker's kiosk and once Moon caught sight of its open doorway, he scuttled into an alley and watched the hara enter and leave the premises. Some of them were of the

Jaguar clan, but Moon didn't really know them. He, Snake, and Raven never took part in group Jaguar activities. In this place, it seemed that apart from him everyhar knew one another. It was impossible for a stranger to enter that closed world.

A group of young hara came down the alleyway behind him, and Moon began to head back in the direction of the Reliquary. But then somehar called his name: "Jaguar har!"

He turned, reluctantly. The hara behind him all wore the distinctive curling facial tattoos of the Firedog clan, but what he noticed more than that was their grinning mouths. He saw scorn and a desire for sport in their expressions. One of the hara approached him. "What you looking for?" he asked.

Moon shrugged. "Nothing."

"Snake sent you."

"No."

"What's he want with us?"

At this point, Moon registered a startling fact. This har was slightly afraid of him and thought he carried dire news. "Snake hasn't sent me," he said. "He doesn't want anything."

"Then why are you here?"

"I came for a drink," Moon said, "that's all."

"Can you tell the future?"

"No."

"Bet you can. Tell mine."

Moon stared at this young har, with his silver-white hair, his pointed elfin features. "You will break many hearts," he said. "If you are not careful, you will die among the pieces, because they are sharp."

The har pantomimed a double take. "What's that supposed to mean?"

Again, Moon shrugged and wished he hadn't said anything. He couldn't play this game.

The har's companions were ambling off toward the inn and one of them called, "See you in a bit, Em."

The har waved at them without looking behind him. "Tell me more," he said to Moon.

"I can't," Moon said. "I have to get back."

"It must be an omen," said the har, "Snake Jaguar's son coming here. I want to know what it is." He touched Moon on the shoulder, which Moon knew was a form of Firedog greeting. "I'm Ember Firedog. What's your name?"

Despite his limited experience of life, Moon knew when the universe throws you a line. He knew it would be stupid not to take hold of it, so he agreed to go with Ember into the inn, on the condition he didn't have to tell anyhar's fortune.

They bought drinks and sat at a table in a smoky corner. The other Firedogs sat nearby, but didn't attempt to intrude on the conversation. "Why will I break hearts?" Ember asked, his expression revealing he knew the answer only too well.

"Because you look good," Moon said. "And you know it."

Ember laughed. "It doesn't always work that way, Moon. You clearly have a lot to learn."

"Too much," Moon said, more to himself than his companion.

"Your father has kept you closeted away. Hara think you're strange. You're not though, are you? You're just very shy."

Moon didn't want to reply to this. He wasn't sure whether being thought shy was worse than the somewhat more glamorous idea of being thought strange.

Ember was watching him very closely, which wasn't pleasant. "I know why you're here," he said at last.

Moon squirmed and stared into his drink.

"It's okay," Ember said. "It was going to happen sooner or later. You're brave. It must have been hard coming here." He laughed. "But you've met me, so that's all right. Will it be your first?"

"No," Moon said. He didn't like this at all. There was something cold and clinical about it.

"We could leave here now, if you like."

Moon stood up, knocking over his drink in the process. "You're wrong," he said. "I don't know what you think, but you're wrong."

He fled out into the night, and somehow, in a kind of pitiful delirium, found his way back home. He sat panting on the steps of the Reliquary, hating every fiber of his being and wishing the world was a different place.

In the morning, Ember Firedog came to find him. Moon discovered him wandering through one of the galleries, apparently hopelessly lost.

"I might look good," Ember said, "but I'm rubbish at seductions, as you noticed. I'm sorry. I have the sensitivity of a fish that is not only dead, but little more than a pile of maggots because somehar left it out in the sun. Or so I'm told. Can we start again somehow? This is a really weird place to live. Is it haunted?"

Ember's direct manner often got him into trouble: Moon could see that. But this very Leviathan-at-full-speed approach to life also had its charm.

"I was scared of coming here," Ember said as Moon showed him around the unfortunately ghost-free depths of the Reliquary. "I thought I'd run across

Snake and he'd put the Eye on me. But I knew I'd screwed up and my friend Sand told me off about it. He said I should come and apologize or something, because hara can be really sensitive and stuff when they've just been through feybraiha. Not that I was."

"Are you ever quiet?" Moon asked.

"Not often," Ember admitted. "Does it put you off?"

"A bit, yes."

"Oh." Ember was quiet for some moments after that. "You see," he said at last. "Looking good isn't everything."

Moon laughed. "I'm learning."

"You're really quiet because you're shy and I'm noisy for the same reason, I guess. That's what Sand says and he really understands me. Silence is a weird thing. It's full of thoughts and some of them might be wrong."

"How old are you?"

"Eight—well nearly. You?"

"Seven." Moon sighed deeply. "How do we get from here to there?"

"To where?"

"Being like older hara. I want to skip this bit. It doesn't feel right."

"Hmm. No way around it. My hostling says I have to make mistakes and learn from them. Then he gets pissed off with me all the time. It's very confusing."

"Want to see my room?"

"Sure."

After only a week, Moon could barely remember the days pre-Ember. The Firedog filled his life, changed it utterly. Moon began to make friends, some of them from his own clan. He spent his days at the docks with other young hara, helping to unload cargo from visiting ships, and went drinking in the evenings with the Firedogs. It seemed like he'd lived this way for a long time. In Ember's presence, even Snake was different: more amenable, on occasion almost cheery. Ember had wanted to meet Snake, of course, no doubt to boast among his clan friends of having braved the serpent's lair. So, late one afternoon, they met together in Snake's dusty cavernous room, surrounded by the tart scent of Snake's favorite strong tea that came from the south on Unneah trading boats. They sat amid the rubble, because Snake hadn't bothered to clear up after the earthquake and Raven had been too preoccupied to notice. Spiraling motes danced in beams of sunlight that came down through cracks in the ceiling, and the clink of the delicate china cups that Moon had once taken from a display case in the Reliquary sounded strangely nostalgic for a time Moon had never experienced.

Snake told stories, because harlings loved stories, and no matter how much Moon and Ember wanted to believe they were grown-up and serious, they really weren't. Ember had come like a flaming brand into the dark corners of the Reliquary and Moon dared to believe that everything—everything in the world—was going to be all right, touched with light, scintillating with hope.

Snake knew Ember's family, because a long time ago he'd traveled north with them. Moon wondered why his father had elected to shut himself away, when it was clear he had once had friends. Had Silken's death done that to him? Somehow, Moon thought it had to be more than that. Snake could talk of Silken easily and when he spoke of his lost beloved it was not with bitterness and grief, but with a kind of wistful peaceful remembrance.

Ember liked Snake a lot and after a time even felt brave enough to ask if he could see the Eye. Reverently, Snake removed his patch, and revealed that savage feline gaze.

"It is beautiful," Ember said softly. "Like a jewel."

Sometimes, when Ember came to the Reliquary, he would visit Snake's chambers first, and once Moon was astonished to find him there, sitting on the floor before Snake's chair, rubbing his withered foot with soothing oil that Ember's hostling had given to him for the purpose.

Ember said, "Fawn invites you to dinner at the clan house, you and Moon and even the Raven."

"Perhaps soon," Snake said.

"Fawn says it is time to come out of the shadows."

Snake only nodded, then noticed Moon standing stunned by the door and beckoned him forward. "Represent our family with the Firedogs, Moon. Eat with them and come to tell me about it."

Later, Moon—and not without a tinge of envy—said to Ember, "You reach him in a way that I never have."

"You're too close," Ember said. "He is afraid for you."

"Afraid of what?"

Ember, for the first time ever in Moon's presence, appeared furtive. "History," he said. "That's all my hostling told me."

Moon was alerted then to the possibility that Fawn Firedog might be able to enlighten him concerning things about which Snake would only remain silent.

The Firedog clan lived in a shattered tower that was covered in dark green creepers. Vines had crept in through holes in the masonry and broken windows and grew over the inner walls. In the basement was a walled-off chamber, where twenty human bodies lay. Ember said they had killed themselves rather than be killed by Wraeththu. It had happened a long time before the fleeing Uigenna had come to the city. In another room, if you tore the creepers away from the plaster, there were pictures of what the city had looked like before. It was very different: austere lines and lots of hard stone. Now, it was softer and green. Humans had built this place, but since they had gone there had been no more building. Wraeththu lived in the ruins, made no mark upon the landscape. *It looks better now,* Moon thought, but at the same time he found himself wondering what it would be like to build a house to live in, one you had thought up all by yourself, that was filled with the things you liked.

"It is all still there, beneath the green," Fawn said. "Eventually it will be buried deep."

Fawn was a gentle har, chesna with a battle-scarred warrior named Hawk, who was not Ember's true father, even though Ember called him that. Hawk, like Snake and Raven, was damaged by past experiences and Ember said he was often prone to unpredictable rages. "He sees things we don't," Ember said, "but Fawn thinks they're not real. Hawk has a hole in his head."

The head of the Firedog clan was Cloud Wolf, and it was perhaps because of his patronage that Hawk was tolerated by the rest of his hara. Moon couldn't understand why Fawn stuck by Hawk, because he was never anything but surly. But it was from Hawk that Moon eventually learned a little about his family's past.

Biding his time, Moon didn't ask any direct questions until he'd visited the Firedog clan several times. He understood that to most hara of the clans the past was taboo, filled with sorrowful memories. Hawk, however, provided a convenient cue.

One evening, as Moon sat on the floor with Ember and his parents eating dinner, Hawk pointed at him with a chicken bone and said, "You are Silken's son."

"Yes," said Fawn, "we know that, Hawk. This is Moon Jaguar. Remember?"

"What was he like?" Moon blurted out. "Silken? I mean. I can't remember him."

"Hara fought over him," Hawk said, his attention returning to the plate at his crossed feet. "Like cats, like jaguars. Snake won him."

"Hawk," Fawn said in a warning kind of tone.

"It was what happened," Hawk said.

"Yes, well . . ." Fawn began, but Moon interrupted him.

"I wish he hadn't died. I wish I'd known him properly."

"He screamed," Hawk said unhelpfully.

"When he died?"

"No, when Snake took him."

"That's enough!" Fawn said. He turned to Ember. "Take Moon outside."

Ember obediently got to his feet and pulled on Moon's arm, who was most reluctant to leave. He wanted to hear what Hawk had to say, no matter how unpleasant it was.

"We are what we are," Hawk said. "You are the gentle Fawn, but once you weren't."

"Things are different now," Fawn said. He looked at Moon. "We were young and stupid. Don't listen to him. It has no bearing on your life."

"They were chesna," Moon said. "They were."

"Yes. Don't worry. Hawk doesn't remember things properly."

"I remember *that*," Hawk said reasonably, "and so do you. Snake did it to impress Wraxilan, because he didn't want hara to know how he felt."

Fawn put his face in his hands and sighed. After a moment, he raised his head and said, "Ember, take Moon outside. Now!"

Ember's hostling might now be the gentle Fawn, but his son clearly understood when to do as he was told. He virtually dragged Moon from the room.

Moon felt stunned. He didn't know what to think, sure only of the fact that he wanted to know more. Outside, the ghost of the old city hung around in the streets and birds off the lake wheeled silently between the broken towers. Moon didn't want to speak. His chest was full of feeling, hard complicated knots and small silverfish wrigglings: it was almost sensual. Ember put his hand on Moon's shoulder and together they walked out into the night. Sometimes, fires were burning, but nohar sat around them. Somehar, somewhere, high up, was singing: a soft wistful song. Dogs nosed through rubbish and bats flickered around like phantoms on the edge of sight. There was peace in this old, sad city: peace and death. It was hard to believe the clans had once been these terrible things, these warriors and rapists, these Uigenna.

Moon and Ember slept in an empty building they found, Ember pressed tight against Moon's back. They hadn't spoken a word since they'd left the Firedog clan house, which given Ember's love of chatter was almost surreal. Moon held on to Ember's hands and tried to convince himself they were real and solid and not likely to disappear at any moment. He didn't want to think his friendship with Ember was just a pleasant fantasy he had and that he could wake up out of it to something bleak and depressing.

In the morning, Moon said, "I want to speak to Hawk. Take me to him. Find us a place where we won't be disturbed."

Ember sighed, scraped back his hair, and said, "I didn't know about Snake and Silken, Moon. I really didn't. Maybe you shouldn't find out more."

"I have to know about our family," Moon said. "All of it, anything Hawk can tell me."

They found Hawk sitting in the middle of what might once have been a playground or a parking lot. The concrete was still in the process of being broken up by determined plants. Hawk sat staring at the sky, his legs straight out in front of him like a harling.

"Let me talk to him," Ember said, and Moon was happy to agree to this. Ember was familiar with Hawk's moods.

Hawk's tattoos were faded, as if the ink had run beneath the skin because Hawk himself was in some way melting. When Ember spoke his name, he did not react. Ember hunkered down beside him and started pulling out weeds from the concrete. Moon hovered nearby, his heart on tornado-beat.

"What was it like when you first came here?" Ember said to Hawk.

There was a short silence, then Hawk said, "Pretty much the same."

"Was it a long journey to get here?"

Hawk didn't reply, but then turned around and looked directly at Moon. "I can hear you," he said. "You shout to me from the inside."

Moon came forward a few steps. "Will you talk to me?"

"Fawn says it should not be so."

"I don't care," Moon said, wondering then whether that was the right thing to say.

"Snake has a lot to live down," Hawk said. "A lot. He cannot forget his kin, because of what they are. And nohar will let him forget."

Moon squatted down in front of Hawk. He could see this was not going to be easy. It was like hearing words from a distance, through a strong wind. "Tell me about my parents."

"Silken was a spoil of war, that is all. It began one way and ended another. It was not uncommon."

"Did . . ."

"Why should you want to know about this?" Hawk interrupted. "It happened long before they made you. You should worry more about the kin from Beforetime."

Moon paused, then said, "My father's brother, the Tigron."

Hawk jumped in such an exaggerated way it was difficult for Moon to contain his amusement. "Don't say that name," Hawk said. "It opens doors."

"Did you know him?"

Hawk shook his head. "No, none of us met him. I was not of Snake's kind. All I know is that he is dedicated to destroying what is left of Uigenna, and that Snake is a light we have to keep covered. You should ask him about it."

Moon thought it was none of Hawk's business that Snake had already mentioned this matter. "Can you tell me anything more?"

"I can tell you that once we were great. The Uigenna were hunters, not carrion eaters. This land was ours. Now we hide in ruins. If I am mad, it is not because of old injuries, but because I have no hope, because I know the end will come, and there will be no broken stones to hide us. If Snake has the sight, so do I, but there is no comfort in it. I see, as he does, the shadow behind the throne in Almagabra. Our way was to fight it, to unmake it, to become ourselves. The Gelaming are ignorant. They are the enemy of all Wraeththu. Enjoy the sun, harlings, enjoy it while you can. Now I have said enough and the words are sour."

Hawk got to his feet and walked off slowly. Neither Moon nor Ember sought to detain him.

Ember puffed out his cheeks and exhaled noisily. "Nothing like good news, is there!"

Moon stood up. "They live in the past too much, all of them. Who would want to come here and take what we have? What is there to take?"

"Hara," Ember said, also rising to his feet. "There is always that."

Moon went home alone to the Reliquary and directly to his father's rooms. Snake, as usual, was sitting in his chair with his eyes closed. He must do that for most of the time. Did he live in the past or in some other realm?

Moon sat down in a ray of sunlight before his father and for some moments studied Snake's countenance. He wasn't wearing his eye patch and his face was the most serene that Moon had ever seen it. Snake was a mystic, gentle like Fawn. It was impossible to imagine he had ever been any other way. "Father," Moon said. "I must speak with you."

Snake inhaled through his nose. "I know," he said, without opening his eyes, although a crease appeared in his brow between them. "I had a dream last night. An old dream. You are too curious."

"Is it true?"

Snake opened his eyes and gazed at his son. The serpent eye glowed with its own fire, the pupil enlarged. Moon hoped he wouldn't have to be more specific. He hoped Snake was intuitive enough to sense what he meant.

"Yes," Snake said at last. "I do not know why the Firedogs believed it was a good idea to tell you that, but yes, it is true. Life was very different then, Moon. You cannot imagine it."

"But I *was* conceived in love, wasn't I?"

Snake smiled and leaned forward to touch Moon's face. "Yes, there is no other way. In the beginning, we were all playing a game, perhaps Silken as much as I. It was a cruel children's game, a legacy of what we had been before. He and I always wanted each other, but there was pretense and pettiness. There was rivalry among tribes, bitter feuds, and betrayals. We grew up, Moon. You did not grow from the cruelty, but from what came afterward."

"Tell me about your brother."

"A sorcerer came and took him from us. He must have been a Gelaming agent. This was before I was Wraeththu, but not long before. For a long time, I believed my brother to be dead, but then I saw him reborn. News came to me of the Tigron in Immanion and he bore my brother's name. He has never changed it."

"Hawk spoke to me of the shadow behind the throne and that because of it Gelaming are the enemy of all Wraeththu. What did he mean?"

"It is not a proven theory, but rather an assumption. It is believed that whoever or whatever created Wraeththu controls the Gelaming. Uigenna have always believed that. They did not want to be controlled. They wanted to be free. They would not be puppets and because of that their excesses were often extreme. They sought to overturn order, to create chaos, to break down all that was, so that true rebirth could occur." Snake smiled sadly. "For those who talked about it, that was the justification. Of course, for the majority of Uigenna hara, they simply enjoyed being in control themselves. They enjoyed being bullies." He leaned back in his chair again and stared up at the cracked ceiling. "Our leader, Wraxilan, climbed a mountain one time, because his campaigns exhausted him. He needed solitude. Alone, he had a vision and it changed him. When he returned to us, he was not the same, and soon he left us. The tribe fell apart, for although it was comprised of many different factions, Wraxilan was their heart. He held them all together."

"What was his vision?" Moon asked.

Snake shook his head. "Nohar knows. He had many secrets and I was not close to him. He took his secrets with him and remade himself."

"Like your brother."

"No. Wraxilan did what he did in full awareness, but my brother did not. He was used. This I know for sure."

"How?"

"Perdu," Snake said. "I spoke to him in trance and he told me."

"Who is he?"

"A spirit, maybe. A dead har. A guide. A god. A living har with a strong ability. I have no idea. He is like an angel of doom. He speaks to me only when something terrible will happen."

"You've spoken with him recently, haven't you?" Moon said.

Snake nodded. "Yes, it was he who told me a seer had found me. Soon the Gelaming will come. I know you don't feel it, and think older hara are paranoid, but it is inevitable, Moon."

"We could leave," Moon said. "We don't have to stay here and wait for the end."

"We do," Snake said, "because it is not the end."

"Are you afraid?"

"Yes, because of what he will have me do. And I am afraid for you, because he will want you close to him. You look like he did when he was young. He will look for himself in you."

A thrill coursed through Moon's body. Until that moment, the Tigron hadn't had a face for him. "Will he hurt me?"

"I doubt it, although he will lead you into danger, because he is in such danger himself. Hawk isn't wrong, Moon. There is more to Wraeththu than any of us know. We, the clans, are free, but not for long. I don't want to be part of what will come. I want to live and die in this place, alone with my memories. In Wraeththu, the Cosmic Joker shook the world and the outcome could have been paradise or hell. It just happened to turn out to be hell."

"How is it hell?" Moon persisted, sensing finality in Snake's words and therefore the possibility he would be dismissed.

"Humans were asleep; they were sheep. Wraeththu were born with open eyes, but most of them chose to close them. That is hell. Stupidity, greed, selfishness, fear—most of all fear. Hara seek to emulate the great empires of human history. It is a travesty. Everything has sunk back to how it was before, except the things that made humanity great have been destroyed. We live in a rubbish heap."

"We don't build," Moon said. "I thought about that recently."

"A lot of hara do," Snake said gently. "What you see here does not reflect the rest of the world. The Uigenna are broken, Moon. Many hara of the clans were once Gelaming captives, victims of sophisticated forms of torture, who were later released like viruses to infect their communities. Infect them with terror, despair, and weakness. Raven is such a har."

"And Hawk?"

"Yes, and Hawk. He cannot remember it, but we are all sure that is what happened to him. It is what happened to Terzian, leader of the Varrs. It happened to many strong hara. The Varrs were our strongest allies, but once Terzian died they became Gelaming, whatever name they gave themselves. Without hara such as Terzian and Wraxilan, the rest of us were lost."

"We still have leaders," Moon said. "What about Great Jaguar Paw and the others?"

Snake was silent for a moment, then said, "Imagine that all hara of the clans have been blinded and maimed by Gelaming, but that our conquerors have allowed a few hara to keep one eye, one hand, and one foot. Those are our so-called leaders, Moon."

Moon reached out and touched his father's withered foot. He said nothing, but tears filled his eyes.

"Yes," Snake murmured softly. "Now you see."

For several weeks after this conversation, Moon watched the lake and the roads into the city. Many had been closed with rubble by the humans who had sought to protect themselves, and since then, the clans had created toll gates on the remaining arteries into the city. Moon did not know what he was looking for, or even if the Gelaming, should they come at all, would arrive by conventional means—on a boat or by road. But one thing his conversation with his father had given him was a sense of imminence. He did not doubt Snake's words. He knew the Gelaming would come. He imagined them as a mighty army that would set fire to the clan houses, round up all hara as slaves. But as is so often the case with anything you imagine in advance, the reality when it arrived was somewhat different.

CHAPTER TWELVE

Roselane is a harsh country late in the year. Its raw and primal landscape channels the energy of encroaching winter in blistering winds, flesh-stripping rain and storms that can pull the most ancient oak from its roots and toss it across a valley to lie like a slaughtered giant upon the cold, unforgiving earth.

Parazha and hara of the Roselane make preparations quickly for the dark months. The dehar of summer dies early upon the mountain slopes and his harsh winter brother stocks up his arsenal even before the last leaves have fallen from the trees. But lights in Shilalama are bright at night, fires are stoked high and doors locked fast against the storms. It makes a har feel truly alive to walk into a heated kitchen, stamping the cold from his feet, to discard his thick coat and gloves and sit down to a meal in convivial company. So it was for Pellaz and Cobweb, because Pellaz made no formal announcement of his arrival in Shilalama, but went directly to the house of his friends, Flick and Ulaume Sarestes, and his sister, who lived with them. Mima had not seen Pellaz since Cal had disappeared from Immanion, and had not even set eyes on Cal since the day he'd seduced her brother away from home—it might as well have been a million years ago. She was fiercely protective of her kin and not short on opinions. Pellaz knew he'd have to endure her ranting scorn (which was merely the outraged voice of her love for him), and did so stoically. He could sense that Cobweb was surprised he endured her tirade without defending himself.

"You are a fool," Mima said, even before the first course was finished at dinner. "You should never have let him back in. I knew something dreadful would happen." She cast fierce glances in the direction of Ulaume and Flick, whom she felt confident shared her view.

"You think Opalexian can help you," Flick said to Pellaz. It was not a question.

Pellaz nodded. "I think so. I am not completely sure that what happened to Rue was anything to do with Cal."

Mima snorted eloquently. "You just never grew up, that's your trouble. A teenage crush has informed your entire life. Now, you have risked ruining everything because of it. Well done."

"Mima, that's enough," Ulaume said, which was unusual, because he was the first to say bad things about another har, given the opportunity.

"She's right," Pellaz said simply. "But knowing that doesn't change anything. Now, I have to make changes."

"What do you think, Cobweb?" Flick asked, diverting attention, which was entirely usual, as he was always the first to put balm on a wound.

"I think we are close to facing what we really are," Cobweb replied. "Thiede was a shield. Now he's gone. The Gelaming are not all powerful, and the world isn't ready to drop like a ripe fruit into their hands. What happened to Pell's child is the beginning, that's all. I've a feeling something important has been overlooked." He turned to Pellaz. "It's strange, but I feel very uncomfortable about being away from home. It's connected with Galhea, I'm sure of it. Something threatens us."

"What do you mean?" Pellaz said.

Cobweb furrowed his brow. "I don't know. Just a feeling of vulnerability. Perhaps I think of myself as Galhea's shield. I can't be away long."

"What would threaten Galhea?" Mima asked. "The problem, as far as rogue hara see it, is Immanion. Surely, there aren't enough autonomous Uigenna left in Megalithica to be a worry?"

"It isn't Uigenna," Cobweb said. "I don't know what it is, or even if it derives from this plane of existence, but it's there, like a shadow. I can almost see it."

"The otherlanes," Pellaz said abruptly. "Is it like what I experienced there?"

"I sensed nothing on the way here," Cobweb replied, "and I was intentionally on the alert, but then the otherlanes are infinite. That doesn't prove anything."

"Pell," Flick began, then frowned and shook his head.

"What?" Pellaz asked.

"I don't know, it's going to sound insane, but do you think you should try and contact Lileem?"

"That's impossible," Pellaz said. "You know it. She made her decision to leave this world and she's gone. I can't go and rescue her again. For a start, she doesn't want anyhar to."

"Opalexian said that she thinks Lileem will return to us, with important knowledge, when she is needed. Perhaps that time is now."

All were silent for a moment. The mention of Lileem's name made those who knew her remember how and why she was no longer with them. She had broken the first rule of Kamagrian and had taken aruna with a har, namely Pellaz and Mima's brother Terez, which had opened up a portal into a strange otherlane realm. Lileem and Terez had been sucked right into it. After some years, Pellaz and Mima had managed to bring them back to earthly reality, but the risks had been great. Also, Lileem could no longer be happy in the world of her birth. Eventually, she had found a way back to the realm she'd left behind. Her intention had been to devote her life to study in a bizarre black library of stone books she had found there. She had been convinced the secrets to all creation had lain hidden there.

"It wouldn't hurt to mention it to Opalexian when you see her," Flick said into the silence.

The following morning, Pellaz and Cobweb went to Kalalim, Opalexian's temple palace in the heart of Shilalama. The Kamagrian leader had been aware of their presence in the city, but had given Pellaz time to orient himself. The truth was that she had been waiting for this visit for a long time. It didn't make it any easier once it was upon her, however.

She received her visitors in a small parlor, where the light was dim and the air very hot, owing to the voracious fire that raged in the hearth. "This year, I feel the cold," she said to Pellaz and pulled a thick woolen shawl closer around her shoulders. Her hands looked very white, and the delicate tracery of veins within them was clearly visible.

Pellaz thought that Opalexian appeared worn thin. She was Thiede's sister, in type if not in blood, so perhaps that was hardly surprising. She might have orchestrated his removal from the world, but Pellaz suspected she missed him too. Perhaps also, because of their relationship, Thiede's absence diminished Opalexian in some way. "Will you talk to me?" Pellaz asked.

Opalexian sat down in a chair next to the hearth and put her slippered feet on the fender. "I will always talk to you."

"Honestly," Pellaz said. "The truth."

"As much as I can," Opalexian said. She glanced at Cobweb. "You can attempt to read me as much as you like. It will make no difference."

Cobweb said nothing.

"It has occurred to me I was a fool to trust you," Pellaz said. "It is possible you took advantage of my feelings, when a more honest parage might have attempted to make me see sense. You indulged me, and now I wonder whether you should have done. I don't think it is a puzzle to you at all. You always knew, didn't you?"

"I knew that Thiede should be removed from power in Immanion," Opalexian said, so ready a confession that it came like a smack in the face to Pellaz. "But I also knew that the power should be transferred to you—and to Cal. It was the way things were meant to be. Thiede shouldn't have made you in the first place, if he wasn't ready to relinquish his power to you. He chose well, Pellaz. I have never doubted that, but I'm not sure he projected his mind into the future to see what you would become. He didn't know what he created."

"Flattery won't work," Pellaz said. "The truth is that I'm out of my depth and have no idea what to do. That's why I'm here now, being honest with you. For the good of all our people, I would appreciate the same courtesy. I'm assuming you're aware of all that's transpired in Immanion?"

Opalexian inclined her head. "Naturally, my agents have reported to me."

"And your thoughts on this matter are?"

Opalexian smiled rather grimly. "If you are expecting me to confess I ordered a pearl to be cut from the belly of your consort, you will be disappointed."

"I will be more disappointed if you don't deny it."

"No, I did not do that, nor did I order it. Although I can appreciate why you would see me as a suspect." She stretched her toes toward the fire. "I don't know who or what did that, Pell, but we must all accept the fact that the child might still live."

"You sound as if you think that would be a bad thing," Pellaz said.

Opalexian nodded slowly. "I know. It's because I wonder who has it, and what they intend to do with it. What I don't know is how much Thiede knew, how much he hid from us all, or what he knows now. I've thought about it a lot. I've wondered whether that was why he could never step off the stage to make way for you. He lived alone with his dilemmas."

"Do you regret what you did?"

"Yes," Opalexian answered shortly. "I can see that you're not ready to take on Thiede's mantle."

Pellaz went cold.

"You asked," Opalexian said. "You wanted honesty. Does knowing the truth make you feel better?"

"You are as powerful as he was," Pellaz said.

"It's not just down to power. Knowledge is equally important. Awareness. The strongest warrior can be bested if he is attacked in the dark from behind. If he is shot from a distance."

"So we are defenseless against whatever threatens us?"

"Not entirely. But I'm afraid we have to wait for them to make another move. Believe me, I have worn out my seers trying to scry and quest for information. I have been in trance myself for days, to no avail. Something runs before me in the darkness. Sometimes, I hear its laughter."

"Are you with me?" Pellaz asked, aware even as he spoke of Cobweb's mistrust for the Kamagrian leader. But Pellaz had to trust her. He did not have enough faith in himself.

"I am not against you," Opalexian answered. "But you know I have made decisions about my life and also Kamagrian as a whole. I do not know how much I can offer you, other than my thoughts."

"That is not good enough," Pellaz said. "Neither for Wraeththu nor Kamagrian. You can't hide away anymore, Lex. You got rid of Thiede, now you must face up to your responsibilities."

"It was never that simple," Opalexian said sharply. "You make it sound like a petty feud."

Pellaz did not respond.

Opalexian rubbed her face. "I truly believed that once you and Cal were reunited, you'd discover your full potential. I forgot you were living creatures of flesh and blood, with mundane concerns as well as more elevated ones."

"You thrust too much on Cal," Cobweb said, speaking for the first time. "He couldn't cope with it. I don't think he even knew what was required of him, and maybe, if he had, he would never have come to Immanion."

"He wasn't ready either," Opalexian said. "I pushed him through healing and training too quickly. At the time, it seemed essential. Now, I wonder." She shook her head. "Flick knew. He warned me. Thiede and I suffer from the same faults. We think we know what's best. Always."

"And your greatest strength, which perhaps Thiede never had, is that you can admit it," Pellaz said.

"Thank you for that," Opalexian said. "You would be right to condemn me. I knew that you would stand here before me one day and that I'd have to speak the truth."

"We all make mistakes," Pellaz said. "You are not a goddess, Lex. Perhaps you are not that different from any of us, and you and I are no different to those we believe we lead. If we can both look upon ourselves simply as every-day folk, with all their limitations, then perhaps we have more of a chance."

Opalexian stood up and embraced Pellaz fiercely. "You are Tigron," she said. "Wraeththu's hope. Never doubt it."

Pellaz drew away and held her at arm's length. "You must be with me now, on all levels. It can be no other way. You are Kamagrian's hope."

"No," Opalexian said. "You are wrong. That is Lileem."

"Is it time to bring her back?" Cobweb asked quickly.

Opalexian paused before answering. "I don't think it is up to us when she returns, if indeed she ever does, but I feel strongly she is working for us."

"What threatens us?" Pellaz asked. "What is its nature?"

"I believe it concerns those who made us. I don't know. Battles for territory. Experiments gone wrong. Millennia are the blink of an eye for some beings."

"Have you tried to communicate with Thiede?"

Opalexian glanced away. "Yes. He is aware of the problems. He can't re-turn to you, Pell."

"I didn't expect him to. What must I do?"

"Wait," said Opalexian. "None of us has enough information. Keep your scryers at work, as I will keep mine."

"I don't feel comfortable just waiting. I want to take action."

"You have no choice."

Opalexian insisted her guests stay for lunch and for a short while Cobweb and Pellaz were left alone, while the Kamagrian leader made arrangements with her staff.

"Well?" Pellaz demanded. "What do you think?"

"She's telling the truth, or some of it," Cobweb said. "She seems distracted, anxious."

"We don't know who our allies are, do we?" Pellaz said bitterly.

"Not really," Cobweb agreed.

In the afternoon, as low sunlight spread across the gardens of Kalalim, Pel-laz walked across the sloping lawns with Opalexian. He had sent Cobweb back to the Sarestes house, because he needed to talk to the Kamagrian alone.

"Please tell me," he said, "about Cal."

"I've already told you everything, you know that. I did what I could with him."

"I don't mean then. I mean now."

"I can't tell you anything, Pell." Opalexian sat down on a lichened stone seat that looked as if it had grown out of the earth. Below her, lakes dreamed, in glassy-eyed stillness. There was a chill to the air, though the sunlight was mellow.

Pellaz sat down beside her. "Where is he? I've tortured myself wondering. I've always believed we were meant to be together, that our union was somehow sacred, different . . ." He sighed. "Everyhar in loves thinks that, perhaps every parage too."

Opalexian laid a hand over Pell's own, which were clasped in his lap. "Never give up hope," she said. "Your belief will be challenged, Pell. I can almost smell it, like I can smell the pears in my orchard down there." She nodded in the direction of the ancient trees that stood to the right of the lake.

"I can smell them too," Pell said. He absorbed the comfort that flowed from the Kamagrian's fingers, found himself thinking of Thiede, then of his own long-dead mother, and an overwhelming desire to be held close. "I won't give up."

Opalexian closed her eyes, drew in her breath through her nose. "The flavor of the season is that of denial," she said. "Of love and desire frustrated. I can feel it. This energy will fan the flames to temper Wraeththu's strongest weapons." She opened her eyes, looked at him. "Including your own."

CHAPTER THIRTEEN

Cal knew he was being watched: he always knew. Thiede observed him continually. In this strange realm, Cal rarely saw the har—or creature beyond har—who taught and guided him. His lessons came in dreams, and in bolts of inspiration. Now, in a room of polished obsidian, in its center, he sat cross-legged on the floor. The chamber was spherical, its floor a transparent platform of black glass. Cal could not see below the glass, because he had not elected to illuminate his working space. He was working on an idea that had recently come to him. Before him, at eye level, he had constructed from pure intention an eye into the realm of earth. It was like an egg of indigo stars.

Then a voice came from above him.

"Do not look too deep, Cal."

He glanced up and saw that, in the darkness, a gallery had become visible, some twenty feet above his head. Thiede stood there, clad in close-fitting dark clothes, which was unusual, because on the few occasions Cal had seen him, he generally wore flowing robes. Perhaps he had been traveling. A flight of spiral stairs appeared and Thiede descended them.

"You have learned well," he said, "but do not be tempted."

Cal did not close down the Eye. "I think I should know what is happening. You won't tell me."

Thiede put his hand above the Eye, then closed his fingers over it, drew his hand into a fist. When he opened it again, a drift of sparkling motes fell to the glass floor and lay there winking, before going out, one by one. "It is not your concern. You are here to train, to learn, but not of that."

Cal rested his elbows on his knees, put his chin between his hands. "I'm going out of my mind here. I feel I've learned enough."

"Restless," Thiede said. "Yes, I know."

"Give back to me the ability to travel the otherlanes. I can't stay here any longer."

Thiede folded his arms. "I have removed it from you for precisely this reason. You must stay away from Immanion, Cal. It will do no good you returning there, for if you do, certain events will not take place that are essential."

"Are you capable of doing anything but using hara?" Cal asked. He got to his feet. "I've had enough. I wander around in this dream of yours, and nothing's real. I don't know what's become of my son since I brought the pearl to you. I don't know what's happened to Pell or Rue. I can't live like this."

Thiede drew in a long breath through his nose. "It won't be for much longer. Learn to be patient, as patient as a lioness stalking her prey. Haste and impulse only waste good energy. We have all the time we need here."

Cal made an angry gesture with both arms. "You've kept me in stasis, like you did with Pell. For all I know a hundred years have passed. Sometimes, I wonder whether this is yet another tower you've confined me in. Another sentence for what I did to Orien." Cal knew he was speaking in haste and impulse, and that it was most likely unwise. He had never spoken Orien's name to Thiede before, nor alluded to his murder. He realized he was trying to provoke a response, to anger Thiede enough to change things.

Thiede regarded him expressionlessly. "Do you think I'm still angry about that? Strange. Surely now you must know that the experience of earthly incarnation is limited. Orien isn't dead. It's impossible to destroy the essence of a har. It is possible only to destroy vehicles of flesh."

"Have you brought him back, like Pell?"

Thiede smiled. "No. It does not work quite that way. Orien lives again, but he does not remember his previous life. Why should I be so cruel as to remind him?"

Cal ran his hands through his hair. "How did you do it, Thiede? I've never asked you. How did you bring Pell back? How did you know he was different? The har he is now is not the one I knew before, and yet he is."

Thiede held out a hand. "Walk with me, Cal. Walk outside."

Cal had never ventured beyond the warren of strange buildings that comprised Thiede's haven. Parts of it were extremely alien to behold, while others were very similar to structures in Immanion. But as to what lay beyond it, Cal had not yet discovered. He had supposed it was a lightless void and that the haven existed only in Thiede's mind, manifested as a dream. Perhaps there was nothing beyond it.

Now the glass floor began to descend, shrinking as it did so, until they stood at the base of the sphere. A light appeared in the wall, which expanded, until it looked like a ring of flame, spreading outward. It left a hole, through which Cal could see the world outside.

"Come," Thiede said. The hole was now big enough for them to step through.

It looked like an ancient world, very similar to the one that Pellaz had described, where he'd found Lileem and Terez. The light was dim and a red sun hung in the sky, bloated and surrounded by a nimbus of purple flame. But, unlike in the realm of the Black Library, the landscape here was flat, an endless vista of shining lakes, surrounded by drooping trees that were not willows, but like them.

Cal glanced behind him, saw an impossible structure rearing up, and had to look away, for it made no sense and taxed his mind.

"You are right, I have partially created this realm," Thiede said. "It is my playground and my retreat. I imagined it into being."

"Did you create Immanion this way?"

"Partly. I had help."

"From who or what?"

"I will tell you all you need to know before you return home. You asked about Pellaz, and it is of him I will speak now." Thiede began to walk toward the nearest lake and Cal followed him. The air was neither cool nor warm. There was no breeze.

"Orien was the first incepted Wraeththu," Thiede said. "It was he who saw our potential before I did. It was he who dreamed of tribes and progress. We lost control of things very quickly. We underestimated how quickly Wraeththu would grow. We did not foresee the collapse of human civilization. We thought we'd have more time to realize our dreams."

"Who made *you*, Thiede?"

Thiede stopped walking and raised a hand. "Let me speak. Events occurred that enabled me to begin building Immanion. Orien helped me stock it with first-class hara."

Cal made a noise of disgust and Thiede reached out briefly to touch his lips.

"Be silent. I know how much that idea offends you, and always has. I do not need to hear your complaints about it now. Just listen." He lowered his hand

and began to walk forward again. "Eventually, I came to know that a Tigron should be made, and I learned how. Many hara believe it was a petty conceit of mine, that Pellaz was my creature, my cat's paw, but this is not the case. I learned that, one day, the Tigron would have a great purpose. He is not a fig- urehead, but a faculty of Wraeththu, like an eye or an ear."

"And now there are two of us," Cal said. "Has that ruined your plan?"

"There is only one Tigron," Thiede said. "You and Rue are his limbs, per- haps, but Pellaz is the brain. He has yet to realize his full potential. Even I did not realize how great that could be. I have many abilities that most hara do not possess. But I also have my limitations." Thiede sat down beside the water and motioned for Cal to join him. "I can remember the very moment when I realized Pellaz was the one. I had received a message from Orien. "Come quickly," he said to me. I could not wait: I had to look at once upon this boy Orien had found for me. So, I constructed a device very similar to the Eye you just created back there. I saw Pellaz fighting with Seel and Orien in the Forale House at Saltrock. I saw his strength of will and the flame inside him that was contained, held back. He was magnificent, like an unbroken colt, but I had no desire to break his spirit, to tame him. Hara always misjudged me about that. He needed discipline, for a long time, but only in order to learn self-discipline. The har he is now is the result of that training. The pain he felt over you was equally important."

Cal nodded. "I understand that now. What I went through, at the time it was pure hell, but if I hadn't experienced it all, I wouldn't be who I am now. And I quite like the har I am."

Thiede laughed. "I'm pleased to hear it." He took one of Cal's hands in his own. "You might not be the Tigron Pellaz is, but you are just as vital to Wraeththukind. I believe that you and Pellaz share a soul. Nohar, or any being of any realm, can sever that link. And that is partly why you will protect him. If he dies on earth, part of you will die with him."

"What must I do?"

"I don't know that. You will have to find out, follow your instincts, but I do know there will come a time when he needs you in order to survive. A conflict is coming."

"What are we fighting, Thiede?"

"Beings you cannot kill. But you won't have to kill them. You are not an as- sassin. Your job is to learn how to displace entities, to flick them from their place in space and time."

"A useful skill," Cal said dryly.

"Indeed. Once you have learned it, you may return to the earthly realm. To- gether, we will examine certain areas of that reality, so you will go there informed. But resist looking into Pell's life, Cal. Put him aside for now. Your love for him must grow and change, as you have done. It must mature into its proper form before you can go to him."

"Are he and Rue all right?"

"Yes. Caeru has regained his health and Pellaz begins to learn many things. They are sad about the pearl, of course."

"Yes, what of our son?" Cal demanded. "May I see him?"

"Perhaps eventually," Thiede said. "He has already left this realm."

Cal pulled a sour face. "Thanks for telling me. Where is he?"

"Safe," Thiede said. "I won't tell you where, because it's dangerous for you to know. What you don't know, you can't reveal."

"I understand that," Cal said. "Must he be hidden away forever?"

"No," Thiede replied. "Only one har in the earthly realm knows the harling's identity and he can be trusted completely. The child will not be told of his heritage. He must discover it for himself. And if he doesn't, then that is meant to be."

"So basically, if I ever want to see him, I have to wait for him to find me."

Thiede nodded. "That is a fairly accurate assessment."

"I think he will."

Thiede stood up. "Let's go back inside. We'll begin the next stage of your training, and later we'll indulge ourselves with good food and wine. We have spent little time together, and you won't be here for much longer. Remember, you have a son who you *can* see, very soon. We should talk about him."

"Tyson?" Cal grimaced. "He probably hates my guts."

"He regrets you cause him so much inconvenience," Thiede said, "or he will do, at any rate. I realize now that he is the most important har in Galhea. I had always believed it would be Azriel. I like surprises. It would get very boring if I knew everything."

Cal glanced at Thiede sidelong. "Training, then more talk," he said. "I want you to tell me what you know about Tyson."

"My pleasure," Thiede said. "That is something we can discuss freely."

CHAPTER FOURTEEN

It was a few weeks after the autumn equinox, when the mists from the lake were at their most concealing, and the air smelled of burning and ripe fruit. Moon and Ember went apple gathering in the sprawling old gardens at the edge of the city, where wasps were getting drunk on the windfalls. Moon polished the best of the fruit with his shirt and Ember arranged them in baskets. They intended to take them to the dock to sell to boat-hara who might pay a few chips for refreshment before moving on to the more intoxicating delights of the ale houses.

Business went well and by early afternoon, they had earned enough to buy steaming mugs of spiced milk from a teahouse and sit for a few hours at a table outside to watch hara come and go along the lane. It was close to the docks and many travelers wandered by to sample the wares of the refreshment booths, cafés, and inns. Moon became aware of being watched only when a shiver unaccountably fizzed up his spine.

For a moment, he felt totally unsafe and dizzy, then glanced to the side. It was one of those life-defining moments. The lane, the hara all around, faded into a blur. Sound seemed dulled. All Moon saw was a pair of eyes gazing back at him intently. He knew them and yet he didn't. His face went hot and he had to look away. Leaning closer to Ember, Moon whispered, "That har over there is staring at me in a really weird way."

"Where?" Ember asked, neck craning.

"Don't look!" Moon hissed. "To my right across the street."

"I have to look," Ember said. "Otherwise how can I see what you mean?"

"Be discreet."

After a few moments, Ember said, "No har's staring at you."

Moon dared to look himself. "He isn't *now,* but he was. The pale-haired one."

The har in question had, like Moon, leaned closer to his companion, a dark-haired har dressed in black, who was sitting with his back to the street. Even as Moon and Ember looked on, the dark har turned in his seat and gazed right at them.

Moon felt a chill in his flesh. "It's the Tigron!" he said. "Look at him!"

"Don't be ridiculous," Ember said, although his voice did not sound certain. "He does look like Snake, though."

"Why are they staring at us? Who are they? Are they Gelaming?"

"They are too scruffy and ordinary to be Gelaming, surely," Ember said. "They look like wanderers, hara of no tribe. They're probably traders and they're only staring at us because we're staring at them."

"That one looks like Snake. You said so."

"You want to talk to them?" Ember asked in an unusually sharp tone. "Go over, then. It's no big deal."

"I don't want to talk to them," Moon said. "I think we should go." He had told Ember very little about his family history, even though he knew Ember was aware of the basic details, and he'd said nothing about how Snake feared the Tigron would soon come for him. Moon thought it would sound too improbable and dramatic and that Ember might think he was stupid, or else get into the idea far too much and then it wouldn't be private anymore.

"Just ignore them," Ember said. "You're drawing attention to yourself. What's the matter with you?"

Moon moved his chair a little, so that he wasn't so visible, but he didn't feel comfortable. If the Tigron had come looking for his brother, maybe he'd be in disguise. Maybe he'd pretend to be a trader. There could be Gelaming warriors hidden all over the place. He finished his drink quickly. "I have to go."

"Moon, what's got into you? You look scared."

"I *am* scared," Moon said.

"Why?"

Moon shook his head. Perhaps the time had come to confide in Ember a little more, but not here. He wanted to feel safe first. "I'll explain later. Please. Let's go."

"Okay." Ember got to his feet. "Oh . . . too late."

"What?"

Moon glanced around and saw that the dark-haired har was coming over to them.

"We could run," Ember suggested.

Moon couldn't move. Half of him yearned to comply with Ember's suggestion but another part was brimming with curiosity. This har looked so much like Snake it was uncanny. Snake would have looked like this before he'd been injured.

The har halted a few paces from where Moon stood and regarded him inscrutably.

"Yes?" Moon snapped defensively.

"I am from the south," said the har, "looking for family in these parts. Forgive me, but you look very familiar. My companion tells me there is a strong resemblance between us."

Moon was so stunned by these words, he didn't know what to say.

"Are you the Tigron?" Ember asked, a question so bizarre in its directness and honesty that Moon almost laughed.

The strange har, clearly more at ease, laughed spontaneously. "No! Do you think the Tigron would walk the streets of a Uigenna enclave so freely?" He paused. "Why would you think that?"

"Don't say anything!" Moon cried.

"Who are you looking for?" Ember asked, folding his arms.

"A har named Dorado."

"We don't know anyhar of that name," Ember said.

"He may well have changed it. You do not have to be suspicious. I mean him no harm. He is a relative of mine, from the old times."

"He looks like you," Ember said to Moon. "Maybe you are related. Perhaps you should take him to Snake."

"Ember, shut up!"

The pale-haired har had sauntered over to join them and now stood with his hands in his pockets observing the proceedings. He jerked his head in Moon's direction and said to his companion, "You're so alike he could be your son. This can't be coincidence."

The dark-haired har nodded thoughtfully and asked Moon, "Who are your father and hostling? Please tell me, it is important."

Moon wanted to resist and be silent, but the dark stranger's gaze was compelling, his voice commanding. "Snake Jaguar is my father," he said. "My hostling, Silken, is dead."

The pale har frowned at his friend. "Does that mean anything to you?"

The dark har grimaced. "No, but that is no indication." He ducked his head to Moon. "I would like to meet your father."

"Who are you?" Moon demanded.

"Terez," the har said. "I was known as Terez Cevarro."

This name meant nothing to Moon, because his father had never told him his old family name, nor had he ever mentioned any members of his human family apart from Pellaz. Was it possible this event was entirely unconnected with Snake's fears about the Gelaming?

"I was incepted to the Uigenna," said the dark har. "I am no enemy of yours."

"Take him to Snake," Ember said. "I really think you should."

"I don't know . . ." Moon was so shaken up he couldn't think straight. These hara were both so tall, looming over him. He felt weak.

The pale-haired har said, "Look, we just want to find Dorado. Maybe your father can help us. Then we'll be on our way."

Moon looked into this har's face and felt a strange sensation. It was the shock of recognition, which was what had made him feel so odd when he'd first noticed the strangers. He'd never seen this har before, or anyhar like him, yet it was as if he had memories connected with him. "I could ask Snake for you," he managed to say at last.

"I would rather speak to him face-to-face," said the dark har. "This is most important."

"You're really not Gelaming?"

The pale-haired har grinned. "My father was a Varr, my hostling Uigenna. Is that pedigree enough for you?"

It should be, but Moon remembered what Snake had told him about Gelaming torture victims. He was still torn as to what to do.

"Ask him if he will see us," said the dark har. "We will wait here for word from you."

"Is that wise?" asked the pale-haired har.

"Let it be a mark of trust."

Leaving Ember with the strangers, Moon ran all the way home. It was nearly dark by the time he stumbled up the Reliquary steps. He felt light-headed, his mind filled with the image of the two strangers. They had affected him deeply. He wanted to return to them with pleasing news.

Snake met Moon on the stairs outside his rooms. Moon was taken by surprise, because Snake so rarely left his private warren. It was like coming upon a ghost in the darkness. Moon knew at once he didn't have to explain too much. Snake's fierce and wide-eyed expression revealed he already knew somehar had been asking about him.

"They are not Gelaming," Moon said hurriedly. "They want to meet with you. One is named Terez. He is looking for a har named Dorado."

Snake's expression was now unreadable, although Moon was sure an utter storm of feeling was thrashing about beneath the calm surface. "It is time," he said. "Bring him to me." With these words, he moved back toward his rooms.

"Wait!" Moon said. "Is this Terez connected to the Tigron? Do you know him? Was I wrong to speak to him? Tell me!"

"He is the Tigron's brother," said Snake. "And this I did not foresee, but I will be very surprised if he has come of his own volition."

"Who is Dorado?"

Snake inhaled long and slow through his nose. "I am," he said. He went into his rooms and slammed the door.

Moon could tell from very early acquaintance with his hura, his father's brother, that Terez was not a har prone to displays of emotion. Normally, he would conceal his feelings beneath an impenetrable exterior. But when he first laid eyes on Snake, the defensive mask was ripped away and what Moon saw was naked shock. Moon hadn't thought to mention it on the way to the Reliquary, but of course Terez had no idea what had happened to Snake. He didn't know about the injuries.

"You think I'd be better off dead," Snake said dryly. "Kindly contain your thoughts. They are insulting. Pellaz has sent you. Say what he intends you to say."

"He needs you."

Snake laughed coldly. "Thank you for being honest, for not pretending you are here for any other reason. My answer, for what it's worth, is that I do not care. Now you may leave, although I know you won't."

"Dorado, you should hear the story. I can imagine what you think but you know so little."

"I am Snake Jaguar. There is no Dorado. I left him, and the rest of you, behind. This is what I am now. Pellaz took the hand that was offered to him and it has served him well. He has won much. Now he must deal with the consequences himself."

"We are still brothers," Terez said. "I have learned enough not to deny my blood. Speak to me alone. I ask only this."

"I knew you went to him," Snake said, "but that was all. I never thought he would send you, although that was perhaps the obvious plan. You do deny your blood, Terez, because you have denied your Wraeththu heritage. You are Gelaming now, whatever you've said to my son. And you bring a Gelaming sorcerer with you." He glanced coldly at the pale-haired har. "I know that face, although I can tell he is second generation. That is Cal's spawn, if I'm not mistaken."

The pale-haired har uttered a choked laugh. "I am not a Gelaming sorcerer! I am Varrish. Cal is my hostling, Terzian was my father. You know of him, of course."

Snake raised his eyebrows. "That is an interesting heritage. Now you are one of the Tigron's cat's-paws. Your father's spirit must be proud. You have no right to call yourself Varrish. It is an insult to his memory."

"You speak in ignorance," said the pale-haired har. "Many Parsic hara still revere Terzian's memory. We are a conquered people, as are you. We are not that different."

"I think we are," Snake said, his voice full of implications. He drew in his breath. "Moon, take this turncoat somewhere and keep him busy. I will talk to Terez for a few minutes. Keep away from Raven. He must not know we have visitors."

Moon could think of nothing to do with the stranger except show him around the Reliquary. He had to carry a flaming torch because night had come.

"I'm Tyson," said the har. "In a way we are related too. The Aralis dynasty has close connections to the House of Parasiel and my hostling is a consort of the Tigron."

This sounded like gibberish to Moon, who still couldn't think straight. He thrust the torch toward a shattered cabinet full of old bones.

Tyson obligingly peered into it. "The family likeness between the Cevarros is astounding," he said. "Terez and Dorado have a sister too, called Mima. She is Kamagrian, which is a kind of Wraeththu offshoot. She lives in Shilalama."

"Don't tell me all this," Moon blurted out.

"Why not? Aren't you curious? Or is it that your father has forbidden you to know the truth about the past?"

"I don't want to know it," Moon said. "There's too much of it. It makes my head reel. You are the enemy of all Wraeththu."

Tyson laughed. "That's right. I've been told that before, but perhaps you are mixing me up with Cal. He's far more deadly than I'll ever be."

Moon realized he was being mocked. "The Gelaming are the enemy. I won't go with you, and neither will my father."

"Your father will not be able to resist Terez's powers of persuasion, I assure you. Why deny your heritage? It seems senseless to be living here in a shantytown when you could have so much. Aren't you the slightest bit curious?"

Moon paused for a moment. "Do you know the Tigron?"

"Yes, sort of. You probably look just like he did when Cal stole him away from his home and made him Wraeththu. Full circle. It seems like no coincidence that here I am now, Cal's son, ready to steal you away too."

Moon was unsure how to interpret these remarks and thought it best to ignore them. "Snake knows the Tigron will put us in danger. He knows these things. He is never wrong."

"Perhaps we are all in danger," Tyson said. "Is your father afraid of what he knows?"

Moon knew he shouldn't answer that. He shrugged awkwardly.

"If you are in danger, little friend," Tyson said softly, "part of it is because you are unaware of your own power, or the potential for it. Pellaz seeks to gather the Cevarros together and he has been very successful so far. Dorado, your father, was the last one, but now there is you as well."

"What does the Tigron want Snake to do?"

"I don't know all his plans and if Terez knows, he would never betray a confidence. If you heard the whole story, of how Pellaz became Tigron, and what happened after, it might help you understand. I could tell it to you."

"In a few minutes?"

Again, Tyson laughed. "Terez will be busy for quite some time. Trust me on that."

There were few comfortable places to sit in the Reliquary, so Moon took Tyson to his own room. For the first time in his life, he was aware of how musty and dingy it was. Tyson glowed like a clean flame within it. He was sleek and fit and had lived a privileged life. Perhaps he had seen the buildings that other hara had made. Perhaps he had built one himself. As Moon made coffee, which was always a lengthy process, owing to the primitive facilities, he filled the awkward silence with this question. "Where you come from, have hara made new buildings?"

Tyson grinned, although he looked a little bemused. "Yes, although my family live in a very old house."

"Have you worked on buildings?"

"I've had a hand in building stuff around the estate, yes. Why?"

"Nohar builds here. It's all ruins."

"Do you have a dream of being an architect or something?"

"An archi-what?"

"Somehar who designs buildings."

"Oh, no, not really. I'm just interested. I thought about it once, what it must be like to live in something you'd thought up and made yourself."

"You could learn a lot about that in Immanion, I expect. It has hundreds of new buildings." Tyson shook his head. "This is the most bizarre conversation I've ever had. What a weird obsession you have."

"It's just something to talk about."

"Oh, I see. I'll tell you the story I promised, then. It's very romantic. A story of doomed lovers, who were of course Pellaz, and Cal, who fell in love with him."

Moon wasn't sure how much of what Tyson told him was true. It sounded extremely unlikely, not least that Pellaz was supposed to have risen from the dead. But the tragedy of Pellaz and Cal, and the pain they had suffered in order to find each other again, seemed very real. Moon had sometimes wondered whether such intensity of feeling could exist. He could imagine it and remembered how he'd tried to weave fantasies around Raven, which had never worked. There was no great power behind his relationship with Ember: it was far too comfortable. There was no yearning, no excitement, no tension. Moon's entire being was consumed with the idea of the ultimate love spanning space and time, so much so he didn't really take in much of the end of the story.

"Thiede has left us now," Tyson was saying, "and Pell needs help. That is why we're here."

"They've been taken from each other again," Moon said, still lost in a dream state. "Pellaz must be in agony."

"Hardly," Tyson said dryly. "He's made of diamond. You can't even scratch his surface. He wasn't always that way, but his position means he's had to learn to become it."

"You are a sorcerer," Moon said. "My father was right."

"How so?" Tyson asked.

"You have made me want to meet the Tigron. I'd vowed to myself I'd never feel that way."

"He is a wonder. He will overwhelm you. You'll think you've died and ended up in some kind of Paradise. Terez felt that way. He's told me about it."

"Are you chesna with Terez?" To Moon that would make complete sense.

"No. Why do you ask?"

"Cal and Pellaz are completely intertwined. You and Terez are part of the twine."

"Don't read too much into it. Every romance has its dark side. Cal might simply have run away because he couldn't bear his new life." Tyson stood up. "I'm going to get back to the inn we're staying at, because I'm starving. If Terez shows his face, tell him that, will you?"

After Tyson had gone, Moon sat on his bed in a daze. He felt he knew Tyson, and now because of the stories, he knew Terez, Pellaz, and Cal too. His family had suddenly become so much bigger and it didn't feel bad to be part of it. His images of the Gelaming had been of sinister, unearthly beings, but in most ways they were just like other hara. He remembered what Hawk had said: that Snake was a light the clans had to keep covered. This was why. Snake had always been part of this, but had denied it.

CHAPTER FIFTEEN

Like Terez, Tyson had always been very good at concealing his true feelings or pretending he felt something else—a necessity, in fact, in a household where he and Seel were usually facing each other off in hostile situations. When he first saw the young har sitting across the street in the open-air café— a ridiculously cosmopolitan idea for a shanty town, he thought—he didn't at first notice any resemblance to Pellaz or to Terez. He'd simply nudged Terez and said, "By the Ag's blood, will you look at that!" He had expected a similarly lascivious and appreciative response.

Terez, however, had stiffened at once and murmured, "Here we are, Ty. This is it."

Making a quick and accurate assessment of the situation and Terez's inevitable reaction should he confess the real reason he'd mentioned the young har, Tyson changed tack and said, "He looks *so* like you. That's too weird."

It was not surprising that Tyson did not make the connection immediately. He had never seen the Tigron as a young har, and the expression Pellaz usually wore around Tyson was a kind of tight-lipped, stretched-to-the-end-of-patience tolerance. Tyson had not met the spontaneous, free-spirited individual who had ensnared Cal's heart and therefore did not recognize any ghost of that in Moon.

Tyson had not expected they'd come to the end of their journey in the city by the lake. He'd imagined that Pell's older brother would be holed up in an isolated spot, revered by local hara, who might leave food out for him and other gifts. That Snake lived in a tumble-down museum with his phenomenal son was a surprise.

Shocking rather than surprising was the word to describe Dorado Cevarro's appearance. Tyson had never seen a crippled har before, mainly because harish bodies are far more adept at repairing themselves than human frames ever were. Therefore, the sight of this maimed har was more upsetting to Tyson than it was to Terez, who of course remembered these things from the old times. If Snake had picked up a disgusted thought, it had most likely come from Tyson rather than Terez. It had taken a great deal of self-control to remain in the room and talk normally, and Tyson had been inordinately grateful when he was dismissed. As he'd walked into the depths of the Reliquary with Moon, unable to appreciate proximity to this morsel of delight because he was so shaken, Tyson couldn't rid himself of the image of Snake's withered limbs. He wanted to ask Moon about it, but also shrank from doing so. He didn't want to hear the details of what might have happened to Snake, even though he was morbidly fascinated by them.

Moon, he decided, was definitely wasted in this environment, and he could see the sense of getting him out of it. Tyson was unimpressed by the other young har who had been sitting with Moon at the café: he considered that without the facial tattoos Ember would look like a rodent. The hara in this place were all damaged, physically and mentally. The farther north they'd traveled, visiting the edges of Uigenna retreats, the more Tyson had been faced with this. Terez had told him that Cal had wanted to help these hara, a sentiment Tyson felt ambivalent about. He thought most were beyond help. Cal had come from these hara though, and that was difficult to credit.

Halfway through telling Moon the story of Pellaz and Cal, Tyson lost heart in it. He could tell he had an attentive audience, but the details seemed somehow irrelevant. No doubt thousands of hara had experienced similar heart-wrenching relationships in the early days, when circumstances had been even more uncertain and chaotic than they were now. When the Tigron had finally been reunited with the object of his obsession, Tyson believed he had been disappointed, even if he wouldn't admit it. The dreams of youth had not survived into the cold reality of the present moment. It was obvious, if you thought about it.

Therefore, Tyson had left the Reliquary feeling jaded and cynical. He had even lost the urge to flirt with Moon. There seemed no point to anything.

Terez did not come back to the inn until quite late at night. Tyson was still awake, wrestling with harsh thoughts. He was thinking he was glad they could go home soon. The journey had been interesting, and he'd enjoyed Terez's company, and earning Pell's approval had certainly not been a waste of time, but now Tyson realized that the world beyond his narrow existence in Galhea was not as mind-shatteringly enlightening as he'd thought it would be. He missed his friends and family, and faced with the often abysmal food and accommodation provided by the northern territories, he even missed the cozy comforts of Forever. He and Terez had taken aruna together, simply because it was convenient, but it was no more meaningful than sharing supplies. Just for a moment, earlier, Tyson had felt his spirits lift, when he'd caught sight of Moon for the first time. Suddenly, the air had smelled cleaner and had seemed full of anticipation and excitement. Tyson wished Moon had not been Snake's son. He sensed that made the har taboo.

Terez came into the room and threw himself onto the rickety bed. Something sharp protested at the weight and thrust up through the unsavory mattress to poke Tyson in the back. He sat up. "Well? Did you convince him?"

Terez rubbed his face and groaned. "He is stubborn and, I think, broken. Why should he care about Pell or me? Only the dehara know what he's been through. He's just waiting to die, and that could take a long time."

"I take it the answer is no, then," Tyson said. "Great. Now what?"

"We'll stick around. I need to win his confidence, somehow inspire him with hope, or at least interest. I think that, in his head, Pellaz is still a grubby upstart of a kid who, inexplicably, our parents adored more than the rest of us. He's not surprised Pell is Tigron. He wouldn't expect anything else. He just thinks hara are stupid to fall for the glamour." Terez glanced at Tyson. "Dorado and Pell were never really close, as you've probably gathered."

"I was shocked when we first saw him," Tyson said.

"Me too. It was the last thing I expected. Poor bastard."

"Did he tell you about what happened to him?"

"It was one of the few things we could discuss, yes. He could tell I was squirming as he talked, and I think he liked that."

"Okay, don't make me squirm. Don't tell me about it."

"Healers in Immanion might be able to help him. I don't know. I'm too tired to try and contact Pell now, but I will do tomorrow."

There was a silence, then Tyson said carefully, "The harling is something, isn't he."

Terez did not respond immediately. "Yes, I suppose so. He might be young enough not to have been too affected by Uigenna despair. We can't force him to leave here though. That's his choice. Pell sent us for Dorado, and that is who we'll secure for him. Leave the harling out of it. Moon's future is between him and his father."

Tyson heard a warning in those words, and then wondered whether he was being paranoid.

Still, over the next few days, Tyson could not avoid spending a lot of time in Moon's company. Sometimes, Ember was there too, which was annoying, because Tyson could barely endure the constant inane chatter. Moon showed him around the city while Terez spent time with his brother, trying to rekindle old loyalty. Snake had not forbidden Terez to call, which must be taken as a good sign. Terez said they spent most of the time reminiscing, and that he was proceeding carefully. Interestingly, Snake had sent his companion and guard on a spurious journey east for some kind of rare herb. Snake had confessed this to Terez, explaining that Raven would not be so hospitable, and if he was around, Snake could not be responsible for their safety.

Inevitably Great Jaguar Paw was interested in Snake's visitors, and sent a har to the Reliquary to inquire about them. Tyson thought it was intriguing that Snake lied so easily to his leader. He did not deny that he and Terez were related, presumably because anyhar could see that, as they looked so alike, but there was no mention of Pellaz or the Gelaming. The Jaguar clan appeared satisfied by Snake's explanation of a long-lost human relative, who was now Uigenna, looking him up.

Tyson discovered quickly that Moon was greedy for knowledge. After their meetings, Tyson's throat was often sore because he had to talk so much. He went to the Firedog clan house, at a time when most of the clan were absent, and there Ember and Moon showed him the wall paintings of how the city once had looked. "It's not quite right," Moon said, while Ember was absent, fetching them some refreshment. "I mean, it's all broken down now, and it needs re-building, but not in the old way. It needs to be a mixture of the old and the new."

"Organic," Tyson said, "blending with the landscape."

Moon nodded. "Blending, that's it."

"Some hara build that way, so I've heard."

"Really?"

"You need to go to school," Tyson said. "Go to Immanion. Learn about architecture. Get a life. Pell would give you anything you wanted."

"We don't need anything Gelaming," Moon said, but Tyson could tell he was thinking about it. It was clear he'd not told Ember anything about who Tyson and Terez really were.

One morning, Ember turned up very early at the Reliquary before Moon had woken up. The way he burst into the room was suspicious—Moon wondered what Ember thought he might find. "Why are you here so early?" Moon asked. "It's still dark."

"I want to spend some time with you," Ember said. "Just the two of us. Can you manage that today?"

Moon stretched. "I have to look after Tyson. Snake has asked me to. You know that."

"He doesn't need looking after," Ember said in a sulky tone.

"What would he do if he wasn't with us?"

"What any other traveler would do. Why should you care?"

"Don't you like him?"

Ember uttered a caustic laugh. "It's not what *I* think."

"Meaning?"

"I'm sick of hearing you talk about him, that's all. It's boring. Anyhar can see what he wants, but if you think anything will come of it, you're mad."

"You're jealous!"

"Maybe I have reason to be."

Moon got out of bed. "This is ridiculous, Ember. Stop it. Terez's visit is important to Snake. It means a lot to him. I can't believe you're trying to make things more difficult, when they're difficult enough as it is." He regretted his harsh tone, because he noticed Ember was close to tears. "What are you so afraid of? This doesn't affect us."

"You don't know how much I care for you, Moon. I'm scared these hara will take you away."

"Why would they do that?"

"I think they're Gelaming, and you're too blind to see it. Everyhar is suspicious of them but for you and Snake. I think the Tigron has sent them. They're bewitching you, and even Snake. I can see it happening before my eyes, and I'm powerless."

"I'm not going anywhere," Moon said, then paused. "Even if I ever did, there's no reason why you can't come with me."

"Oh, yes, there is," Ember said in a low voice. "If you can't see that, you're deluding yourself."

Moon sighed deeply. "Ember, come here. Stop torturing yourself." He took Ember in his arms and kissed his face. "I'm here. I care for you too."

Ember was feeling needy. He wanted contact and clung to Moon as if he were hanging on to life itself. Moon tried to comfort him in the only way he knew how, but it felt like a lie. Ember lay beneath him, passive and fragile, and

Moon was ouana, supposedly to bring strength, but his mind was somewhere high up above the Reliquary, soaring in the pearly dawn sky on sun-tipped wings. From up there, the world was so big and clear. It wasn't gritty or musty or dark. Ember's need was a smell, hot and salty. His fear was sweat and fingers that clutched too tightly. Moon found himself thinking of Pellaz and how Tyson had told him he looked so much like the Tigron. There was power in that idea and a certain amount of pride. He wanted to be stolen away by a beautiful har and made into a king. It was the best fantasy.

Moon knew that he should indulge Ember and spend the day alone with him. After all, the chances were that Snake would refuse to meet Pellaz, and then Tyson and Terez would go away. The dreadful fears Snake had had about being kidnapped by Gelaming seemed absurd now. It was obvious Terez was simply trying to persuade his brother to help him, and that there was no grand plan to whisk him away from his clan, never to be seen again. In any case, Moon was sure that Tyson would not be around for long and wanted to be with him while the chance was still there. He could tell that Tyson liked him, but believed the older har would make no move toward him because of his age and because he was Snake's son. That didn't matter. Simply being near Tyson was enough. It was difficult not to resent Ember for his neediness and insecurity.

They walked out of the city into what had once been suburbs but was mostly now wilderness. It was a beautiful fall day, the sunlight mellow gold and the trees in full festival costume. Ember wouldn't leave Moon alone, as if he were trying to imprint himself on the very core of Moon's being. He couldn't tell that his attempts to rekindle their closeness were only driving Moon farther away. All Moon could think about was Tyson: his sinewy wrists golden against the white of his shirt, his beautiful hands, the way he smiled so wide, so that one cheek dimpled. He was the image of his hostling, Cal: Snake had said so. Moon lay in damp grass, his head full of the scents of the season and felt delirious. He could endure whatever Ember wanted them to do, because at the end of this day was a return to the Reliquary and the chance Tyson would be there. The possibility that he might not be made the anticipation all the more exquisite.

Ember wanted Moon to return to the Firedog clan house with him for the evening meal, but Moon made up a lie about how Snake had told him he must eat with himself and Terez that night.

"Will the other one be there?" Ember asked sharply.

"How should I know?" Moon replied. "He's been wandering around on his own all day."

These words only kindled a desire in Ember for more aruna. At this point, Moon had to shake him off. "I have to get back. It's late."

"Do you love me, Moon?"

"What? Oh, please, Ember, don't do this. Don't claw at me like this."

"I guess that's my answer, then."

"All right. I love you. Do you feel better now?"

"I don't know. Those are just words."

"Exactly. We've been together for months. Doesn't that say enough?"

This seemed to satisfy Ember, because his mood improved. On the way home, he chattered on about plans for the future, which were not big plans, but involved trips out to various landmarks near the city. Perhaps they could sail to the south on a boat and visit an Unneah community. Moon complied with all suggestions to keep the peace. Privately, he was thinking, *Tyson will leave soon. I just need to get through this. Then everything will go back to how it was before. I can't let him go without touching him, but then it will be over. Just once. Is that so bad? I couldn't live if he left here and we'd never touched.*

It was like an infection, and it had been getting more vicious as the day progressed. Now, Moon was feverish. He was sure he'd soon be hallucinating.

Tyson was not at the Reliquary. Moon's crushing disappointment about this meant that he could barely take an interest in the fact that Snake and his brother appeared to be getting on very well. Snake had got his liquor out and by the time Moon joined them to eat, both Terez and Snake were on the way to being drunk. Now, their memories of the past conjured laughter rather than bitterness. Terez appeared happy to join in with Snake's often spiteful recollections of Pellaz's childhood indiscretions. Moon had never seen this side of his father before. He was more at ease than Moon had ever seen him. He reached out to touch Terez a lot, squeezing his shoulder, patting his hands.

"Where have you been all day?" Snake asked Moon.

"Out with Ember. He wanted some time alone with me. I don't know what's got into him. He's jealous of Tyson."

Moon noticed Terez direct a sharp glance in his direction. The atmosphere condensed a little. Terez took a drink from his glass with one eyebrow raised. Moon wondered what he'd said wrong. "Is Tyson here?"

Terez shook his head. "No. It's probably for the best. You shouldn't upset your friend."

"I didn't," Moon protested. "He upset himself."

Terez put down his glass. He appeared to be about to say something significant, then clearly changed his mind. "I brought hot pork from the food market. Are you hungry?"

Moon wasn't, but forced himself to eat. He wanted to ask where Tyson was, but sensed that would be a bad idea. He managed to endure an hour of his father and hura's company, then fled for the open air. He went to sit at the edge of the lake, where a road of moonlight slid over the water. The air was chill, so he'd thrown on a huge woolen sweater full of holes that smelled of mouse droppings. He rested his cheek on his knees, breathing in the rank scent of the wool, and wondered if it was possible to have a clear mind. What had happened to him? It felt like sickness, worse than the time when feybraiha had come upon him.

"Find me," he said aloud. "Find me."

He called upon the magic of the stars and the moon, he called upon it with all his strength. He projected every ounce of will and intention he possessed into the call. *Find me, Tyson.*

And he did.

Moon heard the footsteps approach and could tell that whoever they belonged to was sauntering in reality, but running in their heart. He didn't raise his head. He closed his eyes. It was impossible for it to be anyhar but Tyson.

Somehar hunkered down beside him and Moon opened his eyes. Tyson was staring out over the water, then he threw a stone. "Have a good day?" he asked.

"No. Hell."

"Oh, dear. I've been very bored. You are cruel to abandon me."

"I didn't have a choice. Ember threw a hissy fit."

Tyson laughed. "That must have been a sight. Did he grow whiskers and a hairless tail?" He mimicked a rat's teeth and twitching nose.

Moon gasped in both shock and delight. "That's not nice! He's jealous of you."

"There's no reason for him to be."

"I know that. He doesn't, though."

Tyson threw another stone into the water, then sat back on his heels, his hands dangling between his knees. His fingers looked pure white in the moonlight.

"Ember thinks you and Terez are going to take Snake and me away. Is that going to happen?"

Tyson shrugged. "Who knows? Terez wants Snake to meet with Pell, but what happens to you is between you and your father. He might make you stay here."

"You said I should go to Immanion."

"That's just my opinion. I'm not your guardian, Moon. I have no say in it."

"I'd like to see Galhea, where you live."

Tyson sighed and scraped both hands through his hair. "I'd like you to see it too. But . . ."

"But what?"

"Okay, I'll be straight with you. I've been warned off, subtly. Do you understand what I'm saying?"

"I think so."

"You're still a harling, Moon. Nohar should take advantage of that."

"I'm not a harling! Who said that to you?"

"Nohar. It just is." Tyson shook his head slowly. "I'm sorry. You don't know how much."

Moon was silent for a moment, then gathered all his courage. "Nohar need know, Ty. You'll be gone soon. Nohar will know."

Tyson turned and blinked at him. "I presume this is some kind of wild dream and in a moment I'll wake up."

"No. You heard me right. I'm stuck here in the back of beyond and probably always will be. I want a taste of something. Is that so bad?"

Tyson rubbed his face. "I don't know. I don't know. Things can get out of hand . . ." He sighed again. "By Aghama, you are temptation itself."

"Cal didn't think twice, did he?"

"I am not him, and you are not Pell. I knew it was a bad idea to tell you that story!"

Moon got to his feet. He wondered what would happen if he just jumped into the water. Tyson's head was lowered. Moon could see his neck where his hair parted and fell over his shoulders. He wanted to touch the knuckle of spine there.

Tyson looked up at him and Moon held his gaze for long seconds. Then Tyson stood up. He made a sound of distress and rubbed Moon's arms with his hands.

Do it! Moon thought loudly.

When they finally shared breath, Moon felt as if he turned into a silver liquid, which slipped down through Tyson's arms and ran all over the ground at their feet. There were no physical sensations and hardly any images, just this quicksilver feeling of being set free. We could walk the road of light to the moon. We could keep on walking.

Moon couldn't see properly once Tyson released him. His mouth was numb. His jaw ached. He could feel Tyson's fingers digging into his upper arms.

"I have to go," Tyson said. "Moon, I have to."

Moon pulled him close, pressed his face against Tyson's shirt. "No. Don't. Please."

He felt Tyson's arms curl around his back, Tyson's lips against his hair. They stood like that for what seemed hours. Then a piercing whistle startled them and they jumped apart.

Somehar called: "Ty!"

Moon recognized Terez's voice.

"Fuck," Tyson said in a low voice. He turned and waved. Terez was standing on the Reliquary steps, hands on hips.

"Now, I really have to go," Tyson said.

"I'll see you tomorrow. Ember can just go throw himself in the lake."

Tyson said nothing to this. He touched Moon's cheek briefly with his fingers, then ran toward Terez.

Terez didn't mention what he'd seen until they'd nearly reached the inn, but his silence was excruciating.

"Have you won Snake around now?" Tyson asked.

"Almost."

"He'll come to Immanion?"

"Galhea might be better."

"Good idea. Have you communicated with Pell?"

"Yes."

"What did he say?"

Terez stopped walking and stared at Tyson for some moments. Tyson returned his gaze. He would not flinch.

"Okay, what exactly were you doing by the lake?" Terez asked.

"Nothing. You saw. Moon needed reassurance. He's scared."

"Right. Well, I have one thing to say to you and it is this: no. Got that?"

"No what?"

"Tyson, you are a predator as your illustrious hostling is a predator. You're gorgeous and no doubt every young har in this forsaken place is panting to get near you. But Moon is my sori, the son of my brother, and this is a delicate situation and you will keep your paws off. Be sure you don't want to cross me on this."

Terez started to walk off, but Tyson grabbed hold of his arm. "If we're speaking so plainly, then it's my turn. Why, Terez? What business is it of yours?"

"It's my business if Snake is offended and, trust me, he will be offended by you. He remembers what Cal did to our family."

"That's insane. If it wasn't for Cal, Pell would have ended up Uigenna."

"Which Snake is. Think about it. Just don't go stepping into this territory.

There's too much history attached to it. Also, I'm concerned for Moon. He doesn't need his head or his feelings scrunched up into a little ball to be thrown away by you."

"Excuse me! You've no right to say that. I've no intention of hurting him."

"I'm sure Cal had the same feeling for all of his casualties too."

"I can't help who my hostling is!"

"Of course you can't. How sad. Back off, Ty. I mean it."

"If you had a heart instead of that black piece of coal in your chest, you might not be so draconian."

"Oh, is your heart involved? Surely, it's too early for that. I imagine it's more to do with the throbbing collection of sex organs that currently have a gun pointed at your head. Heart indeed!"

"It *is* possible, Terez. Normal hara feel that way sometimes, you know."

"I'm sure they do. If you really *feel that way,* you can wait, can't you?"

"You're asking me to prove my intentions are honorable? We're not human, Terez. Moon and I are second generation. Don't go dumping all your ancient history shit all over us."

"I don't care what you think. If you touch that har again, you will regret it deeply. I have nothing else to say on the matter."

Terez, in fact, had nothing else to say at all. That night, he and Tyson lay side by side in simmering silence. Tyson couldn't get to sleep. He felt angry, exhilarated, joyous, and bereft. He knew Terez was right: if anything happened between him and Moon it could upset the delicate negotiations with Snake. But it was so difficult to ignore his instincts. *Try,* he told himself. *Use a political solution, as Pellaz would. Organize it so that Moon comes to Galhea with his father.*

Perhaps that calm affirmation was a prayer in itself. Perhaps something heard it.

CHAPTER SIXTEEN

The following morning, Moon was again woken early, but this time by Snake. It must have challenged him to negotiate all the stairs and galleries to reach Moon's room, even though he'd used a walking stick. He was quite out of breath when he sat down heavily on the end of the bed.

Moon, instantly awake, dreaded that Snake was about to say something concerning Tyson. "Son, we must talk," he said.

Moon sat up and nodded. It was beyond him to speak.

"Raven has returned," Snake said.

Was that all?

"I have also come to a decision," Snake continued. "Terez will not take no for an answer. All he wants me to do is meet with Pellaz. He assures me I will be made to do nothing against my will, and I'm inclined to believe him. It's been good having him around these past few days . . ."

Snake's voice trailed off and his gaze became unfocused. Moon wondered whether he was thinking about his childhood, in the days when his body had been whole.

"Will you go to Immanion?" Moon asked, juggling scripts for how he might include himself on such a trip.

"No, to a place called Galhea. It was the Varrish stronghold, years ago." His tone became disapproving. "Terzian's family is very close to the Tigron. Both Terez and I consider it would be best if Pell and I met on neutral territory—or as neutral as it can get in Galhea."

"Can I come with you?" Moon asked, bracing himself for an argument.

Snake stared at him for some moments. His Eye was uncovered and Moon was sure it could see right into his soul. "I wouldn't feel happy leaving you here alone."

Moon dampened the spontaneous desire to shriek with joy. "What about Raven?" he managed to ask in a level tone.

Snake shifted uncomfortably on the bed. "He is my protection. I'll not travel without him, and this is where a slight problem lies."

"He hates Gelaming."

"It's rather more than that. I've asked Terez and Tyson to come here mid-morning. I want Raven to meet them. I'm not sure how this will end, but it is a bridge to be crossed before we can even think about traveling."

Moon paused a moment, then said, "Snake, you were so afraid before Terez came. Were you wrong to feel that way? I didn't think it would ever be this easy for him to persuade you."

Snake smiled and reached out to touch his son's face, in exactly the same place where Tyson had touched it before leaving the previous evening. "Nothing has changed. Well, except for one thing. I did not anticipate the happiness I'd feel at being reunited with my brother. I'd forgotten so much. That alone is a strong persuasive factor. Now that I've found him, I realize I'm reluctant to lose him again."

"I understand," Moon said earnestly.

"There may be storms ahead," Snake said. "There will be danger, of that I have no doubt. But a new realization has come to me: we will not face these dangers alone. We cannot avoid them, because as Terez had made clear to me, we are part of the web of destiny. The Cevarros are no ordinary family, Moon. It is no coincidence we have ended up as we are. You are part of that. It is time for you to become acquainted with your own destiny."

Moon scrambled over the bed and hugged his father. Snake felt fragile and when Moon drew away, his face looked so young. Moon stroked it with both hands. He saw Snake was weeping. "Why are you sad?" Moon asked.

"Pellaz will see me as I am," Snake answered. "I can't bear what I'll see on his face. It'll be what I saw on Terez's face when he first came here, or perhaps worse, because Pell was always so vain."

"You are beautiful," Moon said, "as beautiful as your brothers could ever be."

"I'm not meant to be alive," Snake said. "That is the truth of it. That is why I've hidden here for so long, denying you a life."

Moon had experienced many "firsts" with Snake recently, but this was a confidence he would never have dreamed of hearing. He had no idea Snake worried about his disabilities. He'd always assumed his father was above such things.

"I'll be with you," Moon said. "Let Pellaz be frightened of your differences. Why should you care? It'll only be for a short time. Once hara get used to the way you look, they don't even notice. Remember Ember? He was obsessed with your Eye until he saw it. He's never mentioned it since."

"The gods blessed me with you," Snake said. "And it is only because of this threat to our routine that we've started to get to know one another." He used his stick to haul himself to his feet. "Help me back to my rooms," he said. "Raven will prepare us breakfast. Say nothing to him about the Gelaming. I want to speak to Terez before Raven finds out about them."

Snake organized it so that Raven was out attending to the animals when Terez and Tyson arrived. Moon was already installed in his father's room, his heart beating in such an erratic way it felt life threatening. He glanced once at Tyson, and that was too much. It was as if the room were full of electricity.

Tyson and Terez sat down on the floor by Snake's chair, both respectfully quiet, as if they sensed Snake needed to be in charge for this moment.

"I will come to Galhea," Snake said to Terez.

Terez ducked his head. "I'm glad. I will do all that I can to make the journey comfortable for you."

"Hmm." Snake appeared introspective as if he hadn't actually considered that aspect of the plan. "However, before any arrangements can be made, there is another matter to be addressed. I wish for my companion, Raven, to accompany me."

"Of course," Terez said, "whatever you desire."

"It is not that easy," Snake said. "He has a visceral hatred of all things Gelaming, because he was once tortured by them."

"I see."

"No you don't, Terez. You don't see at all. A long time ago, Raven was known by another name, as was I. He had a love, who was taken from him. Like Cal did with Pellaz, he believed this har to be dead. When the Gelaming took Raven into captivity, they set about destroying him. As is their signature, part of that destruction, along with more obvious forms of torture, involved revealing to him the har he loved still lived. I presume you already know the Gelaming shine at that kind of thing. They know where best to turn a hook in flesh. They told Raven that he would never see his friend again, because now the Gelaming had him too. More than that: they had made him one of them."

"I can see why that would cause problems with us," Terez said smoothly. "What can we do to help ease the situation?"

"That is up to you," Snake said. "Handle it as best you can." He turned to Moon. "Fetch Raven now. Be quick."

Perhaps Snake should have warned Raven, Moon thought later, but if he had, the chances are that Raven would have fled. So, he walked into Snake's room in ignorance, unaware of what he was about to face. Nohar knew the truth of it except Snake. Moon closed the door and as he did so it was as if he trapped an icy ghost in the room. The air became hard. He could barely breathe. Terez stared at Raven and Raven stared back. Shock, horror? It was difficult to discern. Eventually, Terez said, "Agroth . . . ?"

Raven sank to his haunches by the door, one hand braced against the floor. His whole body trembled.

"I'm sorry," Snake said, "this had to be done. All of life is a series of cycles, Raven. Be glad the universe sees fit to help you close this one."

"What's going on?" Tyson asked. For the first time, he and Moon locked gazes. Moon shrugged at him. He didn't know either.

"He incepted me," Terez said. "He was known to me as Agroth. I presume I am the har Snake was referring to, who was taken in by the Gelaming, although it was not quite that straightforward . . ."

Tyson got to his feet. "Wonderful. What do we have now: three hours of recriminations or ritual combat? Choose your weapons."

"Tyson Parasiel, have some respect," Snake said coldly. "This is a bitter history."

Raven fixed Snake with a manic stare. "How could you not tell me of this? How could you?"

"You must face it," Snake said. "As I have had to face many things. This meeting had to take place before any other plans were made. Raven, we are to travel to Galhea. I have decided to meet with the Tigron."

Raven appeared so punch-drunk he clearly couldn't take in what Snake said to him. Once Raven had been a normal har and had had normal feelings for others. At the time, the revelation of this in such uncompromising terms was more shocking to Moon than the idea of what the Gelaming had done to him.

Terez had recovered his composure quickly, every inch the Tigron's diplomat. He inclined his head to Snake. "You were right to arrange this meeting." He addressed Raven. "We were together only a short time, but it was poignant. You were correct in thinking I was abducted, because that is true, but obviously I did not die. I will give you as succinct an explanation as I can. My inception was arrested by my sister, Mima, who had no idea what was happening to me. All she could see was that most of her family was dead and that she had a chance to save me. This was a gross error.

"For a long time, I was lost, a mindless thing. Then Mima met some hara and underwent a bizarre kind of inception of her own. She and her friends finished the inception process for me and nursed me back to health. As soon as I was able, I went to seek you out, for my whole being was imprinted with yours. As far as my body was concerned, it had just woken up from althaia and was desperate for you. You can imagine this was not a comfortable time. I made contact with the Uigenna and discovered you had been taken prisoner by the Gelaming. Once I became reunited with my brother Pellaz, I made inquiries in Immanion as to your whereabouts, but by that time, you'd been released. You covered your tracks well. I am the most adept of the Tigron's trackers, and I never found you."

Raven still said nothing.

"I was incepted to the Uigenna," Terez said, "but the process was never completed. Those who helped me afterward were Sarock and Kakkahaar. My brother Pellaz is Gelaming. I have a mixed pedigree, if you like, but to me the bond of blood is thicker than any other, tribe or no tribe. Snake, Pell, and Mima share my blood, and yours mingles with mine in my veins. I am glad to see you well, and appreciate this must be a great shock. It is to me too, but we have work to do. I trust we can come to a civilized understanding. I will, of course, be glad to discuss anything with you, if you so wish."

Given that Terez seemed so concerned with blood, Moon was astounded he could be so *bloodless* about such a traumatic situation, but of course that was one of the reasons why he was so useful to the Tigron.

Raven simply nodded his head. He looked as if he'd just been beaten with sticks. He turned slowly toward Moon, in an almost drunken way. "I think we did this," he said. "I think we made it possible."

"Perhaps," Moon said carefully. He wasn't sure how best to answer.

Raven smiled crookedly, a gleam of mania in his eyes. "The sky fell in. And now it has again."

"Get Raven a drink, Moon," Snake said.

Moon went to fetch a measure of Snake's liquor, and then knelt beside Raven. He put one hand on the back of Raven's neck as he drank and thought, *He is so ill. He always has been.*

Tyson was leaning against the far wall, almost invisible in shadow. Moon could tell he longed to make a run for it. It was as if they were dissecting Raven. They might as well have had him spread-eagled on the floor. Emotionally, they had opened him up. Guts were spilling everywhere.

Terez got to his feet. "I think Tyson and I should leave now," he said to Snake. "I will begin to make arrangements. Would tomorrow be too soon?"

Snake shook his head. "Do as you see fit."

After Terez and Tyson had departed, Raven leaned heavily against Moon and Moon wrapped his arms around him. Raven's breathing was ragged and wisps of it entered Moon's body like threads of nightmare. Raven was reliving his torment with the Gelaming. Then he was thinking of Terez when he'd first met him, and the feeling had been so similar to how Moon felt about Tyson: the excitement and anticipation, the yearning. He was thinking of oceans of wasted time, of half life, of denial. He was thinking of when he'd taken aruna with Moon and how it had seemed as if sealed passageways in his mind had opened up, allowing a tsunami of suppressed feelings and thoughts to crash through the fragile labyrinth, tearing down walls in its wake.

Moon squatted beside Raven for so long, his whole body became wracked with pain, but he dared not move. He dared not interrupt this process, because he sensed it was healing. Snake sat silently in his chair and bars of sunlight moved slowly across the floor. A scent of apples came in from the garden, far below.

Eventually, Raven stirred and tried to sit up.

"Moon," said Snake softly, "take Raven to his bed."

Moon glanced at his father and Snake nodded.

Raven allowed Moon to lead him like a tiny harling. The things in his room—a cell—brought a lump to Moon's throat. They were just things that Raven used every day, but now they seemed to highlight Raven's fragility: a neatly folded face flannel on the cracked washstand, two pairs of boots lined up side by side next to the bed. An old book open on the coverlet, facedown. Moon pushed Raven down gently onto the bed and went to the washstand. When he turned the only working tap, the plumbing groaned and shuddered, but presently a thin trickle of discolored water came out. Moon wet the flannel and then went to sit beside Raven. He dabbed at Raven's face, which was hot, with the cool cloth.

Raven simply stared up at the ceiling. His whole world had just changed.

"Do you want to talk?" Moon asked. He was completely nonplussed as to how to deal with this situation.

Raven turned his head and looked Moon in the eye. His gaze was full of pleas.

Moon stroked his face and then lowered his head. He put his lips against Raven's own and breathed into him a soothing stream of images. *For a short time, let reality fade away. Think of pleasant things that feel good. Go to the land of dreams, where everything is golden.*

I feel like an adult, Moon thought, *because I am controlling this. It is what Snake wants me to do. He trusts me with this task.*

Moon shared breath with Raven until he felt light-headed, and by that time Raven had drifted off to sleep, as Moon had intended. Moon lay with him for the rest of the day, listening to the slow but persistent drip of the tap. He was alive in his being and desperate for the future. The golden land was all around them.

Although Terez had delivered a command performance in the Reliquary, once free of its musty environment, he did the nearest to falling to pieces it was possible for him to do.

"Get me drunk," he said to Tyson, "then take aruna with me until I'm unconscious."

"Do you really think you should do that?"

Terez uttered a low growl in his throat. "This is the last thing I ever expected. At this very moment, I feel I've just woken up to find Mima telling me she's Wraeththu and I'm wondering what the hell is going on, looking around desperately for Agroth. No, you can't possibly understand, so don't even try."

"Well maybe I can understand a little, Terez," Tyson said meaningfully. "Welcome to the world. Is it your heart or gun-wielding sex organs?"

Terez at least had the grace not to argue with that.

Once they got back to the inn, Terez somehow found the equilibrium to contact Pellaz and to tell him they would set off for Galhea tomorrow.

"He should send *sedim*," Tyson said. "Snake can't make a journey by normal horse. We'll have to find a cart or something. That will really slow us down. Tell Poll to send *sedim*." He was sitting on the bed pulling off his clothes, while Terez slumped, looking drained, on the dusty wooden floor.

"Pell won't do that," Terez said. "He'd never let somehar like Agroth—sorry, *Raven*—loose on a *sedu*. They aren't for everyhar, Ty."

"It'll take us twice as long to get home."

"I know. I have mentioned this."

"What did he say?"

"Nothing."

"Has he been to Roselane?"

"Yes, but I don't yet know the outcome."

Terez clambered onto the bed and lay facedown, groaning. "I feel like I've just run a hundred miles."

Tyson lay down beside him and stroked his back. "How will you handle this Raven business?"

Terez turned onto his side. "I have no idea. He's as much of a mess as Snake is, only in a different way. He's not the same har as the one I knew. Longevity has its downsides. Horrors from the past can keep turning up looking the same as they did decades ago."

"Then forget Agroth and get to know Raven. Maybe it'll be worth it, maybe not. Another downside of longevity: too many memories perhaps? Let go of the past."

Terez laughed. "I don't believe it: wise words from the son of Cal."

"I'm Tyson. It would please me greatly if you'd allow me my own personality."

Terez stared at Tyson for some moments. "I can remember the day so clearly when Cal came to our home. When I look at you, I taste that day. It was the end of our lives as we knew them. It didn't take long for the Uigenna to find us. It wasn't good, Ty. A lot of it I wrapped up in memories about Agroth, and the way he made me feel, but before that I had to watch what happened to my parents, my sisters . . . It's a wonder any first-generation hara are sane. What happened to us was insanity."

"Hush," Tyson said. "You are completely sane. I couldn't have done what you did today. It was outstanding."

"Quick thinking," Terez said. "My life often depended on it, although I've trained myself to be diplomatic. Mima—my sister—spent years telling me how often I said the wrong thing at the wrong time." He paused. "I was harsh with you last night, but I meant what I said. Please leave Moon alone, at least for now."

"That's okay. I'd already come to that decision."

"Good. It might be irrational, but I feel uneasy with the idea of you being with him. Not for just the reasons I gave you, either. Perhaps it's because the pair of you look like Cal and Pell so much. I get a hideous feeling that history might repeat itself."

"We're not them," Tyson said, "but just forget it. Think about yourself for now. You don't have to worry about anything I'd do."

"I'm glad we're friends. I enjoy discovering things about you."

"Let's see what we can discover today, then."

"We need these times," Terez said. "It will all change soon. I'm sure of it."

CHAPTER SEVENTEEN

Desire, when it is not satisfied, becomes a physical pain. There is no position you can find in which it is comfortable to sleep. Every waking moment, the mind is consumed with thoughts of the beloved. Whole days can be wasted staring into space, dreaming up improbable fantasies. Every possible scenario is played out in the imagination, leaving almost no room at all for something to happen in reality, because real events very rarely emulate a fantasy. A glance, a tone of voice, a chance comment becomes imbued with meaning and portent. The beloved becomes an oracle with the key to your destiny.

Three days of travel, with Tyson barely acknowledging his existence, sent Moon into a spin of confusion, lust, and unbearable longing. He could barely pay attention to the fact that Snake was stoically enduring what must be excruciating conditions in the back of a rough cart that Terez had secured for him. The atmosphere between Raven and Terez swung between being incandescent and glacial. It was as if violence could break out at any moment. They were all on their way to Galhea. Life had just become a thousand times bigger than it had been before.

Moon didn't care about any of these things. He'd done or said something to offend Tyson. How could somehar change so quickly? That night at the lake Moon had been sure Tyson desired him. Now this. It was agonizing.

He tried various ploys. First, he attempted to act normally and addressed Tyson in general conversation as he would anyhar else. That didn't work. Second, he opted for withering disdain and ignorance, which made no difference either. Outright sarcasm was met with bland unresponsiveness. It was as if he'd ceased to exist. Moon had nohar to talk to about it. Even though Tyson had already told him he'd been warned off, the heat of Moon's passion, which was unswervingly selfish in its desire to survive, excised the memory from his mind. The reason for Tyson's indifference couldn't possibly be so mundane. It had to be something to do with Moon himself.

Moon had rarely ventured beyond the city limits, and even when he had it had not been far, but it was impossible to take any interest in his surroundings. He sat with Snake in the cart and played cards with him to pass the time, but Snake won every round. He eventually became bored and berated Moon for his lack of concentration. "Don't worry about Ember," Snake said. "He'll not forget you."

Moon merely gibbered in response. He doubted Ember would forget him, but neither would he forgive him, since Moon had left home without telling Ember he was going. He wished that Snake would use his clear sight to work out what was wrong. It seemed inconceivable to Moon that it wasn't obvious. Although he couldn't bring himself to confide in his father, he had already decided he would be open to questioning should the occasion arise, but unfortunately it didn't.

They'd been traveling for four days before the Tigron contacted them. No doubt Pellaz had been sitting at home, brooding about the state of his brother, consumed with curiosity, but also concerned that Snake would be difficult and prickly. Eventually, it seemed, his curiosity overcame any misgivings and he manifested before them, in a manner that could not fail to impress, on a glorious white *sedu.*

Terez realized that a portal into the otherlanes was about to open, because he was familiar with the signs. The air became oppressive, like before a storm, and the clouds in the sky ahead of them appeared sluggish and sickly.

"A portal," Terez said, "perhaps Pell has sent us *sedim* after all." He did not look entirely convinced with this explanation, however. "Ty, have the weapons ready."

"Why?" Moon asked, scrambling forward to where Raven was driving the cart.

"It might not be Pell," Tyson said, staring ahead. "It could be anyhar."

"Snake is Pell's brother," Terez said. "Our purpose on this journey is to keep him safe."

Moon stared at the horizon without blinking until his eyes ran. It felt as if tiny shivers of electricity were running over his skin. His hair had lifted on his head. He could feel the power. Presently, the thick clouds became shot with threads of blue lightning. Terez indicated to Raven that he should steer the horses to the side of the road and the cover of some trees.

Thunder rumbled in the heavens, slow and rolling, then all was silent. The crack, when it came, was like an explosion. There was a flash, both blinding and weirdly invisible to the naked eye, and something flew out of the clouds. It was impossible at first to discern what it was, but after a few moments, Moon could see two white horses galloping toward them upon the road. They appeared real and solid but at the same time weirdly spectral. They were surrounded by a streaking vapor, and even from this distance, Moon could smell ozone. Only one of the horses bore a rider.

"He's come alone," Terez said in surprise. "I really wish he wouldn't do that. He has no sense for security."

"Is it Pellaz?" Snake asked.

"Yes," Terez answered. "Look at that. He is Tigron, yet he travels alone." He shook his head.

"He has another *sedu*," Tyson said, "but only one. I wonder who that's for?"

Moon climbed back to sit beside his father and took hold of one of his hands. Snake's expression was unreadable, but Moon could feel that he was full of tension.

The Tigron brought the *sedim* to a halt and dismounted. He was dressed in a plain riding costume of dark brushed leather, his hair bound back. At a distance, he would pass for any traveling har. It was only when he drew closer that you realized there was nothing ordinary or plain about him at all. Laying eyes on the Tigron for the first time, Moon realized that sometimes great beauty can be terrifying, if not horrific. It is almost alien, and difficult to look upon. When Pellaz paused to inspect Moon, it felt as if a great searchlight passed over and through Moon's flesh. He was in no doubt that the Tigron could see to the core of him and beyond. And yet this was his hura. The idea seemed impossible. This was not the har of the stories Tyson had told him.

Terez had also dismounted and now made the introductions. "Our brother and his son, Moon," he said.

Pell's gaze rested for just a while too long upon Moon before turning to Snake. Moon guessed at once this was because Terez had already told Pellaz about Snake's disabilities. The Tigron was hoping he wouldn't wince, wouldn't betray any reaction likely to give offense.

Pellaz inclined his head respectfully. "Snake Jaguar. Thank you for agreeing to this meeting."

A perfect opening.

"It was supposed to be in Galhea," Snake answered, his tone giving nothing away.

"I know, and it will be . . ." Pellaz placed a long-fingered hand on the rough wood of the cart. "You shouldn't have to travel this way. I have come to offer you an alternative. The *sedim* can take us both to Galhea."

"What about the rest of us?" Tyson asked.

Pellaz flicked him a cold glance. "The meeting is between Snake Jaguar and myself." He turned to Terez. "I will return for you, if you wish. Tyson can escort Snake Jaguar's party to Galhea."

"No," Terez said. "That won't be necessary. I prefer to remain with this party."

Raven had jumped down from the driving seat and now stood protectively behind Snake. "You should not go alone," he said.

Snake raised a hand. "There is no need for concern. I will go with the Tigron. I am curious to experience his method of travel." He fixed Terez with a savage stare. "I place Moon's well-being in your hands."

"It couldn't be in better ones," Pellaz said.

Raven assisted Snake to mount the *sedu,* which stood placidly, switching its tail. Everyhar present politely averted their eyes, except for Moon, who went to hold the saddle straight. He wasn't happy that his father was leaving and yet it would have been unbearable if he'd had to go to Galhea, leaving Tyson behind.

Now, the four of them could ride rather than use the cart, which could be sold at the next settlement. Terez's packhorse would be rather weighed down, but they would still be able to travel more swiftly.

That night, they stayed at a farm run by a group of what were presumably ex-Varrs, although they took care not to betray their origins. Moon and his companions were greeted in the yard by a har wearing hoop earrings, his head wound in a blue scarf. He was used to providing accommodation for travelers. He boasted of many guest rooms. Once they were shown to these rooms, their host departed. He said that a meal would be laid out for them after dark.

Moon was intrigued by the house, because it was the nearest thing to his dreams of a self-built home that he'd ever seen. As the sun sank, he wandered around it on his own. It was strange that the house seemed so empty. Whoever lived there must be out working on the land, and there clearly weren't many, if any, other paying guests there at present. Moon prowled along the narrow passageways and ran through the dank dark parlors. There were lots of small dark rooms, where clocks ticked as they had ticked for centuries, now marking the lives of creatures alien to those who had built them. Sometimes, in some of the rooms, Moon would hear small scurrying sounds, as of mice and rats rushing for cover. In one room, he found a dresser covered in old photographs of humans who had most likely once lived here. Moon wondered why the new Wraeththu owners had kept the pictures. Perhaps they never used this room.

Time seemed to move more slowly in the farmhouse. When Moon went to the window to look out upon the darkening fields, he wouldn't have been surprised to find the house hanging in a dark void and that the real world had slipped away. He was not frightened by these feelings or even discomforted. He was enjoying his new adventure. Eventually, when most of the house had given up its secrets, he went back to the kitchen where he discovered that the table had been laid with four places and that food had been left out for them. Nohar else was around. Perhaps ghosts had prepared the meal.

Moon went up the tiny winding stairway to the bedrooms. He might as well find the others and tell them there was a meal waiting for them. The first room he visited was Raven's but it was empty. For one stultifying moment, Moon wondered whether he really was entirely alone and that his companions had vanished. He went quickly to the room that Terez occupied and flung open the door.

Raven and Terez had become like a statue carved of wood, painted to look real. They sat upon a sofa beneath the window, as motionless as stone and utterly silent. They looked dead, but he knew they weren't. Joined lip to lip, sharing secrets deep and dark, a lifetime of information perhaps. Moon stood at the threshold for some moments, unsure of what to do. It seemed rude to interrupt such an intense process and he doubted whether Terez or Raven would even hear him if he did speak. Darkness was beginning to claim the room as the last of the twilight faded. It was like an entity in itself, alive and sentient.

Moon closed the door and stood in the corridor. That left only Tyson. A few minutes ago, knocking on Tyson's door, to tell him food was waiting had seemed an easy thing to do. Now, it was different. Moon wasn't sure what reception he'd get, yet surely Tyson must be hungry.

Not that hungry, obviously. When Moon knocked upon the relevant door and received no answer, he opened it and found that Tyson was lying facedown on the bed, snoring.

The darkness was beginning to get a bit creepy now, but the prospect of the kitchen, with the warm range in the corner, seemed more inviting than the gloomy corridors and bedrooms upstairs, so Moon went down to eat alone. Clocks ticked slowly around him and the night stole in. Moon wished some of the hara who lived in this place would make an appearance. It was as if they'd vanished like spirits. A beam in the ceiling creaked and Moon almost jumped out of his chair. There was nothing else to do but go to bed and hope that in the morning everything would be normal.

Moon didn't undress, but only took off his boots and got into his bed fully clothed. It was cold in the room and he could see his breath misting by starlight. Fortunately, the covers were thick and warming. He snuggled down into them, but felt far from drowsy. Noises came through the wall: creakings and sighs. Moon was so convinced the place was haunted, it took him some moments to realize he was listening to the sounds of two hara taking aruna together. Raven and Terez had clearly resolved their problems.

Moon put his hands over his ears. He didn't want to hear those sounds. They only reminded him how alone he was. He could smell the season creeping in through gaps in the window frame. He could smell apples and wood smoke. He could hear the house breathe, exhalations of centuries, and mingled with these sensations were the sounds of hara in love. Moon screwed up his eyes, bit the inside of his cheek. He felt hot and feverish. He was the heart of a volcano, churning with lava, ready to blow. He couldn't lie there suffering. His body wouldn't let him.

Moon could already see Tyson before he even went back into that room. He could see him lying there, right inside the bed now, a mound of blankets, curled up like an animal. The brass door handle was so cold Moon had to pull his hand from it firmly. The ice went into him. He couldn't tell if his skin ripped or not. He was thinking of a house in the desert, and in his imagination, something rattled outside in the night breeze. He heard a coyote sing to the stars. He smelled dust and the reek of sage. He thought of Pellaz, who was more beautiful than any living creature had a right to be: an unreal thing like a dream or a fantasy. Moon still couldn't believe he'd met him, or that he could in any way resemble this paragon of harishness. But at one time, Pellaz had been young and guided by instinct and desire. He had stooped to pluck a bright flower from the desert floor, and the perfume had been like wine, and its thorns had been like poisoned steel.

Moon closed the bedroom door and leaned against it. His heart seemed to be beating inside his face. His eyes were throbbing. There was a chair near to the bed, where Tyson had thrown his clothes. Moon crossed the floor, every board creaking beneath his feet, and sat down in it, on the garments that had recently been close to Tyson's skin. Moon put his hands on the faded chintz of the arms and stared at the bed. Tyson was still snoring, invisible in his warm musky nest. *I could sit here all night,* Moon thought. He could no longer hear any sounds from elsewhere in the house. His breath misted on the air, hanging in clouds around his head. He could see the blankets on the bed moving slightly with Tyson's sleeping breath.

"Ty . . ." Moon's lips were so cold, he couldn't feel the word come out, and yet the inside of him was raging heat.

He knew this softly spoken word penetrated whatever deep realm Tyson explored in his sleep, because the mound in the bed suddenly became utterly still and silent. After a moment, Tyson poked his head out.

"What is it?" he asked, looking startled. "What's happened?"

Moon saw there was to be no dreamy realization of his desires, no replay of a romantic history. "Nothing," he said. "I had to get away."

"From what?"

"Raven and Terez. They are in the room next to mine and it's a roonfest in there."

Tyson sat up and yawned, pulling the blankets around his shoulders. "You shouldn't be in here. You know that. Terez would have my skin."

"Tyson?"

"Yes?"

"What have I done wrong?" Moon thought it was the most important question he had ever voiced.

"Nothing," Tyson said softly. "You know that too."

"Don't send me away."

Tyson sighed deeply and ran his hands through his hair. The blankets fell from his shoulders, revealing more than Moon could cope with. Smooth skin, an amulet on a thin chain. "Being with you, inviting you into my bed—it's what hara would expect of me," he said. "They never see me. They see *him.* Always. And if he were here now, he would bring you to his bed, and you would be lost. You would never leave that bed, not in your heart. It would haunt you for the rest of your life, and that is a long time. Do you understand?"

"I don't know who you're talking about. I don't know that har."

"I want to be different," Tyson said. "I want Pellaz to be pleased for us, give us his blessing . . ." He shook his head. "It will never happen. If I ever do any of what I want to do, I'll be judged for it, because nohar will see me. They'll see Cal, the mother of my being. My tainted hostling."

"*I* see you," Moon said. "It's all I see."

"Don't do this to me. It's not fair."

Moon saw then that a door in Tyson's protective sanctuary had opened just a chink. He had betrayed weakness. He had betrayed that the unfairness was because he wouldn't be able to resist for much longer. "I love you," Moon said. "I have always done so. It's in my blood."

"No," Tyson said. "It's not. Dorado never fell for Cal. Quite the opposite. Don't delude yourself."

"I'm not in love with Cal."

"You're not in love with me. It isn't that, Moon. It's just us—Wraeththu, hara."

"It's the selfish creature," Moon said. "It's aruna. Is that what you're saying? It has a life of its own, I know. It thinks."

Tyson laughed uncertainly. "Well, that's a new take on it. But yes, maybe. I'm not sure myself, Moon. I'm not sure of what I feel. I only know there would be consequences involved in us being together, and maybe we should wait until we're sure."

"You are so not like your hostling," Moon said. "Can't you see it? You once said to me that we are not Pell and Cal. I know that. We're not even symbols of them. What happened to them won't happen to us. I know it. You don't have to be afraid. I'm no starry-eyed virgin, Ty. I know how it is."

"You are a Cevarro," Tyson said, "and you want your own way. You all do. Soon you'll be calling yourself har Aralis, and you'll be different. It will come easily to you. Pellaz could live his life again through you. He could punish Cal through me."

Moon considered that this exchange, though conducted in level tones, was really a kind of raging argument. He should give up, leave the room, close the door. There seemed no way forward. He would go to a new life and accept all that was offered to him. It would be the easiest course. He stood up. "I'm sorry," he said. "I was wrong." Even as he made his way across the room, which had suddenly transformed into a gigantic space, he knew he hadn't made a fool of himself. That was perhaps the saddest part.

"Wait," Tyson said.

Moon really hadn't expected that. He turned around, said nothing.

"I knew someone once," Tyson said, "someone not quite har, but certainly not human."

Moon remained silent.

"Her name was Lileem," Tyson continued. "She made me see that I didn't have to be like Cal. For a long time, the strength she gave me changed everything, but she's been gone so long, I think I've forgotten it."

Moon went to sit on the end of the bed. "What happened to her?"

"It's a long story," Tyson said. "She's not in this world anymore, but I don't think she's dead either. She's Kamagrian, like your father's sister, Mima."

"Why are you telling me this?"

"I don't know. I just thought of Lileem. I know what she'd say if she were here now, and yet I knew her so briefly, really. She'd tell me to go for it. Maybe she *is* here." He put his hands against his face, his elbows resting on his raised knees through the blankets.

"Are you afraid of Terez?" Moon asked. "Of what he might do to you?"

"I'm afraid of his disappointment in me," Tyson said, through his fingers. "I've won him. I've worked for his friendship. I've made him see me as I really am."

Moon reached out and dragged Tyson's hands from his face. He leaned forward and kissed Tyson briefly on the mouth. "I understand," he said. "Don't worry about it. There's no need. Maybe what I feel is lust and maybe it's love, but whatever happens, you can't stop me feeling it. I love you enough to let you go. I love you enough to fight aruna's demands. I hope that means something to you." He stood up. "I'm leaving now. Don't stop me this time."

Once the door was closed behind him and he stood in cold dark corridor Moon expected that he'd want to weep, but he felt strangely detached. He went back to his room and crawled into the bed. In the room on the other side of the wall, Terez and Raven were silent, perhaps curled up asleep in each other's arms.

Clarity is bitter, Moon thought. *It tastes like gall.*

He felt he had reached the longed-for place of maturity that he and Ember had once talked of. He was no longer a child in any way.

CHAPTER EIGHTEEN

By the time they reached Galhea, the last of the leaves were falling from the trees, and the horses trod upon a sodden, fading carpet of gold and bronze on every road. Rooks called from the high bare branches and the fields beyond the roads looked wide and empty.

Moon had not really been surprised to discover that Raven was now a changed har. Moon had never heard him sing before, but now Raven's deep honeyed voice carried them into the future. It was the theme music of their journey, and Moon would never forget it. Eventually, he'd look back fondly on that aspect of their travels. Raven and Terez sang continually, and seemed oblivious to any iciness in their companions. It seemed to Moon obscene that Raven should be so released, so happy, for Moon felt quite the opposite. He was brittle and offhand with Raven, even though it was clear Raven felt he should now take on the mantle of hostling, which Silken's death had left lying on the floor long ago to go moldy: until now, Raven had simply walked across it every day without noticing it. Moon felt uncomfortable with this joyous stranger, because every gesture of affection or concern was colored by Raven's own happiness. He couldn't really see that Moon was suffering, because in his bright new world there was no room for such things.

Moon did not speak to Tyson again, about any personal matter. In the morning after confronting Tyson, he'd woken from unrefreshing sleep filled with anger. Downstairs in the farmhouse, normality had been restored. Moon and his companions ate breakfast with a rowdy group of hara who told them they'd been celebrating somehar's feybraiha nearly all night at a nearby farm. While Raven and Terez chatted easily with their hosts, Tyson never spoke a word. He didn't even look up from his plate. Moon simmered with rage. He thought Tyson's piety was false. He'd put Terez first. His feelings for Moon could not be that deep. Despite this, it was clear that Tyson was not happy either.

After they'd left the farm to resume their journey, Moon could see the great effort Tyson put into being sociable with the others and he felt vengefully pleased about it. But whatever small gratifications Moon derived from Tyson's discomfort were eclipsed totally by what he had to endure himself. He had discovered aruna's savage side.

The spirit of this thing, which had absolutely no consideration for any living har, was vicious in its desire to be satisfied. It was a black hag gibbering at Moon's back every step of the way. It clawed his body, made him feel sick, gave him headaches. A more experienced har could have told Moon this was because he was young and aruna had only recently become a part of his life, and that part of growing up meant aruna was an itch that needed to be scratched fairly regularly. Denied, it got nasty. Terez or Raven could have told Moon this, but Moon was in such a state, and so envious of them, he couldn't go to them for help or advice. If he tried to relieve himself, the demanding spirit of aruna viewed it with contempt.

Think you can get rid of me that easily, fool? Think again.

Some hara might have been able to cope that way, but Moon was not one of them. He wondered whether he had to resign himself to the prospect of going mad. It didn't help that the object of his desire was so close to him physically, yet so distant. Eventually, as the days passed, the need became so great that Moon knew he'd have to find somehar to be with the next time they visited a settlement. Unfortunately, that might not be for a couple of days. Moon was really afraid now that he couldn't last that long. The dark spirit was killing him. He could almost see it at night, a shadowy blue-black phantom at the corner of his vision, waiting with clawed hands to attack him. He could no longer sleep properly and his dreams, when he had them, intensified his frustration.

One night, as he lay awake, he realized he was not himself anymore. He had a disease that was eating him away. He was afraid that he'd lose his mind completely and do something terrible, only to come to his senses with blood on his hands. The terror condensed in the small bivouac he occupied. The canvas pressed down on him, smothering his breath. Very soon, the dark spirit would take over, and then Moon would be lost.

Panicking, he fought from his sleeping bag and clawed his way out of the bivouac. He stumbled to where Raven and Terez were sleeping and scratched at the stiff tarry fabric that covered them. "Raven, Raven . . ." He was nearly in tears.

After some moments, Raven opened the bivouac and, uttering a sound of concern, took Moon in his arms. Moon gratefully collapsed against him, sobbing. "You have to help me. You have to . . ."

"What's wrong?" Raven murmured, stroking his hair.

Later, Moon wouldn't remember exactly what he said, but he knew that in his desperation it was graphic. Terez had also come out of the bivouac by this time and both he and Raven listened to Moon's hysterical outpourings without comment. Moon was vaguely aware, on the edge of his perception, that Raven was faintly shocked. The expulsion of the words alone was something of a release and once he'd got it all out, Moon lay weeping against Raven's side.

"You should have said something before," Raven said. He sighed. "This is my fault. I should have noticed. I should have been caring for you, as Snake wanted me to."

"I knew this would happen," Terez said darkly. "It's like a curse."

"Neither of them gave in to it," Raven said in a rather sharp tone. It was clear he and Terez had discussed the matter of Moon and Tyson.

Raven took Moon's head in his hands and made him look at him. "I didn't teach you well, did I? I'm sorry. This is normal, Moon. It's just part of life. You fixed yourself on somehar and it didn't happen. This is the result." He let go of Moon and said to Terez. "Would you mind . . . ?" He jerked his head in the direction of Moon's camping site.

Terez shook his head. "Of course not." He began to head to the place where Moon had tried to sleep.

"No," Raven said. "Go to Ty, Terez. I think you should."

Terez nodded. He went off into the trees, to the spot where Tyson had pitched his bivouac, some distance from the others.

"Are you okay with this?" Raven asked Moon.

Moon now thought he had made too much of a fuss and felt stupid. He knew that Raven meant to take aruna with him, and part of him was embarrassed by the whole thing, while another part of him was relieved. "Don't let me be ouana," he said. "I'm afraid of what I'll be. I can feel it like a dark tornado. It's worse than an earthquake."

"That's Uigenna blood for you," Raven said. "Keep to your own, Moon. Forget these Gelaming."

"You are with one."

"That's different, and you know it. Tyson is a fool."

"He's only doing what Terez wants him to."

"I don't know what he's doing," Raven said dryly, "but I think it's more do with himself than anyhar else."

Moon didn't entirely agree with this, and for some reason felt he should spring to Tyson's defense, but said nothing. He knew only one thing: Raven was right about the Uigenna blood. He remembered the story of his parents and it filled him with dread. He was horrified to think he might have followed a similar path. Still, Raven had the power to heal and used it wisely. Once it was over, Moon felt more like himself again and deeply ashamed. "How do we control it?" he asked Raven. "That feeling. It's evil. It's so selfish."

Raven held him close and said, "You were led on, Moon."

"No, I wasn't. It's in me. It scares me."

"Try to forget him," Raven said. "I know it's easy for me to say, but I'll help you. When we get to Galhea, find some new friends, some nearer your own age."

"I love him," Moon said, and it felt like the biggest confession in the world.

Raven made a soft sound and kissed the top of Moon's head. "You're young," he said. "You'll heal yourself of it. In years to come, when you look back, it won't seem real."

At least Raven hadn't denied Moon's feelings or tried to tell him they were something else. "You are with the one you loved years ago," Moon said. "That happened for you."

"Sometimes the universe is kind," Raven said. "Sometimes, it forgives. Sometimes, things just aren't meant to be and then the universe will do all that it can to prevent anything happening. Tyson identifies with his hostling too much. He's reliving a history he never had and yet at the same time he's fighting it. You're well out of that, Moon. Take my advice: keep far away. The thing that keeps you apart is your guardian spirit."

Moon buried his face in Raven's braids and inhaled their dark, buttery, musky perfume. "You're so different now," he said.

For the rest of the journey, it was testament to Raven's and Terez's generosity that they took their wayward companions in hand and spent less time with each other than they wanted to. Terez generally rode on ahead with Tyson, while Raven hung back with Moon and tried to keep him in good spirits. He taught

Moon a lot of old songs, spiritual ones from before he was har, which his family used to sing. Every evening, he'd ask Moon if he wanted to be alone that night or needed company. Moon took advantage of the offer only when he was afraid the bad feelings would come back. He didn't want to be in the way of Raven's newfound happiness. He realized that the best thing to come out of the whole sorry situation was that he and Raven had become close. Even though they occasionally shared a bed, Raven felt like family, the nearest Moon had had to a hostling. Moon learned to love him, but not in the way he loved Tyson. He was looking forward to telling Snake about all this. He was looking forward to Snake seeing how much Raven had changed.

Tyson, on the other hand, failed to find any positive aspects in the situation. He felt torn apart, faintly ridiculous, and full of bitter regret. Terez had said nothing aloud to condemn him, but Tyson was aware of an air of contempt in Terez's manner. Tyson had done what he could to earn Terez's approval, but in the event, he might as well have not bothered. Terez held him responsible for Moon's feelings, and clearly had very little regard for Tyson's own. Now, the possibility of him and Moon ever being together seemed shattered. It was all a horrible mess that made him wince with shame. Like the others, he hadn't considered Moon's state of mind. He'd thought only about himself and with more than a faint whiff of burning martyr. He wanted to forget the whole thing, but on those occasions when his gaze accidentally scraped across the space that Moon occupied in the world, he was filled with painful longing. He knew now it wasn't about aruna. It was about taking the hand of a har he adored and saying, "This is you and me against the world. Together, we are bigger than we are when we're apart. You are the sun that keeps my world alive." Moon's youth no longer seemed an impediment. It was the magic of wonder, a rejuvenating balm, and for the sake of nothing, Tyson felt he had denied himself this miracle for all time. The last leaves falling from the trees were the last tears. Beyond them, lay winter, barrenness, and cold.

When Moon first saw his father again, he was surprised to see how much better Snake looked. The Parsics had given him healing and although they couldn't mend his body completely, they had taken away a lot of the pain and stiffness, which meant that Snake could move more easily. He stood taller and now he never covered his seeing Eye. There was an emotional reunion with Raven, during which Snake shed tears of happiness. It seemed that everyhar, but for Moon, had seen their lives transform into a wondrous new territory. Hope, strength, and harmony filled the air. Whatever problems the Tigron might have, this company of forceful souls must be able to help him vanquish any danger.

The Tigron's family remained in Galhea only for a few more days, before Pellaz summoned more *sedim* so that the five of them could travel to Immanion swiftly. The days were so filled with social gatherings and trips to view particular sites of interest that they passed for Moon in a whirl. He barely caught sight of Tyson, who disappeared into the depths of Forever, or else into town, and did not reemerge. Moon had to meet so many new hara that some of his emotional pain inevitably subsided. He made particular friends with Aleeme, the consort of Swift's son Azriel, and spent one unforgettable night with both of them in their bedroom, during which he learned so many astonishing things that hara could do together, it made him laugh aloud at odd moments for several days afterward. He said nothing to Azriel or Aleeme about his feelings for Tyson, and even managed to stop himself asking any questions. He knew that Raven was right. He should forget about Tyson. It would never have worked.

If only we'd had just that one night, Moon thought. *It would have been enough. Now, I will never know.*

He thought the pain afterward would have been worth it.

On their last night in Galhea, Cobweb threw a party in the style of which only he was capable. The house heaved with guests and there was so much food and drink Moon was sure that most of it would go to waste. Visitors came from near and far, and Moon was intrigued to meet his father's sister Mima, who arrived with Aleeme's parents from Roselane in Jaddayoth. The Cevarros sat together, a captivating and raucous tribe. But there was no Cal and there was no Tyson. There were holes in the gathering that no amount of laughter and wine could fill.

All evening, Moon felt his eyes drawn again and again to a particularly beautiful har, who appeared to be a friend of Cobweb's although he was considerably younger. Moon even entertained the idea, fueled by wine, that he might strike up conversation with this har very soon. He might as well attempt to make his last night in Galhea as memorable as he could. He was about to ask Aleeme who the har was, and had even leaned across the table to do so, when his heart almost froze. Tyson had come into the room. He looked heartbreakingly gorgeous, dressed in black leather trousers and a soft white shirt, his hair clean and sleek. All of Moon's feelings for him came back in an unwelcome and instantaneous flood. Tyson stood in the doorway for some minutes, while Moon debated with himself whether he should go over and speak. Was there a possibility they could remain friends? Aleeme and Azriel had already invited Moon back to Galhea at some time in the future. If he was to accept their invitation, then surely it would be more comfortable for everyhar if he and Tyson were on speaking terms. But before he made a decision, the har he'd been eyeing up all evening left the table and went to where Tyson stood at the threshold. Moon's chilled heart went even colder. He saw this har reach out and touch Tyson's face, and he did not pull away.

Moon grabbed Aleeme's arm. "Who is that?" he demanded, pointing.

Aleeme appeared bemused and puzzled, then said, "Oh, him? That's Ferany. He's Ty's chesnari, or was. Nohar really knows what's going on between them now."

It was blindingly apparent to Moon what was going on.

"Why?" Aleeme asked.

Moon shrugged. He turned away, but not before he saw Tyson and Ferany embrace to share breath, not before he saw that Tyson was gazing right at him over Ferany's shoulder.

"Moon?" Aleeme said cautiously. "What is it? You look very strange."

"Nothing," Moon said. "Really, nothing."

Aleeme stared at him hard for some moments, and in that time, Moon believed his new friend intuited a little of what was going on. "You will come back, won't you?" Aleeme said.

Moon smiled with difficulty. "Yes, I want to."

"Will you talk to us then? About the things you've not told us and maybe should have done? Explain that look Tyson just gave you?"

Moon raised his eyebrows in what he hoped was a flirtatious manner, shrugged carelessly, and took another drink of wine. "Maybe. I'll see."

"Secrets," said Aleeme. "I love them."

CHAPTER NINETEEN

❯─┤◀❯─◆─❮◆├─❰

Moon came to believe that Immanion existed in a different time stream to the rest of the world. After living there a week, it felt like months had passed, and by the time the winter solstice festival arrived, he might as well have lived in the city all his life. Even so, it felt like there weren't enough hours in the day to accommodate all that he wanted, and was required, to do. Tutors came to his apartment in Phaonica for four hours every day, beginning after breakfast. These aloof hara instructed him in basic skills. In the afternoons, three days a week, Moon met for two hours with a high-ranking har who was in charge of his magical progression. In the City of Ghosts, nohar had been concerned with caste ascension: Moon didn't even know the names of the different levels. Now, the instruction he received astounded him. He'd had no idea Wraeththu could learn to become seers like Snake, and to manipulate energy and affect the world around them.

As well as these skills, Moon was trained in the art of controlling a *sedu* and the more taxing art of court etiquette. Pellaz might well have derived from a humble background himself, but now he held the reins of power in a tightly structured administration. He had been forced to learn quickly how to negotiate the twists and turns of Immanion's social complexities and clearly felt his brother's son, his sori, should be given a similar education.

It was obvious to Moon that not everyhar in Immanion approved of Pellaz bringing former relatives into the city; many frowned upon his desire to maintain contacts from his previous human existence. Perhaps, in seeing Pellaz dote upon his sori, many found themselves thinking wistfully of old family ties, and this bred resentment. Therefore, as Pellaz had done when Thiede had first brought him to the city, Moon had to be especially vigilant about how he behaved and what he said. Sometimes, alone at night, he became angry with himself for even caring about such things, but in the light of day it was almost impossible not to seek Pell's favor. A smile of approval from the Tigron of Immanion was like seeing a prayer answered before your eyes. Moon's old life in Megalithica became increasingly remote. He had been plucked from it, as Ember had once feared, and now he barely remembered how he had felt and what he'd believed.

Snake, meanwhile, did not fall completely beneath Immanion's spell. He was ill-at-ease in company and scornful of Pell's colleagues. He did not fit into the city's landscape particularly well and spent most of his time either alone or with his brothers. Moon was lucky if he saw his father once a day. He did make the effort to visit Snake's apartment in the palace whenever he could, even if only for an hour in the early evening. Most nights he was whisked out into the city night by hara who could not exactly be termed new friends, but who had an interest in him because of who he was. Moon was being trained for a position within the Hegemony Department of Buildings. Moon guessed that Pellaz didn't want him to leave the city long-term, such as if he'd been more attracted to the military, and had therefore been delighted to learn of Moon's interest in architecture. Sometimes, the way Moon's life had been taken over and changed was disorientating and frightening to him. Sometimes, it was wonderful.

Snake seemed appreciative of Moon's opinions and kept his own to himself. Moon knew that Pellaz was making his father work hard, because Snake often looked very tired, and on those days all the healers in Immanion could do nothing to ease the aches in his withered side. Moon himself had been taught healing techniques as part of his magical training, and whenever he could, he practiced them on his father. As to what Snake and Pellaz actually discovered from their work together, Moon remained unenlightened. On some level, he didn't want to know, because the idea of the Tigron being in any kind of trouble seemed unthinkable. Immanion was so huge and secure, as if it had stood for a thousand years. Nothing bad could touch it.

Often Moon thought of Tyson, even though he tried hard not to. Raven had attempted to speak to him about Tyson some weeks after they'd arrived in Immanion, but Moon didn't feel capable of discussing the matter. He felt strangely ashamed, as if his feelings were an unsavory secret he didn't want to share. Once he sneaked into the rooms that had belonged to Cal. The drapes were drawn against the windows, almost like an act of mourning, and Moon imagined that Pellaz must have done that. The air smelled of nothing, and what few possessions Cal had had still remained in the drawers and on the shelves. Despite this, Moon could sense no presence of another har in the rooms. He knew that Pellaz's security staff must have inspected it thoroughly and had perhaps wiped all etheric evidence of Cal away. It was hard to believe this enigmatic har had ever existed. Harder still to believe the story he'd once been told, in a dark old room that smelled of mildew, when a clean white flame that was a har from another world had turned the air to gold.

Soon after Snake had settled into the rooms in Phaonica that were too large and orderly for him, Pellaz took his brother to Caeru's apartment. Here, while Caeru sat on the terrace staring at the sea and thinking involuntarily of autopsies, Snake moved slowly from room to room, pausing in each one to close his eyes and draw in a deep breath. Pellaz said nothing, waiting at the threshold every time. In the place where Caeru had been attacked, Snake hunkered down, leaning on the new cane that Pellaz had given to him, which was crowned with a serpent's head. He put one brown hand flat against the floor and remained there for some minutes. When he opened his eyes, his golden eye glowed like a cat surprised in candlelight.

"Anything?" Pellaz asked softly.

Snake drew himself slowly to his full height, which even given his disabilities was taller than Pellaz. He nodded, his lower lip stuck out a little. "Yes," he said, still nodding. "It was here."

Pellaz already knew that and stifled the pang of impatience that shot through his chest. "Can you see . . . ?"

"I do believe the job was not quite finished," Snake pronounced.

Pellaz came fully into the room. He sensed a presence behind him and glanced around to find that Caeru had finally forced himself to face whatever might be revealed.

Snake tapped the floor with his cane, in the very spot where Caeru had struggled with his assailant. "Somehar came here to take the pearl, you don't need me to tell you that, but something happened they did not anticipate. Not here, but when they left this realm. Some residue of the event trickled back through. There was something else—a har? I'm unsure. They were hidden well, so well that their complete absence in this case reveals their presence."

Pellaz did not question Snake's assessment. He remembered what Cobweb had told him about his brother. "Is there anything we can do to find out more?"

"I will try," Snake said. "That is all that can be done." He limped to the doorway and Caeru shrank away. "Don't be afraid," Snake said to him. "Give me your hand."

"I don't want to see . . ." Caeru began.

"Do it," Pellaz commanded in the kind of smooth, even voice that cannot be disobeyed.

When Caeru tentatively extended one hand, Pellaz thought he could see the ghost of blood beneath his consort's fingernails, dark smears on the pale skin of his wrist. Caeru had closed his eyes, perhaps because he could see that too.

Snake took hold of Caeru's hand and drew in a slow deep breath. His brow furrowed. After some moments, he released his grip and shook his fingers as if to rid them of something noxious. "You are extraordinary," Snake said to Caeru. "You created within you something that many hara—and perhaps other creatures—want desperately. The moment of its conception was a shout to the world." He glanced at his brother. "Like the moment when you were born into this life another time."

"Who did it to me?" Caeru asked.

Pellaz already knew it was pointless to ask questions. Snake would reveal what he'd learned in his own time.

"Perhaps we should be asking 'what,'" Snake said. "Many things are unclear to me. Something took the pearl, and still has it, I'm sure, but I do not think it was the one who attacked you. They were responsible for removing it, yes, but they were interrupted in the otherlanes. The way they travel is different to using *sedim*. For this reason, the portal did not close up entirely immediately." He shook his head and then glanced at Pellaz. "I'm surprised your investigators didn't pick that up."

"They are not as adept as you," Pellaz said, "and from this moment I would very much like you to start training some of them."

"Cobweb would have found that," Snake said. "Instead, you went to all that trouble to hunt me down."

"Cobweb has great respect for you," Pellaz said. "He believes your skills far outrank his own. As you know, it was he who suggested I look for you."

Snake shrugged. "I admit the pieces of the puzzle fascinate me. If something did attack you in the otherlanes, was it Rue's attacker or the other shadowy presence? I will need to go deeper into the inner world to try and find out more."

"You look tired," Caeru said. "Don't do it yet. Rest awhile."

Snake smiled rather coldly. "I know that, tiahaar. I had no intention of working further today. I might be crippled but I'm not an idiot."

Caeru hadn't meant anything insulting in what he'd said, and Pellaz could see that his consort was stung by Snake's words. Caeru was easily hurt nowadays, even more so than before; his skin was as thin as a butterfly's wing. "And your condition is no excuse for being rude," Pell said lightly to Snake. "Rue meant no wrong, you know that."

"You haven't changed," Snake remarked and left the room.

"He has," Caeru said to Snake's retreating back, "more so than you."

Following this incident, Pellaz visited Sheeva in the Infirmary to ask if anything could be done for Snake's condition. "He feels it badly here in Immanion," Pellaz said. "He thinks we're all perfect."

"I could examine him," Sheeva said carefully.

Pellaz intuited that Snake would never agree to such a thing, mainly because he'd know what Pell had gathered from Sheeva's tone: nothing could be done.

Snake didn't like living in Immanion: he never would. The only time Pellaz had seen him relaxed was in Galhea. For this reason, he suggested that the Aralisians should spend the winter solstice at the House of Parasiel. "You could perhaps work with Cobweb," Pellaz said to Snake, "seeing as you think he was capable of seeing what you did. Together, you should make a formidable team."

"I never work with others," Snake said, "but I would like to return to Megalithica. I miss the air."

In Galhea, during the years of Varrish reign, the feast of the winter solstice had often been known simply as Festival, for the majority of Varrs had not been greatly spiritually inclined. But those of them who tended the land, and who were left alive after Ponclast was routed, were more in tune with the tides of the seasons, and the ancient rites of reverence were revived. For all, Festival became Natalia, celebrating the return of the light. On the night of the longest day, the dehar Solarisel gives birth to the pearl of Elisin, the child of light, Lord of the Sun. Solarisel's sleek white hounds streak across the sky baying out the news to the world, and in the morning harlings look for their slender footprints in the snow.

Even in the days of Terzian, Cobweb had always made sure that the winter festival was celebrated in full, following the ways of his own tribe, the Sulh. This tradition had expanded over the years. Now, on Natalia eve, virtually the whole of Galhea congregated at Forever. High-ranking hara gathered in the house, while others, including the human residents of the town, celebrated around a huge bonfire in the gardens, where the snow fell softly in pillowy flakes. The celebrants carried torches, their bodies wrapped up in thick coats. They sang new songs of the season that already sounded hundreds of years old. The air was full of the scent of cooking meat from the huge barbecue pits and the aroma of mulled sheh: apple liquor enlivened with the juice of oranges from the south, a sun fruit, symbolizing the return of the light.

Moon had imagined with dread and excitement that he'd see Tyson again, and was therefore both disappointed and relieved to hear he'd elected to accompany Ferany on a visit to some friends of Ferany's parents farther west. Moon knew how important it was to Cobweb to have his family around him at festival times, so he guessed Cobweb had also thought it would be for the best if Tyson was away during Moon's visit. Aleeme must have said something about his suspicions concerning Moon and Tyson. Both Azriel and Aleeme were keen to hear what further disclosures Moon might make on the subject, but he played it down. He felt embarrassed about it now.

It was clear to Moon that Snake felt far more at home in Galhea than he did in Immanion. He appeared less drawn and tense. At breakfast on the festival day, when everyhar rose late because of the previous night's party, Cobweb remarked on Snake's appearance in front of everyhar. "See how good the air here is for you? You are twice the har you were when you arrived two days ago."

Snake smiled, in a way Moon had rarely seen. "Forever has cast its spell upon me. I do feel better. The heat in Almagabra is too much to bear. I'm no longer used to a hot climate."

Cobweb was silent for a moment, then addressed Pellaz. "Here's a suggestion. Why doesn't Snake stay here for a while?" He glanced at Snake. "What do you think? You could continue your investigations and I could help you."

"Well . . ." Pellaz began, clearly the introduction to a refusal.

"An excellent idea," said Snake. "I would appreciate your help."

"You told me you always worked alone," Pellaz said.

Snake shrugged. "Usually . . ." He turned to Cobweb. "If you could find me a little house somewhere . . . I'm not a great one for company."

Moon caught Aleeme's eye and grinned. He had never seen Snake so animated.

"Raven will not want to leave Immanion because of Terez," Pellaz said. "And I certainly can't do without Terez."

"Raven has found a life for himself," Snake said. "I'm glad for him. I no longer need him to look after me. I'm sure that Cobweb will find hara who can tend to my modest needs."

"There is a house you could have," Cobweb said. "And it's in the grounds. It's an old lodge. We could renovate it. It'd be perfect."

"What about Moon?" Pellaz asked.

"I think Snake should stay here too," Moon said, thinking of how it would prevent Pellaz pushing his father too hard. "I can visit him here regularly, can't I?"

Pellaz appeared sour. "It seems to have been decided."

"Good," said Cobweb. "I'll take you over to the lodge later, Snake, so you can look around it."

Three days later, Moon returned to Immanion alone with the Tigron, who grudgingly accepted his brother's desires. Before they left, Aleeme drew Moon to one side in the stable yard, where the snow had been swept away. "Do you have a message?" he asked, stamping in the cold air to try to warm his feet.

Moon pretended ignorance. "What?"

"For Tyson. I wasn't supposed to tell you, because Cobweb says we shouldn't encourage you, but it took weeks for Ferany to persuade Tyson to go with him out west. Cobweb kept asking why he wouldn't agree to it and Tyson said it was because he didn't want to leave the family at Natalia. Cobweb didn't accept that, because he knows Tyson gets bored at big family functions. We all think he wanted to see you. I don't know what the fuss is about. Why can't you see each other? So, any message?"

"Just say . . . hello," Moon said, awkwardly.

Aleeme raised his eyebrows. "Can't you do better than that? We're starved of gossip here."

"He's with Ferany," Moon blurted. "What else can I say?"

"Ferany is a convenience," Aleeme said, then rolled his eyes. "Listen to me! I shouldn't say these things. Will you be back soon?"

"Maybe," Moon said. "I'll come to visit Snake."

"I think it'll work out one day," Aleeme said. "Between you and Ty. I just have a feeling."

Moon smiled with difficulty. He couldn't imagine such a day. "Just tell him I said hello."

CHAPTER TWENTY

>—+—◆>—●—<◆+—<

Ponclast did not reveal his feelings to Diablo, but he was extremely anxious about the reaction of their new allies once they discovered he had failed to take the pearl, never mind devour it. He was prepared for a fight, and intended to speak out on Diablo's behalf, in case he should be given the blame. It was wrong that they had been allowed to proceed without foreknowledge that there might be opposition to their plans. Diablo could very easily have been killed, and as Ponclast had become fond of him, he was angry about that. He had not been told how to communicate with his allies, but neither was he prepared to wait for them to contact him.

Ponclast spent a lot of time with Diablo now, but sent him from the cave in order to work alone. He took himself into trance and hit the ethers with a loud call. *I don't summon you, fair enough. But hear this!*

It is very dangerous to shock a har out of trance, especially when his mind is extended far into the ethers. But Ponclast was ripped from his meditation by a sharp slap across the face. It felt as if his lungs filled with icy water and he fell into a fit of coughing. He opened his eyes, wondering what har had the effrontery and courage to strike him. But what stood before him was not har. He saw only what appeared to be a small human girl child, who was clearly not really human because she had blue skin and hair. Her eyes were white, with pinpricks of azure in their centers.

"We do not obey a summons!" she said in a petulant yet proud tone. "You've been told that."

"I have information for you," Ponclast answered, his head still reeling. "Something has stolen the pearl. My son was attacked in the spirit paths and nearly died."

"We know of that," said the child. "The matter is now out of your hands. Think no more of it."

"Actually, I cannot accept that," Ponclast said, realizing he felt brave because of the apparently fragile form of the entity before him. He also realized this bravado might not be sensible. "Who attacked Diablo? Who else wants the pearl?"

"We are not prepared to give you this information. You cannot ask questions. Be thankful our masters do not blame you for the episode. Their retaliation is swift, if needed."

"You said you would help me. Will this still occur?"

"Yes. Presently, you will leave this forsaken place. We have a use for you in this realm. You will be given a *teraph,* which is an entity that will carry you through the spirit paths."

"Like the Gelaming use *sedim?*"

"The *teraphim* are kin to the *sedim.*"

"I wish to return to my fortress, Fulminir, to rebuild it."

"Where you go is your decision. Attack your enemies as you see fit. Our desire is only that you do what you do best, and most effectively. You will receive further instructions at a later time."

"That is satisfactory. One thing I must ask. Is there any danger to me, or my hara, from what attacked Diablo? If so, you must warn me of it, protect me."

"It will not come for you here. It did what it wanted to do."

"I see." Ponclast paused for a few moments, while the child stood passively before him. "Are you aware that the Tigron's son came to me? He assisted Diablo after he fell from the spirit paths."

"We have no interest in that. It is your affair. Use him as you see fit."

"I would appreciate your opinion. He carries the Tigron's blood, which presumably *is* of interest to you, seeing as you were keen to possess the pearl. I have wondered whether it might be of use to create a pearl myself with this har. It is, after all, one of the things I do most effectively, and Abrimel har Aralis is of far better stock than my poor ruined Varrs."

The child's strange blind-looking eyes widened. He could see he had pricked her interest. For some moments, she was silent, and Ponclast received the strong impression she was communicating with some other being. Eventually, she said, "We are told it would be pointless for you to do such a thing without the higher energy."

"What do you mean?"

"Hara use this energy, but you do not. You use something else."

"I don't understand you. Speak in terms I know."

"Learn to love," said the child. "Do not attempt to call us again." She vanished.

Learn to love? Ponclast snorted at the idea. He knew very well how to love. He loved all of his hara and believed it was this emotion that had helped keep them alive in Gebaddon. He could not, however, love a Gelaming, not in that way, but perhaps the blue child hadn't meant that. She had spoken of passion.

I remember that, Ponclast thought wistfully. *But what am I now to inspire passion in a harish breast?*

He sat and pondered for a while, recalling how just for a moment he had looked upon Abrimel with desire, only to be rewarded with an expression of revulsion in the Gelaming's horrified stare. How to change that? Presently, Ponclast came to a decision. He sent out a mind call to Diablo who came running at once.

"Diablo, my sweet, can you take me to the place where you found Abrimel har Aralis?"

Diablo narrowed his enormous eyes. "No. I cannot transport our hara from Gebaddon. I have tried to. There are limitations placed upon my abilities."

Ponclast was somewhat astounded his son had been conducting his own experiments in private. "You should have told me this before," he said. "But I'll overlook this secrecy for now. Bring Abrimel to me."

"At once."

Diablo did not exaggerate. He vanished before Ponclast could even draw breath to speak further.

The last time Ponclast had seen Abrimel, they had parted with the understanding that Abrimel would provide information as and when the Teraghasts needed it. Ponclast had felt strangely soiled by his brief union with the Tigron's son. Possibly, this was because when he'd lain against that perfect body he'd been reminded too painfully of his own condition, and that of his hara. He had decided not to see Abrimel again and that Diablo must deal with the Gelaming when necessary. Now, that decision had to be revised. He must proceed with caution. Even though Fulminir was no doubt as much of a ruin as Ponclast thought himself to be, the disaffected son of the Tigron might well be tempted by the offer of becoming the consort of the har who would rebuild it. He could help destroy the Gelaming, and his ignorant parents, who had no idea what danger their indifference might have put them in. *That is the way,* Ponclast thought. He would appeal to Abrimel's bitterness and resentment. He would be sympathetic. He would remember the art of seduction.

CHAPTER TWENTY-ONE

It began with a communications breakdown. Cobweb was naturally suspicious of Gelaming technology and never used the psycaller device in Forever to contact Immanion. If he needed to speak to Pellaz, he would walk the Tigron's dreams. Swift was generally the only har who used the psycaller, and in all truth it had gathered a layer of dust, somewhere beneath a pile of papers in Swift's office.

But one particular evening, late in the spring of ai-cara 32, Cobweb asked his son to send a message to Phaonica. His instincts urged him to do it, although at the time he voiced the request, it seemed merely mundane: invite the Tigron to Galhea for the summer solstice. He could bring Moon and Raven, because Snake would no doubt like to see them.

Swift went to do this at once, but his efforts to use the psycaller came to nothing. He returned to the sitting room, where Cobweb was conversing after dinner with Azriel and Aleeme, and said, "It's strange. I can't get through."

Cobweb experienced a brief but telling chill throughout his flesh. "I will attend to it," he said, his words imbued with the unspoken message that Gelaming devices were unreliable and suspect. "We have the natural ability to communicate over distance, so we might as well use it."

"Not *that* much distance," Aleeme said.

Cobweb did not respond. He went directly to his room, drew the drapes over the windows, and lit three candles. He composed himself cross-legged on the floor and closed his eyes. Drawing in deep breaths, he was for a moment gripped by a bizarre thought: he would change. He would have to become something different.

Dismissing this to analyze later, Cobweb descended into trance. For him, it was as simple as diving smoothly into a deep dark pool: he caused barely a ripple. He swam through the ethers, as was his usual practice, to discern any nuances or messages that might float there for him to pick up. But that night, he found not the familiar mindscape he knew, but an unknown and impassable territory. The ethers were disturbed. It was as if they had been ravaged by a mighty storm of energy so that all the usual channels were blocked or hidden.

Shaken, Cobweb brought himself back to normal consciousness. Instinctively, he went to the window and threw open the drapes. He peered through the darkness, searching for he knew not what. The night was calm, the air breathless. Perhaps it was too still out there for comfort. He could see himself reflected in the window: a slender har, shawled in dark hair, his loose trousers and shirt glowing pale in the dark. He looked at himself and, for a stultifying moment, saw a human woman looking back. That was what Terzian had made of him, this virtual "she." He felt she might be about to die.

Some of the curtain hooks ripped from their rings as Cobweb fiercely closed the drapes once more. His entire being was filled with terrible foreboding. *Too long have we hidden,* he thought. *Too long have we gazed into painted mirrors.*

Around him, the house felt uneasy and skittish, its timbers groaning, its pipes shuddering. Outside, the night hounds began to bay all at once, an ululating cry rising and falling in alarm. Cobweb ran down to where members of his family still sat together. They looked up in surprise as he burst into the room, for Cobweb was a har who usually moved slowly and with grace. "Summon the Watch, Swift," Cobweb snapped. "Have Ithiel check the gardens."

Swift got to his feet, while Azriel said, "What's wrong?"

"Much as it pains me to admit it, your Gelaming device wasn't at fault," Cobweb replied. "The ethers are closed to me too. The dogs are howling."

"I heard that," Aleeme said, "but sometimes they do just howl."

Cobweb fixed Swift with a stare. "Summon the Watch," he said again. "Something isn't right."

The night hounds were virtually choking themselves upon their chains trying to break free, until Ithiel ordered them to be loosed. They streaked out into the night, chasing shadows. Hara on horseback went after them, only to find nothing amiss.

While the search was under way, Cobweb stood before the long windows in the sitting room, rubbing his arms for they were cold, despite the fire burning hungrily in the hearth nearby. He felt powerless, and that was not a comfortable feeling for him. Something was going on and he had no idea what it was, only that it stank of threat. When Swift returned to the house to report on his findings, Cobweb said to him, "Summon Seel and Tyson from the town. Bring them home. Do it now."

Swift did not question his hostling's command.

It was Cobweb's custom to allow other hara, such as his son, his highson, and their militia to deal with matters of security. His job was to run the household, to care for others. But that night, Cobweb found himself thinking of Caeru har Aralis, and what had happened to him in his own home. He knew that sometimes the ouana-might of the more masculine-aspected hara was of no use in matters of protection.

Cobweb went to the kitchens and the small room where boots and coats were stored. He dressed himself for the outside and then went to the stables. There were no grooms on duty at that hour, so he saddled his horse himself, something he had not done for many years. It reminded him of times long past, fleeting images of a different life, when he had spent more time on horseback than on the ground. He remembered his life with the Sulh, and the acrid smoke of ruin always on the air. Humanity was contained now, and the green had crept back with subtle fingers over most of their civilization. The world breathed more easily, but that night Cobweb's breath was all but stilled in his breast. He feared history was a tidal wave and it was coming back, hundreds of feet high.

All the animals were stamping restlessly in their stalls, grunting and snorting. Cobweb mounted his horse and urged it to gallop out into the night. A wind had started up, strangely warm. Snake Jaguar now lived comfortably in the house in the woods, quite near the garden walls: once it had been a lodge to the main house when humans had occupied it. He was reclusive, which the Parasilians respected. Sometimes, he turned up at Forever seeking company, and on those occasions he was welcomed and indulged, but there was an unspoken rule between them all. Snake's privacy was not be intruded upon. Quite often, Raven and Terez came to visit him and sometimes the three of them would socialize with the House of Parasiel, but the times when Pellaz visited Snake alone meant the door would be securely locked against others.

Cobweb knew that Moon visited his father too, and then Azriel and Aleeme would be invited to dinner to the house in the woods, but Moon seemed reluctant to visit Forever. Cobweb knew the reason behind this, but believed that time was a great healer. Moon must get over his childish crush. In Cobweb's opinion, Tyson was not chesnari material, not yet. His ongoing behavior with Ferany was testament to this: Cobweb had spent many evenings listening patiently to Ferany's heartfelt outpourings of disappointment and complaint.

Snake spent his time traveling the ethers, seeking any information that might be helpful to his brother. So far as Cobweb knew, Snake had yet to discover anything of use, and he had carefully sidestepped most of Cobweb's offers of assistance. They had worked together on a couple of occasions, at Forever, but Cobweb could tell that Snake preferred to work alone. Whatever threat had loomed over Immanion had either sensed Snake's investigation and gone into hiding or else had disappeared. Cobweb knew Snake was not unhappy, that he enjoyed the simple life so close to the fecund earth. In Galhea, Snake had found peace. Raven was no longer there to care for him, but he did not need such care. Healers had assuaged the aches in his withered limbs and he was mobile enough to look after a small garden and no domestic chores were beyond him, other than chopping wood. Cobweb had logs delivered regularly to the little clearing where Snake's house stood. Cobweb had never visited since the days when he'd supervised its refurbishment. Now, he had a pressing need.

Dim light glowed from one of the windows. Cobweb dismounted and went to knock upon the front door. He knocked several times and then called, "Snake, it's me, Cobweb. I have to speak with you at once."

Cobweb heard movement inside the lodge and presently Snake opened the door. His expression was guarded, but Cobweb was not deceived. He could tell that Snake feared this was bad news about Moon, for what else could impel a Parasilian to come riding to his house in the dark?

"It is not as you fear," Cobweb said, crossing the threshold. "Moon is fine, but I must speak to you urgently."

Snake nodded silently and indicated for Cobweb to enter the small room, which served as both kitchen and parlor.

"Have you noticed anything unusual tonight?" Cobweb asked, sitting down in one of the two chairs before the stove.

Snake limped over with a kettle of water, which he placed on the hot plate. "I was wrapped up in reading," he said, and gestured at the pile of books, which he had taken from Forever's library last time he'd visited. "The knowledge of our forebears shouldn't be lost. There is much wisdom there."

Snake was the only har Cobweb knew who referred to humans as forebears. "The ethers are disturbed," Cobweb said. "There's a shiver in the air.

Something smells dank. Animals are fretful. I would appreciate you investigating this phenomenon and giving me your opinion on it."

"There will always be nights like this," Snake said. "You know that. It is the way of wyrd, when forces move in the world beyond our comprehension. But they are a part of the world and not to be feared."

"This is different," Cobweb said. "I know *that*."

Snake again nodded without speaking and went slowly to his front door. Cobweb waited while Snake peered into the night, no doubt extending his senses. After a while, Cobweb could not resist making tea, because the kettle had begun to boil, and Cobweb's instinct was to do such things. He was drinking the tea when Snake returned, frowning.

"You're right," Snake said. "Tonight, I was lost in the world of the past, and didn't sense it."

"What does it mean?" Cobweb asked.

Snake shook his head slowly in puzzlement. "Many things," he said unhelpfully.

"In your opinion, is this connected with Phaonica or the Aralisians, anything to do with what Pellaz has experienced?"

"It's difficult to tell. There's certainly a taint to the air, and it feels familiar, but it is also shrouded. Something or somehar is aware of us and our abilities. We should be vigilant. It's all we can do."

"I don't think that's enough," Cobweb said. "I feel it in my bones. I want to contact Pell about this, but it's impossible. I'm concerned this is a deliberate attempt to prevent us communicating with Immanion. The otherlanes are closed to us."

"We can work together, you and I, to create a barrier of protection around your domain," Snake said. "That's the immediate course of action that suggests itself to me."

"We'll do this," Cobweb said. "Tomorrow, Swift must send riders to Imbrilim." He paused. "I'm afraid, Snake. I never feel afraid like this. Something approaches."

Snake was not a har to extend a reassuring hand. Instead he said, "We will do all in our power to protect ourselves, and what greater power is there in the world than you and I combined?" He smiled, and then sat down carefully.

"Shall I send healers tomorrow?" Cobweb asked, expecting a rebuke or a refusal.

Snake grimaced. "Yes," he said.

"You shouldn't wait," Cobweb said. "When the pain returns, you should come to us. It's senseless to suffer needlessly."

"I don't often notice it," Snake said. "But when it gets too bad, I come to Forever. Say nothing more."

"Let me help you now, before we work."

"No," Snake said. "Tomorrow will be soon enough."

Cobweb knew that Snake did not want to be touched, especially by hara he knew well, other than his immediate family, with whom he was quite affectionate. Except for them, he tolerated only the hands of the healers. It was clear to Cobweb that Snake feared being close to hara, mostly because of his disabilities. Perhaps deeper, less visible hurts were equally responsible. But despite whatever demons might cackle deep in Snake's mind, he was a pleasure to work with. When he and Cobweb sat together and extended their senses, it created a source of power that was easy to manipulate and project. If Snake's body rejected contact, his mind did not. The barrier they created took much energy, but once they came back to normal consciousness, Cobweb did not feel depleted. Snake was all that Cobweb had intuited him to be: a psychic of immense power, who could shape the energy of creation as easily as river clay. Cobweb could see virtually with his physical eyes the dome of silver-white energy they had conjured into being. It would take a power of equal force to breach it.

"The barrier will decay over time," Snake said. "We'll have to replenish it for as long as we need to."

"I hope that the Gelaming will help us," Cobweb said. "I'm not content with simple protection. I want to know what threatens us and why. We should seek its face."

"I will go to Pellaz," Snake said. "He will hear me."

"You can't," Cobweb said. "The route is closed."

Snake smiled again. "I will go to him," he said. "When out of my body, I can climb the highest, darkest mountain. I can break through walls of rock. It will take time perhaps, but I'm confident. Trust me."

Cobweb returned to Forever to find that the household had retired for the night. He'd spent more time in Snake's lodge than he'd thought. Before retiring himself, Cobweb walked through the house, entering every room. At the windows and thresholds, he drew symbols of protection in the air, and all the time the bones of the house creaked and groaned around him.

The stairway looked long and dark, the corridor above wreathed in shadow. Cobweb ran up the stairs, his flesh prickling. He did not like to feel the house so disturbed. It should be a safe haven and that night it did not feel safe, despite all the precautions he'd taken. He went to his room and gratefully opened the door. Beyond, a dim lamp was lit next to the bed, and a shadowy figure stood in the bay of the window.

Cobweb was momentarily paralyzed. He remembered the nights when Terzian had come to him in that room, and had stood looking out of the window in just that way, his hands clasped behind his back.

"Swift . . ." Cobweb said, and waited for the figure to turn to him, to reveal itself as known and ordinary. But instead, he found himself looking only at an empty space. There was nohar there.

That night, he dreamed of Terzian. In the dream Terzian was not dead. He came back to Forever, having been lost on a long journey. He said to Cobweb, "You have betrayed me. I will not forgive you. I must take from you all that you love."

And Cobweb saw a hill where once a home had stood, and it had become a pyre, its summit a mass of roaring flame.

Tyson could not feel things the way Cobweb did. He was impatient with having been hauled from a convivial evening at the barracks in Galhea and could see no reason for it. Cobweb was spooked. So what? Seel had been visiting friends, and he also appeared to be slightly put out at having been ordered home. For once, Seel and Tyson were in accord.

"What's this all about?" Tyson asked Seel.

Seel shrugged. "Can't say. I hope that Cobweb is wrong, that's all. We should all hope that."

In the morning, all seemed normal. Tyson went down to the dining room for breakfast where Cobweb, Swift, and Seel had already gathered. "Has the storm of ghosts passed?" Tyson asked Cobweb.

"The air feels a little better today," Cobweb said. "Take that look off your face, Ty. I wasn't wrong last night."

Tyson sat down. "I was on a winning streak at cards when I was dragged back here. The next time I might not be so lucky and I shall hold you responsible."

"If that's the worst that can come from last night, I will be happy," Cobweb said. "Where are Azriel and Aleeme?"

"Sleeping late," Swift said. "Perhaps they were on ghost watch all night."

Tyson laughed and even Seel grinned into his coffee.

"Go and rouse them, Ty," Cobweb said.

Tyson rolled his eyes, "Oh, for the Ag's sake, why? Let them sleep."

"Tyson!"

Tyson sighed and got to his feet. "Okay, okay, I'm going."

At Azriel's door, Tyson knocked and called out, "Stop whatever you're doing, if you're doing anything. Cobweb has summoned you."

No voices answered him.

Tyson knocked again. "Az?"

Again, silence. Tyson opened the door. It took a moment for what he saw to register. He didn't go inside.

Tyson's feet barely touched the stairs as he ran back to the dining room. "Swift!" he cried.

Swift was on his feet in an instant and together he and Tyson ran back upstairs. They didn't speak. They didn't need to.

The room was a mess. All the windows were broken and ragged drapes flapped against the shattered frames. Half the furniture was turned over, and the floor was covered in ripped bedclothes and shards of glass. The bare mattress was daubed in gouts of red.

"Search," Swift said.

Tyson obeyed this command without question. He felt light-headed. This wasn't real.

Cobweb and Seel appeared at the threshold and Cobweb uttered a strange hoarse cry.

"They're not here," Swift said. "They're not here."

"This isn't possible," Seel said. "Where are they? What happened?"

"Your father . . ." Cobweb said. He was hanging on to the door frame as if he were trapped on a sinking ship.

"What?" Swift barked.

Cobweb shook his head. "He was here. Your father."

"No," Swift said. "No ghost did this. Stop it, Cobweb." He rubbed his face with both hands. "Did any of you hear anything last night?"

"No," Seel said. "Nothing."

Swift touched the broken window frame. "Somehar or something broke in, that's obvious. Why didn't we hear anything?"

"Oh, God," Seel said, using an oath that was little heard nowadays. "It's happened again."

"What?" Swift snapped. "Speak."

"When Cal killed Orien . . . In Saltrock. None of us heard it. It was like a bewitchment."

"No!" Swift said. "Not that. No more of that. The past is done. This is now. Tyson?"

"What are you asking me?"

"You and I are the only ones not squirming beneath a ton of history," he said. "What do you think? Tell me."

"I think somehar broke in and . . . oh, how should I know? Have they been kidnapped, murdered?"

Swift pushed past the others, making for the stairs. "We'll search the grounds. Come. Hurry. All of us. I'll fetch Ithiel."

The search revealed nothing more than Snake, who was making his way in painful slowness to Forever. Cobweb, who was searching with Swift and Tyson, met him beneath the yews in the gardens. Cobweb went to him at once, in such a state he didn't register the fact that touch-resistant Snake took hold of his hands.

"What has happened?" Snake demanded. "I feel it. What has happened?"

Cobweb explained as succinctly as he could.

Snake nodded, his expression grim. "It has come," he said. "Our barrier was no match for it."

"What?" Swift demanded.

"An opposing force," Snake said shortly, releasing Cobweb's hands. "An enemy. It comes from the otherlanes. We were negligent last night, Cobweb. The threat was greater than either of us thought. We didn't do enough, didn't investigate the matter as fully as we should have done. We shouldn't have slept. The danger came when we were not alert."

"That's my thought too," Cobweb said. "I'm furious with myself, but that changes nothing. Now we must decide how to act."

"Why take Azriel and Aleeme?" Swift asked. "What is the motive? Ransom?"

"A warning," Snake said. "That is my opinion. Kind of them. Or perhaps it is simply arrogance."

"They could be dead," Cobweb said bitterly. "I can't tell."

"If murder had been the objective, surely they'd have left the bodies for us to find," Swift said. "No, I think we must assume that Azriel and Aleeme have been taken as currency."

Snake made a growling sound in his throat. "You're right. Muster your forces, Lord Swift. Secure your domain and prepare yourself."

"For what? Attack? But from whom?"

"It will begin here," Snake said, "but I believe the real focus is Immanion. Galhea is its strongest ally. Subjugate Parasiel, then move on Imbrilim, and you destroy the heart of the Gelaming's hold in this country. From there, with otherlane access, the way to Almagabra lies open to you."

"Who are these enemies?" Swift demanded. "Do they have the use of *sedim*? Does that imply they are rogue Gelaming?"

"They're not Gelaming, as far as I can tell," Snake said. "My thought is that some remnants of Varr or Uigenna have found their way to a power none of us believed they'd ever possess."

"How?"

"If I knew that, I would tell you," Snake said coldly. "I'm not sure, in any case. It's just a theory. I, more than any of you, know how what is left of my tribe view the Gelaming. Only months ago, I would cheerfully have joined a campaign to oust them myself!"

"Did you contact Pell last night?" Cobweb asked.

Snake frowned. "I don't know. I tried as best I could. I just hope the message got through." He smiled without humor. "I am arrogant myself. I thought that no barrier could hold me back. I was wrong. However, the Gelaming use the otherlanes all the time. We can only trust they have encountered the same phenomenon and are alerted, as we were."

"I will send a party to Imbrilim today," Swift said. "We cannot rely on vague hopes."

"Is there really any evidence of an imminent attack?" Tyson asked. "This could be a personal issue, somehar who has a grievance against our House."

"If that's the case, they also have a grievance against the House of Aralis," Snake said. "The taint I feel in the air around me is the same I felt in the apartment of the Tigrina. I also feel power massing. It creeps upon us like a slow-moving storm. It's a hurricane over the waters of the otherlanes and soon it will break against the land." He turned to Cobweb. "We have much work to do today. I want to see the faces of our enemies. Then we are in a better position to help Azriel and Aleeme, supposing they still live. Help me to the house."

CHAPTER TWENTY-TWO

Immanion's discovery of the strange otherlane phenomenon was, in fact, far more dramatic than that of Galhea's. As Snake had pointed out, the Gelaming used the otherlanes continually. Therefore, when the blast of hostile energy blocked and destroyed the most familiar of its labyrinthine paths, many Gelaming were in transit. Some were expelled into earthly reality instantaneously, while others were less fortunate. Some were trapped in trackless void, and yet more were killed, the atoms of their being blown apart by the searing energy that hit them. The screams of the *sedim* gushed out of the otherlanes and rattled the towers of Phaonica. Every har in the city was shaken awake in his bed. The Gelaming woke from dreams into nightmare, into paralyzing fear. Heads sizzled with pain, limbs were numb. Something terrible had happened.

Eyra Fiumara was the member of the Hegemony whose responsibilities revolved mainly around otherlane traffic. His staff was called the Listeners, sensitives of Algoma caste, whose inner eyes and ears were finely tuned to the ethers. Eyra was the greatest of Immanion's seers and he turned up at Pell's apartment in Phaonica before the Tigron had even gathered his wits enough to summon him. The Listeners were already busy working on the problem, trying to unblock the otherlanes in order to rescue trapped Gelaming and discover who or what had instigated the obstacles.

Pellaz received Eyra in his dressing room, still wearing his night robe. "What has caused this?" Pellaz demanded. "We know so little of the other-lanes. Thiede took too much of his knowledge with him, never having shared it. Is this a natural phenomenon, a disaster that was waiting to happen?"

"That is not my belief," Eyra said. "Something has shaken the otherlanes, but from those who managed to escape I've learned they felt a rush of hostile force. It was like a blast of heat to them. They are lucky to be alive."

"Is there any indication where this hostility came from?"

"Not yet. The ethers are equally in chaos. We can't communicate with any of our settlements or allies. We are, in this instance, alone with the problem."

"It seems senseless to send ships to Megalithica to give and receive news," Pellaz said. "It would take weeks for them to reach it." He paused. "What of the *sedim*? Is there nothing we can learn from them?"

"The *sedim* have always kept their own counsel," Eyra replied. "They communicate with us only to the extent of enabling travel. If they have any other agenda, or even the ability to communicate with us fully, it is unknown."

Pellaz sat down, frowning. "If only we knew how Thiede acquired the *sedim,* or exactly where they came from." He glanced up at Eyra. "How many have we lost?"

"Sixteen," Eyra replied.

Pellaz shook his head and sighed. "That's far too many. We cannot replace them."

"We still have over five hundred, tiahaar."

"Five hundred that are apparently male so cannot breed. If we're under threat, it's not inconceivable an enemy has worked out that the most effective form of aggression would be to disable our transport system. If we lost the *sedim* we would lose much of our power and virtually all of our mobility. Think of our major settlements. Imbrilim, for example, would be alone, and most of its citizens are refugees, not military."

Eyra nodded thoughtfully. "The most distressing aspect of this whole business is that it seems likely somehar or something has access to the otherlanes without *sedim*. Of course, the threat itself might derive from some other realm. Our incursions into otherlane territory might be perceived as a form of aggression. We have no way of knowing."

Pellaz remembered when he and Mima had entered another realm via the otherlanes to rescue Lileem and Terez some years back. Nohar knew who or what had built the structures on that world. Perhaps, unwittingly, the invasive presence of Wraeththu had caused this problem. Perhaps the entity that had confronted Pellaz in the otherlanes more recently derived from that event.

"I had a strange experience in the otherlanes sometime back," Pellaz said. "I should have discussed it with the Hegemony, but I didn't foresee the seriousness of the situation. Terez and I were working to discover the cause of the problem, but everything had quietened down."

"It would perhaps have been wise to inform your colleagues," Eyra said carefully.

Pellaz ignored the implied criticism. "We have also to consider whether these events are connected with the attack upon Rue."

"It is feasible. Whatever attacked him was not of this realm, in my opinion."

"How can we defend ourselves?" Pellaz asked, thinking aloud. "We face an enemy that can perhaps strike at any time without warning. What should we expect now?"

"At the very least, we must construct firewalls of protective energy around the city," Eyra said. "We have to hope we are given breathing space, in order to plan and for my hara to conduct their investigations."

"Messengers must be sent out immediately to all towns and cities," Pellaz said. "If they have to ride to Jaddayoth and beyond, then so be it. Late news is better than no news at all. Everyhar in Wraeththudom must be warned to protect themselves in whatever way they can. We don't yet know how great this threat might be, so we should prepare for the worst. We must trust that the Kamagrian are also aware of this problem and are already working, as we are, to solve it."

Eyra bowed his head. "The Hegemony must meet as soon as possible. I have already sent messages to summon them."

"They won't need summoning," Pellaz said. "Go to the Hegalion. I'll meet with you there as soon as I can."

Eyra hesitated before leaving. "Tiahaar, I don't wish to offend you, but we should perhaps address the possibility that Tigron Calanthe's disappearance is associated with this disruption."

"I'm glad you don't want to offend me," Pellaz said. "I will see you shortly, Eyra."

Pellaz was still dressing when Caeru arrived in his apartments. The Tigron was in no mood to answer the Tigrina's questions, but bit his tongue and reminded himself that Caeru was as much a part of the Hegemony as he was. He relayed all he could remember of his conversation with Eyra, other than the final exchange about Cal.

After he'd finished speaking, Caeru was uncharacteristically quiet.

"What is it?" Pellaz asked. "What are you thinking? I can tell you're thinking something."

"I don't want to voice it," Caeru said. "But I know I must. Pell, how much can we trust the Hegemony?"

Pellaz stared at his consort in surprise. "What in the Aghama's name are you suggesting?"

Caeru took a deep breath before speaking. "That some members of the Hegemony are still resentful of the way Thiede brought you to power, that they are not completely trustworthy."

"What makes you think this? What have you heard?"

"It was something Velaxis said once."

"Something Velaxis said," Pellaz repeated in a scornful deadpan tone. "And you saw fit not to tell me this before?"

"I didn't think of it too deeply. At the time, you and I weren't speaking."

"What did Velaxis say?"

"I can't remember exactly."

"Should I have him arrested?"

"What? No! He is not your enemy. He's just very adept at getting information."

"Then perhaps you should apply yourself to a similar task," Pellaz said. "I have no time to consider this now. Will you undertake the responsibility? I'm not sure your suspicion has any grounds, but it would be stupid to ignore it."

Caeru nodded. "I will. I'll come to the Hegalion with you now. I can speak to Velaxis some time this morning. He will, of course, be there."

"I have something to attend to before I go," Pellaz said. "I'll meet you there."

"What are you going to do?" Caeru asked.

Pellaz held the Tigrina's gaze for some moments before answering. "Say nothing of this," he said at last. "I want to try and communicate with Peridot. I'm hoping the night's events will have shaken him enough to want to talk to me."

"You think he's really capable of that?" Caeru asked.

"I have to find out," Pellaz answered. "Now is the time to break down the barrier between the *sedim* and ourselves. If we lose them, we are easy meat for an enemy with otherlane transport."

Pellaz went to the stables where Peridot was housed. Phaonica kept two dozen *sedim* on the premises, although most of them were stabled in the barracks on the outskirts of the city. As Pellaz approached, he could sense the *sedim*'s unrest. It hung as the sour odor of sweat on the air, the sweat of terror. The sight of Peridot's huge powerful body trembling in his stall affected Pellaz greatly. The *sedu*'s coat was dark and wet. Froth hung from his nose.

Pellaz went up to him and caressed his ears. Peridot pressed his broad fore-head against the Tigron's chest. He uttered a low, grunting sound. "Hush," Pellaz said. "I am here. Let's go out together."

He opened the stable door and swung onto Peridot's back. They trotted out into the early dawn light, the city spread out below them. It looked so beautiful and peaceful, as if nothing could touch its marble towers. Pennants flew in the morning breeze, which carried the scent of the ocean to Phaonica's heights.

Pellaz urged the *sedu* to gallop from the city, out to the hills beyond. Peridot ran so fast it was as if he was trying to exorcise his fear, to burn off anger. Pellaz let him have his head, his hands buried deep in the *sedu's* thick mane. Eventually, Peridot came to a shuddering halt in a grove of poplars. He collapsed to his knees as Pellaz vaulted from his back. For some moments, Pellaz watched the creature. Peridot's sides were heaving and his eyes were closed, his chin resting on the ground. A horse in distress could not have emanated the intense emotional energy Pellaz felt streaming toward him.

The Tigron went to sit beside Peridot and stroked his flank. "It's time we spoke, you and I," he said.

Peridot held his breath. The air around them was perfectly still.

"I know you understand me," Pellaz said. "As I know that, for whatever reason, the *sedim* are content to work with and for us, though will not communicate with us fully. I do not ask for an explanation, Peridot. I ask only that now, in the face of whatever threatens us, we can work together for the safety of all, your kind and my own."

There was only silence, and Pellaz felt no hesitant touch in his mind.

"Why are you afraid?" he asked, in his head. "There is something that Wraeththu must not know, isn't there? Something that the *sedim* know."

He continued to stroke Peridot's damp coat, and then leaned forward to rest his head against it. "We have seen a lot together," he murmured. "I look on you as a friend, as more than a friend. Trust me now, great Peridot. I am a child in the face of your wisdom, I know, but I think we need each other."

Stand back!

The words came as a blast to Pell's mind. He jumped up at once and staggered backward.

Peridot rose slowly to his feet, and then shook his entire body. He tossed his head and uttered an unearthly screech, like that of some giant mythical bird. The air around him grew hazy, as a milky energy, shot with violet threads of light, formed around him. He was transforming.

Pellaz was filled with an indescribable horror. He had witnessed many unimaginable things in his life, but now he felt he was being faced with something that would be difficult to bear: Peridot's true form. He already knew that the *sedu* appeared only as a horse in this reality, as he'd beheld a strange transformation in the realm he'd visited with Mima. Also, in the otherlanes, to a trained consciousness, *sedim* appeared as formless vehicles of energy. But Pellaz knew he was about to be shown something different, something more real. He wanted to see it and yet he didn't. If you gaze upon the true face of the gods, you burn.

For some moments, he could see nothing but an immense ball of radiance before him, and then something stepped forth from it.

Pellaz dropped to his knees, hid his face. He began, uncontrollably, to weep, because he had never beheld anything so magnificent or so frightening. He wanted to run, but he could not move.

"Now you see," Peridot said to him. "Now you see."

"You are an angel," Pellaz said, his eyes still shut tight.

"Some have called us that. Gaze upon me, Tigron of Immanion. You called to me, now have the strength to face what you invoked."

Pellaz raised his head. His eyes were streaming and not just from emotion. The image before him was blurry: a radiant figure ten feet tall. "I can't look upon you," he said, turning his head away. "You know that."

"If any can, it is you," Peridot said. "But you have seen enough. Turn your head from me and speak your heart. In this form, I can speak to you in return. Is that not what you want?"

It took strength for Pellaz to speak, but perhaps there was not much time to ask all the questions that ranted inside him. "Yes. Tell me now. What threatens us?"

"An old bitter enemy," Peridot replied. "He aims to take what is yours, but he is twisted and guided by greater forces."

"Who?"

"He who was hidden in the forest. Lord of Varrs."

"Ponclast?" Pellaz exclaimed. For a moment he glanced at Peridot again, and then regretted it. His head spun and he turned away once more. "How is that possible?"

"Some secrets are not yours to own, in this life. I cannot give you all the knowledge you seek."

"Can you help us?"

"My brethren scream in torment. I cannot go to them. The ways are closed by those greater than I. The *sedim* will help you, child. You did not have to ask. We are already helping you, though we tremble in fear. We are lowly creatures among our kind, though to you we are as gods."

"How did Thiede find you?"

"We found him, the most beautiful of the children of Hermaphroditus. Our kings sent us to be with you, to guide you along the ways. We are here in the nursery of Wraeththu to watch over those who grow."

"Did we do wrong in visiting another realm, Peridot? Should we have left Lileem and Terez to their fate? Was that the cause of what is happening now?"

"No. The one you call Astral and I did wrong in taking you there, but we were lucky and were undetected. We broke the laws of our kind carrying you to another realm, for the time is not yet right for Wraeththu to be given such knowledge. We did it for love of you."

"Can the ways be opened again?"

"Yes. No force is mighty enough to disrupt them for long, although in earthly time it might seem so."

Pellaz was silent for a moment, then voiced the most prickly question that beat upon his mind. "Where is Cal?"

Peridot answered without hesitation. "With Perdu," he said.

"Who is that?"

"You cannot ask me that."

"Was he abducted? Did he run away? What happened to him? Peridot, if you know, you must tell me. You know you must."

"He is safe," Peridot replied. "He lives. That is all I can say. His part is yet to come. Do not ask me of this matter, which is so close to your heart. Ask me what is vital. I must revert very soon to my earthly form."

"What must be done now?"

"Defeat Ponclast," Peridot said, "though that task is not yours alone. Galhea will fall, as the phoenix falls. From the ashes will come that which shall bring victory. I will carry the son of your brother to the great continent once the ways are open to me."

"Moon?"

"Yes. Have him be ready."

"Why? What is his part?"

"He is your avatar and you will need him. I can say no more on that. You should know that the *sedim* are sure your enemies will not move upon Immanion until the last of Parasiel is dust. You have time, though you are disabled. Summon a meeting of tribes. The *sedim* will work diligently to open a channel of communication to those on this continent, as far afield as is possible for us at this time. These troubles will bring all Wraeththu closer together. Look for the one from the north, he who is brother to the wolf and the hare, for he has much to teach you. Now, you must ask me no more. I have said far more than I should. It is not our way to interfere in the affairs of hara, as it was not our way to interfere in the affairs of humans."

"Perhaps you should have done," Pellaz said softly.

"Our interference would have had grave consequences," Peridot said. "You do not realize how much. Know only this: in revealing myself to you in this way, we shall henceforth be closer in mind. For now, you must say nothing to another living har of our conversation. I trust you to remain silent."

"Silent? Then how will I explain to the Hegemony about Ponclast? If I reveal this information without giving the source, it will look suspicious, and the Tigrina already believes I have adversaries in the Hegalion."

"At the strike of three after the noon bell, a message from your brother will come to you. Be ready for it. That is the information you need. I must take on the flesh of the beast again now. The air here stings me."

"Thank you, Peridot," Pellaz said. "You have given me far more than I dared hope for."

In Galhea, there was much argument over who should go to Imbrilim. While Cobweb and Snake concentrated on gathering information from the ethers, Swift met with Seel and his right-hand har, Ithiel, in his office. Swift wanted Ithiel to remain at home, as he was the most trusted of Swift's hara, and had once been a general of Terzian's armies. Swift thought it made sense for Ithiel to protect Galhea while he himself rode to Imbrilim, because he wanted to talk face-to-face with the Gelaming. Ithiel, predictably, disagreed, saying that if there were indeed enemies about, the leader of Parasiel riding in only a small party was an obvious target for attack, and because nohar knew how they'd managed to infiltrate Cobweb and Snake's barrier of protection and break unheard into Forever, it was likely they could attack without warning.

"We must send a high-ranking har," Swift said. "I can't trust any but you or I to negotiate with them. They can be slippery fish, as we know. If there is trouble, I wonder how much aid they'll be willing to lend any but their own tribe."

"You cannot trust me?" Seel asked. "Remember I am Gelaming before I am Parsic."

"I didn't mean you," Swift said.

"Then I will go. I know the ways of Gelaming intimately. Also, I think you underestimate how much they value the House of Parasiel. They will give us aid, should it be needed."

"Seel, it could be dangerous. I don't want to risk your safety."

Seel laughed. "I have lived a dangerous life, Swift, long before I met you. I'm probably the best equipped for this task, other than Ithiel. Also, I want to make sure every effort is made to find our son. I want to do this myself, and I know that the Imbrilim commander, Arahal, will not refuse me whatever I ask for."

Swift sighed deeply. "I'm not happy about this, but your words make sense. Go at once, Seel. Take a dozen armed hara with you. Take the best of our horses. Ride fast."

In an upstairs room that Cobweb liked to use for meditations, as it overlooked the wildest part of the garden, he and Snake sat opposite each other on the floor, their minds fighting with what felt like wet silk mesh that tried to obstruct their investigations at every turn. Cobweb drew strength from Snake. Every time his will faltered, he concentrated upon a point of light that was the essence of Snake's being. It drew him back to the path, which was so difficult and vague. Sometimes, Cobweb heard terrible screams, which he knew emanated from the otherlanes. Cobweb lacked the ability to travel the otherlanes in astral form. He could only wander the ethers, which are comprised of layers of thought of every living being, past and present. If the otherlanes are like roads upon a world, then the ethers are the memories of those roads. They cannot be traveled to reach a destination, merely used to view countless potential destinations, to give glimpses of what might be found there.

Cobweb saw many perplexing images before his mind's eye. Some were so alien he could not even identify their components, but then, in a flash, he saw an image of Terzian. It was enough to make him jump partially out of his trance. The dreams he'd had the previous night still haunted him.

"They have got out," Terzian said, and vanished.

His voice had been so clear it was as if he were standing at Cobweb's shoulder in reality. Cobweb gasped and opened his eyes. It felt as if his body had forgotten how to breathe: he had to make a conscious effort to do it.

Opposite him, Snake opened his eyes. He looked dazed. "What is it?" he asked. "What did you see?"

"Terzian," Cobweb answered. "He spoke to me."

"Did he speak of the black fortress?"

"No . . ." Cobweb rubbed his face. "He said, 'They have got out.' Black fortress . . ." Cobweb shook his head. "No, that cannot be possible. What did you see?"

"I saw a memory: Seel and Swift before a great citadel. Many hara. Engines of war. I saw the radiance of magic, of grissecon. Energy. I smelled blood."

"Fulminir," Cobweb said. "Can it be that?"

"The Varr stronghold?" Snake said. "I have heard of it."

"Who hasn't of our generation?" Cobweb said dryly. He pursed his lips. "There is an interpretation of what we've both seen, but I don't like it."

"Which is?"

"Ponclast's forces, or what was left of them, were contained in an area south of here, sealed off by an energetic barrier. Thiede assured us it could never be breached, that Ponclast's hara would live there forever until they died. They had everything they needed to survive. It was not as brutal as it sounds."

"Any form of cage is brutal to the one trapped within," Snake said. "Do you think this was what Terzian referred to?"

"It seems too much of a coincidence, you seeing Fulminir. Terzian and Ponclast were very close." Cobweb paused. "Do you know, I've not thought of those hara since the day Thiede told me what he'd done with them. I don't think anyhar has. They are the forgotten tribe, the embarrassment we'd rather forget. They were the scapegoats, who carried all Varrish sins into the Forest of Gebaddon for eternity. There were countless other Varrs, who no doubt now hold high positions and great wealth, and who were probably no better than them. The hara of Fulminir took the brunt of Gelaming wrath. In retrospect, I can see this was not entirely just. They should have stood trial, like many others did. Not all of them could have been evil. They just followed orders, as everyhar did, like Ithiel, who is now one of the most respected hara in Megalithica. At one time, he was on the Gelaming's most wanted list."

"I have always been aware of the injustice," Snake said. "I lived in the eye of its devastation."

"I know," Cobweb said softly. "Is this the face of our enemy, Snake? Is it Ponclast, or one of his hara?"

"The evidence points that way."

Cobweb frowned. "Then how have they broken out of Gebaddon? Is it because Thiede is no longer here? Was it his power alone that kept them contained?"

"These are all interesting possibilities," Snake said.

"Gebaddon was a place of strange forces," Cobweb said. "Who knows what the Varrs might have uncovered there."

"The only force I feel is hatred," Snake said. "Loathing for their enemies. If Ponclast lives, it is safe to assume he is far from chastised."

Cobweb stood up. "We must tell Swift of our findings at once. Gebaddon must be checked."

"I feel it is too late for that," Snake said. "It is Fulminir that should be checked."

"It was razed."

"I lived in ruins," Snake said. "Remember that."

Cobweb nodded. "Come. We will tell Swift this."

"You go," Snake said. "I want to try and relay this information to Pellaz."

"Of course. Do you want me to stay and help you?"

"No, I do this best alone. In the ethers, I perceived chinks in the dank fog that occludes them. I think I can get a message through, if I pick my way carefully."

"I wish you luck," Cobweb said. Impulsively, he leaned down and kissed the top of Snake's head.

Snake's body went rigid. "You must go," he said.

CHAPTER TWENTY-THREE

Although nohar else knew it, the devastation in the otherlanes was not a deliberate ploy. It was merely a side effect. Ponclast's unseen allies ripped the barrier to shreds and their violent presence in this reality shook the fibers of the otherlanes into chaos. At the moment when the barrier around Gebaddon finally crumpled and fell, and Ponclast's Teraghasts burst out like black blood from an infected wound, the whole of creation screamed. The ethers went into convulsions and entities on every strand of the web of wyrd were made aware that a cataclysmic event had occurred. For some, it was of no more import than of hearing an explosion in a distant place, while for others it meant the end of everything.

Ponclast rode a golden horse, which was kin to the *sedim,* though of darker substance, despite its radiant appearance. The beast was a son of the *teraphim,* and before him all *sedim* would tremble. Ponclast's mount carried him overland to the ruins of Fulminir, where once the worst of Varr atrocities had taken place. It was no longer a blasted patch of scorched earth, spiked by shattered towers. The green had poured over it, slowly and inexorably, and now flowers bloomed among the tumbled masonry. To Ponclast, this seemed both fitting and just. It represented just how much the Gelaming could not contain living essence. The monument to their enemies, which they'd intended to let stand as a warning to all those who might oppose them in the future, was now a garden, its harsh lines softened. Ponclast too had changed.

He rode alone to his old home, leaving his hara in the outer courts, and found that much of it still stood, although several of its halls stood open to the air and young trees grew upon the stairways. As he rode the *teraph* through this place, Ponclast heard no ghosts of screams and combat. He heard only the song of birds. It was, in fact, quite peaceful.

He found for himself an intact room, which would be his headquarters. It had to be fairly comfortable because here he would continue to deliver his pearls—or at least the one that he still carried. It might be that procreation must be stalled for a time, while other matters pressed upon his attention, but the pearl he held within him now was special. He realized he cared about it, something he'd never felt before. It was also Abrimel's child.

The seduction of Abrimel har Aralis had not been as difficult as Ponclast had feared. Over time, the Gelaming had got used to Ponclast's appearance; Diablo had carried him to Gebaddon at least once a week, sometimes more. For some time, Ponclast had merely talked to Abrimel, flattered him discreetly, encouraged him to speak his heart. One night, as they'd consumed wine that Abrimel had brought with him from Imbrilim, they had ventured into the scarred territory of Abrimel's childhood. He could remember in distressing detail the Tigron's cruelty to Caeru. He remembered his terror when Pellaz had shouted and his even greater fear of the violent energy that had poured from his father's body. Ponclast gently nudged him to deeper revelations, and eventually Abrimel put his face in his hands. At that moment, Ponclast furled an arm about his shoulders. "Pellaz har Aralis will regret what he did to you, this I promise."

Abrimel had looked up at him then. "Whatever has been done to you, you are more beautiful than my father."

"I know what I am," Ponclast said, "but that will change also. Before I met you, I rarely considered my appearance, but now it is important to me."

"You have shown me more kindness than any other har," Abrimel said. "I know what you are, through and through, and it does not matter." With these words, he took Ponclast's face between his hands and shared breath with him.

Ponclast pulled Abrimel back until they lay on the cold floor. He almost swooned as Abrimel carefully opened the crimson robe and covered his starved body with kisses. Each kiss was a gift of life. Ponclast felt as if he were filling out, regaining himself, with every caress.

"There is no part of you I will not taste," Abrimel said, somewhat drunk.

"There is not," Ponclast agreed. "The deepest secrets of my being are yours."

It was a pleasure to guide Abrimel to the moment of creation, so different from all other occasions when Ponclast had kindled new life within him. Abrimel was no ravaged being, like the sorry Teraghasts, but a vital healthy har in prime condition, mentally alert and emotionally susceptible. For the first time, Ponclast understood some of what he had once despised in other hara. For the first time, the father of the pearl was important, wanted, and needed. The pearl would be very different to any that Ponclast had borne before. The harling within it would not hatch to be twisted and warped. It would be pure and perfect, with a heart as fierce as an angel. It warmed Ponclast greatly to know that the Tigron's own blood went against him, but there were also other benefits. Abrimel truly saw beauty in Ponclast. Because of this, the Tigron's son was more prized by Ponclast than he'd ever guess.

Now Ponclast called for another of his sons, who he also treasured, but for different reasons. He called psychically to Diablo.

Diablo came quickly to his hostling's private room, even though he had not set foot in Fulminir before. He knelt at Ponclast's side to be caressed, for this was one of the few pleasures in Diablo's life.

"Was your mission in Galhea successful?" Ponclast asked, knowing he did not really have to ask. The episode with the Aralisian pearl had been a glitch, because other forces had been involved.

"Yes," said Diablo.

"Was our merchandise damaged?"

"Hardly at all. A little. I did as you said."

"Who have you brought for me?"

"Two. One is a son of Parasiel, of Swift the Betrayer."

"You have excelled yourself. Who is the other?"

"His consort, who is from afar. I smelled his blood and it is strange. It carries the taint of the serpent."

"That's interesting," said Ponclast. "There's a tribe of serpent hara, my sweet, and they are called the Colurastes. They are rarely seen by others. The Kakkahaar leader, Lianvis, owned one once. I wonder if I'm to be equally fortunate."

"I do not know these names," said Diablo.

"You will," said Ponclast. "I see I must educate you." He lifted Diablo's sharp chin in his hand, gazed into his son's dark eyes. "You must relearn yourselves, all of you, my children. You must not be groveling imps but proud warriors. You must learn to stand tall. I have neglected you."

"I will do as you ask," said Diablo.

"Good," said Ponclast. "Bathe yourself. I have another job for you."

Diablo appeared somewhat confused.

"Immerse yourself naked in water," Ponclast said, "for some time."

"I will," said Diablo.

"Return to me just before sundown. I have something to attend to. After that, I will view the prisoners."

Once Diablo had left, Ponclast composed himself in a meditative state to deliver the pearl he carried. It was slightly before term, but he had a need to rid himself of it now, because he had to be at his most agile. It fought him a little, because it was not ready to leave its nest of warmth and safety, but he knew these last few days were merely a luxury to it. If it learned early the harsh reality of existence, it could only be of benefit to its development. Ponclast squatted on the dirty floor and focused his entire being on expelling the pearl. When it fell, eventually, into his hands, some fresh blood came with it, but not enough to worry about. Ponclast held the pearl close to his breast while he concentrated upon healing himself. He closed ripped blood vessels, soothed torn flesh, gazing inside himself as a surgeon might do, but using only his mind.

For nearly an hour he sat staring into space, the pearl still held close in bloodied hands, thinking about how much work he had to do. Fulminir must be rebuilt, but not as it had been before. If he was to take on the Gelaming and their fawning allies, then he must meet them on equal terms. He would create for himself forces like theirs, but seen through a dark mirror. His own allies would help him.

The *teraph* had remained with him throughout the birth, an immense yet immobile presence in the shadows of the room. It had come to Ponclast only minutes before Gebaddon had been breached. Ponclast realized he must forge a relationship with this creature. "You are Golab," Ponclast said to the *teraph*. "I name you so."

The *teraph* stamped and came forward, head hanging low, its hooves thudding heavily against the old wood floor. It nosed at the pearl, its lips tickling Ponclast's hands. Its breath was warm. Ponclast remembered the instruction that the blue child had given to him: do not attempt to contact us again. He could not heed it. They had sent the *teraph* and breached the magical barrier around Gebaddon, but this was not nearly enough.

"I have little time," Ponclast said to the *teraph*. "The hara from the old days are crippled by memory, and those of the new are ignorant creatures. Help me shape them, Golab. You have seen with your own eyes the state of things here. If my request is justified, go to your masters and bring me aid."

The *teraph* lifted its beautiful head and shook its mane. It made a chewing sound, as any normal horse would make. Then before Ponclast's eyes, it opened up a portal and went into it, leaving only a chill breeze behind.

At the appointed time, Diablo returned to the room of his hostling. Ponclast had already wrapped the pearl in a drape he'd torn down and now it was incubating in a corner of the room. Ponclast showed it to Diablo. "I appoint you as guardian of your brother," he said. "Every night you will sleep with this pearl, warming it with your body. When it hatches, you must put the life of the harling within it before your own. Do you understand?"

"Yes."

"Where are our hara gathered?"

"In the outer courts of this citadel," said Diablo. "They are preparing food and await your presence."

"Bring two of them to me immediately. They must guard the pearl while we are at our business."

"I will."

"Choose well."

Diablo ducked his head and slipped from the room. Ponclast could not hear him going down the stairs. He smiled.

The Parsic prisoners were confined in another room of the citadel and, as Diablo had said, were not too damaged. They had fought against their captor so Diablo had been forced to spill a little blood, but their injuries were not serious: a slashed arm, a shallow wound to the belly.

Ponclast stood before them and was pleased to note they were defiant and uncowed. It brought no pleasure to Ponclast's heart to torture a beaten har. They might be disorientated after Diablo had dragged them, without the agency of *sedim,* through some of the darker back alleys of the otherlanes, but at least they were in possession of their senses. "Do you know who I am?" he asked them.

They stared back at him, silent, wrapped in each other's arms. They were afraid, but somehow determined, not yet resigned.

"I am Ponclast. You might know this name. Which of you is the highson of Terzian?"

Again, he was met only with furious silence.

"I can find out very easily," Ponclast said. "You might as well tell me. Why bring needless pain to yourself? I am being courteous, for the sake of your highfather's blood."

"I am Azriel Parasiel," one of them said.

"And this is your chesnari, is it not?" Ponclast asked, gently nudging the other har with his foot. "Are you Colurastes, har? You don't have a look of them, although I am advised you carry the serpent taint."

"I am Aleeme har Sarestes," said the har, "half Colurastes."

"Thank you for being so compliant," Ponclast said. He fixed Azriel with an unblinking stare. "This serpent har will be taken to my quarters. If you wish to ensure his relative safety, you will be cooperative."

"If you intend harm to our tribe, we are prepared to die before we'll cooperate," Azriel said.

Ponclast was not deceived. He could tell that Azriel did not want to die, but also that he and his chesnari had discussed their circumstances while they'd been left alone. They felt they should do the noble thing and sacrifice themselves, but they did not have the courage to take their own lives.

"You have no choice," Ponclast said. "Believe me, death is the least of your worries. You might be surprised at how quickly you'll want to cooperate, should I decide to persuade you."

"You are insane," Azriel said. "The Gelaming will crush you."

"Your gauche opinions are endearing. I almost wish, for your sake, that they were realistic. But they're not."

"What do you want us to do?" Aleeme asked.

"You? I will use you to create a new strain of har. Have you borne a pearl before, Colurastes?"

"No!" Aleeme spat. "And you cannot make me do that, no matter how much pain you inflict upon me. You should know that. It is beyond me."

"Actually, it is not," Ponclast said. "As you will learn. I prefer to carry the pearls of my sons myself, but that condition will be inconvenient to me for some time. Therefore, I shall have to create new hostlings."

"That is not possible!" Azriel said. "Pearls cannot be created in hate."

Ponclast laughed harshly. "You think not? You should know your own tribe was once very familiar with the process of creating pearls on demand. You've not heard of the Varrish pearl farm, I take it?"

"Oh, we know of that abomination, Ponclast," Azriel replied. "We also know how the Varrs abandoned their breeding slaves to starvation once the Gelaming declared war in this country. It was not a farm, it was a pit of torture."

"Hardly that," Ponclast said. "The hostlings there were reared for their vocation. Also, though I have no need to justify myself to you, we had no choice but to abandon our workers. At the time, our forces were being massacred." He paused a moment before continuing. "You know, it amuses me greatly the way you refer so scathingly to 'Varrs.' You are one yourself, no matter what fancy title your father chooses to plaster over the past. Perhaps you too would make good breeding stock, Azriel *Parasiel.*"

"You are obscene!" Azriel cried.

"No, simply realistic. I do not view the world through a comfortable rosy glow, Parsic, and do you know why? I have been confined in hell for years. Your father, lapdog of Thiede that he is, saw to that. But now Thiede is no more and I am freed from my prison. It's difficult to be sentimental after such an ordeal. Harlings are a resource, not romantic expressions. Your highfather knew this also, as you will come to know it."

"You killed your own son," Azriel said. "If you were in hell, you created it yourself."

"I have many sons now," Ponclast said mildly. "Loyal ones. They are legion. Believe it. When your father comes for you, my sons will tear his body into a thousand pieces, so small they will be impossible to devour and dogs will lick up his blood."

Azriel uttered a growl and spat at Ponclast, the spittle striking his robe at the knees. "Hmm," Ponclast said, "for that affront, I bestow a new honor upon you. I will allow you to witness just how easily your beloved chesnari can create pearls in hate." He inclined his head to his captives and left them to their grief.

Satisfied with the interview, Ponclast went to his hara, who were gathered around fires in the sprawling outer courts of the citadel. Before he made his presence known, he spent a few moments observing them. They were underfed, having sustained themselves only with the poisoned fruits of Gebaddon for many years, but even so they were fit, as they'd spent most of their time fighting among themselves. Now, it seemed, they had rediscovered how to be of one mind, and for those of second generation a new way of living was being revealed. So few of them though, merely six hundred at most. Their strength would have to be as swift-striking assassins, rather than ordinary troops. Ponclast needed more hara, and even if he had a thousand hostlings bearing pearls for him, the harlings would grow too slowly to be of use in the foreseeable future. Subjugation might be the only way. How many hara of Megalithica were truly happy with Gelaming rule? It could be that once Ponclast had obtained a few victories, in particular the conquest of Galhea, some Parsics might cast off the shackles they wore and regard themselves as Varrs once more. And what of the Uigenna? Where were the remnants of his greatest allies? Had the Gelaming destroyed them all or was there another Gebaddon somewhere, waiting for his liberating hand? Now, he gazed upon his ramshackle army, clad in rags, with their bones poking through their skins, and had to fight hard to dispel the sinking sensation that gripped his belly. They were all he had. They would have to suffice.

He stepped out of the shadow of an archway and stood before his hara, at the head of a short flight of steps. They all turned their heads toward him and went silent. Ponclast saw the need in their eyes for reassurance and promise. He held out his arms to them.

"Welcome, hara of the Varrs, to your freedom. You have cast off the chains that bound you. You can remember without fear the glories of the past and look forward to greater victories. Those who enslaved us will feel the force of retribution. The scavengers will be gutted in their beds, for you will strike swiftly and in silence."

Ponclast hoped for some show of enthusiasm and bloodlust at his stirring words, but his hara continued to stare at him, perhaps with some measure of distrust. He realized most of them were probably grateful only for their freedom and had plans to melt away into the world, invisible, to live their lives in peace. This was not, in Ponclast's view, part of their destiny.

"Where is your pride?" he asked them. "Where are the tall warriors of Fulminir?"

"You know the answer to that," said a har, rising to his feet. Ponclast did not recognize him, but he was clearly of first generation, sinewy and scarred. "Part of us died in Gebaddon. We are no match for the Gelaming. If we attempt to confront them, they will destroy us. We should take what we have and hide."

"What is your name?" Ponclast asked.

"Kyrotates, tiahaar. I was a general in your army."

Ponclast walked slowly down the steps. "It is wise to ask questions, to be aware," he said. "Your fears deserve a response. Think about how you escaped your prison. Think about how I now have the son of Swift the Betrayer in my custody. We are not powerless. We have stronger allies than the Gelaming ever had."

"Who are these allies? We've seen nothing but the deaths of those consumed by the dark forces that emanated from your dwelling, tiahaar. It seems to many of us that our allies might be worse than our foes." A rumble of agreement came from the hara around him.

"They are," Ponclast agreed, "but nonetheless, they are allies."

"Who are they?" Kyrotates persisted. "Will they show themselves? What is their purpose in freeing us? What do they want of us? If they are so strong, then surely they don't need the assistance of starved and underequipped hara like us."

Ponclast would not allow control of the situation to slip away from him, but unfortunately he did not really know the answers to the questions Kyrotates wisely asked. "They have already given you so much," he said. "Through my son Diablo, our kind travels the otherlanes at our own free will. Through him, we achieve things of which we could only once have dreamed. The Gelaming do not possess this ability. The walls of Gebaddon were destroyed. We all breathe clean air. Are these gifts worth nothing to you?"

Kyrotates inclined his head. "They are, tiahaar, but what is their price? If, through luck and assistance, we destroy every Gelaming and traitor in this land, who will rule us afterward?"

"I have sent a messenger to our allies," Ponclast said. "Soon, you'll have the evidence you need. Trust me, Kyrotates. The Gelaming hoped we would be poisoned and would die in Gebaddon, but we did not. They thought we would dwindle and fade, but we did not. Through my own body, I have kept our tribe strong, even though many of our comrades at arms sickened and succumbed to the toxins of the forest. I have given myself to you all, every atom of my being. I stand between you and any danger. That will never change."

Kyrotates bowed his head at these words. It was inconceivable that any har present could doubt Ponclast's sincerity, because he did indeed mean every word.

However, once he had left his hara to their meager meal, his body was swamped with weariness. He stood in the shadows of a damp dark corridor and supported himself with one hand against the wall. He missed Terzian badly. If he was here now, he'd be the one cajoling the troops, kindling the fire of belief. Ponclast remembered how he and Terzian had often fought, especially over the issue of alliance with the Kakkahaar. Dimly, Ponclast turned this idea over in his head. Where did the Kakkahaar stand now? Was it possible that alliance could be reforged? Diablo must be sent out to bring Abrimel to Fulminir. The Aralisian would possess the information Ponclast needed in this respect, and it was time now for him and Ponclast to be together continually.

Straightening up, Ponclast returned to the room he had found for himself. His body ached, perhaps at last protesting about the premature delivery of the pearl. Diablo was present in the room, and had dismissed the guards he had selected, having returned there as soon as he'd shown his hostling where the prisoners were confined. He squatted in a corner, stroking the pearl.

"Has the *teraph* returned?" Ponclast asked.

Diablo looked up and shook his head, then resumed his careful caress of the pearl.

Ponclast sighed. The events of the day had taken their toll; he felt weak. He must sleep. But there was no soft bed to support his body, no deferential hara to attend to his needs. Only the dank and the dark, and an imp of a being squatting in the shadows. The enormity of how much he'd lost washed over Ponclast in a paralyzing wave. It was as if the strange air of Gebaddon had kept the past at bay. He had existed in no-time. Now, it came crashing back.

"This was once a place of strength and power," he said to Diablo, and sat down on the floor to lean against the wall.

Diablo came to his side, his luminous eyes wide.

"It will be so again," Ponclast said, hoping he could believe it. He patted Diablo's bony shoulder and closed his eyes. He felt Diablo's sharp paws on his face. His son was stroking away tears. Perhaps he had never seen them before. "*They* will give it to you," he said.

"Yes," Ponclast murmured. He was so tired, he could barely think.

"They want to give it to you now."

Ponclast said nothing. Sleep was coming for him like the approach of night.

"*Now,*" said Diablo and shook his hostling roughly.

Ponclast felt a chill cut through his entire being. He opened his eyes.

There were seven of them before him, standing in a V formation: figures eight feet tall, clad in silken shirts and trousers of cobalt blue. Scarves were wound around their faces and they wore strange high headdresses of black and blue feathers. Each carried a curved blade, carved with shining symbols. The strangest thing was that their presence could not be felt. Ponclast had sensed nothing of their arrival. They were simply there.

One of them stepped forward. "We do not recognize a summons," he said. "We cannot be invoked."

"Yet you are here," Ponclast said. He pushed the tiredness away, concentrating every last shred of his energy into dealing with what he supposed were the emissaries of his mysterious allies.

"It is time for it. We are the Hashmallim, the Lights of the Faceless Ones. I am Abraxis, Foremost of Lights. I will assist you in certain matters."

"I thank your Masters for delivering us from Gebaddon," Ponclast said. "As you see, the experience has taxed me. I ask for strength and health, for myself and my hara. I ask that Fulminir be rebuilt and equipped."

"The hara here are leavings from beneath the table," Abraxis said. "They are weak; they are dogs full of parasites."

"They have suffered," Ponclast said carefully. "Their greatness has been sucked from them."

"We will do as you ask," said Abraxis, "for the Faceless Ones desire it." He sheathed his sword and glanced over to where the pearl lay hidden in its nest of soiled drapes. For a moment Ponclast was terrified for his developing son. "You seek to make another like the one that was stolen," Abraxis said. "Your efforts are commendable, but you lack the composition required. However, it is our will that the one who breaks from the pearl should match in strength the one who would oppose him. In this, we shall assist also."

"Thank you," Ponclast said. He did not like to feel so powerless and ineffectual. Before these beings, he could not swathe himself in the armor of belief he had built in order to survive.

"Come to me," Abraxis said. "There are things that hara inherited from our kind, but they are a weak reflection of what is. Learn now of the truth and of potential."

Ponclast got with difficulty to his feet. He could not exercise any show of independence or authority. He could merely obey.

Abraxis pulled the scarf away from his lower face. There was no monster hidden beneath the cloth: he looked har, like the best of hara. Now he stooped and put his mouth against Ponclast's lips. This was more than a sharing of breath. There was no sharing. Abraxis blew into Ponclast's body a white fire that threw him backward. He hit the wall and collapsed on the floor, his flesh aflame. It felt as if he had spontaneously combusted. He would soon be nothing more than ash. The Hashmallim stood silently and observed his writhings. Diablo ran around his hostling, uttering squeaks of alarm. Occasionally, he paused to hiss at the motionless giants standing before them. But presently, the fire subsided and Ponclast lay quiet. His own breath sounded very loud in his ears.

"Rise," said Abraxis. "Go to a reflective surface and look upon yourself, for you are now equal to your greatest enemy, and will become more powerful than he. I carried the fire with me from our Masters. It is their gift to you. You can be Tigron of Varrs, if such is your wish."

Ponclast sat up and held his hands out before him. They were glowing.

"It will fade," said Abraxis. "Savor this moment. Look upon yourself." He indicated a far corner of the room and there Ponclast saw a cracked mirror leaning against the wall. He went to it and bent down. He looked into it, but uttered no words. It was like the best of dreams, the hateful, spiteful dreams where all is perfect and then you wake to cold reality. Only he knew that this time there would be no awakening, because he was not asleep.

He stood up. "Give some measure of this to Diablo also." He pointed at his son who was gazing at him stupefied. "Wake him."

Diablo screeched like a terrified monkey as Abraxis lifted him in one hand. He struggled and wriggled, spitting and clawing. Abraxis put his free hand over Diablo's distorted face and a light came out of him. After only a few seconds, the Hashmal dropped Diablo from his hold. Diablo fell to the floor like a rag doll and lay motionless. He looked dead. Abraxis wiped his hands together. "Your request is fulfilled."

"What of my hara. Can you do this to all of them?"

"Take me to a place where I might observe them without being seen," Abraxis said. "My brethren will remain here."

Ponclast led the Hashmallim leader to a window that overlooked the courtyard where his hara were gathered. It took longer than he thought it would, because so many of the passageways were blocked by fallen masonry or destroyed. Sometimes they had to leap over gaping dark abysses. When they reached the window, night had fallen and the sky was occluded by cloud. Only the flickering flames of the cooking fires gave any light.

The Hashmal did not speak, but unsheathed and lifted his sword. He held the weapon before him, and its bright surface reflected the flames from below. "Watch," said Abraxis. "I will transform your hara with the soul of fire." His sword drank the light, condensed it, made it stronger. Then Abraxis turned the blade slightly and a beam of intense red radiance spilled out of it. It roared like an inferno over all who sat below the window. At once, they were thrown into panic. Many hid their eyes, others uttered cries. Ponclast watched in horror as his hara writhed and screamed in agony, to all appearances being destroyed by the fire of the sword. He knew how it felt, and although it tore at his heart to witness it, he remained silent.

After some moments, Abraxis lowered his arm. The fire in the blade ran like liquid through the markings upon it before shrinking to a point and disappearing completely. Outside, Ponclast's hara were unconscious, piled upon each other like corpses on a battlefield. "Come sunrise," said Abraxis, "you will have what you desire."

"They wish to see you with their own eyes," Ponclast said. "They doubt."

"Tomorrow, they will be beyond doubt," Abraxis said. "I have given to them the ability that was given to your son Diablo before the walls of the Gebaddon were breached. This is your army of shadows. You will use them wisely. We will not and cannot show ourselves to them."

"And will your Masters ever show themselves to me?"

Abraxis smiled grimly. "They are faceless," he said. "They cannot be seen."

That night, Ponclast lay in his makeshift bed on the floor, with one arm around Diablo, the other around his pearl. He slept fitfully, conscious of the smoldering presence of Golab in the corner of the chamber. He replayed feverishly in his mind everything that had happened that day, until he was unsure whether he was dreaming or awake. But then the dawn came and Diablo stretched against him, opened his eyes.

Ponclast gazed upon this strange har, who in the early light appeared supernatural. He would never look like a normal har, but the Hashmal had transformed him. He no longer appeared pitiful or wretched. He was alive in his own skin, unique and flawless, a new template of perfection.

"How do you feel?" Ponclast asked him.

Diablo sat up and examined his hands. "They fed me."

"Yes," Ponclast said, still lying on the floor. "We have all been fed."

"We can't dress in rags. Not anymore."

"Indeed not. We'll take what we need from elsewhere: clothes, supplies, weapons. There is much to do. Go to Imbrilim and bring Abrimel here. Can you ride the *teraph*?"

Diablo stared at the creature, which appeared to be dozing in the corner. "It should be easier than what I'm used to."

"Then bring with you as much as you can carry from Imbrilim. Bring food, blankets, whatever you can."

"I'll tell Abrimel to gather things for us. I'll make as many trips as it takes. Abrimel can come last."

"Those are good ideas," Ponclast said. He sat up and placed the pearl in his lap. Already he could perceive huge differences in Diablo. "Don't overtire yourself. The spirit paths are very unstable at present, and although the *teraph* is better equipped than most to travel them in this state, it might still be hazardous."

Diablo smiled. "The way they are now, the spirit paths are perfect for me. They're like Gebaddon. Their darkness and strangeness are known to me."

Ponclast reached out and stroked his son's arm. "Still, be quick and be careful."

"I will go now."

"You should eat first."

"Abrimel can feed me. He has better food than we have here. I'll bring something back for you to eat, before anything else."

Diablo made so many trips to Imbrilim, transporting goods that Abrimel had collected as discreetly as possible, it wasn't until the late afternoon that Abrimel himself arrived in Fulminir. Ponclast had spent the day talking with his hara, all of whom had recovered from their ordeal of the previous night. Their enthusiasm for life had been rekindled, as had their self-belief. Kyrotates came to Ponclast and said, "I was wrong to doubt you. Forgive me."

"Then trust me in future," Ponclast said.

His hara did not want to be Varrs again; in their pride and anger, they wanted to remain Teraghasts. Let the Gelaming and their allies know that they were not as strong and all-powerful as they believed themselves to be. Let them know that the victims of Gebaddon were free and transformed.

As he walked among his hara, Ponclast observed their animated discussions with amusement and affection, occasionally offering his own remarks, before passing on to the next group. They were like harlings who had just been given their hearts' desires. In no way did he want to quash that zeal. For today, he'd let them celebrate. Some of them went out into the countryside to round up animal stock. There were many feral herds of sheep, cattle, and horses nearby, some from earlier human farmsteads but several, no doubt, from Fulminir itself, when the Gelaming had razed its farms. Other Teraghasts set about clearing living quarters and inspecting the water supplies. There was much work to be done, and they did it independently of Ponclast's command. They had come home at last.

Ponclast dressed himself in Gelaming attire that Diablo had brought for him. He found a long belted robe of supple crimson velvet, which he presumed Abrimel had procured for him specially. He brushed out his hair with a carved wooden hairbrush that bore the insignia of the Aralisians. His heart hammered in anticipation. He felt exhilarated, yet nervous.

Abrimel came to him at sundown. Diablo left him at the door to his hostling's chamber and departed. Abrimel stared at Ponclast without words. He looked almost sorrowful.

"Speak," Ponclast said at last. Was he deluding himself and was now more of a monster than he'd ever been?

"How can I speak?" Abrimel said. His eyes shimmered with unshed tears. "I should fall to my knees before you."

Ponclast went to him and took him in his arms. "You helped make me," he said. "You gave me hope. Our pearl is born. Come, see it."

He took Abrimel to the alcove where the pearl lay in its nest. Abrimel reached out and let his hand hover over it. "Can we ever be happy?" he asked. "Will we be granted that privilege? Will we see our son growing up? Will there be summer days and laughter? Will there be peace in our world?"

"Bree," Ponclast said softly. "We'll have those things. Do not fear."

"It has to be different this time," Abrimel said. "Then, perhaps we'll deserve them."

"What do you mean?" Ponclast asked sharply.

"You *know*," Abrimel said. "Fulminir's dark history. Many oppose the empire of the Gelaming, but the Gelaming are clever. They present themselves as light and good. The Varrs were not. What was found in this place . . ." He shook his head. "It cannot be that way again. Not if you want victory."

"You know nothing. The Gelaming did many unspeakable things that hara don't know about. Their methods were simply different from mine."

"It's what hara see that matters," Abrimel said. "You know exactly what I'm saying. Don't deny it."

"I never lied or deceived," Ponclast said. "Perhaps that's a talent I should adopt." He laughed bitterly. "The Parsics sneer at the idea of Varrish breeding facilities, but what were you, Bree, other than a planned strategic birth?"

"I was an accident," Abrimel said.

Ponclast raised his eyebrows. "Really? You believe that? There are no accidental conceptions among hara. Think about it. Think about Azriel har Parasiel also. Before Thiede sealed me into Gebaddon, he told me how he'd arranged for Swift the Betrayer to breed with some Gelaming minion."

"Azriel was presented differently to the world," Abrimel said. "Thiede acted so carefully, so manipulatively, that Azriel was conceived in love and desire. The end result was the same. Think about *that*."

Ponclast nodded. "I see your meaning." He kissed Abrimel's cheek. "You give me good counsel. Thank you."

Abrimel was silent for a moment, then put his hands upon Ponclast's shoulders. "Am I your consort?"

"In every way," Ponclast said.

"Take the blood-bond with me," Abrimel said. "I feel strongly we should do that."

"In some ways, I am traditional," Ponclast said carefully. "A blood-bond is insoluble."

"It must be done," Abrimel said. "Some of your hara will be suspicious of me. I must prove I am one of them. If needs be, I'll cast off my Aralisian birth before every har in this citadel."

"Appearances aside," Ponclast said, "is this what you want, personally?"

"Before you, I have never loved," Abrimel said. "It *is* what I want." He smiled. "My place is here, with you. I won't stay in Imbrilim for much longer."

"I need you there, Bree. You must report to me on whatever you hear of the Gelaming's plans."

Abrimel took in a deep breath through his nose. "I don't belong there."

"I know, and as soon as we know what action the Tigron plans to take, you'll move here permanently."

"Very well. I'll stay there for now. I have my dreams to sustain me."

Ponclast took Abrimel's face in his hands. "You are of my heart," he said. "The ceremony will be a formality. We are already bonded in blood."

CHAPTER TWENTY-FOUR

Cobweb had always known he was a creature of intuition and insight, even before he was har. When his flesh shivered in a particular way, when the stars in the night sky seemed harder and brighter than usual, and a dead crow was found beneath the cedars by the lake, he knew something bad, something life-shaping, was about to take place. He had never imagined his instincts could fail him, that his forewarning system might not work.

After Azriel and Aleeme were taken, nothing happened for several weeks. Seel went to Imbrilim, and while he was away, the channels in the ether opened again, much as they'd been before, albeit with cloudy pockets of scrambled information and upsetting glimpses of things so strange there were no words to describe them. Sometimes, a bank of murk stole through the channels, making communication difficult or impossible for several days, but there were clear days too. A message came from Seel to say that the Gelaming were indeed aware of the problem, were not taking it lightly, and that the Tigron had summoned a Council of Tribes in Immanion. The Gelaming *sedim* were still having trouble accessing the otherlanes as freely as they were used to, but at least Immanion was once again in contact with its settlement in Megalithica. Arahal was on alert and was preparing for the worst. Ponclast's name had already been associated with the events, and now it had been proposed that he had been responsible for the attack on the Tigrina. He might also have taken Cal in the way that Azriel and Aleeme had been taken. The Gelaming had sent agents to Gebaddon, but they had yet to report back on their findings, because they'd had to travel overland rather than through the otherlanes. The enemy had a name, but as yet there was no hard proof the name was correct.

Cobweb could tell that Swift was suffering far more than he revealed to his family. Swift feared for Seel, he feared for his son, he feared for Aleeme, he feared for Cal. Nohar dared conjecture what might be happening now to those who had vanished. If Ponclast was involved, the possibilities were too dire to contemplate.

Swift said only one thing to his hostling, "If it is true, if the Varrs have escaped Gebaddon, they will not have forgotten who put them there."

Cobweb had placed one hand upon his son's shoulder in comfort. He was only too well aware of that fact. "Azriel and Aleeme are not dead," he said. "I am sure of it."

It might be that Ponclast was mustering his forces, or perhaps he was incapable of doing more than he had already done, but Cobweb could not help but feel that they were being played with. The silence, stretching interminably into the hot reaches of balmy summer, was intolerable. It was worse than attack. It was worse than the most terrible of news.

When news finally came, it was not on a windy, moaning night or a miserable morning when rain slashed the earth turning everything gray, it was on a motionless afternoon, with sunlight the color of honey splashing against the walls of Forever. A horse came galloping up the curving driveway from Galhea, its hectic sweating rush totally inappropriate on such a glorious afternoon. Its rider urged it madly into the sleepy yard behind the house, where horses rested their chins on stable doors and flies looped drunkenly around their eyes.

Cobweb, who was painting in the garden, watched the horse approach. He put down his brush, set aside the creamy white parchment he was working on, and went with purpose back to the house. By the time he reached the stable yard, Swift, who happened to be home at the time, was already out there. Cobweb saw a shuddering har hanging in Swift's rather stiff-limbed hold. He heard Swift barking questions, but could not hear the words.

"What is it?" Cobweb asked, and his own voice seemed to come from another world. He already knew.

Swift released the messenger into the hold of two of his staff who had followed him out of the house. "Amber Ridge has been attacked," he said.

This was a Parsic settlement some miles south of Galhea. "By what?" Cobweb asked.

"By shadows," Swift answered, "shadows with knives."

"What?"

Swift did not answer. He was already walking back into the house, calling orders to the rapidly expanding group around him.

Cobweb soon stood alone in the peaceful afternoon, while a groom led the shuddering horse to a stable for water and a blanket. He looked up at the sky, though his vision was blurred, but all that drifted there were tame clouds, not a single black bird scrawled against them.

The attack had come in the early morning, just as hara were rising from their beds to attend to their day's work. It had taken some time for them to realize they were, in fact, being attacked, because each assault came secretly: in the yard of a home, in a back alley, in a bedroom where the curtains were still drawn. It was only when the cries began to resound from different points of the small town that hara realized these were not isolated incidents. Even as a har died, his throat opened like paper, he could hear the cries of a neighbor dying upon the pales of his fence next door. A harling shrieked in terror as his hostling's life blood pooled in dead eyes on the kitchen floor, only to hear his best friend groan his last, while his parents helplessly tried to free him from the hold of an assailant they could barely see. Smoke beasts: that's what they were. Blurry shadows that flashed with silver, the metal of their weapons. They made no sound, they had no smell, you could not touch them. The first attack took only five minutes at most, and even while the residents of the town were still reeling from it, weeping over their dead, trying to organize their stunned thoughts, the second assault came, more deadly than the first. The town governor sent a rider to Galhea, moments before he was gutted and crucified upon the eaves of his own house.

Cobweb heard the details later, when he interviewed the messenger alone after Swift had made him tell the story several times. The messenger seemed only too relieved to be able to speak of the horror again and again. The details never changed. They did not have to be exaggerated.

"What will you do?" Cobweb asked Swift.

Swift was dressing himself in steel-strengthened leather armor, pulling on black gloves that looked as if they belonged to an executioner. "Investigate," he said. "Cobweb, you and Snake work on our protection. You're all we have, I think. Send messages to Seel, to Pellaz, wherever you can. Send messages to any har who can hear you."

"I will," Cobweb said. "But how can you protect yourself?"

"These shadows strike with blades of metal, not ether," Swift replied.

"They move quickly, but if they attack an armored har, we have to hope this protection will afford enough time for us to defend ourselves."

"How many are there, do you think?"

Swift shook his head, sighed. "Only a few hundred were confined in Gebaddon, all those that were left of Ponclast's forces. I can't see who would ally with them now. As they appear to have otherlane access far different to that of the Gelaming, I think they're making quick guerrilla strikes, with only a few hara. Our task will be to try and capture one of them. We can't answer this attack with might. We must find other means."

"They will have a weakness," Cobweb said. "Everyhar does."

"Yes . . ." Swift paused. "I have spoken to Ithiel. He will remain here with you. He and his staff will speak to everyhar in town to ensure they take precautions. I think our enemy will attempt to pick off outlying towns before assaulting Galhea. They could have come for us first. They didn't. There must be something here they fear." Swift reached out and touched his hostling's face briefly. "Take care. Take especial care."

"If I cannot protect this house, I deserve to die," Cobweb said. "This is my domain. None shall breach it."

"Extend that protection," Swift said. "There is more than this house at stake."

As Cobweb stood on the front steps of Forever, watching Swift lead a troupe of hara down the driveway, he could not help but be reminded of the times when he'd stood in exactly the same place watching Terzian depart on some campaign or another. One time, Terzian had not come back. *Do not think that,* Cobweb told himself. *Don't risk making it real.*

He went back into the house and found the Kamagrian housekeeper, Bryony, in the hallway. "The staff are worried," she said. "Nohar will tell us anything."

"Bring all of them to the kitchens," Cobweb said. "I'll speak to them. Send somehar to fetch Snake Jaguar and to find Tyson."

Bryony went at once to do so.

For some moments Cobweb stood alone in the hall, his head in his hands. His heart was pounding painfully fast, his breath was shallow. This was an ordinary day. Nothing was different. And yet everything was.

The messenger from Amber Ridge had insisted on joining Swift's forces, so Cobweb had to relate the story to his staff in his own words, as best as he could remember. His vision was filled with a blurry sea of round, panicked eyes. He tried to keep his voice level, to instill confidence. While he spoke, pans containing vegetables for dinner bubbled on the stove. Life went on, it always would. Forever lived up to its name. Whatever happened at Amber Ridge was a glitch, a mistake. Other hara might have died, but Galhea was safe. Still, it appeared the staff did not share this view. Cobweb could smell the heat of their fear. He realized, for perhaps the first time in his life, what the responsibility of being a leader of hara really involved. He could not betray weakness or anxiety. If those feelings chose to gnaw away at the certainty everything would be all right, he had to be his own consoler. Those who stared at him wanted to believe he could protect them. It was the job of the House of Parasiel. It was why they lived in this big house, why they were respected and obeyed.

Once Cobweb had finished relating what he knew, Bryony said, "This is ridiculous! Ponclast and his butchers are no match for the Parsic forces. What are they thinking of? The Gelaming put them in Gebaddon, it'll be easy to put them back."

Some heads nodded in agreement around her, but Cobweb could tell that most of them harbored a superstitious fear. Perhaps, like him, they had begun to question just how fair it had been to fling the Varrs into Gebaddon in the first place, and how a har's mistakes might come back to haunt him later, once everything was forgotten, and life was deceptively rosy.

Once Snake arrived at the house, he and Cobweb worked together on a newer, more potent shield of protection. Cobweb was slightly shocked how much energy Snake demanded they pour into it. It felt to him as if his life energy were being drawn from his body. All that they were, they poured into a shield for others. It left them depleted, and Cobweb had never experienced that before with Snake. Both of them fell asleep exhausted on the floor of Cobweb's trance room.

Some hours later, Cobweb was awoken by what he thought at first was the crash and rumble of an electrical storm. He was fully alert at once and sat up. The room was in darkness, but flashing light from outside sporadically filled it. He got to his feet and went to the window. He could see with his physical eyes a dome of silver-white radiance over the town, which was unusual to say the least. He realized this was only possible because something was striking the shield. It was not the shield he saw, but the hostile energy splashing against it.

"Snake!" he cried.

Snake was beside him in an instant, moving more quickly than Cobweb had believed him capable of. "It comes," he said. "We must reinforce the shield."

"We need more strength. We need others," Cobweb said desperately. His own energy reserves were so depleted there would be little he could do to sustain their defenses.

"Then go and find them!" Snake ordered. "Hurry!" He winced and gripped his chest.

"Snake . . ." Cobweb reached out a hand in concern, but Snake backed away from him.

"Do it!" he growled. "Go at once."

Cobweb ran out of the room. The only resources he possessed were the household staff, who were untrained and of low caste. He ran into Tyson on the stairs.

"I was coming for you," Tyson said. "We're under attack."

"I can see that, Tyson," Cobweb answered sharply. "Where is Ithiel?"

"He was here earlier but went into town when the show started."

"Is Ferany with us?"

"No."

"Then fetch him immediately. I need both him and you to help me. You're no great magus, Tyson, but you're going to have to learn very quickly."

"What?"

"Find Ferany. Quickly. Bring him to my trance room. But if you can't find him at home, return here without him. We have no time."

Tyson left the house, while Cobweb went to the staff quarters where he found Bryony and Yarrow, the cook, attempting to keep their anxious hara under control. "I need those of you with any psychic ability whatsoever to come with me," Cobweb said.

They all stared at him speechless.

Cobweb sighed. He could see they were all senseless with fear. "Yarrow, you," he ordered. "And pick whoever else you think can help."

He turned to Bryony. "I must ask this of you. Your Kamagrian essence may be of great help."

Bryony nodded and sighed, her face set in an uncertain smile. "I always meant to start . . . training. I should have done. I really should. But I'll do what I can."

"That is all I ask," Cobweb said. "Come to my trance room. We have to feed the shield with our energy. Put fear aside. Focus on this task. It is all that matters."

Cobweb didn't wait to see how Bryony and Yarrow dealt with the staff. He went back into the family area of the house, unsure of what to do next. He had an intense urge to search for something, but he didn't know what. It was as if he'd forgotten something vital, something he'd meant to do that had slipped his mind. He went from room to room, reinforcing the protection glyphs at the windows and doors and hearths. Outside the night was alive with light. It was beautiful to behold. He was almost compelled simply to stand and watch it. Bewitching. Nothing had ever touched Galhea, not even in the days when Terzian had waged war wherever he could. Galhea had always been the safely protected heart. How would Terzian deal with this if he were still here? And where was Swift? Why hadn't he returned? Amber Ridge was not that far away. Had he been lured from home so that it could be attacked in his absence?

Cobweb pushed his fearful thoughts away. He could not dwell on them. The danger was immediate. He had been brought to Forever simply to be a hostling, to give Terzian sons. He had become a domestic leader in the house, but now he knew he had to become more than that. He had to remember who he was, how he had once been wild and warlike himself. So long ago. Too dim to remember. The woman in him had slipped one night into the chamber of the warrior and had slit his throat as he slept.

"This is not my job," Cobweb said aloud. "Aghama, Thiede, help us. I cannot do this."

He put his hands against his face, pressed hard. It seemed a strange, soothing atmosphere came into the room. The deafening crackle of energy from outside became muted.

"Do you hear me?" Cobweb said. "Thiede, are you there? Tell me what to do. Give me strength. Come back to us. I am not the har for this task."

There was a moment's silence, and then a soft voice behind him said, "You are."

Cobweb turned around so quickly, he stumbled. He did not really expect to see Thiede standing there, but neither did he expect to see the har who now came toward him from the darkness of the room: a tall har with white-gold hair.

"Cal . . ." Cobweb's initial reaction was to be flooded with a feeling of relief so intense he nearly lost his senses. Acting on impulse he threw himself against the har before him, gripped his clothes. "Don't vanish. Don't you dare vanish!"

"I am here," Cal said. "I'm no illusion."

"You heard me. You have come to help."

"I have come to help," Cal said gently. "Let me go. You've grabbed flesh as well as cloth."

"How . . . ?"

Cal shook his head. "Now is not the time to explain. It would take too long."

Cobweb released his grip. "Ponclast's Varrs have escaped Gebaddon. They are attacking us. Swift is gone, with many of our forces. Seel is in Imbrilim.

Azriel and Aleeme have been taken. The shield is foundering. Snake and I . . . we are . . . Do you know what I'm talking about?"

"I know you are under attack and that your defenses are weakening. I know we can ensure the shield will hold for this night. That's all we must think about."

Cobweb nodded silently, then said, "I don't know why, but I'm not surprised to see you."

"We must start work," Cal said.

"Come to my trance room," Cobweb said. "Pell's brother is there. Not Terez. Dorado. He is called Snake now. He is powerful, but drained, as I am. We made the shield."

"I know. Lead on. I am anything but drained."

Cal didn't say anything more as Cobweb led him to the upper part of the house. It was hard to believe it could really be him, and not some supernatural manifestation. *Too many questions and no time to ask them. Be thankful for what you are given. Take it and be glad.*

By the time they reached the trance room, Yarrow and Bryony had already taken a number of the staff there and Tyson and Ferany were also present. The expression on Tyson's face when Cal came into the room would remain with Cobweb forever. It was comical, but in that situation there was no space for humor. Cobweb wondered whether this was difficult for Cal, whether he cared.

"We have unexpected aid," he said lightly. "Most of you know Cal, of course." He gestured toward Snake. "Cal, this is Pell's brother."

"We have met," Snake said in an enigmatic tone.

Cal merely inclined his head. "Well, let's get started. It might well be a long night."

As the group composed themselves in a circle, Cobweb was amused by the way they arranged themselves, how Snake and Tyson chose places far from Cal's hands and how Ferany made a point of sitting next to him. Cobweb sat on Cal's other side and the whole group joined hands. Cobweb led them into a trance state, all the while conscious of the familiar yet strange energy that coursed into him through Cal's warm, dry fingers. It was as if he had left Forever only yesterday. For a while, secretly, Cobweb had believed Cal could be a second Terzian for him. They had experienced an intense and complicated relationship while he'd lived in Galhea. Now, it was difficult not to remember those times. Cobweb was also aware he was doing little to guard his thoughts. If Cal picked up on them, he gave no sign, but then he was used to hara being in love with him. For Cal, it was a life hazard. His devotees in Forever formed an exclusive club, but few of them had any idea Cobweb was part of it.

One of many, Cobweb thought, and because he did not like to be such a thing, he curbed his fond recollections. His companions were ready to project their energy toward the shield. That was the only consideration.

Cal's presence was like an amplifier. Cobweb was sure that none present found it difficult to project their intention with power and authority. Cal's strength filled them all. He had been changed, but by what or who? Where had he been all this time?

In his mind, Cobweb visualized the energy dome around Galhea becoming hard as steel, hard as diamond. Whatever struck it would be sent back to whoever hurled it in their direction. *Take it back,* Cobweb thought, *and be aware we will fight you with equal strength.*

An hour or so before dawn, the attack subsided. Cobweb sensed this and picked up a brief mind touch from Snake. *End it now.* Cobweb's low voice called to his companions, bringing them back to normal consciousness. Their work was over. Far from being exhausted the group felt strangely exhilarated. They all commented on it. Those with little experience were overwhelmed by what they had achieved. The atmosphere in the room was one of celebration and triumph.

Yarrow was the first on his feet. "Breakfast," he said, and gestured at some of his staff. "We all need a good meal."

"We'll be down shortly," Cobweb said. "Thank you, all of you, for being here. Galhea has much to thank you for."

"What would have happened if the shield had been breached?" Bryony asked. Now it was safe, she obviously felt comfortable asking the question.

"I don't know," Cobweb answered, "but can only imagine it would have been something like what happened at Amber Ridge. Unseen assailants?" He shrugged. "It doesn't matter. We held them off." He paused. "Now we have family business to deal with. I'll see you all later."

The staff filed from the room quickly, and Snake also got to his feet. Cobweb was concerned because of all of them, he seemed the most unsteady. "You don't have to go," he said.

"I would prefer to," Snake answered.

Tension came into the atmosphere. Cobweb let him go, leaving only Tyson, Ferany, Cal, and himself behind.

"Do you want me to go also?" Ferany asked.

Tyson shrugged as if he didn't care either way. He was staring at Cal. "Did you come to me last year? I thought I saw you."

"I was thinking of you," Cal said carefully. It was clear he had no idea how to relate to Tyson. Perhaps this was because of all the hara in the world, Tyson was the only one that Cal couldn't use arunic wiles on. "It's like looking in a mirror. I'd know you anywhere," he said. "You've turned out well."

Cobweb winced inside.

"I have spent my whole life so far convincing hara I'm not you," Tyson said, but he didn't sound bitter. "Looking at you now I wonder why I bothered."

Cal laughed. "It amuses me to think of Seel having to see you every day. I'm grateful to you for that. I have remembered many things."

"Like what?" Tyson asked.

Cal shook his head. "Details. Not important. Well, now we have met again and I'm relieved to discover you're not some screwed-up ball of resentment ready to go for my throat. Pellaz bullied me about us meeting, you know, and frankly I was terrified of it. I'm quite aware I'm not exactly a model parent."

"I never resented you leaving me," Tyson said. "That's the truth. I'm too like you not to understand."

"Does Pell know you're back?" Cobweb asked quickly before Cal could respond.

"No, not yet," Cal said and there was a guardedness in his tone that made Cobweb uneasy.

"When . . . ?"

"I don't know," Cal interjected. He glanced at Tyson and Ferany, then clearly came to the decision he felt comfortable speaking plainly in front of them. "I don't know whether I will return to Immanion."

"Oh," Cobweb said. "I see."

"I hope you do. Some would call it healing. I've learned to be realistic."

Ferany spoke up in a cool voice. "All of Wraeththu will be disappointed. Your love for Pellaz is . . . was . . . legendary. Your reunion was supposed to be the happy ending."

Cal grimaced. "I prefer to be something other than a legend. My home is in Galhea. It always has been, since the day I first came here."

Cobweb was astounded by these remarks and not altogether pleased. Pellaz was, after all, one of his best friends. "What happened to make you change your mind?" he asked coldly.

"You just walked out on him, didn't you?" Tyson said, before Cal could answer. "You weren't spirited away, or kidnapped."

It was obvious to Cobweb that Tyson was delighted about that. "Do you know what happened to Rue?" Cobweb asked.

"I heard," Cal said. "I'm sorry for him, but essentially it was the best thing that could happen. What we did together was wrong."

Cobweb gazed at Cal in shock for some moments. "Do we get to hear the full story?" he asked at last. "Where have you been?"

"Receiving an education," Cal answered. "The one I should have had before I was sent to Immanion in the first place. If I'd had it then, things would have turned out very differently."

"Would you have even gone there?" Tyson asked.

Cal fixed his son with a stare. "I really don't know," he said. "Let's just say, if I had, my motives would have been different."

"I don't believe this!" Cobweb snapped. "You are denying Pell completely? This isn't you, Cal. I don't believe it."

"I deny nothing," Cal said, "but hara change. I was deluded. Even Rue told me that. The Pellaz I was obsessed with is long dead."

"You've been indoctrinated," Cobweb said. "You must have been. Who put these things in your head?"

"Orien did," Cal said laconically. "Or rather the memory of him. Shall we leave it there? There are more important things to discuss than my obsessive past. Pellaz doesn't need me at the moment, Cobweb. Leave idealistic romance out of it. We have important issues to address."

"Excuse me," Cobweb said, "but in this matter I am obsessive myself. I won't let you duck out of it. We're family, Cal. For the Ag's sake, what the hell has gone on?"

"I have been with Thiede," Cal said.

"What?" Cobweb drew in his breath. "He's not dead, then, as Pell wasn't dead. I see. Who *is* dead? Will Terzian show up again? Will Gahrazel?" He laughed coldly. "Maybe you could bring Orien back, while you're at it. This is insane."

"Thiede is Aghama," Cal said reasonably. "You know this."

"Oh," Cobweb said. "I get it. You've been with a god. Makes sense. Only you could do that."

"Why are you angry?"

"Angry?" Cobweb couldn't even respond. "We should eat. We're all hungry."

He began to leave the room and noticed Tyson pat his hostling's shoulder. Cal reached for his son's hand, squeezed it briefly. Allies instantly. Typical.

Snake didn't come down to the dining room, so Cobweb asked Bryony to take him a tray. Later, he would visit Snake, who was sleeping in one of the guest rooms. For now, he still wanted to get the truth from Cal. It was disorientating to be sitting at the dining table with him, where he placed himself in the very seat where once he had stabbed Terzian right through the hand. Cobweb swallowed bitter saliva. He remembered how he'd felt then, so jealous and frightened. He remembered Terzian's desire for Cal, which had been so strong it had filled any room they were in together like smoke. He wanted Cal to be the same as he had been back then, the wild creature, whose madness was barely contained: the angel of vengeance doomed to a desperate love that was almost sacred. He didn't approve of this new, contained, and very obviously sane and sorted Cal. It diminished him, made him too safe.

There were only four of them seated at the big table. Cobweb felt all the absences deeply.

"So this is your chesnari," Cal said to Tyson, smiling at Ferany. "You are fortunate."

Ferany had already been reduced to a shuddering mass of quivering eyelashes and coquettish glances. Cobweb groaned inside. He was also curious as to how Tyson would answer.

"We've been together for a while," Tyson said, applying himself with rather too much concentration to the food on the table.

"He hates the word 'chesna,'" Ferany said. "He thinks it makes him sound too ordinary and boring. That's your influence, I expect."

Cal laughed. "Probably. For that I apologize. But I hope that despite his lack of commitment, the experience is worth it."

"Oh, *yes,*" Ferany said, "he gets that from you too."

"So," Cobweb interrupted firmly. "About your story, Cal. Will you tell us now?"

Cal was crumbling a bread roll onto his plate. "Some of it," he said. "I can't tell you everything, Cobweb, not yet."

"The smallest particle would relieve me greatly."

Cal drew in a deep breath. "Okay. I didn't leave Pell voluntarily, not exactly. I had to leave, because there was something I had to do, that only I *can* do. It's my work now and I can't speak of it entirely. Shall we say it's classified, but it's to do with what's happened in Gebaddon and what is now happening in Fulminir?"

"How did you find out about this *vocation?*"

"Somehar came to me. I met him in Immanion and he convinced me."

"Who?"

Cal shrugged his shoulders. "Sorry . . ."

"Thiede?"

"No. An agent of . . ." He sighed. "This is very difficult. I can only say an agent of individuals who have Wraeththu's well-being at heart."

"Conspiracy, how lovely," Cobweb said mordantly.

"This is important to me," Cal said. "I have purpose now, and direction. I've never had that."

"So what will you do next?"

Cal gazed at Cobweb for a few moments. "I think we should discuss what you should do next."

"You have plans for me? How sweet."

"You must take your hara and the human community from Galhea, Cobweb. You must take them to a safe place. They are not safe here."

"We can protect ourselves. We did so last night."

"That was nothing. That was Ponclast testing the water. He has allies you cannot imagine. He will go to them now and next time he attacks, you won't be able to hold him off so easily, not even with my aid."

"It's impossible to move an entire community. It would take months of planning."

"Then you'd better begin today. You don't have months."

"Ithiel is in charge in Swift's absence. You must speak to him of this matter. I would be interested to hear his opinion."

"I will speak to him today. It's imperative that Galhea is evacuated. It is perhaps the only way to preserve it."

Cobweb shuddered, remembering his dream of Forever in flames. In his heart, he sensed that Cal spoke the truth. "How do you know this?" he asked.

"If you knew who Ponclast's allies were, you'd know it yourself."

"Well, I don't, do I?" Cobweb said. "Because you won't tell me."

"I hope you never know," Cal said. "Trust me. I said I was here to help and I am. This is the best advice I can give you. Ponclast wishes to destroy the House of Parasiel. He burns with hatred for Swift and by default for all those who honor him."

"I can't leave here without Swift," Cobweb said. "We don't know if he's safe."

"He is safe," Cal said. "You will receive news very soon."

"What happened at Amber Ridge?" Tyson asked. "Do you know?"

Cal nodded. "A little. They were attacked again, after Swift's forces arrived there. As far as I know, he held them off, but didn't manage to take any prisoners."

"How do you know this?" Cobweb asked.

Cal smiled. "Colleagues keep me informed."

Cobweb uttered a derisive snort. "I hate this. It's so stupid. Just tell us the truth, Cal! What could possibly be so dangerous in being honest?"

"What you don't know can't harm you," Cal said. "That's all I can say. At one time, I despised Orien for this kind of behavior, and the irony is not lost on me, but I'm sorry, I can't say more. We must concentrate on the problems here for now, evacuating Galhea."

"But where could we go?" Ferany asked. "Where could we take an entire community so that Ponclast couldn't find us?"

"You must think about it," Cal said, gazing at Cobweb. "Think hard."

"If you're here to help, *you* think!" Cobweb snapped. "Can we get to Immanion?"

"No, the otherlanes are still disturbed and you'd need too many *sedim*. I doubt Pellaz can spare them."

"Imbrilim?" Tyson suggested.

"Prime target," Cal said.

"We could go to the forests, I suppose," Cobweb said, "but how would we feed everyone?" He shook his head, then paused. "Wait . . ."

"You've thought of somewhere?" Cal said.

"A possibility," Cobweb replied, "though it's a couple of weeks ride away, through the cloud forests."

"Where?" Tyson asked.

Cobweb pulled a sour face. "When Ponclast was in power the Varrs had . . . breeding facilities. It was a disgusting concept, quite grotesque. The Gelaming liberated one of these harling farms some years ago, the only one that ever really became 'successful,' and I became friendly with the har who was left in charge of it once the Varrs abandoned them. It became an education center and a kind of orphanage, but still has the advantage of being fairly hidden and I know they already have some basic facilities . . ."

"Like what?" Cal asked.

Cobweb rubbed his temples, eyes closed to conjure up old memories. "Fields nearby, where the visiting soldiers would stay, a covered pavilion, fireplaces and some running water built in, a few showers even." He looked up. "Running water in the facility too, more indoor sleeping space than they need these days, a small farm, kitchens . . . And I know they've stockpiled on supplies—Lis is paranoid about that. It's possible . . ." He frowned. "But no, it won't work . . . It's not really big enough, certainly not designed to handle an entire community like ours."

"But it sounds the perfect place," Tyson said. "Way off in the wilderness, supplies even . . ."

"I doubt Lisia could, or would, help us," Cobweb interrupted. "He is fiercely protective of his hara."

"Whoever this har is, he's obliged to help," Cal said. "You are in extreme need. If this is the best you can think of, and I agree with Tyson this does sound feasible, you must go there."

"Can you try to contact him, Cobweb?" Ferany asked.

"I could try, although the ethers are still not too reliable, and I haven't communicated with Lisia for quite some time. I'm not sure we are attuned as much as we used to be."

"We could just go there," Tyson said. "Turn up unexpectedly. Then he could hardly refuse to help us."

Cal smiled. "Good thinking. But less of the 'we.' You'll be going somewhere else."

"Oh? Like where?"

"With me," Cal said. "To Fulminir."

"Great," Tyson said, "and this suicidal mission is for . . . ?"

"To free Azriel and his chesnari," Cal said. "Had you forgotten them?"

"*You* will do this?" Cobweb asked, surprised. "You won't help us evacuate the town?"

"That is your task, and Ithiel's. We have to get Azriel out of Fulminir fast. We believe that Ponclast intends to use the Sarestes for some abominable purpose. Too many harlings are being created like perverted machines. The mingling of the blood of the snake and what Ponclast has become is too dangerous."

"Does your harling still live?" Cobweb asked. "The one that Rue hosted?"

"Yes," Cal said. "He does."

"How? Where . . . ?"

Cal raised a hand to silence him. "And Ponclast seeks to create somehar similar. We know that, but not everything. Some areas are cloudy. When we heard he had taken Aleeme Sarestes, we feared the worst. The Colurastes hide their light, and their considerable powers. There is something in their blood. Not even Ulaume is aware of everything about his tribe."

"You know about . . ."

"We know Ulaume and Flick are in Shilalama, yes," Cal said, "although I was stringently prevented from meeting them when I was there. I wish I had. I should have seen Flick. He would have persuaded me that what I intended to do was wrong, but . . ." He sighed. "It no longer matters. We cannot change the past. We can only change the future."

All were silent for a moment, then Cobweb asked, "The harling you created, Cal, what has he become? What is he? Why was he taken and by who?"

"He was a mistake, a product of the Tigron's arrogance."

"The Tigron's fear," Cobweb amended curtly.

"What we did was wrong. Two hara create pearls, not three. It was . . . sickening, an abuse of Rue's body. Every time I looked at him afterward, it was as if I could see that *thing* . . . the pearl inside him, sucking out his life, greedy and monstrous, so much bigger than a pearl should be. Pellaz was rash and ignorant to persuade us. We trusted him."

"Pell felt he had to do it, you know that," Cobweb said. "He felt he needed to create somehar special. It was instinctive."

"Maybe that is true, but the motive changes nothing. The harling is safe now, where he can do no harm."

"You make him sound like a monster, but he's as much your son as Tyson is."

Cal closed his eyes briefly. "I know that. But I trust the hara who care for him."

"Pell and Rue should know about this," Cobweb said.

Cal shook his head. "No. I should not have told you. You must say nothing."

"I can't promise you that!" Cobweb snapped. "Rue was ripped apart, Cal, literally. He deserves to know."

"Does he?" Cal asked sharply. "I won't discuss this any longer." He turned to Tyson. "After we've finished breakfast, take me to Ithiel."

In the event, they did not need to, because Ithiel came to the house before they'd left the table. He was shocked to find Cal there, but listened to all Cal had to say. At the end of it, Cobweb said, "I want to speak to Ithiel privately. We have a big decision to make."

"Of course," Cal said. "I understand that." He stood up. "I'd like to go down to the town, Ty. Care to show me around? I wonder how much it's changed."

"Quite a lot, I expect," Ferany said. "I'll go home, give you two time to get reacquainted."

"Beautiful *and* considerate," Cal said.

Ferany actually blushed at that and left the room quickly.

"Some things never change," Cobweb said darkly.

He took Ithiel out into the gardens, not least because the thought of having to leave them made him want to spend time there while he still could. "What do you think?" he asked Ithiel as they strolled down a graveled path.

Ithiel did not answer immediately. "I don't know. It's a big move, and from what I saw last night you and Snake held the shield together."

"Cal thinks we might not be able to do it again, though."

Ithiel stopped walking, wrinkled his nose. "I don't know. Maybe we could get local farmers to move the herds to higher pastures, make some kind of arrangements for a possible evacuation. It wouldn't do any harm to be prepared."

"No, I agree, but I don't think we should just scare every har and human in this town into taking flight. What would Swift do?"

"He'd be cautious, but also prepared. I think perhaps we could evacuate harlings, and the human children and older humans. The forest lodges could accommodate them."

"That makes sense. Will you see to it?"

"I will, though I doubt it will go down well. Galhea trusts this house, Cobweb. It believes you can keep it safe."

"Precautions are never amiss," Cobweb said. "This is what you must impress upon the hara and people."

Ithiel took hold of one of Cobweb's arms. "And how are you bearing up?"

"Managing," Cobweb answered. "Thank you for asking." He stopped walking. "Come to me tonight, Ithiel. I need comfort."

"I will be there," Ithiel said. "It has been too long."

"I am unfair to you. I snap my fingers and you always come to me. It feels like I'm using you, but I'm not."

"I understand," Ithiel said. "I know the boundaries. Don't concern yourself with it."

"There are things, perhaps, I should have said to you."

"Hush," Ithiel murmured. "Save it for the time when all this is over. You have enough to worry about. I'm not one of those things."

"You are a good friend," Cobweb said.

They went back into the house.

Cal did not approve of Cobweb and Ithiel's caution. "You should begin preparations for a wholesale evacuation now," he said. "If you don't, it might be too late."

"You don't really believe the Gelaming are unable to contain this problem, do you?" Cobweb said. "I can't see the point of such an upheaval if the danger is to be eradicated sooner rather than later."

"And how long will your shield hold against attacks?" Cal said. "It could happen again tonight, and you don't have the strength for it."

"I do. We'll get more hara from town to help us. Snake and I can take it in turns to lead them. I don't see that as a problem. One of us will always be on alert. I'll sleep this afternoon."

Cal sighed. "Well, at least you're getting the harlings out. It won't be enough though. I just hope you're not dooming most of them to being orphans."

"I appreciate your concern, and of course you know things that I don't, but unless you're willing to share that information with me, I am yet to be convinced complete evacuation is necessary. Amber Ridge was taken by surprise. We are forewarned. We know what to expect and so does every resident of this town."

Cal shrugged. "I was going to leave for Fulminir today, but will remain here one more night. I've a feeling that's all it's going to take to convince you, if indeed you survive it."

"I wonder whether appearances are deceptive," Cobweb said. "You look sane, but only a mad har would attempt to sneak into Fulminir, surely? What hope have you of success? I don't approve of you involving Tyson."

"I have my methods," Cal said. "You shouldn't be afraid for us."

"How did you get here?" Cobweb said, suddenly aware of the obvious. "You don't have a *sedu*."

"No," Cal said. "I don't need one."

"And you can transport Ty in the same way?"

"I think so."

"Think?" Cobweb laughed scornfully. "That's not good enough."

CHAPTER TWENTY-FIVE

Moon, like most of the young hara of his acquaintance, was excited by what was happening rather than frightened. Every day, parties of hara from different tribes were arriving in Immanion for the council of war that Pellaz had called for. Some were uneasy allies and the city filled with a strange sense of friction and anticipation. It would take time for everyhar to arrive, but already discussions were being held in the Hegalion. Moon could not attend them, but friends of friends did, and from them he learned some of what took place. Gelaming agents had investigated Gebaddon and had found it empty of Varrs, but for a few dying, insane individuals, from whom no sense could be wrenched. Now those same agents were riding north to Fulminir, but it would take time. Moon felt restless. He wanted to be involved.

One morning, he was summoned from his schooling by the Tigron, a development that filled him with hope. He knew that Pellaz was very busy, so it must mean something important would be asked of him. The Tigron received his sori in his office in Phaonica, and his manner was brusque and formal. "I would like you to go to Megalithica," he said.

Moon experienced a chill at these words. His idea of involvement had been to work in the Hegalion, perhaps looking after important visitors or running errands. He didn't believe he'd be asked to leave Almagabra. "Why?" he asked, a little impertinently.

"I wish for you to go to Galhea," Pellaz said. "Your father will need you at this time."

"But how?" Moon persisted. "How will I get there? A sea journey would take forever."

"My *sedu*, Peridot, can take you there. We have been investigating the otherlanes, and have found a route. It might not be the most comfortable of journeys, but I'm confident of Peridot's abilities."

It occurred to Moon then that Pellaz knew what he suggested was fraught with peril. Why would he risk the life of his own flesh and blood in this way? Moon couldn't believe it was simply because Snake had need of him. But if there were another reason, why wouldn't Pellaz just say it?

"What must I do there?" Moon asked.

"Snake will no doubt find work for you."

"Has he asked me to come to him?"

"Not in so many words. He wouldn't believe it was possible for you to reach him, but it is. I wish you didn't have to go alone, but Peridot cannot get more than one har through." He fixed Moon with a stare. "It is important, Moon. I can't tell you why, only that I feel it strongly. There is work for you in Galhea. My instincts tell me so. I wouldn't dream of asking you to do this if I wasn't convinced it's vital."

Moon laughed uncertainly. "Don't know how much use I'll be, but of course I'll go. If you think Snake needs me, I have no choice."

There was no outward sign of Pellaz slumping in relief, but Moon sensed that was how the Tigron felt inside. "I'm pleased to hear it. You are of my blood, Moon. You are very dear to me."

Moon knew in his heart that Pellaz had never said those words to his own son. He'd heard all the gossip about Abrimel and his relationship with the Tigron. Now, Moon felt sorry for this har he had never met. He felt he was stealing something that rightfully belonged to Abrimel, which was strange. If the accounts were correct, Abrimel didn't care one way or the other what Pellaz thought of him.

Before he left Immanion, Moon knew he should at least say good-bye to Raven, but couldn't face the prospect of Raven's worry and complaints. If he was going to go through with this, he'd leave without seeing anyhar. If he didn't say good-bye, it meant he'd surely come back.

Pellaz took him to the stable block in the palace and together they walked out of the city leading Peridot. Pellaz clearly didn't want anyhar to see Moon leave, and Moon intuited this was because nohar knew that the otherlanes were at least partially negotiable. Hidden among the hills, Pellaz helped Moon onto Peridot's back. Moon had never ridden a *sedu* without harness before. He felt unsafe and hoped his anxiety wouldn't affect the creature. He dug his fingers deep into Peridot's thick mane. He wanted to leap to the ground, beg Pellaz not to make him go, but at the same time he wanted the Tigron to admire and respect him.

"It is not shameful to be afraid," Pellaz said. "Your courage will not be forgotten." He laid a hand briefly on one of Moon's legs and then stood back. Peridot began to walk forward. Moon's last image was of Pellaz raising a hand in farewell, and then reality shattered.

Pellaz had not exaggerated. It *was* the most uncomfortable of otherlane journeys. Peridot enfolded Moon totally in his being, but even so, Moon was aware that many times their headlong flight was arrested by insurmountable obstacles. His very soul felt sick at the constant twists and turns, the abrupt halts, when it felt as if his essence would be torn to shreds, and the unimaginable treacherous leaps through what felt like nothingness—gaps in the path. It should take only minutes to reach Megalithica, but it felt like hours. Time does not exist in the otherlanes as it does in normal reality: Moon was only aware of how long the journey was taking because he felt himself losing all sense of identity. If it didn't end soon, he'd disappear completely. It was like dying, slipping away. Perhaps Peridot couldn't find a way out. But then a portal opened and the *sedu* plunged through it. Moon could not repress a scream of pain. It was like being dragged through a maze of broken glass.

Peridot crashed down onto hard earth with such a jolt that Moon finally fell from his back. He curled into a ball and lay there shuddering, so full of fear his being was consumed by it. His whole body was covered in a crust of ice. Gradually, he became aware of Peridot's hot breath on his face, the *sedu's* long whiskers tickling his cheek. Reality came back to him and he was able to struggle into a sitting position, shrugging off the melting shards that clung to his clothes and hair. Peridot had brought him to the gardens of Forever. From the position of the sun, Moon could see it was late afternoon. Everything looked normal. There was no sign of conflict and for that he was grateful. Using Peridot's broad flank for support, Moon got to his feet. He could see that a har was already running from the house, no doubt having felt the portal open. Peridot nudged Moon with his nose and then walked away into the trees. He opened another portal at once and disappeared through it. Moon hoped the *sedu* would find it easier to travel without a passenger.

The har who had come running from the house was Cobweb. "Moon!" he exclaimed. "How did you get here?" He was looking around, no doubt searching for a *sedu*.

"Peridot brought me," Moon said, "but he went straight back into the otherlanes. Pellaz wanted me to come here."

"Why?"

This question was delivered too sharply for Moon's liking. He shrugged. "I don't really know. I'm sorry if it's inconvenient."

Cobweb shook his head. "No, no, I'm glad to see you and so will Snake. Come into the house. You look dreadful. Whatever was Pell thinking of, shoving you through the otherlanes when they're in such a state?"

On the way to the house, Cobweb informed Moon of everything that had happened. They were under attack, and yet the day was so calm and beautiful, the sunlight dripping like butter off the eaves of Forever. There was no feeling of threat to the air, nothing at all. Only Moon could see that Cobweb had bitten through his beautiful lips, and they were ragged, marked with blood.

"Cal is here," Cobweb said.

Moon wasn't sure what he was supposed to say to that. He knew only that the name immediately brought an image of Tyson to mind and for a moment he wished he hadn't come, only for this feeling to be followed by one of great anticipation.

"He's been missing for a reason," Cobweb continued, apparently talking more to himself than to Moon. "He's here to help us."

Cobweb ushered Moon into Forever through the window doors that led into the main sitting room, which was shady at that time of day. "Does Pell know Cal is here?" Cobweb asked.

Moon shrugged. "I don't know. He didn't mention it to me. He's never talked about Cal to me, in fact. I'm here because he thinks there is work for me in Galhea."

"We might have to evacuate the town," Cobweb said. "Ithiel is sending the harlings to the forest lodges today."

"Have hara been killed?" Moon asked.

"Not here," Cobweb replied, "but despite appearances, we are in danger, or so Cal believes."

Now, they were in the hallway and Moon wondered where Cobweb was taking him.

"Swift has taken a fair-sized force to Amber Ridge," Cobweb said. "The house feels so empty. Everyhar's gone."

Maybe Tyson had gone with his brother. Moon realized he was afraid of seeing that face again, even though he yearned to. The thought made him remember the musty smell of the Reliquary, the way he'd felt, the strange tremulous excitement. He should be over it. He was the Tigron's sori, a har of importance. Pellaz would never betray such weakness.

Perhaps some of these thoughts leaked out of his mind. Cobweb turned to him and said, "It's not your fault, Moon. It was never your fault. He just wasn't ready." Then he walked away quickly, beckoning for Moon to follow him, so that Moon wondered whether he had really heard those words at all.

They went into the kitchen, and Cal was there talking to Bryony. He was sitting on the table, amid a pile of scrubbed pans, eating a raw carrot. Moon expected to feel some kind of rush, but was strangely unmoved. This was a har of dreams, a legend, yet he was not Tyson. There could be no mistake. Cal, however, appeared momentarily horrified when he caught sight of Moon.

"This is Snake's son, Moon," Cobweb said, and then added rather pointedly, "Pell has sent him to us."

Cal laughed uncertainly. "Here to check on us?"

Moon knew instinctively that what Cal had seen was the image of Pell from long ago. He might have thought a ghost had come into the room to accuse and stare. "No," he said. "I'm here for my father."

"You shouldn't have been sent here. It's not safe. If Pell can get *sedim* to Galhea, he should consider getting these hara out of here, not adding more."

"He doesn't know about what's happened here," Moon said.

"He will do," Cobweb said. "Snake will contact him. Eventually."

Moon didn't feel comfortable at all. He wanted to see his father. He didn't like the scrutiny of this lazy-eyed har, who might well be concocting ridiculous ideas about him. He wasn't a spy. He wasn't part of the past. He wasn't an omen.

Cobweb seemed to be in a daze. Why he'd taken Moon to meet Cal, Moon wasn't sure, because only minutes later, he was telling Moon to follow him upstairs to Snake's room. The longer Moon spent in the house, the more he could sense that nothing at all was right. You could tell so many of the family were missing, even though Forever was often empty of hara on summer afternoons.

Snake was pleased to see his son, but angry that Pellaz had sent him into danger. Moon was shocked by his father's appearance. The last time he'd seen him, Snake had looked better than he ever had. Now, there were blue shadows beneath his eyes and his face was drawn. He could barely rise from the seat by the window, and as he did so, shakily, a book fell from his lap to the floor. He could not bend to pick it up, so Cobweb did so.

Moon went to his father's embrace. "I warned you once," Snake whispered in Moon's ear. "I told you I was afraid of what my brother would have me do."

Moon gazed into his father's gold eye. "Don't do it," he said.

"I have to," Snake said. "It is no longer just for Pellaz."

"Perhaps you can help us tonight," Cobweb said to Moon. "Give your strength to your father."

"I'll do whatever you want me to," Moon said to Snake, and Snake nodded, saying nothing.

Cobweb went to his room to sleep for a few hours and Moon remained to talk with Snake, relaying gossip from Immanion and snippets of news about Raven. But Moon could see that his father could barely concentrate on what was said to him. Eventually Moon stopped speaking. "You've hardly heard a word I've said. You should get some sleep too. I can see you need it."

"I will," Snake said. "Maintaining the defenses is hard work, Moon. Even Wraeththu are not built to sustain such effort."

"Perhaps Cal is right and everyhar should leave Galhea," Moon said.

"I fear he might be," Snake replied. "If an attack comes again tonight, we'll have no choice."

Moon went out into the gardens and walked down to the lake. He felt melancholy, because his life had changed so much for the better, now Fate seemed to want to ruin it. If there hadn't been a threat, of course, Pellaz would probably never have looked for his brother, but if only Snake had been strong enough to vanquish that threat. That would have been the perfect end to it.

The waters of the lake, stirred only by an occasional ripple as fish broke the surface, were inviting. Moon took off his clothes and waded out from the bank. The water was so clear, he could see white pebbles on the bottom. He could see the quicksilver fishes flashing away from his legs. Moon dived beneath the surface and swam underwater for as long as he could hold his breath. The cold brought clarity back to his mind. He must do what had to be done, as Snake was doing. He must take each moment, one at a time. The shard in his heart was strength, not weakness. Each time it pricked him, it reminded him he was alive and feeling. It was real.

He broke through the surface, gasping, treading water. His hair felt very heavy over his shoulders and at once the hot sun burned against his skin. He swam back to where his clothes were lying, and saw that somehar was sitting beside them, perhaps waiting for him. *Did I invoke him?*

"Hello, Tyson," Moon said. The pain of instinctive longing was actually exquisite, nothing to be feared.

Tyson didn't even glance at him, and seemed quite abashed to find Moon naked. "I thought we should speak before tonight," he said, staring at the ground. "I didn't want to embarrass you. Ferany will be here."

"Why would that embarrass me?"

Moon could tell that if anyhar was embarrassed, it was the one sitting in front of him. He decided he would not dress himself at once. He could dry off first. Tyson's discomfort was a soothing balm. The least Moon could do for himself was enjoy this spurious pleasure for a short while. He sat down beside Tyson and stretched out his legs, leaning back on straight arms.

"Oh, come on," Tyson said. "You know what I mean. I didn't want you to think . . ."

"Think what?"

"That I was putting you in a difficult position."

"You're not. Forget what happened. It was eons ago. Part of growing up, I guess, that first crush. I must have been a pain. Don't worry about it. The thought of it makes me cringe."

"Well . . . good," Tyson said. He stood up. "I should get back. I just wanted to make things clear, that's all."

"Thank you, I appreciate the courtesy, but there's no need."

Tyson nodded distractedly and went back along the path to the house. He hadn't looked at Moon once. Moon leaned back, lifting his face toward the sun. He felt numb. He wasn't sure whether he'd said the right things or not.

The sun had done something to him though. That night, as he dressed himself for dinner in the room that Cobweb had given him, Moon was pleased by the way his reflection seemed to glow in the mirror. It was as if sunlight were captured within his skin. He felt remarkably good about himself, hardly feverish at all, and glad he would be spending time in Tyson's company that night, Ferany or no Ferany. He would enjoy the tricky nuances of interaction. *This is power,* he thought. *Tyson doesn't know what he feels, but he feels something.*

This certainty was compounded by Ferany's cool behavior. He gave Moon a measured stare across the dinner table, a dismissive and disapproving gesture, which spoke volumes. Moon wondered whether, on some drunken night, Tyson had told Ferany what had happened between them. He must have heard something, from somehar.

Moon noticed Cal observing him too, but his expression was guarded. "How is Rue?" Cal asked.

"Okay, I think," Moon answered. "I don't see him much."

"Did everyhar think I was responsible for the attack upon him?"

Silence descended over the room like a moldy shroud. Tyson coughed.

"I don't think so," Moon said, glancing at Snake, who was clearly distancing himself from the situation. "My father told them it wasn't you."

"So did I," Cobweb said.

"Pell thought it though, didn't he?" Cal said.

"He feared it," Cobweb said. "That's different."

Cal raised a sardonic eyebrow and went back to his meal.

Cobweb sighed deeply. "After dinner, I'll put more energy into the shield. Snake, you rest. Ferany, Tyson, you come with me. Cal, you work with Snake later."

Cobweb had recruited more hara from the town, including Ferany's parents, so that the defenses would be supported by individuals with more experience and ability. Moon could tell that Cobweb wasn't convinced another attack would come, but even so, every resident of Galhea was on alert, each focused on protecting their own space, should the worst happen. The population had allowed their offspring to be escorted to the forest lodges without too much complaint. Most had been scared witless by the events of the previous night, unable to sleep because of the deafening onslaught that had lasted nearly till dawn. Humans and hara alike gathered in groups of ten or more. None would be left alone this night. Strength lay in numbers. Ithiel and his hara would patrol the town, while Cobweb and Snake concentrated on maintaining the shield. It all seemed organized and efficient.

Moon offered to take part in the first reinforcement meditation, even though he'd previously promised his strength to Snake. He wanted to be in trance in the same room as Tyson.

Ferany had obviously been thinking about the situation, because as they prepared themselves to work he adopted a friendly front. "Sit by me," he said to Moon. "I've done this before. I'll guide you."

It seemed like an easy job to Moon. He was surprised to find how deftly Ferany guided him, like a soft silken hand. He could see the shield in his mind's eye, the dim patches where the energy was weak. He and Ferany concentrated on repairing certain of these areas, feeding them with life force that they drew from the universe itself, while their companions put their efforts into different areas. Even as he was concentrating on this task, Moon's mind was busy with other thoughts. It was obvious why Tyson was with Ferany: he was just so easy and smooth to be around. He reminded Moon of aromatic mild coffee spiced with cinnamon, topped with cream—and that was without even sharing breath. He realized it would make it easier for him if he liked Ferany. He could not feel so envious or jealous then.

How strange it is, Moon thought. Hara in permanent relationships often take aruna with others, but sometimes, just sometimes, there are hara who are off-limits, taboo or threatening, and that's when feelings are involved, deep feelings. Sometimes a light comes out of a har that blinds you to all others, even those you might love and who might love you in return. There can be no sharing then.

He had learned something.

Perhaps Ferany had too. When they came out of the trance, he leaned over and whispered in Moon's ear, "I can't let you have him, Moon. I hope you know why."

Moon squeezed Ferany's fingers, which were still interlaced with his own. He knew.

"I think it will be safe for us to relax a little now," Cobweb said. "The shield holds strong, so if anything hits it we'll have time to prepare ourselves."

"I could do with a drink," Tyson said, "a strong one."

Cobweb fixed him with a stare. "No, Tyson. Keep a clear head. Just in case."

Moon felt he had to be alone, so he excused himself from the others and went to his room. He decided to get a couple of hours' sleep before Snake went on duty. He still intended to assist his father. His body felt on fire; perhaps the sun had burned him more than he'd realized. He drifted into an uneasy sleep, where fragments of dreams drifted through his mind. He dreamed of Cal coming into the room and saying, "I don't like you being here. That face doesn't belong to you." And then somehar else came, who was a complete stranger, yet Moon felt a strong sense of recognition. "I'm glad you came," he said and the har merely smiled and said, "Why would you doubt it?"

Moon didn't know what woke him. There were no suspicious or threatening noises, no strange lights, not even a flex to the air. He just woke up, instantly fully alert, and full of dread. He'd gone to sleep wearing his clothes, so paused only to pull on his boots before leaving the room. The corridor beyond was quiet, yet the lamps on the walls appeared dim, as if energy were being sucked from them. Something was wrong.

Moon went directly to Snake's room and found his father sitting on the window seat, his face nearly pressed to the glass. He glanced around as Moon came over to him.

"What's happened?" Moon asked. "Has the shield been breached?"

"Not that I can tell," Snake answered, "but something has happened. I heard . . ." He shook his head. "I don't know what I heard. Find Cobweb for me. Tell him to send Tyson and Cal into town."

"Right away." Moon headed back to the door.

"Return here as soon as you can," Snake said.

Cobweb and the majority of his helpers were downstairs in one of the sitting rooms, where Yarrow and Bryony had provided food for them. It was clear to Moon, from the moment he crossed the threshold, that Cobweb was already aware something had happened. Hara were stationed at the windows, peering into the darkness beyond. Moon relayed Snake's message.

"Tyson and Cal have already left the house," Cobweb said. "Ferany has gone with them."

"Do you know what's happened?"

Cobweb shook his head. "No. The shield seems fine. It could be a more traditional form of attack, of course. At the moment, that would take us more by surprise." He laughed coldly. "Ironic, really."

Moon didn't want to go back to Snake's room. He wanted to find out for himself what might have happened. "Do you know where Cal and the others went?" he asked.

"I expect they went to the barracks . . . I don't know. It would depend on what they found down there."

"I'll go to help," Moon said, steeling himself for Cobweb's objection, but Cobweb only nodded distractedly.

"Protect yourself," he said. "You'll find equipment in the storehouse off the kitchen. One of the staff will show you." Cobweb was not himself. He seemed half in trance. "We need to protect the house. Find out what you can and report back to me."

In the kitchen, Yarrow helped Moon don a jerkin of reinforced leather armor with a throat guard. Moon noticed that most of the staff were similarly attired. "Take a horse from the stable," Yarrow said. "Do you need help with that?"

"No," Moon said. What did the Parsic take him for, some pampered Gelaming who could not even saddle his own horse? "I know where everything is kept."

He chose a horse he knew belonged to Aleeme, one that he had ridden before on previous, happier, visits to Galhea. Once he was outside, Moon could hear distant shouting coming from the town below the hill, and also the occasional crashing noise, as if barrels were being turned over and windows smashed. He urged his mount to gallop down the driveway and into the wide avenue beyond the iron gates.

Before he rode past the first dwellings, he could smell smoke. He guided his horse toward it. A large storehouse had been set on fire. Moon could see dark shapes running about, heard cries and orders being shouted. Two hara held a spurting fire hose toward the flames. The hose appeared to struggle in their grip like a water serpent. There was a hiss, a pause, then the leaping fire seemed only to gain in strength. Moon rode on. He knew he was looking for Tyson.

Ahead, he could hear cries, the unmistakable sound of combat. He reined in his horse. It would be folly to gallop headlong into conflict without first assessing what was going on. He guided the horse into a side alley between high dark buildings. There was nohar around and the windows of the buildings were dark. The sound of the horse's hooves echoed from wall to wall. After some minutes, Moon perceived a faint blue glow ahead of him, perhaps in the entrance to a backyard. As soon as the horse saw it, the creature refused to move any farther. It danced on the spot, uttering groans, so Moon dismounted to silence it. He approached the blue glow cautiously. It wasn't normal. He knew it didn't belong in this place. Instinctively he drew the knife he had strapped to his belt, even though he suspected the weapon would be of little use to him.

The light was the most beautiful color, a deep peacock hue, seeming to hang about eight or nine feet above the ground. Surely such a thing of beauty could not be dangerous? It was like the balefire that sometimes Moon had seen as a child, coiling over the waters of the Sea of Ghosts. He was hypnotized by it. But then a tall figure stepped out of the shadows, and Moon could see that the amazing light came from its eyes, enveloping its whole face in radiance. It was more than tall: it was a giant. Moon could perceive no other details, but his instincts reacted severely. What stood before him was the personification of terror. For the merest instant, he froze, but then he was running, running as fast he could, filled with a desire to flee so great he couldn't fight or control it. The horse he'd ridden had vanished, no doubt escaping the moment Moon had climbed down from its back. Animals often had more sense than hara.

Moon ran toward the end of the alley ahead, drawn by the familiar sounds of harish voices, and the flicker of flames. Anything, no matter how terrible, would be safer than what lay behind him. Even to look upon it was forbidden, not part of this life, this reality.

He was moments away from the alley mouth, he could see hara running about, the leap of flames from burning roofs. Smoke burned his mouth and lungs. He was just about to leap into the small square ahead of him, but then a strong arm curled itself around his neck from behind and lifted him from the ground.

Moon was choking, dangling in midair, sure that at any moment his neck would snap. He could hear—and feel—a rumble in the thing that held him, a deep frightening sound that shook the fibers of his being. It was like a voice building up, coming from far away, and if it was heard in this world, it would be devastating. Buildings would collapse. The sky would fall. This was the end. Moon was angry, more than frightened, suddenly filled with Uigenna bitterness and Uigenna ferocity. He fought for life, managed to utter a vicious roar of fury.

The creature shook him and he kicked backward, striking the pillars of its legs with his heels. He sensed it pause, as if it were suddenly interested in him in a different way. Words that dripped like poison into his mind hissed: *"Uigenna puppy!"*

How this dialogue might have continued Moon could not guess, because at that moment somehar leapt into the alley, wielding what appeared to be a weapon made entirely of glittering water in both hands. The strange blade swept through the air, shooting off droplets or globules of energy. It struck his captor in the side. Moon was released at once and fell to the ground with a bone-jarring crash. Not even bothering to register whether he was hurt, he scrabbled away to the side. Pushing hair from his eyes, he saw Calanthe har Aralis, Tigron, limned in blue radiance, standing fearless before the smoking-eyed giant. Baring his teeth in a snarl, Cal plunged his weapon into the creature's chest and it vanished.

"You killed it!" Moon cried.

"No," Cal said. "Moved it." He lowered his weapon. It looked like metal now. Whatever had animated it had come from within Cal himself. "What the fuck are you doing here?" He didn't appear to want an answer, as he was already glancing around himself, presumably for more hostile creatures.

"Same as you," Moon said. "Brief me."

Cal gave him a short but considered glance, then nodded his head once. "They haven't broken through the shield. It simply isn't there to them. These are not hara, although they have hara with them . . . got them through."

"What are they?"

"Abominations," Cal said. "Parasiel cannot fight them. They are leaving now. They have achieved their desired result: terror."

Moon followed him out of the alley. The square beyond was fairly quiet, for the conflict had moved on. Hara were attending to fallen comrades. From farther away, the sound of cries persisted. It was the howl of a maddened creature, a creature trapped in a pit, showered by spears, but even as Moon listened to it, it began to ebb away, cries becoming sobs, becoming silence. Moon looked around himself, saw many buildings on fire. He could smell blood, cooked meat, and worse stenches from deep within harish bodies that had been opened to the air.

"I *told* Cobweb," Cal muttered, apparently to himself. "They should have listened to me, all of them."

Moon had to agree.

They went to various areas of the town to assess damage and assist where they could with the injured and dying. Moon helped stanch wounds, held the hands of a har as he breathed his last. He could feel Cal watching him.

Moon had hoped they would come across Tyson and Ferany, but there was no sign of them. Moon checked every corpse he could find, fearfully.

Cal said, "Ty's not hurt, Moon. You won't find him here. Stop fretting."

Moon glanced at him, saw Cal's sly smile, and felt heat creep up his neck. Fortunately, it was unlikely Cal could perceive that in the ruddy light of burning buildings. How had he known though? Was it so obvious?

After a couple of hours, Cal suggested they go to an inn at the edge of the town, which was undamaged. "We need a drink," he said. "We've earned it."

The innkeeper, dealing with a heavy influx of shocked clientele, who would no doubt keep him up all night, gave Cal and Moon ale on the house. They sat outside on the ground to drink it, surrounded by other groups of hara who still could not believe what they'd just lived through.

"Bizarre that you are Uigenna," Cal said conversationally. "But I should have guessed they would reach Pell's old home eventually. I imagined his people as dead, but not incepted. Stupid really. When I look at Terez, I wonder why on earth I didn't take him with me to Saltrock too. Could have saved him some pain."

"You were blinded," Moon said. His throat was so sore from smoke, his voice sounded husky. "You had eyes only for one Cevarro."

"Yeah."

They drank for some time in silence.

"You are some har, Moon," Cal said eventually. "You look so young, yet you showed real guts back there. Nothing fazed you. I can tell you are a har to rely on, and that means a lot in this world."

"I was terrified of the giant . . . thing," Moon said.

"You were kicking hell out of it, yelling like a berserker!" Cal laughed. "Still, I wasn't going to simply watch, much as you might have been able to take that thing out eventually."

"I couldn't have done that," Moon said. He paused. "It *knew* me. It recognized the Uigenna in me, even though I'm not really that now."

"Makes sense," Cal said.

"What is that weapon you've got?" Moon jerked his head toward the apparently normal blade that was now sheathed and hanging from Cal's belt.

"It's called a sword," Cal said, smiling.

"Oh, come on. It's more than that."

"No, it's not. What you saw was a particular aspect of Agmara, life force, which I channeled into the metal. For a time, the metal became something else, a form of energy that can repel certain other kinds of force, such as the thing that had you in its fists."

"Did Thiede teach you that?"

"Yes, he did."

"Can you show me how to do it?"

Cal laughed. "I could, if you have a spare lifetime."

"You haven't been gone that long."

"Time is different where I was."

Moon took a deep breath, then had to voice the question on his mind. "Have you really forgotten Pell?"

Cal ruffled Moon's hair, a distancing gesture. "Impertinent minx!"

Moon pulled away, affronted. "Well, have you?"

"No, of course not. We are one, he and I."

"Then, why . . . ?"

"I'm not going to discuss it with you, so be quiet. We should get back to the house." Cal put his empty tankard down on the floor between his raised knees. "I have a suggestion, which you might like."

"What?"

"How would you like to come to Fulminir with me?"

"Why?"

"I like what I see in you. I think you'll be useful."

"Oh." Moon hesitated. "Isn't Tyson going with you?"

"Yes. It will be dangerous, and your father will no doubt raise a barrage of objections, but I have a feeling about you. I think you should be given the opportunity to show what you can do."

"That's flattering," Moon said. "I'm not sure though." He thought for some moments about how his first instinct had been to come to the town that night, not hide away. He wasn't frightened of facing danger. Perhaps Cal was right about him, but there was also the possibility Cal had a secret agenda, concerning his son, or even himself. Moon didn't like the thought of that.

"Don't be getting the wrong idea," Cal said, clearly intuiting Moon's reservations. "I meant what I said. Whatever's between you and Ty is your business, but I don't think you should let it interfere with your decision. Nohar more than me knows what it's like to be governed by emotions and desire. Take my advice. Don't be like me. It won't get you anywhere but a cold dark place."

"Okay, maybe I will come with you." Moon grimaced, visualizing clearly Snake's reaction to this news.

"You are not a harling," Cal said dryly. "Nohar can tell you what to do now. It's nohar's decision but yours."

"He will hate you for it," Moon said. "Snake, that is." And Pellaz too, no doubt, once he got to hear about it.

Cal nodded. "Oh, well, no change there. I'm used to it."

"You must teach me things, though. I want to learn."

"It will mean we must travel overland, because I can't transport three of us through the otherlanes, not in the state they're in now, at any rate. Also, I now think we shouldn't get to Fulminir too soon."

"Isn't that risky? Ponclast might kill Azriel and Aleeme."

"He won't. That isn't in his plans for them. Their blood is valuable to him. He will breed with them."

Moon shuddered. "That's disgusting."

"Yes. But it'll ensure their safety for a while. I don't know what the end of this will be, but it won't be some huge war. At the end, it will be down to Ponclast and Pellaz. That is Thiede's feeling, and mine also. Pellaz needs to earn his title. This will be the greatest initiation. And he needs to go through it alone."

"I see," Moon said. "He must do as you did. I understand now."

"Good." Cal got to his feet. "Come on, I have an intense desire to raid Yarrow's kitchen. I'm starving. It must be time for breakfast."

CHAPTER TWENTY-SIX

Cobweb did not sleep that night and Ithiel did not come to him. He stood at a window, right at the top of the house, in a neglected area that pulsed with memories. He saw the flames shooting into the sky, and the strange blue lights that moved with slow and inexorable purpose around the town. He could feel in every atom of his body that hara were dying. They were powerless, and whatever resistance they put up was pointless, just a final act of defiance, before the culling ceased.

After dawn, Cal returned to Forever with Moon. Tyson and Ferany had got back to the house moments earlier and were sitting with Cobweb in the dining room.

"Do you see now?" Cal said to Cobweb. "Do you understand why I advised you to leave?"

"You can't strike them," Tyson said. "They are not harish. They just took who they wanted and left."

"How many casualties?" Cobweb asked.

"That is still being estimated," Cal said. "I would imagine several hundred."

"I just thank the Aghama my parents were here at Forever," Ferany said. He paused, his mouth tight-lipped. "Our house is gone. It's a ruin."

"They avoided Forever, avoided Galhea's heart," Cal said. "They are wary of your power, Cobweb, or Snake's, or the pair of you combined."

"We have little power left," Cobweb said. "Today, we must leave Galhea, as you said. We'll go to Harling Gardens and trust that Lisia can and will help us. Where is Ithiel? He must begin organizing our people at once."

"I don't know," Tyson said.

"Then go and look for him," Cobweb said. "Put out a mind call. Do it now."

Tyson went to attend to this task, while Ferany sought out his parents in the guest rooms.

Moon said to Cobweb, "Do you think Snake will be able to stand this journey?"

Cobweb sighed. "I don't know. He has to. I wish Pell could send Peridot to carry Snake back to Immanion. Perhaps I should ask him."

"I don't think Snake could manage the otherlanes journey either," Moon said. "It wasn't easy. His condition has deteriorated. I don't like it."

"I know," Cobweb said. "I will give him healing myself this morning."

"There may not be time," Cal said.

"There *is* time," Cobweb snapped. "The rest of you get everything ready. Yarrow and Bryony will help. You know that."

"You are leader of Parasiel at this moment," Cal said. "Everyhar needs to see you. You should go . . ."

"No," Cobweb said. "My place is here, with Snake. He has sacrificed himself for us. I'll not let him . . ." He shook his head. He didn't want to say the word "die" in front of Moon.

At that moment, Bryony came into the room. Her expression was odd: shocked yet blank. "You must come," she said to Cobweb. "You must come at once."

"Why?" Cobweb snapped.

"Tyson has brought Ithiel here . . ." Bryony rubbed her face with both hands. "Cobweb . . . Cobweb, he's dead."

Cobweb went utterly still. It was as if another har walked inside his body, took over. Without saying anything, he followed Bryony to the kitchen. Tyson stood next to the table, along with two other hara from the town, and the majority of the household staff. They had laid the body of Ithiel there. Cobweb swallowed sour saliva: his tongue felt too big in his mouth. Hara stood aside to let him reach the table. Nohar said a word.

Ithiel's face was covered in blood. His eyes were open, as was his throat: the guard that should have protected it had been ripped away.

Cobweb looked down at this dead har who had been so big a part of his life for so long, taken always for granted. Ithiel, the right hand of Parasiel, who had served Terzian, then Swift, with unfailing loyalty and efficiency. Cobweb could see himself falling upon the body in tears, tearing out his hair, uttering laments. He could see himself curled in a corner, shuddering with terror, alone. It would be so easy to do it, and so comforting. What did hara expect of him now? Although he had always been discreet, it was no secret that the har who crept at night to Cobweb's room when he needed company was Ithiel. They had never been chesna, just friends who'd been comfortable in each other's arms. Cobweb was not even sure what he felt now. If anything, it was a crushing sense of inevitability, but something else also, like a door opening. Strange. He couldn't work out what it meant. Everyhar was staring at him; he could tell without glancing up. The moment he had been dreading had come. He could never be the same again.

"Wash his body," Cobweb said, gesturing at Bryony. He turned to some of the other house-hara. "Dig a grave, now, and with haste. Do this before you prepare to leave." He realized he hadn't yet announced to anyhar that they were definitely leaving. He had relied on Ithiel to do it.

The house-hara, however, did not question his words. They left at once.

"Bryony," Cobweb said. "Find what is left of Terzian's ceremonial uniform. I believe it is in a chest in the first attic. Dress Ithiel in it when you are done with preparing his body. I will conduct a Ceremony of Passing, but there is something I must attend to first. Do not disturb me. I will come to you when I am ready. Tyson, you and Cal must organize everyhar and human in town to be ready to leave, as soon as possible. They must take only essential supplies, for a journey of two weeks. Everything else must be left behind. We must suppose that one day we can return."

"Cobweb . . ." Tyson said softly, extending a hand.

Cobweb took a step away from him. "Tyson, get to work. There is much to do." He leaned down to kiss Ithiel's brow. "In blood," he said hoarsely. "Beloved of Varrs." He reached out and closed Ithiel's eyelids.

Everyhar was silent as Cobweb left the room. He didn't think, could barely breathe, but made for the stairs and climbed slowly toward Snake's room. Every step took great effort. When he opened the door to Snake's room, Snake was lying on the bed, wide awake. He looked gaunt.

"Ithiel is dead," Cobweb said. His chest felt so tight, he was beginning to feel light-headed.

Snake struggled into a sitting position. "I'm sorry . . ."

Cobweb raised a hand to silence him. "We are lucky we lost nohar else from our family and close friends. Today, we must leave Galhea. I'll give you healing now. The journey might not be easy for you."

Snake stared at Cobweb for some moments. "You can't do this. You must be in shock."

"I must do this," Cobweb said. "I'll not lose you too." He brushed his fingers across his forehead. "I have a salve I can use. I'll fetch it. Undress yourself, Snake. I'll not be long."

Cobweb went to his own room and pawed through the collection of bottles and jars he kept in a cupboard there. His thinking had become a tunnel with hard stone walls. He could focus only on what lay immediately ahead. The most useful of the salves and potions must be packed to take with him on the journey. At random, he began throwing them on his bed, until he found the one he needed. He would not look at himself in the mirror as he left the room.

Snake had stripped to the waist and lay, clearly seething with self-consciousness, on top of his bed. Cobweb took in the sight of Snake's withered left side, the arm so thin, the dreadful scarring that spread in a formation like ice crystals or fungus tendrils, across his chest.

"I didn't want you to see this," Snake said.

"I have just seen one of my oldest friends lying like cold meat on the kitchen table," Cobweb said harshly. "You might be scarred, but you are alive. That's all I care about." He uncapped the jar in his hands and gestured with it toward Snake. "This will help. I've used it in conjunction with hands-on healing many times. An old Sulh recipe, from my homeland. It's very ancient, from long before Wraeththu times."

He sat down on the side of the bed, astounded at how clearly he was able to think. His feelings were in hiding. He gouged out a dollop of the salve and rubbed it between his palms.

"You were Sulh?" Snake said.

"Yes," Cobweb replied. "Lie back and relax. Be quiet."

Snake's body was tense beneath his hands, every muscle bunched up. Cobweb focused on summoning healing energy. There were no other considerations. *Heal yourself,* he told Snake's body. *Use what I pour into you to do it.*

Snake uttered a soft grunt and flinched. If he'd been human, he'd have died years before. It must take every morsel of his strength to maintain this sputtering machine of flesh, because the scars were not just skin deep.

The rhythmic movements of Cobweb's hands helped lull him into trance. He imagined it as being like creating a cat's cradle of glittering strings, the mesh that would reinforce Snake's flesh and essence. After a while, he turned

Snake over, crossed to the other side of the bed, and began work on his back. The shoulder blade felt jagged and fragile beneath its meager covering of skin. Cobweb realized Snake was weeping, silently, his face in the pillow. There was a deep hole between two of his ribs that Cobweb could push a thumb into.

"Let me do the leg," he said softly.

With difficulty, Snake rolled onto his back. He lacked the strength to take off his trousers but allowed Cobweb to do it, lying with one hand pressed against his eyes. Cobweb knew then why Snake avoided physical intimacy with any har. His ouana-lim had been damaged; it was burned and shriveled. He must have been in agony for a long time after the accident. Cobweb applied salve to Snake's thigh, working it into the skin, while channeling healing energy. He knew it would take far more than this to do much good. Perhaps Snake intuited that thought.

"You should leave me behind," he said in a cracked voice. "I've served my purpose."

"I won't leave you behind," Cobweb said. "Whatever you say will not change that."

"I can't be what I want to be," Snake said, "not to you . . . not to anyhar."

Cobweb knew he must be careful. He doubted Snake had ever spoken this way to anyhar before. "You are everything to us," he said. "Your sight is the greatest gift."

"I should be dead." He gestured angrily with his good arm. "This is not a harish body. It is like a failed inception. It is cruel. Life is agony, yet I also love it."

"Count your blessings. You could be Ithiel."

Snake laughed softly. "That is one thing I could never be."

Cobweb wondered if he interpreted correctly the message in those words. "You could be, if you mean what I think you mean." He let his hands lie still just above Snake's knee.

Snake lowered his hand from his eyes, perhaps searching for mockery in Cobweb's gaze. "I can't endure pity, nor revulsion, and even in a har who loves me, neither would be far away."

Cobweb began to move his hands again, gently. "That is probably true," he said. "I understand."

Snake uttered a choked laugh. He hadn't expected that kind of honesty.

"The scarring is ugly," Cobweb said. "I can understand why you don't want anyhar to see it. I wouldn't either." Yet still he continued to massage the flesh, pouring into it more than simple healing power.

"It doesn't feel ugly at the moment," Snake said. "The salve burns cold. It feels good."

"Then you should have let me get my hands on you before, shouldn't you?"

"I wasn't sure I could stand it."

"Well, now you know you can." Cobweb slid the fingers of one hand briefly between Snake's legs. Snake tensed again, holding his breath.

Cobweb stood up and went to the small washstand to clean his hands. He wasn't sure what he was doing or why. It was like being drunk.

"Have you given up?" Snake asked. "You haven't done the lower leg."

Cobweb dried his hands, looking at Snake's reflection in the mirror before him. "No, I haven't given up, but as you said, the salve burns."

"But it was good . . ."

"Hush," Cobweb said. He lay down beside Snake and stroked his face.

Snake laughed uncertainly. "Is this what I think it is?"

"I don't know. What do you think it is?" He put his lips against Snake's own.

Cobweb realized Snake had always known the attraction had been mutual, which was why he'd avoided contact. He was ashamed of his body, embarrassed about having to explain things. Such feelings were no longer pertinent.

I do not pity you, Cobweb said in mind-touch, deep in the sharing of breath. *Nor do you revolt me. I simply want you. Open yourself to me.*

For a moment, Snake's body tensed again. He couldn't believe this was happening because of simple desire. *Is this because of Ithiel?* he asked. *Do you need aruna, Cobweb? Is this your wake for him?*

No . . . Yes . . . I don't know. Cobweb slid his hand down Snake's belly, gently squeezed the ouana-lim, then moved his fingers farther down, more invasively.

Snake pulled away from his mouth, uttering a gasp.

"Are you hurt here also?" Cobweb murmured.

Snake shook his head. "No, it's just been so long. Don't stop."

"Let me undress."

"I don't care."

Cobweb laughed. "Please! Let me go."

Galhea was burning and Ithiel was dead. The future held no certainty, but it seemed to Cobweb as if a small pocket of tranquility existed in that room. For a while, nothing else existed. He didn't care how little time they might have; he intended to take this slow, give Snake as much pleasure as he could. The whole town could come banging on the door and he would pay no heed. He sensed what they were doing was important, beyond mere surface bliss. This was healing on a deeper level, perhaps essential for the journey ahead. Aruna became trance, the rhythm of tides, or the moon across the sky. It held within it the essence of eternity and the stairs of angels to the stars. Cobweb realized they had ventured beyond the boundaries of normal aruna. There was only one possible conclusion, which would not be right. Snake's body couldn't possibly stand it.

"We must stop," he said softly. "You know that."

"No," Snake said. "Don't. It's not what you think. I can tell." With these words he opened the cauldron of creation within him and Cobweb was powerless to end it then. But what happened was not the conception of a pearl. Something was conceived, and at a very deep level, it was painful. Snake's body was rigid. He could not draw breath. Cobweb was afraid Snake was dying, but he could not move. They were paralyzed together, while something beyond their control took place. Cobweb felt as if his ouana-lim were being torn out by the roots. It was agonizing. Then it was as if he were spat out of Snake's body. He leapt up from the bed immediately, expecting blood, more ruin, but there was none. After a moment, he had to go into the bathroom and vomit. He'd never felt so strange.

When he reemerged, Snake was sitting up on the bed. "What just happened . . . it isn't just for making harlings," he said. Slowly, he raised his damaged arm, held it steady. "Look."

CHAPTER TWENTY-SEVEN

They had come from Jaddayoth, sailing in boats driven by spirit winds, swift as the winds themselves. They had come from forest-covered Thaine, from the hot baked land of Huldah, from the ancient green island of Alba Sulh. Representatives from all of Wraeththudom converged on Immanion, with one purpose in mind: destroy the threat from across the ocean. Many tribes had resisted Thiede's aim to unite them under the banner of Pellaz har Aralis, but as few hara had been unaffected by the trouble in otherlanes, most were now prepared to overlook their doubts and misgivings. They realized they were ill-equipped to deal with whatever faced them, and hoped that, in Pellaz, Thiede had created a leader who could help them.

Pellaz took time to meet each representative personally, even if this meant interviewing groups of them at a time. Already teams of the strongest Listeners were at work on repairing the otherlanes. It might only be days before a sizable force could travel through them to Megalithica. But then perhaps the threat was closer to home than that.

A week after Moon had gone to Galhea, Pell's assistant, Attica, came to the Tigron's office to deliver messages that had been received by Eyra's Listeners. Usually, this job was dealt with by Vaysh, but the Tigron's aide was out of the city, in an advance meeting party for the representatives from Maudrah.

"The tribe of Freyhella has requested an urgent audience with you," Attica said. The ethers were still unreliable. Sometimes, they were impenetrable for days.

Pellaz looked up from his work, unable to keep the surprise from his face. "Freyhella? Didn't they decline our invitation to the conclave?"

Attica smiled rather grimly. He was an unusual-looking har with piebald skin. "They did. There's been a development. A Freyhellan fleet is on its way to Immanion. It's estimated they'll arrive sometime today."

"Their leader: Tyr, wasn't it?"

"Was," Attica amended. "The reason Freyhella are now prepared to be cordial is because they have suffered a loss. The details are indistinct. Their new leader will speak only to the Hegemony in person."

"I see." Pellaz frowned. For a moment, he felt extremely unsafe, a feeling he banished firmly. "Is there any other news this morning, Attica?" He could see, from the tight expression, on Attica's face, that there was. "Well, spit it out. What else?"

"It is of a personal nature," Attica said. "The Listeners have received communication from Galhea."

A wave of cold washed through Pell's flesh. "What?" he snapped.

"Tiahaar Cobweb has evacuated the town," Attica said. "It was attacked."

Pellaz stood up, scattering papers as he did so. "Moon? Snake?"

"They are well," Attica said. "Tiahaar Snake has been unable to communicate with you, for some reason, which is why the message came through Eyra's office."

"Evacuated the town . . . Where are they going?"

"A safe place. Information was withheld, for obvious reasons, but there was one other piece of news." Attica drew a breath. "Tigron Calanthe turned up in Galhea."

Pellaz felt as if the ability to speak was taken from him. He stared at Attica for some moments.

"That was all that was said," Attica said awkwardly. "I expect Tiahaar Cobweb wishes you to know that the Tigron is safe and well."

There were further moments of uncomfortable silence, then Pellaz said in a soft voice, "What time is the Freyhellan fleet due? Will you inform me when it is sighted?"

Attica nodded. "Certainly." He paused. "Would you like the Listeners to try and return a message to the Parsics?"

"Not at this stage," Pellaz said, turning his attention to gathering up the scattered papers on his desk. "I will commune with my brother when he is able." He glanced up and attempted a smile. "I expect Eyra has already attempted to relay this information to Imbrilim. Tell him he must report to me immediately if more news is received."

"I'll go and tell him at once," Attica said.

The moment his assistant had left the office, Pellaz went to a quiet room he reserved for meditation and communication and composed himself to contact Snake. His message was a scream upon the ethers, but it was like trying to peer through fog. His wordless cry broke up and dispersed into the murk. He tried also to establish contact with Cobweb, and for the briefest moment was sure he felt the familiar touch of Cobweb's essence, but nothing more than that. He couldn't bring himself to try to contact Cal.

Cal is in Galhea. Why not here?

In his gut he knew the answer to that was because Cal did not want to be there. And that single thought brought back in shining clarity the moment Pellaz first set eyes on Cal. It brought back memories of Saltrock and first love, like a fist slamming into his mind. He could taste Cal's body. He could smell it.

The news spread throughout Immanion like flames, but only Caeru was brave enough to visit Pellaz. He said nothing about Cal, for which Pellaz was grateful, but radiated a cautious aura of support. "I hear the Freyhellans are coming," he said. "I visited Freygard once, a long time ago. My band played there, in fact." He sighed. "Another life! I thought the Freyhellans were beautiful creatures: hair the color of flax and sea-tanned skin. And very magical. A time in Freygard would inspire the least magically inclined har to take up their training again. You should go to watch the fleet arrive. It will be impressive, I'm sure."

"I thought I'd do that," Pellaz said. "They are an independent breed. I'm fascinated, to be honest."

Caeru laughed. "Not surprised, so am I. They're so independent as to decline the support of Immanion, despite their relatively small numbers? I wondered what happened to change their minds."

"Would you like to accompany me?" Pellaz asked.

"I'd like to, but I'm busy this afternoon. Still working on Velaxis. We are meeting with the Thaine delegation later today."

"Any developments with Shiraz?"

"Not really. I have to be subtle." Caeru paused. "Perhaps you could arrange a dinner with the Freyhellans, here in Phaonica. We could inspect them at leisure, then."

"I'll see. It might be best to keep them at arm's length for a time. We don't want this minor upstart tribe to start making demands. They must know their place."

"I'm sure they do," Caeru said, "in their own world."

Pellaz raised an eyebrow. "You think I'm wrong?"

Caeru reached out to touch Pell's face. "I think the Tigron disapproves of not being given the respect he thinks he deserves."

Pellaz laughed. "Maybe. In some ways, I'm looking forward to some kind of challenge."

In the late afternoon, when shadows lengthened along the streets, horns began to blow at the harbor gate to indicate that ships of importance were sailing toward the docks. Pellaz rode Peridot down to the sea and walked him along the right arm of the great curving quay. The tide was high and the sea gates at the mouth of the quay stood open. The message had said "fleet," but did five ships comprise a fleet? All the same, they were impressive, as Caeru had guessed. They were like something out of ancient history, Viking long boats with stylized snarling wolves at their prows. As they passed through the sea gate, and alongside the quay, so the rowers raised their oars and water poured down from the paddles, glittering in the mellow light. Pellaz rode alongside them for some minutes. He presumed the largest ship, whose sail bore the heraldic device of the tribe, carried the Freyhellan leader. He would be a proud and vain barbarian, Pellaz thought. Somehar to be appeased yet in some way curbed. This could make for lively debate in the Hegalion: a way to vent anger, to exorcise feeling in the swordplay of words. The emblem of the Freyhella was symbolic: strange mythical creatures intertwined, which in some ways reflected ancient art, while in others were completely new.

The hara onboard the ships were mostly brown-skinned yet pale-haired. Pellaz fought a rising sense of discomfort as he watched them at work; most of them were stripped to the waist. None of them appeared particularly interested in the sights around them. Perhaps they had decided not to be impressed by Immanion, which was ridiculous, given the way it rose so majestically and impossibly before them. On the largest ship, Pellaz noticed one har break away from his companions and go to the prow. Somehar at least, then, was curious. Perhaps the Tigron's attention was sensed, because the Freyhellan turned to stare at him. Pellaz asked Peridot to halt. He returned the stare, amused to think that if he had made any impression at all, it would be doubly compounded when the Freyhellan met him again and discovered who he was.

The Hegemony was extremely interested in the Freyhellans, which at first Pellaz found somewhat puzzling. The Hegemony Chancellor, Tharmifex Calvel, came to Pell's apartments, shortly after the visitors had arrived. "You must meet with them tonight," he said.

"Why?" Pellaz asked. "Shouldn't they be made to wait? We shouldn't appear too eager. Also, I wonder why we should be eager anyway. Freyhella is hardly as useful an ally as, say, Maudrah, or any of the Jaddayoth tribes, for that matter."

"They are different," Tharmifex said. "Most of us are pleased they've decided to listen to us. I wasn't the only one who was disappointed when they declined to have discussions over the current crisis."

"Different in what way?"

"Eyra in particular feels they will be of immense help. They are deeply spiritual."

"As are many others. I don't understand it, Thar. From a distance, they do appear striking, true, and have a charismatic air to them. But appearances aren't everything."

Tharmifex fixed Pellaz with a stare. "I sense resistance in you. Is there any reason for that?" He didn't like the Tigron disapproving of any of his plans.

"No. I'm just cautious. I like to form my own opinions."

"Tonight, then. At the Hegalion. We'll invite some of the other representatives. Just so we don't appear too accommodating."

Pellaz inclined his head. "As you wish."

The meeting was formal, everyhar sitting in ranks in the main chamber of the Hegalion, with Pellaz and other members of the Hegemony at the high table. Pellaz had dressed down, shunning any trappings of rank. He wanted to appear no different from his colleagues. Several of the Hegemony were missing, as they were involved in other business. This included Ashmael Aldebaran, who Pellaz wished was present. Ashmael would never accommodate anyhar if they didn't deserve it.

Tharmifex had invited as many representatives as he could from tribes already present in the city. It made for quite a crowd, many of whom were eyeing each other suspiciously. They had all come to listen to the Freyhellans, to find out what had happened to make them abandon their staunch sense of independence from the Wraeththu world. Pellaz understood then some of what Tharmifex felt about the Freyhellans. If they were happy to ally with the Gelaming, then so would many others.

The Freyhellans, perhaps to make a pointed gesture, turned up late, after Tharmifex had made the formal introductions of the Hegemony. When they finally arrived, Pellaz registered a stir at the back of the chamber. The new arrivals, five of them, sat down in one of the far rows of seats.

Once everyhar was settled, Tharmifex stood up. "I would like to introduce Galdra har Freyhella." He gestured toward the Freyhellan party. "Tiahaar, if you would come forward. You may speak to this assembly."

Pellaz watched as a pale-haired har stood up and came toward the high table. It took some time because his party was sitting so far back. He was, perhaps no coincidence, the one Pellaz had noticed on the leading ship that afternoon. The Freyhellan wore leather and fur, and his thick pale hair was loose over his chest, whereas most of his companions wore braids, but he did not appear particularly barbaric. It was clear he was very sure of himself, however.

Galdra executed a slight and rather insolent bow to the Hegemony. "Thank you, tiahaar." His gaze flicked over Pellaz, who gave no sign of having noticed it, although his skin prickled. This was the tribe that should have incepted Cal. He was like them in appearance. What would life have been like if that had ever happened?

"We recognize no authority but our own," Galdra began, addressing the hara before him rather than the Hegemony. His accent was heavy, yet musical. "Events have occurred recently, which have touched every harish soul. Nohar knew their origin, or how much threat they posed. After much discussion, Freyhella saw no reason to concur with Immanion's initial summons to a conclave of tribes. We are capable of defending our own boundaries, and many of us believed that the Gelaming would use this crisis to gain control over tribes who might panic and believe they need help, when in fact the problem might be of short duration and easily overcome."

He paused for effect. Pellaz was astounded the Freyhellan dared to speak so openly. He glanced at his colleagues and found an amusing array of impenetrable expressions on their faces. "Something happened to change your mind," Pellaz said in his most ringing tone.

Galdra glanced at him for a moment. "Yes. It is why we're here now. Freyhella no longer believes the threat is small or of short duration."

"Enlighten us," Pellaz said.

"Our leader was murdered," Galdra said, "along with the crew of his ship, on a routine inspection of our outlying coastal towns. His ship was returned to Freygard in flames. Tyr was . . ." Galdra clearly fought to remain composed. "His body was nailed to the mast. We never found . . . He had been decapitated."

A ripple of subdued murmurs swept around the chamber.

"I'm sorry," Pellaz said, and hoped that sounded genuine.

Galdra nodded thoughtfully. "We were chesna. Freyhella desired me to take his seat in our Council. This I have done, in his honor."

"We are pleased to have you with us," Tharmifex said, "though sad it is under such distressing circumstances."

"We don't know what took him," Galdra said, "or why. There was no sign, other than the ship coming out of the mist to our shore in flames. The crew had vanished; there were no bodies. It sailed into dock as if guided by unseen hands, and everyhar could see the body of Tyr, still wearing his chains of office, upon the mast. As the ship came to dock, the flames died down. We don't know how. It seemed to be a taunt. No other tribe on this continent has—to our knowledge—suffered such an attack. We are curious to learn why we were singled out, and also why no follow-up attack occurred. We have decided, not without reservation, to learn whether the Gelaming can assist us in this matter."

"We will do all that we can," Pellaz said, and found that he meant it. As Galdra had spoken, albeit in quite brief terms, Pellaz had imagined Cal being returned to him in that way, headless upon a flaming ship. He could smell smoke and burning meat. He felt paralyzed by loss.

Galdra stared at him for some moments. "Thank you," he said. "I can see you are sincere."

Pellaz realized he was on the brink of succumbing to emotions he'd held in check for months. He stood up. "All we can tell you is that we believe Ponclast, erstwhile leader of the Varrs, is behind recent attacks and otherlane dysfunction. We believe also he has access to powers we are as yet unable to fathom. But our finest minds are working on it, and now we hope the finest minds of other tribes will join with us. It is time to put aside all fears of conquest and power games. Only by uniting can we move on and learn how to protect ourselves from threat. We have much to learn. We should do it together."

Galdra narrowed his eyes a little. "You are the Tigron."

"Yes," Pellaz said. "That is the office given to me. Now, it is late, and you have traveled far today. I think we should meet tomorrow. I have matters to attend to this night. You will all have to excuse me." He could tell Tharmifex and the others at the high table were somewhat affronted that he intended to leave the meeting early, but he couldn't stay longer. He wasn't sure he could keep control of himself. A few more impassioned words and he'd be weeping in front of everyhar, and no matter how that might endear him or not to the tribal representatives, it was something Pellaz could not personally endure.

As he made to leave the dais, heading for a side door, Galdra put a hand upon his arm. His expression was that of inquiry, but also sympathetic compassion. Pellaz could not speak, but pulled his arm free.

"Until tomorrow, tiahaar," Galdra said, and leaned forward to kiss Pellaz on the cheek.

Pellaz fled the chamber, his vision a red mist. The Freyhellan's gesture had been disrespectful and overfamiliar, but also spontaneous. Observation of formal protocol obviously played no great part in the Freyhellan psyche.

Only when Pellaz was far from the room and the night air had claimed him could he release what he felt inside. It wasn't just weeping; it was like vomiting up his heart. He found his way to Caeru's apartments, almost witless with grief, although he'd managed to stop the tears by then. Long ago, Orien had advised him never to weep in front of others, and it was advice he'd always tried to heed.

Caeru, sensitive as to what was wrong, shooed away the friends who were visiting him and planted a large glass of liquor in Pell's hands. "You don't know the reason Cal didn't come back here," he said carefully.

"I do," Pellaz said. "That's the trouble. I am not Pellaz Cevarro. But he is still Cal. He is better than he was, whereas I am somehar completely different. He ran from me, Rue. I know it."

Caeru sighed and knelt by Pell's chair. He winced a little, for his body was still sore inside. "You don't know that."

"Damn Ponclast!" Pellaz snapped. "I should go to Galhea."

"But the Parasilians have already left there," Caeru said softly. "I think you should be thankful you can't go."

Pellaz laughed bitterly. "I am supposed to be strong and dispassionate; to inspire hara in these troubled times. But I have a heart, Rue, and it's bleeding. I can't give myself the time to grieve."

Caeru curled his fingers over one of Pell's hands, which lay limply on the chair arm. "Pell, I don't know what to say to you. Your grief is a monster, it always has been. The love you and Cal have for each other is often destructive. I understand it now, but it also frightens me more."

"I don't think he loves me, Rue. He loves a dead har. It's so cruel. I wish I looked as different on the outside as I am within. Thiede should have taken it from me. Why didn't he? He could have done anything to me. He could have dissolved that love."

"Perhaps there was a reason he didn't."

Pellaz sighed and stroked Caeru's fingers. "Maybe. But I have to go on. I cannot let it consume me. I managed to control it before, I can do it again. Maybe Cal and I will be together again, maybe not. I am Tigron. I haven't got the time to indulge myself wondering about it."

"It's not over, Pell. Trust me on that."

Pellaz kissed Caeru's hair. "I could never have imagined a day I could come to you like this. I am grateful, Rue."

"Cal gave us that," Caeru said. "Stay here tonight. Talk as much as you want, so that tomorrow you can work with a clear head."

Pellaz nodded. "I will. Thank you." He paused. "The Freyhellans are strange. Galdra, their leader, affected me. He made this emotional outburst happen, although it wasn't intentional."

"Tell me," Caeru said. "Tell me everything in your heart."

The following day, Pellaz attended the Hegalion once more as the tribe representatives applied themselves to devising some kind of strategy. Self-defense was of prime importance. What had happened in Freygard could happen anywhere. As in Megalithica, the strikes could be swift and devastating. The leader of the Sulh representatives, a tall, dark-haired har named Heron, said to Pellaz, "Even you might not be safe, tiahaar."

They would all have heard rumors about the attack on Rue, and Cal's disappearance, of course, although Pellaz resolved to play it down. "Nohar is safe," he said. "Status is irrelevant."

During a break for lunch, Pellaz sought out the Freyhellan leader. The Sulh appeared to have struck up quite a friendship with the Freyhellans, perhaps because of similarities in their spiritual outlook. When Galdra saw Pellaz heading over, he excused himself from his companions. "I understand I behaved inappropriately last night," he said, before Pellaz could speak.

"A little importunate maybe," Pellaz replied. "Might I ask why you felt impelled to do that?"

"You have suffered a loss," Galdra said. "My words brought it back to you. Anyhar could see that."

"And anyhar can pick up gossip in the streets of Immanion," Pellaz said. "My private life is not that private."

Galdra smiled. "It seems strange to be able to converse with you like this. I imagined we'd be commanded to prostrate ourselves before a statue in a temple, or something. I didn't for one minute imagine you as a har of flesh and blood, or one whose eyes would carry such pain. That is honest of you."

"Careless, more like," Pellaz said.

"Am I forgiven the indiscretion?"

"Yes. I have already forgotten it."

"If you should ever want to talk, I can provide a friendly ear."

"And I thought a *kiss* was importunate? Really, tiahaar, you are presumptuous."

"So I've been told. I can't see the point of twisted words. I can't play the Gelaming game of intrigue and duplicity. It is part of the reason I was reluctant to come here."

"Then remember to whom you speak," Pellaz said. He inclined his head and turned away, conscious of the Freyhellan's gaze even when he reached the other side of the room.

It was two weeks later that Pellaz finally gave in to Caeru's suggestion for an informal evening reception in Phaonica for visitors to the city. In truth, he had quite enough of the tribal delegates during the day, when it seemed he spent most of his time smoothing ruffled feathers and nurturing fragile egos. He had no wish to continue that in a social setting. The discussions had brought home to him how much the other tribes saw the Gelaming as a threat. They seemed to need constant reassurance that they were regarded as important. This was not easy because, despite outward appearances, Pellaz was impatient with the way so many of them were easily offended, and in fact seemed to thrive on finding reasons to be affronted.

The Freyhellans had acquired celebrity status among the delegates, but much as Pellaz strove to find it, there was no indication that Galdra, or any of his colleagues, were fomenting dissent among the others. The talks went back and forth, endlessly, yet all they were waiting for really was the ability to send *sedim* to Megalithica or for Ponclast to commit another atrocity nearer to home. Talk did nothing really. Pellaz wished the tribes would just agree that the Gelaming were most suited to commanding the situation and let them get on with it, but that was not going to happen.

Caeru flittered around the edges of the Hegemony meetings, being a charming host and, along with the ever-present Velaxis, entertaining who he referred to sarcastically as the "VIH" (Very Important Hara) in various hotels around the city. He was in his element, and Pellaz was amused when he realized that quite few choice specimens of foreign harishness ended up in the Tigrina's bed. These distractions had succeeded in ridding Caeru of the last traces of illness, and he appeared to be in constant high spirits.

One morning the Tigrina came to Pell's office and repeated his plea for a party in the palace. "Pellaz, you are becoming curmudgeonly," Caeru said. "What happened to your desire for some sparring? Invite the Freyhellans here. You might not have noticed, but that Galdra has his eyes glued to your back. It's about time you brought a little light into your life."

Pellaz had indeed noticed Galdra's constant scrutiny, mainly because his eyes always tended to seek out the Freyhellan in any gathering. He usually found an excuse to talk to Galdra at formal meetings, even though part of him wished he could resist it. "If you are so keen to meet them informally," he said, "invite them to *your* apartment."

"I'm thinking of you, not me. Lighten up."

"I don't want Galdra here, Rue. That's an end to it."

"Why? You talk to him every day. He flirts outrageously. You like him, don't you?"

"Look, I have work to do. I have a meeting in less than an hour. I am sick of meetings."

Caeru grinned. "I think I shall organize a party without you. Then I'll make you attend if I have to drag you there by your hair."

"Do what you like."

"Oh, I *see*. The decision had to come from me. I quite understand."

"Get out, Rue. I'm busy."

Caeru laughed and went his way, so much more like the har Pellaz had met in Ferelithia so long ago. Pellaz sat at his desk and put his face in his hands. He didn't know why he felt so hot. It was nothing.

Caeru sent Velaxis out with invitations for a select group of hara to attend the event. Velaxis was adept at tracking hara down when they were alone to make sure only the right ones were informed. However, his plans went slightly awry concerning the Freyhellans. Caeru was not pleased to hear that when Velaxis had cornered Galdra, literally as he was walking down the street, the Freyhellan had accepted the invitation and then demanded to bring a companion.

"Who?" Caeru demanded.

"Heron har Sulh," Velaxis replied. "I could hardly refuse because Heron was also on your list. Do the implications of this interfere with some strategy of yours?"

"I don't know," Caeru said. "It probably doesn't matter."

Velaxis paused, very slightly, before saying, "You should know the Hegemony look favorably upon the Freyhellan."

"What do you mean?" Caeru asked archly.

"Life goes on," Velaxis said. "Alliances are important. You know exactly what I mean."

"If Pellaz wasn't Pellaz, he'd have had a breakdown by now," Caeru said, more openly than he intended. "He deals with things in his own way. He won't be forced."

"He is har," Velaxis said. "And he's not a raw inceptee who can sustain himself with fantasies. He needs to wake up."

"You're the vizier—try telling him that."

Velaxis laughed coldly. "The Tigron would much appreciate an opportunity to have me locked up. I'm not so stupid. Just think about what I said."

CHAPTER TWENTY-EIGHT

Pellaz knew the party had started because he could hear music drifting up from the lower floor of Phaonica. It wove in through the open windows like an enchantment. *There is no reason not to go,* he told himself. But even so, it felt like entering the salon below would be a betrayal. It made no sense. He didn't know what he feared.

After an hour, Caeru still had not turned up demanding the Tigron's presence, so Pellaz realized he would have to make the decision himself. He told himself he didn't want to attend—the music alone was irritating—yet he felt so restless. After some minutes of fruitless inner debate, he dressed in black and went downstairs.

Once he left the stairs, it was as if he'd walked into a different world. His own rooms above were quiet and peaceful; down here was a bustle of activity. House-hara rushed in all directions carrying trays of food and drink. Everywhere was brightly lit. Voices were loud from the main salon. It seemed that Caeru's gathering was a success.

Pellaz paused at the threshold and was astonished at how many hara the Tigrina had invited. Still, it was easy to get lost in a crowd, which might not be a bad thing. He noticed Caeru sitting with a group of adoring hara and went to join them.

Caeru smiled at him. "I was giving you just ten more minutes before I came to fetch you. Now you're here. Have a drink." He picked up a tall glass of wine from a tray on the table before him and offered it to Pellaz.

"No, thank you."

Caeru sighed. "Don't just sit there and be a ghost at the party, dampening everything with your dire moans. Enjoy yourself. I know you remember how."

Already, hara were glancing in Pellaz's direction and he knew it was only a matter of minutes before they descended on him, demanding his attention. He could remember when he used to thrive on that; now it had become a chore. Pellaz took the glass, which Caeru still held out for him. He sighed.

Inevitably, the hara surged over like a swarm of locusts and proceeded to pick the flesh from the Tigron's bones under the guise of socializing. Pellaz adopted his usual public persona and was able to converse and laugh automatically, while his mind brooded in some dank dark place. He wanted to see Cal so badly, it was a physical pain. He wanted to run from Phaonica and take Peridot into the otherlanes, find a way to Megalithica, no matter how long it took or how dangerous the journey. For so long, he and Cal had been kept apart, with insurmountable obstacles between them. Now, the only impediment was the dysfunctional otherlanes. It seemed ridiculous.

For just a moment, the crowds parted and Pellaz saw Galdra sitting with the Sulh across the room. The group was deep in conversation, for which Pellaz was glad. He knew only too well what he saw in the Freyhellan: the gold-haired rebel, the confident seducer. It was dangerous because it wasn't real, or perhaps it was too real for comfort.

Lost in dismal reverie, he didn't realize he was staring until Galdra appeared to sense his scrutiny and looked around. It was not good, the way the room suddenly seemed empty but for the two of them. Not good at all.

"Pell," Caeru said. He leaned close. "Go to him."

Galdra hadn't dropped the stare and now Heron har Sulh appeared confused, and not exactly pleased. Pellaz turned to Caeru. "Tonight, I might fight my way through your admirers and claim my consort. Am I allowed that?"

"Always, you know that. But I don't think that's what you truly want."

Pellaz traced Caeru's jaw with a fingertip. "Nohar will ever love me as much as you do, Rue. It's a gift I have never deserved."

"You know that isn't true," Caeru said. "Well, maybe you don't deserve my love, but I'm not the only one. You need distracting, that's all. You need aruna to squash your depression. I hate it. It's like horrible black stuff seeping out of your pores."

"Then why not with you?"

"Because I think you need to confront exactly why you're afraid to initiate anything with Galdra. What's the difference between me and him? See. There is a difference, and that's what worries you."

"Leave it, Rue. The night is young. As you said, I should enjoy myself. Tell me gossip."

Caeru was staring across the room. "He's still looking over here. He looks distraught, which is less than can be said for Heron har Sulh."

"Rue, stop it."

Caeru laughed. "I admire your willpower, I really do." He glanced at Pell's glass. "And you've finished your drink already. You must be thirsty. Have another."

"This is not a good idea." Still, Pellaz allowed Caeru to refill the glass. Over the course of the next two hours, that glass was rarely empty.

Occasionally, Galdra would glance around and catch Pell's gaze, but his expression was inscrutable. He did not look distraught, he looked smug. Pellaz was offended by his confidence. The Freyhellan believed he belonged in the Tigron's bed, and he had no right to that. Did he think he'd been invited here tonight for this purpose? The thought made Pellaz wince. They should speak. It had to stop.

Before midnight, Pellaz dismissed all those around him from his attention and summoned Cleis, another of his personal assistants and the brother of Attica, with identical unusual skin coloring. Cleis was standing with a group of house-hara nearby. Pellaz rose to his feet, happy to find he was still steady, and said confidentially to Cleis, "Have Galdra har Freyhella brought to my rooms."

Cleis bowed, his expression bland. "Of course. When, tiahaar?"

"Give me ten minutes."

Cleis nodded and returned to his friends.

Pellaz turned to find Caeru studying him. "I have to go," he said.

Caeru raised his glass. "Good night, consort. Sleep well."

Pellaz couldn't sit down. He had to keep moving. He drank water because he was afraid he was drunk and needed to remain focused. Ten minutes seemed like an hour, although in fact it took twenty minutes for Cleis to bring Galdra to the Tigron's presence.

Cleis left the Freyhellan at the door to Pell's sitting room, where long windows were open to the terrace beyond. Pellaz was out there, staring down at the city, thinking, *Come now. You must come now.* He wasn't thinking of the Freyhellan. It reminded him of the moments before his blood-bond to Caeru, when he'd prayed to any deity in the universe who could hear him. He'd prayed for Cal to appear before him, but it hadn't happened. It wouldn't happen now either.

"You summoned me?"

Pellaz turned at the sound of Galdra's voice. The Freyhellan stood at the threshold to the terrace, his arms folded. "Yes, I summoned you," Pellaz said.

"Is this to discuss a matter of state?" Galdra came toward him.

"In a way. I think you should know I have no intention of succumbing to your overt flirting. It is embarrassing. You are making a fool of yourself."

"You summoned me here to tell me this?" Galdra laughed. "Here's some advice. If somehar desires you and you don't feel the same, try ignoring them."

"I was thinking of your feelings."

"Of course. You've been thinking of them all night."

Pellaz welcomed the hot surge of anger through his heart. "You are unbelievable. How can you think so much of yourself? Have you forgotten who I am?"

Galdra shrugged. "I don't care about your title. Somehar gave it to you. Everyhar knows where you came from. I prefer to see that. And here is something else you should know. I would never embarrass myself by flirting with somehar who didn't desire me."

"You're deluding yourself."

"Maybe I am. It's more than desire. You know it. And you're fighting it, because of the one who abandoned you. The moment you admit how you feel for me is the moment you have to let go of your dreams. And you don't want that."

Pellaz laughed coldly. "And my next line is that you get out of here and get out of this city. I don't care what the Hegemony think of you. The alliance between Gelaming and Freyhella has just ended."

"You don't have the authority to make that decision."

"No, I don't, but it felt good saying it. I *can* order you out of my sight, however."

Galdra sighed. "This is not how it should be. Everything has come out wrong. The Tigron is a big wall to break through to get to Pellaz."

"Don't try," Pellaz said. "There really is no point. In future, you must conduct your discussions with other members of the Hegemony. We can no longer speak. Go now. I've said what I had to." He leaned upon the balcony, his back to the Freyhellan, heard him draw nearer.

"I won't just go, Pellaz. Not until I've said what I want to say too. And it is this. After what happened to Tyr, I didn't think it was possible to feel that way for anyhar else. I was wrong. And I don't see it as a betrayal of Tyr's memory. I saw you on the quay, the first day we arrived here, and I hoped I'd see you again. And there you were, in the Hegalion, clearly of high rank, some lordly position that Gelaming give to themselves. But we connected instantly in a mere graze of a gaze. Then I discover you are Tigron. That title comes between you and any other har. It is a barricade, because you can never see a har for what he truly is. We meet every day and our eyes are like blades across each other's skin. You want to believe, but you can't. You can only see some-har who wants to get close to the leader of Gelaming. I wish you could believe that your position means nothing to me. If I could cut it from you, I would. Some things are meant to be. This is one of them. I'm sorry that you can't see that. I'm sorry that you're in such pain and isolation."

"You have no idea," Pellaz said. His voice sounded hoarse in his own ears. "The one I love is not dead." He swallowed with difficulty. "But he might as well be."

Galdra stood beside Pellaz at the balcony and they stared at the ocean, where lights danced upon the water. Pellaz could smell Galdra's body, a perfume laced with a faint reek of tar and brine. Pell's hands felt numb, too big. He couldn't feel the balcony rail as he gripped it. This was too strong, one slip and the universe could come crashing down on his head.

"You met some friends of mine once," Pellaz said. "They passed through Freygard on their way to Roselane: Flick and Ulaume."

"I remember," Galdra said. "They were running from Gelaming."

Pellaz laughed abruptly. "Yes, but not from me. I'm afraid. You don't know how much."

"I know."

"They live in Shilalama now. It's so beautiful. The mountains are alive there. I can smell the honey dripping from the combs in Ulaume's little shed at the bottom of the garden. It always smells like summer." Pellaz closed his eyes, remembering the holidays he had spent with his friends, the balm of their chosen land. He felt one of Galdra's hands slip beneath his hair. "If I let go . . . I'm not sure where I'll land. Galdra . . ."

"Hush." Galdra pulled Pellaz into his embrace and kissed him. It wasn't sharing breath, for he held that back. It was a simple kiss, slow and languorous. Pellaz realized he'd never been kissed before. Not this way. As har, he'd always shared breath, lost in visions and incense perfume. This was purely physical. The only comparable experience in his entire life was the time when Cal had seduced him away from home, before he was har. And it could be Cal against him now, so easily. It wasn't difficult to imagine. He returned the kiss, holding back on the sharing as Galdra did, until Galdra released, as wisps of smoke, the finest shreds of impressions, like fleeting memories or the ghost of scent. The kiss became deeper, evolving entirely into the full mingling of essence as waves of impressions washed through Pellaz's body. He could hear the crash of the ocean, the scream of gulls. The wind was in his hair. And what could he offer in return, but the very essence of himself, alone and bewildered, caught up in a storm?

Galdra pulled away from him with a gasp, then leaned his forehead against Pell's own. "I love you," he said, "with my being, my heart, my soul. Say nothing in return. I want nothing."

Pellaz did not speak, but rekindled the kiss. It was like drowning, like dying, fading away until every memory was gone. The ultimate betrayal.

He stepped back, wiped his mouth. "You must go now," he said.

Galdra stared at him steadily. "Is that what you want?"

Pellaz shook his head. "No, but it's what must be. I can't do this, Galdra. I can't. I can't give up hope."

Galdra nodded slowly. "I understand. I wish I didn't, but now I do. I lived it in your breath."

"Go to your Sulh," Pellaz said. "He is a lucky har, who no doubt knows it and is sorely upset at your leaving him. Be with him, Galdra. I can give you nothing."

"I meant what I said."

"I know. I'm not offended. I won't stop speaking to you, but not this. Never this."

Galdra said nothing more. Pellaz faced the city and felt the Freyhellan's warmth and light move away, until all that was left was the cold night air. He couldn't weep. The stars danced in the sky, mingling into one, but he couldn't weep.

CHAPTER TWENTY-NINE

⊱—┼◄►—⊙—◄►┼—⊰

The Varrs had done many terrible things during their time in power, and the breeding facilities were one of them. As Cobweb led his hara on the final stage of their journey to Harling Gardens, he had no idea that Ponclast still harbored obsessions similar to those that had inspired the facilities. All Cobweb could think of was the past: the faintest reek of despair clung like disintegrating rags to the trees and fences. Hara had been kept constantly in pearl in these places, hara too young for the task, really. And the harlings from those pearls had been given numbers, not names.

Cobweb urged his horse to the front of the line, as they approached the long driveway to the old facility. He had yet to put out a mind call to Lisia, concerned his old friend would be horrified at the sight of so many refugees. Lisia still harbored deep-seated fears about poverty and starvation, and Cobweb knew they would be rekindled in force the minute Lisia set eyes on those who now needed his help. This was despite the fact that Cobweb had dispatched as many hara as he could to the forest lodges and to some of the eastern coastal towns, with which Galhea had trading links. His party was still a sizable force. They had brought animals with them, and as many supplies as could be hastily gathered from Galhea.

The journey had taken longer than Cobweb had thought: nearly a month. It was grindingly tedious, because progress was so slow. In the ancient forests they'd passed through, the Varrs had once run like wolves. Cobweb could feel their presence still. But then, beyond the forest and darkness, the secret garden. Just as on the day Cobweb had first seen them, the grounds were blanketed with flowers, beds planted along the driveway and spreading out up the hill, where beyond a line of trees was hidden the place Cobweb hoped would be their haven.

Hara at work in the fields put their tools to rest as they watched the procession passing by them. They gathered at the end of the driveway, spilling into the valley road. Some ran to the main complex. Soon, mind call or not, Lisia would know he had visitors.

Cobweb raised his hand to indicate the line should halt—it would take some time for his signal to be relayed to the farthest har. Snake was riding in a wagon farther back and Cobweb directed a brief message to him. *Wait here.*

A small party of Swift's soldiers had turned up at Galhea while everyhar was preparing to leave. They had been led by Leef Sariel, an old friend of the family. Leef had informed Cobweb that Swift had taken his hara to Imbrilim: the rumors were that the Tigron would soon be amassing an army there. Swift had wanted to rejoin Seel and ride to Fulminir. Cobweb imagined how that must feel to Swift: a replay of a past event. With Ithiel gone, Leef had assumed command of the Galhean militia. He had accompanied Cobweb on his journey.

Now, Cobweb summoned him as Leef rode close to him. "Come with me," he said. "Everyhar else must stay put."

They urged their horses into a canter, throwing up pebbles from the dusty road. The gates ahead stood open—they always did now. Beside the gate stood the same sign that had always greeted the Varr soldiers, who had visited the facility to breed: "WELCOME & ATTENTION: No Weapons Beyond This Point." Lisia had chosen to retain the sign, as it was still his preference to keep Harling Gardens a place of peace, growth, and learning.

Cobweb slowed his mount to a trot and led the way up the driveway past the screening line of trees. There spread before them was a familiar tableau, only now, transformed through the time and effort of a group of hara who had chosen to build dreams on memories of pain. There was the grand main building, two stories of red brick, its arched entrances and windows like giant eyes and mouths. In human times it had been a convent and then, with an extension, a parochial school. Off to the sides, several new outbuildings had been constructed, including a barn, a larger stable, and a dozen cabins used by visitors, each of which had its own flower garden. The entire grounds were covered in blooming shrubs and lush foliage. It was truly a garden.

Any diminishment Harling Gardens had once suffered in the face of war and abandonment had been completely eclipsed. Lisia had imprinted himself over the past. But always it was there; Cobweb felt it in his bones. The mere fact this land had not been razed and sown with salt indicated Lisia still had an attachment to his memories. The school and infirmaries that now operated here, established once the original harling residents had been raised and sent into the world, could have been built anywhere. But Lisia had chosen to remain in this spot.

Cobweb slowed his horse to a walk as he and Leef approached the main entrance. Lisia was already standing on the steps, arms folded, his long brown hair tied back, but for the natural blond streak that fell to the side, which lifted slightly in the sweet, flower-scented breeze. As Cobweb had feared, Lisia's face did not register an expression of welcome. He looked suspicious and defensive. Neither did he recognize Cobweb immediately. "Who are you and what do you want?" he snapped.

"Lis, it's me," Cobweb said, moving his horse closer to the steps.

For a moment, Lisia appeared startled. *"Cobweb?"*

"Yes."

"What's happened to you?" He would be registering Cobweb's changed appearance: the tightly braided hair, the clothes of close-fitting black leather.

"Galhea has been attacked. I was forced to evacuate the town. I had to come here, bring many of our hara with me. There was nowhere else." Cobweb dismounted from his horse; he handed the reins to Leef. "Have you heard nothing? You must know the ethers are disturbed."

"We haven't heard anything about an attack but yes, we have noticed the state of the ethers." Lisia came down the steps and embraced Cobweb rather awkwardly. "They say you have brought an army."

"Not that. We are refugees."

"Why didn't you contact me?"

Cobweb risked a smile. "Because I wasn't sure you'd feel able to help us. At Tyson's suggestion, I decided to surprise you."

"Shock is a better word," Lisia said dryly. "You look so different."

"My role has changed."

Lisia didn't appear impressed. "How many hara, Cobweb?"

"Quite a lot. We left the harlings and older humans behind in the forest lodges, and as many able hara and humans to protect them as the lodges could accommodate. I have also sent many to the coastal towns, but couldn't risk everyhar going that way. Harling Gardens is safer."

"How many, Cobweb?"

"A couple of thousand."

Lisia put a hand over his mouth, then lowered it. "We can't possibly accommodate so many."

"I'm aware of that. We have tents and supplies of our own and except for relying on a few of your facilities, we plan mainly to stay out in the fields, where the army parties used to stay. We've brought some of our herds with us."

"Herds?" Lisia glanced with concern beyond Cobweb's shoulder, as if he'd catch a glimpse of these multitudinous beasts trampling on his precious flower gardens.

"We have lost many souls, Lis. The attack was devastating. I had no choice but to flee. I am in command of the party."

"Where's Swift?" Lisia snapped, his concern for Cobweb's son evident in his tone.

"Safe. He's with the majority of our forces, in Imbrilim. He plans to ride to Fulminir with the Gelaming. Communication has been difficult. Seel is also in Imbrilim. Ithiel is dead."

"Fulminir," Lisia said, his voice cold. Apparently he hadn't heard the rest of what Cobweb had said. "Why there?"

"Ponclast has escaped Gebaddon."

"What? And he attacked Galhea?"

"We presume so. After all, he knows who was responsible for his incarceration."

"I see. And now, to escape him—the very har on whose command Harling Gardens was established and who used to visit here—you bring a vast portion of your hara and human population here."

"Many have gone elsewhere, Lis. I did what I could. I had no choice."

Lisia was silent for a moment, clearly wrestling with inner debate. He took a deep breath. "We are old friends, Cobweb. You know I love you, but I can't put my feelings for you and Parasiel before my own hara. I'm sorry. You can't stay here. You can't bring that danger to our door. My life is dedicated to protecting those under my care. Refresh yourself this night, then move on. That's the way it is."

Cobweb regarded this har, who he had known for many years. They had once been so similar, yet now a gulf had opened up between them that was wider than time or distance. "I am acting leader of Parasiel," he said. "Harling Gardens falls in our territory. I'm sorry too, Lis, but I'm afraid I have to insist we stay."

Lisia's lips drew into a thin line and his eyes narrowed. "I don't know you," he growled. "Do what you see fit, as Varrs have always done with us!" With these words, he swiveled around, marched up the steps, and closed the great wooden doors behind him with a resounding thud.

Cobweb glanced over to Leef, who shrugged. "Shall I give the order to make camp, Cobweb?"

"Yes, the fields are ready for us in any case and the water may already be turned on." Cobweb glanced back at the closed door. "I'll give Lisia time to cool off, then speak to him again. He has no option but to cooperate."

"Kind of ironic, isn't it?" Leef said as Cobweb remounted his horse.

Cobweb drew up the reins. "Nothing is the same," he said, and urged the animal back toward the entrance to the Gardens.

The occupants of the Gardens could not maintain a distance between themselves and the new arrivals for long. This was initially because they were hara who were naturally curious: what could have brought such a large group of hara to set up camp just outside the gates? Once a few of the residents had spoken with the field-workers, or had come down to the end of the driveway to see for themselves, they had not been able to keep away, and could not keep from asking questions. The new arrivals were refugees! Some of them appeared wounded or grieving. Several of the facility's students and visitors had come from Galhea themselves and were deeply concerned, desperate for news of their relatives. Before too long, a group of Lisia's own students were helping the Galheans to make camp.

Lisia himself kept away, and his immediate staff were also noticeable by their absence. Cobweb smiled to imagine that Lisia had cornered them in a room somewhere, forbidding them to be too helpful. Harling Gardens was a world of its own, a place of harmony and peace, its hara somehow innocent and untouched, despite what were for some troubled pasts. Cobweb appreciated only too well why Lisia feared for them. Should Ponclast shift his attention to this place, its occupants could not easily defend themselves. Students were mainly there to be taught specialized aruna techniques, learn the birth arts, and study harlingcare. Many of the residents were hostlings rescued from other breeding facilities in Megalithica that had been closed down after the wars. The Gardens was also home to other war casualties: orphans and shattered veterans of the old Varrish campaigns.

Once the campfires were burning and the evening meal was under preparation, Cobweb left the camp and returned to the main building, where Lisia lived in spacious quarters on the top floor. Cobweb could picture the former hostling sitting at his bedroom window, staring out over the grounds, brooding and considering ways to expel the evil that had come to his door.

Cobweb felt exhausted, his temper sour. He did not want to have to justify himself, explain, cajole. He just wanted to rest. Since he and Snake had discovered an unexpected by-product of aruna, they'd had no time to further their explorations. There was no doubt Snake's body was healing itself. Every day he grew stronger, and sometimes he walked beside his wagon for hours at a time, exercising muscles long left idle. Cobweb was sure that if they could only repeat what they'd done before, the healing would be swifter, but even though they slept together and were intimate, the circumstances just weren't right to take aruna that one step further.

It was a phenomenon to be studied, and the one har who was most qualified to discuss it with Cobweb was Lisia. The hostlings at the facility had once been trained to be able to conceive pearls at will. They understood the workings of the inner organs far more than most hara, even though that knowledge had been abused. Surely Lisia would be fascinated by what Cobweb had to tell him, and perhaps this subject could be the peace offering. Still, before such discussions could take place, Cobweb would have to soothe Lisia's feelings. He could understand his friend's reaction. It was only natural after all the Varrs had once put him through.

The hallway of the main building was filled with soft light, which emanated from globes upon the floor set amid foliage plants. The air smelled green and fresh, the only sound that of running water from the ornamental waterfalls half-concealed amid the plants. A place of learning and meditation. This was Lisia's doing, Cobweb knew, for the work had all been done since the facility's liberation. Like the flowers outside, the interior of the building was Lisia's shout to the world about how he had the power to change things, after all. There were no bloody chambers in this place, no surgeons slipping on the slick floors as a production line of young hara delivered and surrendered the jewels of their bodies. But the ghosts were there, because the past would never really go away. If you stood still for long enough and listened, you would hear them weep.

Cobweb breathed deep and absorbed the ambience of the hall. Lisia would know he was there. The trick was to know the rules of the game. Was he expected to wait here or seek Lisia out? He went to the library on the second floor, because he and Lisia had spent many hours in that room, on long evenings, drinking strong coffee and discussing plans for the future. It had been the director's library then, a hall of unspeakable records, locked up. The locks had been broken, the doors had hung loose: one night, one of them had fallen to the floor with a crash. In the darkness where'd they sat, Cobweb had been spooked by the long fingers of light coming in from the hall through the gaping doorway. Lisia had stared out of the window, redesigning his life. He had seen what could be and had made it so.

It seemed a century ago, when Ashmael Aldebaran's Gelaming elite had found this place. It had been part of Parasiel's territory, so Cobweb had become instrumental in its restoration. He had been the nurturer then, the safe one, trusted when everyhar looked askance at Gelaming uniforms. Everything had been so new and raw: Terzian recently dead, Seel lately installed in Forever, Swift becoming an adult too quickly, learning how to frown and worry. Cobweb had thrown himself into helping Lisia, because it had made the transition easier. In lonely hours, he'd remembered his first love for Terzian, the way his heart had clenched like a desperate fist whenever he'd looked upon the har who'd claimed him as his own. Somewhere, in a moldering file, there might have been information about the sons Terzian had sired in this place, on visits Cobweb had never known about. He'd never searched, didn't want to know. There seemed no point. The harlings were probably long dead.

For just a moment, as he walked between the looming dark shelves, Cobweb smelled familiar perfumes of the time when Harling Gardens first began to change: the scent of turned earth, of sappy wood, the musty aroma of cracked brick. A time of building, without salt to scour the ground. It was a beautiful spot. Made sense not to raze it.

Lisia came in soft-footed behind him. "So," he said.

Cobweb turned, saw Lisia as a silhouette against the light from the hall, a slight and feminine creature. The doors were of polished oak, repaired now and always open, pinned to the walls with brass hooks. They had no doubt never been locked since their restoration. Lisia did not like locked doors. "Well, we need to talk," Cobweb said.

Lisia walked past him and sat down on a window seat that was upholstered in green velvet. It had once been bare wood, with splinters. "Why here?"

"It's safe."

"Is it? Will it remain that way?"

"I think so, yes." Cobweb sat down beside Lisia, his feet firmly against the floor.

Lisia was curled up, feet on the cushions, his chin on his knees. "I thought it was all over." He sighed. "Am I so wrong?"

"We have to rely on the Gelaming. We have to believe the future of Wraeththu is not Ponclast, and was never meant to be. We have to believe in the greater good."

"Tell me everything."

Near the end of Cobweb's narrative, a har came into the room, carrying a tray of hot food and drink. Cobweb was grateful. His throat was sore from talking, his stomach growled. The har placed his burden on the window seat, between Lisia and Cobweb, then departed.

"So much has happened," Lisia said, pouring coffee from a slender pot into tall cups. "It's another world to me. I'm so sorry about Azriel and Aleeme." He handed a drink to Cobweb.

"I trust Cal," Cobweb said. "If anyhar can release them, he can. He vanquished Thiede, after all."

"Yes," Lisia said. He paused. "I've missed you, Cobweb. We were close once. What happened to that? It seemed for a while, as if we would . . ."

"Life intervened," Cobweb interrupted. He could not mention how eventually Harling Gardens and all who lived there only reminded him of sad memories. He'd kept away and discouraged contact, living in the moment. He could not forget his first impressions of this place, what he'd seen and learned. At the time, for the first few days, he'd walked around with the taste of blood continually in the back of his throat. He'd made himself inspect the birthing rooms; sepia stains between the floor tiles, a metal drain in the middle of them. His heart had almost broken to hear Lisia's history. He'd wanted to restore Lisia's belief in Wraeththu, in aruna, in life. They had become close, yes, but only for a time.

"It grieves me to see you lonely," Lisia said, and reached out to touch Cobweb's shoulder. Old memories.

"I'm not," Cobweb said, too sharply. He took a breath. "There is something else I'd like to tell you about."

Lisia stared at him, eyes round.

"It's about Snake," Cobweb said. He paused. He could see from Lisia's expression that Lisia had always hoped Cobweb would return here one day. He had fantasized about it, but those fantasies had never included a har like Snake.

"You are chesna with him?" Lisia asked in a clipped tone.

"It seems to be going that way," Cobweb said. "We have discovered something."

"Then tell me."

The story was painful to Lisia, Cobweb could tell. For that reason, Cobweb left out some of the details, made it sound like an accident, casual aruna that had somehow slipped into being something else.

"It makes sense," Lisia said, once the story was out.

"Why do you say that?" Cobweb asked. "Have you ever encountered anything like that before?"

"Not exactly, but you must remember that I was as familiar with opening the cauldron of creation as I was with using my own voice. I could sense things. It was like . . ." He screwed up his nose. "How can I put it? It was like opening the door to a great house, of many floors and passageways and rooms. Conception of pearls took place in the main hall, and you could reach it quite easily by following the widest corridors. But there were other rooms. I had no time to investigate them because for me aruna had only one purpose. And since then, well . . ." He shrugged. "I have never entered that house again."

"Have you never wondered about it? Surely, this should be researched."

"Cobweb, I delivered twenty-four pearls," Lisia said, "and as you might imagine, since then I have avoided getting anywhere close to conception." He refilled their coffee cups. "We do teach aruna arts here, to hara who for whatever reason need help, especially with conceiving, but to be honest, it never occurred to me that healing might be a part of aruna; well, not that kind of intense physical healing. We have other methods we can use, after all, and they are strong enough for most ailments and hurts." His lips thinned. "But this is interesting, very interesting. There are hara here who could benefit from this, if it can be replicated. As you said, you don't really know if it was accidental, a fluke, or what." He smiled. "I have Varrish veterans here who have lost limbs and eyes. Now there would be a challenge!"

"I think maybe too much of one," Cobweb said. "But other things—burns, and such like. Injuries like Snake's. You could use your knowledge, Lis, and that of the other hostlings who remain here."

"I don't think any of them would be too keen to try," Lisia said. "It would make them uncomfortable. It makes me uncomfortable too."

"It was just a thought."

"And a valid one. I *will* consider it." Lisia hesitated. "Bring Snake here. I'll give you a room. You might find the privacy helpful."

"Thank you," Cobweb said.

"I'm still not completely happy about you bringing your hara here, but I trust you'll be able to protect us, should the worst happen. As you appear now, you seem more than capable."

"I hope that will not happen. I won't suggest we create a shield, because that might attract attention. I hope that Ponclast is more interested in those who are a threat to him rather than us."

"I hope that too," Lisia said.

That night, for the first time since they'd left Galhea, Snake and Cobweb attempted to replicate the aruna that had somehow kick-started an unknown healing mechanism in Snake's body. Cobweb was nervous. He wasn't sure whether what had happened had been a fluke. Snake had no such fears and guided them effortlessly into the same, almost trancelike state, beyond orgasm, yet prolonging it. This time, he remained focused, observing as best he could what took place within him. In mind-touch, Cobweb said, *Lisia spoke of different rooms . . . like chambers you could explore. Do you see any of this?*

Snake did not respond for a moment. *I'm not sure what I'm perceiving. I'll try to explain. I can feel your ouana-lim doing something. I feel as if there's an army of ants within me, all working on the same task. Do you understand that? Can you place your awareness inside me?*

Cobweb extended his perception as best he could. *It feels like . . . like sewing . . . A needle with thread, working very fast. But it's not that at all . . . That's the only way I can describe it. I don't feel like it's part of my body anymore. I'm like a generator, providing power. Too much so.*

Cobweb uttered a cry out loud and his senses were hurled back into reality. This time, he did not feel so nauseous, but even so, rolled off Snake quickly. He had to lie motionless, breathing deeply, for some minutes. Snake took hold of one of his hands.

"Cobweb, I can feel it. Heat across my chest. Down my belly. The fabric of my being is changing."

"Mmm," Cobweb murmured, incapable of saying more.

They lay in silence for a while, then Snake said, "There's more to this than healing. I can almost smell it."

Cobweb sat up, rubbed his face with both hands. "I certainly need to work with it more. I wonder if it has to be this depleting. Maybe I put too much of my own energy into it."

Snake reached out to stroke Cobweb's back. "We've done enough for now. I think we should leave it awhile before trying to do it again. But I do think we're on the brink of discovering something amazing."

"We already have," Cobweb said. He ran one hand down Snake's chest. "The scarring is so much smaller than it was. That's amazing enough for me."

CHAPTER THIRTY

On the first night, when Cal, Tyson, and Moon made camp, Tyson asked to speak to Cal alone. They had found themselves a small clearing in the forest, ancient oaks creaking all around them, huge branches lying dead upon the floor. Cal sat down on one of them. "What is it?"

Tyson couldn't really see his hostling's expression in the darkness. He could hear the snap of twigs echoing through the trees as Moon collected wood for the fire. "Why did you bring Moon with us?"

"He will be useful."

"In what way? Surely the more of us there are, the less inconspicuous we are. Moon is so young. I want the truth."

Cal took a tin of hand-rolled cigarettes from his coat pocket, extracted one of the thin sticks, and lit it. Briefly, a ghost of sulphur, a flare of light that illumined his face. "It's not what you think. And I can see what you're thinking. The har has Cevarro strength. He is resourceful. Pellaz sent him to Galhea for a reason. I think that reason was to go to Fulminir. He is Pell's avatar. I must keep him close, but not for the reason you suspect."

"You still love Pell, don't you? Why don't you go to him?"

Cal inhaled deeply, crossed his legs, and rested his arms upon them, the cigarette dangling limply. "We were talking about Moon. If you want to probe infected spots, let me ask this. I see a fire between you that is very familiar, yet you keep your distance. Don't tell me it's because of the unquestionably charming Ferany. Have you taken aruna with Moon ever?"

"No! He was barely more than a harling when I met him."

"Bullshit, he was beyond feybraiha. You are not me, Tyson, and he is not Pell. I think you should follow your heart, discover what you're both capable of. You have a clean start that Pell and I never had."

"It's too late. We missed the tide."

Cal laughed softly. "I wonder what you're afraid of. It is interesting, the way Wraeththu are given this capacity for an experience beyond love and sex, yet so many back off in terror should it become likely to manifest. Perhaps it's a fear of losing your identity, being consumed by the beloved."

Tyson grimaced. "Interesting theories, but nothing more than that. Perhaps it's more to do with circumstances. If I'd ever made a move on Moon, I'd have been judged harshly. My parentage is regarded as suspect, on both sides."

"I lost my identity," Cal said reasonably. "I became nothing more than my desire for a single har, which was wrapped up in bitterness and resentment and stark terror. I know what I'm talking about."

"And this is why you've run from it again?"

"I haven't run from it. Pell and I need to reassess everything. It was unrealistic to assume we could just take up where we left off. I need to find myself first."

"You must be so confident of his love for you."

Cal shrugged.

"Well, you must be. While you're busy finding yourself out here, he might be finding other things too. Have you thought of that?"

"We share a single soul. I have faith in that, yes. I don't feel we're apart."

"From what I've heard, you're alone in that," Tyson said dryly. "You should have seen the state of him when he came to Galhea after the attack on Rue. He was terrified you'd done it. Torn apart. You shouldn't have left Immanion then. It was a ridiculous time to leave."

"I had no idea what happened to Rue when I left," Cal said. "That was coincidence."

"Really? I was taught there are no coincidences."

Cal took a final draw off the cigarette and ground it out underfoot. "I don't want to talk about this. There are more important things to consider."

"Where were you? Were you really with Thiede?"

"Yes," Cal said. "I learned some things." He stood up. "If all goes well, I'll be able to tell you everything. In the meantime, start training that young har. You're not going to be judged for it."

"Training?"

"Get over yourself, and get in tune with him. Grissecon toppled Fulminir once. It might be the most potent of our weapons. I know for sure that guns and steel are useless for our purposes."

Cal wandered off to help Moon with the fire and Tyson sat down on the warm spot on the fallen branch that Cal had vacated. It sounded so straightforward and reasonable and out here, there was no Terez or Snake to judge and condemn, but even so, Tyson was nervous. He would have to back down and he never found that easy. He would have to revive feelings he'd taken great effort to bludgeon to death, or at least into submission. There was a moment in time, by a lake in the dark, when anything had seemed possible. Was it possible to pluck that moment from history?

Abrimel had discovered it was difficult to try to live two lives at once. What had begun as an exercise in survival, mixed with the unpredictable spices of bitterness and curiosity, had now become something of an obsession. In between his visits to Fulminir, Abrimel was haunted by the memory of his last meeting with Ponclast. It no longer had anything to do with Abrimel's feelings for his parents.

Everyhar knew that it was only a matter of days before Immanion began to send hara over to Megalithica. The otherlanes were mostly cleared and there had already been successful tests. The Tigron himself would be coming to Imbrilim, as well as many hara from other tribes. If the Gelaming had a strategy for dealing with Fulminir, they were keeping it secret.

One of the first Gelaming to arrive in Imbrilim from Immanion was Velaxis Shiraz. He came in advance to supervise arrangements for other tribe leaders and one of the first hara he visited was Abrimel.

"Now could be the time to make your mark," Velaxis said, as before making himself comfortable in Abrimel's office.

Abrimel poured Velaxis a drink, concentrating on keeping a tremor from his hands. He could feel Velaxis's eyes upon him. "How?" he asked.

Velaxis made an expansive gesture with both hands. "Nothing like this has ever happened before—so many tribes gathering beneath one banner. I'd like you to work with me, Bree. Abandon your books and fusty lists. Join the administration and make some worthy contacts."

"That's generous of you," Abrimel said, handing Velaxis a glass.

"No more than you deserve. Rue misses you. You should contact him."

"He knows where I am, tiahaar," Abrimel said, sitting down. He realized he was fully in control of the situation and it felt good.

"He might well visit here soon," Velaxis said. "Make the peace, Bree. Family feuds are pointless. There is no threat to your position now. Pellaz is a changed har. Take the place at his side, which should always have been yours."

Abrimel shrugged, pulled a wry face. "Perhaps. I suspect I might still have to fight my way through a throng of relatives, however."

"Snake and Moon Jaguar are here in Megalithica. Terez was never an impediment to you."

"Nor has he maintained contact."

"This is all irrelevant. Stop making excuses. Calanthe is no longer part of the equation. In my opinion, he has made his feelings clear. His loyalties lie with Galhea, and perhaps that is for the best."

"I still find that hard to believe, given everything that's happened."

"Perhaps he served his purpose, and has now moved on."

Abrimel shook his head. "No, Pellaz will never let it lie at that. If you try to convince me otherwise, you are not the har I think you are."

Velaxis regarded him steadily. "Things are in hand. We have a new commodity. Perhaps I should enlighten you concerning Galdra har Freyhella."

"Who?"

"He is a fine har, a born leader. The Hegemony, in the absence of Cal, is keen to persuade Pellaz to take him as consort, as second Tigron."

Abrimel laughed. "If they attempt that, they are insane." He paused. "Do you really think it will happen?"

"Cal went to Galhea. We still don't know where he's been or what he's been up to. The Hegemony is nervous about him. They wonder if he is a threat. They don't trust the Parasilians' judgment. To them, Cal is still an honorary Varr."

"What does my father think?"

Velaxis shrugged. "I have no idea. Pellaz is as close as a sealed oyster. There have been rumors about the Freyhellan and him, but unconfirmed. It's my belief he still has Cal in his eyes, but the Freyhellan is persistent." He leaned forward in his chair. "I am concerned for you, Bree. Please believe me when I tell you I think you should take on more of an official role within your family. Something disturbs me . . ."

"You once said to me that many factions fight for control," Abrimel said. "Can you tell me more about that?"

"Many factions who once fought are now united," Velaxis replied. "Think about that, Bree. Please think hard."

Abrimel looked away. He had a bizarre feeling that Velaxis could look right inside him.

CHAPTER THIRTY-ONE

Sometimes, there is no reason on earth not to go after what you want: sometimes there are plenty. Sometimes the consequences of your actions are so small, it's nothing more serious than a drop of rain falling from the end of a leaf into a river. Nobody cares. But a single drop becomes part of the whole, it flows on down to the sea.

Moon knew there was absolutely no reason why he shouldn't just lie down next to Tyson one night and say, "Here I am." He could tell from the hot glances that singed his skin like a burning match that Tyson had similar thoughts. But there was something, something that made it impossible. The words would turn to stone in his mouth. They'd tumble out onto the ground with a series of thuds. In Tyson's presence, with the possibility of intimacy hanging between them like a lascivious ghost, language lost all meaning. It was senseless yet there it was. Moon felt he had created something impenetrable back in the farmhouse on their journey south. This pious sense of denial was unreal. It didn't even feel like he owned it.

They rode west, toward the place where once Swift had toppled Ponclast's forces. Moon asked Cal what would happen when they got there. Cal only smiled in his typical, feline way. "I am Uigenna," he said. "So are you, and so is Ty, partly."

Tyson laughed. "Are you suggesting we simply ride in there, say hello, and introduce ourselves?"

"Got a better idea?" Cal asked.

"But I look like Pell," Moon said, frowning. "Won't Ponclast . . . ?"

"He has never met Pell."

"He's met you though, hasn't he?"

"As part of Terzian's household, yes. I don't believe I'll have a problem with him. It's doubtful he hasn't heard about me leaving Immanion. If that's not the case, he's no worthy foe of the Gelaming's. He must have intelligence agents at work."

"Still brave," Tyson said.

"I don't think so," Cal said. "In my opinion, Ponclast will believe that the majority of Parsics will welcome the return of the Varrs. I don't think he'd be too wrong in that either. He will expect his old allies to come crawling out into the light."

"It's still a big risk," Tyson said.

Call shrugged. "Really? Why? You are Terzian's son, I am an erstwhile consort of his. Moon is the son of Pell's brother who was Uigenna to the core. I don't think our pedigrees will go against us."

"Still . . ." Tyson appeared worried.

"Just watch me at work," Cal said. "It'll be fine. Trust me."

"What are we going to do there?" Moon asked. "Fool Ponclast into trusting us, then try to get Aleeme and Azriel out?"

"More or less," Cal replied. "I need to find out what Ponclast has been up to concerning his dynasty. We might need to remove rather more than Ty's relatives."

"Why are harlings so important to him?" Moon asked. "Is blood really that strong?"

"We could debate that for hours," Cal said, "but all you need to know is that hara will invest for the future in harlings. That is their strength. Harlings are banners you can ride behind. They represent an idea, sovereignty. The mixing of blood is alchemy. Thiede talked to me at length about it."

Moon could see the sense in this idea. His imaginings of what aruna would be like with Tyson made him appreciate how love, or intention, could contribute toward creating a special creature. It could be a physical expression of this intention, a magical working, a spell.

The walls to Fulminir were now only piles of rubble covered by creeping blankets of ivy. They looked, in fact, like a ring of small hills around the citadel and

its outbuildings. But within them, wooden palisades had been constructed, presumably in haste. Smoke purled from chimneys into the afternoon sky. From a
distance, the sound of stone striking iron could be heard, just a single insistent
beat, like a blacksmith. Hara were at work in fields around the citadel, and it
appeared like any other Wraeththu settlement. Cattle grazed in a meadow of
clover, their tails switching lazily.

"They do not appear to be on high alert against attack," Tyson said. "Do we
know for sure that Ponclast has reclaimed Fulminir? Couldn't these just be ordinary hara who've moved in and made use of the old buildings?"

"How I wish that were true," Cal said dryly. "Our approach has been noted.
Guard your thoughts and your tongue."

Moon felt it as a tickle to the skin. It was as if an invisible wave of energy
moved slowly over him from head to toe. He caught a quick message from
Cal: "Guard yourself!" And he did.

The hara that came to them were thin, sinewy creatures. Moon could see at
once their history in their eyes. A har looked him over and Moon knew that
he'd never basked in sunlight sure of his own beauty, nor swapped glances in
candlelight across a civilized dining table. He had surely killed with his bare
hands.

"We are here to see Ponclast," Cal said in a clear, even voice. "I am an old
friend of his."

The hara said nothing to this. The feeling they gave off, like sweat from
their skin, was a cocky kind of confidence, but also extreme caution. They
were dangerous because of it.

There were to be no formal invitations or gestures of respect. They indicated that Cal and his companions must follow them, that was all.

Was I like them once? Moon wondered, and found pictures of his childhood coming back to him. He thought of Hawk, sitting in the parking lot that
day, when he'd told Moon about Snake and Silken. It could have been a lifetime ago.

It would take a hard har indeed not to be affected by the sights within the
wooden barricade around Fulminir. So much effort had already gone into re-
creating a settlement, and seeing those hara going about their daily business,
hammering nails into wood, clearing out debris, did not give a message of aggression or cruelty. It spoke of desperate individuals simply trying to survive,
to create comforts, a home. At one time, this place had been attacked as Galhea had been. Moon could not find it within himself to be scornful or even
suspicious. But then, he had seen nothing. He'd not even been born when Fulminir's dark secrets had been uncovered. He remembered the last night in

Galhea and framed it deep within his mind. That was why he was here. There were captives in this place.

They were taken to a har named Kyrotates, who held a high position in Ponclast's forces. He said to Cal, "You were in Galhea recently."

Cal nodded. "Yes. I went to see how the land lay."

"We had reports," Kyrotates said. "Some of our hara knew of you. I want you to tell me now why I shouldn't believe you have come here as a spy."

"You can believe what you like, tiahaar. I am here to speak with Ponclast, not you. I expect that is what I'm supposed to say."

Kyrotates did not smile, even though it was clear Cal was trying to lighten the atmosphere.

"This is where you say, 'Who do you think you are?' and strike me?" Cal offered.

Kyrotates exhaled through his nose. "We know who you are, *tiahaar.* You are a Tigron of Immanion."

"And a Tigron would saunter into Fulminir without fear?" Cal said.

"If they did, they would either be a fool or think themselves very clever, which amounts to the same thing. Nohar believes you to be stupid. Why are you here, Calanthe?"

"If Ponclast would speak with me, he would see I am sincere. I am no longer at the side of Pellaz har Aralis. I fled Immanion some time ago. Ponclast must know this. Many hara in Almagabra believe I am responsible for the attack on the Tigrina. For that, Ponclast owes me."

Kyrotates laughed coldly at that.

"At the very least, he must be curious," Cal said. "I have brought my son with me, who is also Terzian's son." He turned to Moon. "And this is Moon Jaguar, from the City of Ghosts: a young Uigenna, born to a brother of Tigron Pellaz."

Kyrotates remained stony.

Cal sighed. "You must know, tiahaar, that I was taken captive by the Gelaming while on a mission to find Terzian. You have no idea of what I was put through, as I have no real idea of the torments you must have suffered. The fact is that we are all victims of the Gelaming, in one way or another. This is what binds us."

"The Gelaming took you in, made you Tigron. That is hardly suffering."

Now it was Cal's turn to utter a cold laugh. "You think so? Please ask Ponclast to speak with me. You are right, I am not stupid, and I would not insult Ponclast's intelligence by coming here as a spy."

Listening to this conversation, Moon could not help feeling that Cal, in some way, was telling the truth. That, or he was the most expert liar Moon had ever come across. He felt uneasy. Why were they really here?

"We have traveled from Galhea," Cal said. "Allow us to rest and then show us how we can help you here. We are willing to work."

"You will be kept in confinement until Ponclast has decided your fate," Kyrotates said. He jerked his head toward two hara who stood guard at the door. "Take them to a secure room."

Cal bowed to Kyrotates. "We will cooperate fully," he said.

Kyrotates said nothing. He turned away.

Ponclast was indeed intensely curious about the arrival of Calanthe har Aralis. He did not trust Cal for one minute, but he also had Cal's measure. Ponclast believed that Cal was the most self-serving har he had ever met. If he was here in Fulminir, he wanted something. Still, it would not give the right message to display eagerness. Ponclast decided he would interview Cal after dinner that night. He had yet to decide what manner he would adopt for the meeting.

Abrimel came to Fulminir early in the evening, and Ponclast told him about Cal's arrival.

"Kill him is my advice," Abrimel said. "He will bring trouble. He always has."

"He was Terzian's consort," Ponclast said mildly. "Terzian loved him deeply. I am also curious to meet Terzian's son."

"Terzian is dead," Abrimel said harshly. "Calanthe is a manipulator. Only the Aghama knows why he left Immanion, but I find it extremely suspicious him turning up here. Also, it was no secret he was in Galhea when our forces attacked it. He was fighting by the Parsics' side. He was seen. Now he is here. The message is plain. Kill him."

"A relative of yours is with him. Moon, the Uigenna's son."

Abrimel visibly paled. "I have no wish to see him."

"That is a shame. You are hura-brothers. I have had reports from the north. It's no secret that the Gelaming coerced Snake Jaguar to go to Almagabra with them. There is talk of threats having been involved. There is also talk that Tyson Parasiel was with the party who met with Jaguar in the City of Ghosts. All these facts spin in my head. I am intrigued." His voice took on a harder tone. "Calanthe is here now, and will be kept secure. He will learn nothing of our plans. He might be here to glean intelligence for Immanion, but somehow I doubt it. He has his own agenda, always."

"Test him," Abrimel said.

Ponclast cocked his head to one side. "In what way?"

"Tell him about Galdra har Freyhella and how the Hegemony has him lined up as Cal's replacement. I doubt he knows about that. If there is any loyalty to my father left within him, this might manifest at the news. You would be able to smell it, I am sure."

"Perhaps you had better tell me about it," Ponclast said. "In detail."

Ponclast had done much to improve his quarters since he'd taken repossession of Fulminir. Most of their appointments had been stolen from Imbrilim by Diablo. Ponclast now had a comfortable office that overlooked the main courtyard. It was situated halfway up a tower whose summit was missing. Here, Ponclast composed himself to receive his new guest. He felt slightly light-headed, not exactly nervous but aware the coming interview must be conducted with care to get the best results. Cal had survived much. He was a supreme example of what Wraeththu could be, but he was unpredictable and unreadable. Ponclast could not fully believe Cal had walked away willingly from Pellaz har Aralis, but neither did he think Cal was here on the Tigron's behalf. He believed it would take wits and cunning to discover the true reason.

When Ponclast's hara delivered Cal to his door, Cal stood at the threshold, bowed respectfully, and touched his brow. "In meetings, hearts beat closer," he said, an old Uigenna greeting.

Ponclast would not reply in kind. "Come in, sit down."

Cal did so, choosing a chair opposite Ponclast's own. Ponclast made a discreet gesture and Diablo appeared from the shadows. He poured wine into two stone goblets and handed them out. Ponclast intended only to take the barest sip of his own cup. He dismissed Diablo from the room.

"So," Ponclast said, once he and Cal were alone. "What are you going to say to me?"

Cal took a small taste of the wine, then put the goblet down on Ponclast's desk. "What do you want to hear?"

"You were fighting for the Parsics mere weeks ago. I presume you have some measure of attachment to the House of Parasiel, despite their betrayal of Terzian's blood."

"The Parsics are a conquered tribe," Cal said. "But if you attack them, they will defend themselves. What did you expect?"

Ponclast sighed theatrically. "I am not prepared to debate their politics. In my view, they are traitors, or at least are led by them. Swift gave our hara to the Gelaming."

"Swift cares only for his hara. He does what he can to protect them and rule them fairly. He is the buffer between them and Immanion. You should not judge him so harshly."

"You think not? You were not here on the day Fulminir fell, tiahaar. I had my fill of Swift the Betrayer at that time. He was Thiede's creature. He went against his own blood."

"He was very young," Cal said. "Anyway, I am not here to discuss Swift. He has made his choices and sticks by them."

"Then what are you here for?"

"I am interested in seeing whether you can convince me that you are as good a force for Wraeththu as the Gelaming."

Ponclast laughed. "Your arrogance is stunning! Why should I care what you think?"

"Because I could be of use to you."

"You are only ever of use to yourself, Cal. I have more acuity than Pellaz in that matter. He has never realized this simple fact."

"Strangely enough, I do care for the Uigenna, or what is left of them. Believe that or not, it is of no consequence. You have acquired strong allies. It is impressive."

"Abandon that thread of conversation, tiahaar. You will learn nothing of them from me." Ponclast paused, took another sip of wine. "Put yourself in my place, Cal. I cannot release you into our community. I cannot envisage you fighting at our sides. Your offer of alliance may be genuine, or as genuine as you are capable of making it, but I will not take that risk. Not unless you have something interesting to offer me."

Cal laughed, leaned back in his chair. "Okay, I appreciate that." He hesitated. "Do you ever wonder what your allies want of you?"

Ponclast said nothing, prepared to let Cal continue.

"You are nothing to them, tiahaar, as the Gelaming are nothing to those who support them. We are all part of a greater conflict. This realm is pivotal, its energies are a resource, but that is that. Humanity endangered that resource. Wraeththu are better guardians. But we are expendable. It is my thought that, instead of being ignorant slaves, fulfilling supply through forced labor, without even knowing we are doing so, we should take command of our resources and trade instead. I would be interested to hear your opinion."

Ponclast had expected nothing like that. He took another drink to cover his surprise, give him time to compose a response. Eventually he said, "And how do you propose we take that control?"

Cal shrugged. "How should I know? I think it's important only that I give you this information. Act on it as you will."

Ponclast smiled coldly. "Ah, I see. You attempt to sow discord between me and my allies."

"Not exactly. Have you ever asked them why they're offering you aid? You don't need to answer me aloud. All I ask is that you consider my words. I think it's useful for you to know your place in the scheme of things."

"And how do you know that? I don't believe you know more about these allies than I do, and I know more than enough to satisfy me."

"When I left Immanion, I made it my purpose to seek out knowledge. I have seen many things during my life, tiahaar. I have always known there is more to the game than we know. Thiede did not build Immanion by himself. That is common knowledge, even if nohar knows who helped him. He was cleverer than most. He worked out that Wraeththu weren't an accident, and he went looking. That's all I can say."

"Not enough," Ponclast said.

"Why do they need us?" Cal said. "Think about that also. How much influence can they have in this realm if they need hara to do their fighting for them? It is my belief they find it difficult to manifest, at least in their own forms, for any length of time. Also, it's possible to remove them from our reality, if only temporarily." Now Cal leaned forward, and gestured emphatically. "Thiede did not build the walls around Gebaddon. He did not possess that power. It was otherworldly, which was why its destruction had such an effect on the otherlanes. Those who call themselves your allies are after a piece of what the Gelaming's benefactors, or masters, consider their own."

Ponclast felt breathless; he could tell Cal spoke what he believed was truth. He swallowed. "Why come to me? Have you given Pellaz this information?"

Cal leaned back again. "No."

"Why not? Surely your loyalty lies with him before me?"

"I am not loyal to you. You should know where you stand, and why, before you take on a war with the Gelaming. You can be sure their allies are as fearsome as yours, and casualties on either side will mean little to them."

Ponclast laughed aloud. "By all that's sacred! You're not here as a peace monger, are you? That is a rich, sweet thought! Will you go to Pellaz next?"

Cal did not share Ponclast's amusement. "At the end, Ponclast, it will be between you and him. I promise you that. There is more than one war. While higher powers jostle for resources, hara of flesh and blood fight for the hearts of all Wraeththu. Somehar must win. Then our future will be set."

"I am equal to Pellaz har Aralis."

"In some ways," Cal said. "I can see that. But what I learned when I first went to Immanion is that true strength comes from opposing forces being in balance, not from the scales tipping too far one way."

"Your fanciful dream will never happen," Ponclast said. "The Gelaming would not have it, and neither would I. There is no common ground between us."

Cal appeared weary now. "As you will. I've done what I set out to do: tell you what I know. You should know that the Gelaming's allies have intimated some of the truth to me. Your own have not afforded you that privilege."

"You are in contact with them?"

"No. It was made known to me by them, that's all."

Ponclast narrowed his eyes. All that Cal had said made sense to him; his own instincts advised him Cal's words were rooted in truth. But he also sensed this was not the whole story. He drew in his breath. "Do I take it the reason you have not gone to Pellaz with this information is because of the Freyhellan?"

Cal's face assumed a bland expression. "No, that is not the reason."

Ponclast gestured airily with one hand. "Strange. I would have thought it would have annoyed you, the Hegemony organizing for somehar to take your place."

"They cannot do that."

"They can make a new Tigron, Cal. You know that."

"It will mean nothing. I have no interest in the Hegemony's schemes. They lack subtlety."

"I've been told he resembles you, this Galdra har Freyhella. He derives from an interesting tribe. I considered disabling them, as it was intimated to me they would prove useful to my enemies. Interestingly, something beat me to it."

"Generous of you to share that information," Cal said.

Ponclast shrugged. "I assumed my allies had taken care of it, and gave it no further thought. Unfortunately, even though the lead wolf of the pack was killed, a cub took on his strength and went howling to Immanion. He is of equal stature to you, Cal. It seems to me you might be here now because you know your avenue into Immanion has been closed with iron gates. You are here because there is nowhere else for you to go."

Cal's mask was perfect, but Ponclast could perceive that from it leaked a strange dark light. He had not known about the Freyhellan. "I cannot imagine where you got this intelligence," Cal said coldly. "The Gelaming perceive my absence as indicative of weakness among the Aralisians. This is some propaganda they have put about for your benefit. They know who and what I am. They know I cannot simply be replaced."

Ponclast nodded, his face creased in apparent thought. "True, true. However, I have an agent in Imbrilim who told me of it. I wonder how far the Hegemony, or indeed Pellaz, will go to keep up appearances, eh?" Ponclast smiled at his guest and lifted the wine flagon. "Another drink, tiahaar?"

While Cal was having his meeting with Ponclast, Tyson and Moon were left alone in a dank room just below ground level, which had a small primitive bathroom that was little more than a cupboard. A grid above their heads let in muted light, filtered through a thick tangle of grass. The afternoon sunlight had brought out the perfume of the greenery, and the musty smell of the old building was tinged with this essence of summer. The room was not too uncomfortable. There were four narrow beds in it, and from a cursory inspection, Moon had discovered that the blankets on them, though of coarse texture, were clean. Water had been left in an old stone urn in the darkest corner of the room, and not long after Cal had been taken away, a Teraghast unlocked the door and brought them a meager supper of rough bread and rather charred meat. He did not speak as he left the food on the small table that stood against one of the walls, and after he'd done this, he went out and locked the door again.

Tyson sat with his knees up on one of the beds, tearing up hunks of bread and stuffing them into his mouth. Moon lay on another bed, his arms behind his head, staring at the sunset through the grille. He did not feel hungry. "We're prisoners," he said.

"Yep," Tyson agreed in a clipped tone.

"I hope Cal works his magic on Ponclast. I don't like being locked up. They could do anything to us."

Tyson sighed through his nose. "I wonder whether Cal is simply insane. This was an insane plan."

"Which we followed willingly enough."

"Well, at least we know Fulminir is being rebuilt. I wonder where Azriel and Aleeme are."

"You should try to sense them," Moon said. "Try to let them know we're here."

"Good idea," Tyson said. He put down the remains of the bread. "We could do it together." He got up from the bed and went to sit in the middle of the floor.

Moon stared at him, unsure of what he thought or felt about this suggestion.

"Come on," Tyson said. "I won't bite."

"What do you want to do?"

"Join hands, concentrate. Think you can manage that?"

"Don't know. I'm not their relative like you are."

"Oh, don't be ridiculous. I know you spent enough time in their bed!"

"What is *that* supposed to mean?"

Tyson gazed at Moon for several long seconds. "Just what is your problem with me?"

"No problem," Moon said, wondering how Tyson could bear to suggest any kind of contact between them after all that happened. Wouldn't it be as painful to him as it would be to Moon? Perhaps Tyson had forgotten that night in the farmhouse. Perhaps it meant nothing to him.

Moon got up and sat down before Tyson, scraped back his hair. He stared at Tyson's hands, which were held out to him. He found himself thinking of the Sea of Ghosts, the night, the moonlight, a kiss. He couldn't do it.

Tyson sighed and withdrew his hands. "What is it, Moon? Are you ever going to tell me? Did I do something so bad? I didn't do anything."

Ponclast can do with us what he pleases, Moon thought. *Who knows what that will be?* "The worst thing you did?" he began. "You want to know what it was?"

"Yes. I'm curious."

"If you must know, it was when you stared right at me over Ferany's shoulder while you shared breath with him. You were trying to punish me, and that was unfair."

Tyson expelled a short gust of laughter. "What? I've no idea what you mean. When the hell was that?"

"If you don't remember . . ." Moon shook his head.

"You said it was a childish crush," Tyson said. "I remember our conversation next to the lake at home pretty well."

"So do I. You made your choice, fair enough." Moon paused. "We can't do this. We cannot work together. Search for Azriel and Aleeme yourself."

"All right. I will."

Moon went back to his bed, turned his face to the wall. His heart was beating too fast. After some minutes, he heard Tyson sigh heavily. "It's no good," Tyson said. "I can't concentrate. Moon, we have to talk."

Moon said nothing. He still felt angry.

"Right," Tyson said, "then I'll talk to your back. You're not asleep so you have to listen. We both know what this is all about—the unfinished business. Well, you should know that there wasn't one moment when I didn't think of you—on the journey from your old home, back in Galhea, and for a long time afterward. But my decision was right. If we'd got together back then, it would have been wrong. And yes, maybe I did want to punish you, just for existing. I went back to Ferany to exorcise you, and that was wrong too. I can't be what he wants me to be. I don't want what he wants. The whole harish family thing turns my stomach. It's not right for me. And here I am, on a lunatic quest, with a hostling I barely know and a har who still sticks a blade in my heart whenever I look at him. I want you, Moon. Does that put a bandage over your pride? Knowing that, can we be civil? You have the upper hand now."

Moon felt sick, not least because Tyson had read him so accurately. He turned over and said savagely, "You can't have me now just because it's more convenient."

Tyson's expression was very close to the way Cal looked sometimes: bland but calculating. "Who says I expect that? I don't always act on my desires. It's something I've learned. The whole experience was tough on you, I know it was. But I can't unmake it, Moon. Neither do I expect you to come running to me now. I'm aware I probably sacrificed that. So resheathe your claws, pretty cat."

"Don't *ever* call me pretty!" Moon said. "I hate that." He sat up. "Thank you for being honest." He paused. "Will you stay with Ferany?"

Tyson's shoulders slumped. "I shouldn't, but . . ."

"Convenience?"

Tyson shrugged.

"He knows about us," Moon said. "He warned me off. Did you tell him?"

"I've never said anything to him about you. He isn't my confidant."

"Well, whoever is must have told him. He's a good har. You're not fair to him."

"Yeah, he's perfect," Tyson said. He wrinkled his nose. "It's strange, I just think that . . . I don't know . . . we're meant for more than breeding like humans. Too many hara are quick to go down that road now. I wonder if it's a distraction of some kind. Can't put it into words really."

"Somehar has to do it, Ty, otherwise we'd die out."

"I know. Sort of. But our life spans are so much longer than humans' were. If everyhar kept on reproducing, the whole planet would be covered in a seething mass of Wraeththu, far worse than anything humanity could have achieved."

"Valid point," Moon said, "but I understand the drive. I understand what it must be like to want to reach for something higher, to go beyond reality . . . with somehar you love."

Tyson nodded. "I understand that too, but sometimes, I just get the feeling that we've underestimated the potential of aruna, that we earth it too much, and the drive to create new life is somehow missing the point." He laughed. "Listen to me. I'm as spiritual as a plank. I've never said these things to any-har before. I've no idea why I've just done so to you."

"When did you start thinking this way?" Moon asked.

Tyson held his gaze. "Oh, around the time I met you."

There was a silence, then Moon said, "Are you in love with me, Ty?"

Tyson paused, pursed his lips. "I think so. I suppose I should say it aloud. I love you."

"Then why are we fighting?"

"Because the potential scares me," Tyson said. "It's like what happened to Lileem, when she took aruna with Terez. I feel I could lose myself somehow. And the strangest thing is that this is only just becoming clear to me, now, this moment."

"We're not that special," Moon said. "We're no different from any other hara."

"No, we're not," Tyson agreed. "Which is what makes it even more terrify-ing. Don't you feel it?"

Moon considered. "No. I don't think I know what you mean. If I was wary of touching you, it was because I wanted it to mean something to you too." He frowned. "But now you've said what you said . . . I don't know. I still don't want to." He laughed shakily. "This is very strange. It's like a nexus point."

"You might as well say it," Tyson said. "Then we can put it in front of us and sit and stare at it while we're locked up here, and try to figure out a mean-ing in which we are not mad."

"Okay." Moon drew in a deep breath. He grimaced. "I can't."

"You can."

"All right. I love you."

"Was that so bad?"

"Not really. How do we stare at it?"

"We don't. That was just a joke. I think we simply accept it and see what happens. Do you feel better?"

Moon nodded. "I think so."

"Me too. How weird. We've probably both just had the most intense ex-change of our lives, and it was . . . I don't know . . ."

"Casual," Moon said. "It's probably just us, pride or something."

Tyson grinned. "In our position, Cobweb would be tearing out his hair and lamenting, being most dramatic."

"Pellaz would probably order somehar else to do it for him. I expect he used to send official messages to Cal."

"Yeah, he would have done. I can't imagine Pell having a romantic moment, casual or not!"

The conversation continued in this lighthearted vein, until Cal returned. Once his escort guard had left them, Cal said, "Why are you sitting in the dark? Our hosts have provided lighting, I understand."

"We didn't notice it had got dark," Tyson said. "How did it go?"

Cal stood at the table and lit the oil lamp that had been left there for them. "So so. Ponclast is suspicious, which is only natural."

"Do we have to stay locked up?" Moon asked.

"For the time being, yes," Cal replied. "We must simply be cooperative."

"Did you find out anything about Azriel and Aleeme?" Tyson said.

Cal was staring at the lamp. "Not yet."

"Then what *did* you talk about? You haven't been away for long."

"I just tried to win his trust. It'll take time." Cal joined his companions, who were sitting on the floor. "He's changed, you know. It was quite a shock to see him. Whether Gebaddon did that to him, or something else, he will certainly be a match for Pell now."

"Changed how?" Tyson asked.

Cal pulled a wry face. "Difficult to describe. He's become more than he used to be." He grinned. "He's become . . . ponclastic!"

Moon and Tyson both laughed at this. Moon was aware that he felt lightheaded, almost on the verge of hysteria. It would be impossible to sleep that night.

Cal fixed him with a stare. "So, moonling, what can you tell me about Galdra har Freyhella?"

"I've never heard of him. Who is it?"

"Nohar. Ponclast mentioned him, that's all. Are you sure you've not heard anything about him in Immanion?"

"Absolutely. A lot of hara were arriving from all over the place before I left the city. I got to hear about the most important ones. You know what Immanion's like for gossip."

Cal grimaced. "Indeed I do. Well, we can only assume this Freyhellan is not that important, then." He braced his hands against his knees. "Ponclast assured me he'd move us to better quarters tomorrow. He doesn't trust me enough to let us have free rein here yet, but I've roused his curiosity. This might be a long game. Be prepared for it. We have to become part of Fulminir. It's what we're here for. Believe it. To do otherwise would be dangerous.

Make friends. Be open, but not too full of questions. Only the right kind of questions. Understand?"

"Won't he be scanning us now?" Moon asked.

"Probably," Cal replied, "but we have nothing to hide, do we?"

Moon glanced at Tyson, who smiled at him. "No," he said. "We don't."

CHAPTER THIRTY-TWO

Pellaz har Aralis traveled to Imbrilim at summer's height. This was long past the solstice, deep in the heavy heart of the season, that magical time when the airs shimmers with ghosts, and the landscape seems to breathe so loud you can hear it. These were the last days of summer. Soon the leaves would turn and the balmy days would be just a memory. Pellaz couldn't help fearing this might be the path of his life from now on.

The Gelaming had sent agents to carry out surveillance on Fulminir, but only one had returned alive. With maddened eyes, he told of flickering shadows armed with knives, creatures that moved so fast it was impossible to defend yourself against them. They had covered the survivor's body with cuts, but had let him live. Somehar had to ride home with the news. Since then Swift and Seel Parasiel had moved their forces closer to Fulminir, to observe the citadel and its traffic from a safe distance. So far, they had reported nothing of importance.

After his attack on Galhea, Ponclast had ceased attacking Parsic settlements. Imbrilim was another matter. Assassins had attacked both humans and hara in the fields outside the town, random raids when they set the fields to burning. However, once *sedim* arrived in Imbrilim, these attacks ceased, mainly because the *sedim* were able to predict when they would occur, being sensitive to movement in the otherlanes. They could move as fast as Ponclast's forces and had even taken a captive, who had cut his own throat before the Gelaming could question him.

At the suggestion of Velaxis Shiraz, Pellaz organized for his household to take up temporary residence in Abrimel's home. Abrimel had agreed to this, and was even present when the party arrived. Looking at him, Pellaz wondered how such a har could ever have sprung from his flesh, or from Caeru's for that matter. Abrimel was a contained and ascetic har, a creature of precise movements and habits. He was icily polite, a stranger. Pellaz considered he might have looked like Abrimel, had he been raised on bread and water by fanatical monks, who scorned life's pleasures.

"Thank you for accommodating us," he said to Abrimel.

"I have plenty of room," Abrimel replied.

"You must tell me about your work," Pellaz said, hoping his son wouldn't take him up on the offer.

"You'd find it boring," Abrimel said. "You have far more pressing matters to think about."

That first night, communication was received from Shilalama. Pellaz had invited the Roselane to the conclave of tribes, but Opalexian had declined to attend. The Gelaming knew, from Kamagrian who worked in Immanion, that some parazha were actually quite eager to join forces with Wraeththu: not all of them were the spiritual mystics that comprised Opalexian's dream of the ideal Kamagrian community. Many of them, who had traveled widely in the world, felt that the only way to deal with the current threat was to strike back. As more than one parage had said to Gelaming friends, "Hiding in a cell, meditating upon the meaning of life, is pointless if something bursts out of the otherlanes and cuts your throat."

Opalexian might not have sent a horde of Amazonian warriors to Immanion after the existence of the Kamagrian became common knowledge, but it was clear there were more than a few willing Amazons waiting to take up arms. Now, a message came from Kalalim, Opalexian's palace, which was received by one of the Listeners. The parage, Tel-an-Kaa, a trusted aide of Opalexian, was on her way to Imbrilim. She would offer assistance in whatever way she could.

"It might not be much," Vaysh said to Pellaz, "but it's a start. I'd never have thought Opalexian would let any of her parazha near our forces."

Pellaz nodded. "That means she's scared," he said.

Every day, more hara arrived in Megalithica: the *sedim* worked without pause to carry both personnel and supplies across the ocean. In addition to these forces, delegations from local tribes began to appear in Imbrilim: Un-neah, Megalithican Sulh, and Froia, to name but a few. Imbrilim's resources were taxed to their limit by the influx.

"Ponclast won't have a chance," Ashmael Aldebaran said to Pellaz. "Shad-owy, otherlane-traveling assassins or not, the Varrs will be overwhelmed by sheer numbers. I can't see what else he can throw at us. He hasn't had time to prepare."

"And if that is the case," Pellaz said, "why hasn't he hidden himself away for some years, to build up his strength? I don't think we should be too confi-dent. He has tricks up his sleeve, I'm sure."

Two nights before the Gelaming and their allies rode to Fulminir, clouds came in from the east and smothered the stars. Rain fell relentlessly in warm heavy rods, turning any unflagged roads to mud. Pellaz felt restless. He could not eat his evening meal and had his staff turn Velaxis Shiraz away when he came to call. Pellaz went out to the stables, seeking solace in Peridot's silent company. *Speak to me, Peridot,* he urged, but the *sedu* only transmitted a sense of under-standing. Pellaz rested his face against the *sedu*'s broad brow and listened to the rain, its different cadences. He could not imagine the future. His body ached for an embrace he could not name. He wanted to be held fast. He wanted to be filled: he supposed he wanted Cal. But as anyhar will tell you, when the spirits of summer's deep hang in the air, shrouded in rain, and a wish goes out to the hidden stars, it is often answered.

When somehar came to the stable door, Pellaz sensed him before he heard or saw him. He glanced and saw a tall silhouette against the lamplit rain. For just the briefest moment, he thought it was Cal, and his heart clenched, then he realized it was Galdra har Freyhella. Pellaz turned back to Peridot, stroked his long nose. His hand was steady, but his heart and lungs were not. It was as if his breath steamed out of him, seeking the mouth of the Freyhellan, full of questions and the desire for answers. The *sedu* stamped his back feet.

Galdra came into the stable, fearless as ever. Perhaps he couldn't sense an at-mosphere. "We just arrived," he said. "The journey was something I'll not for-get."

"Your first *sedu* journey?"

"Yes. Tiahaar Vaysh said you were here. I thought it polite to report in to you personally. Also, I wanted to see you. I am concerned for you."

Pellaz didn't say anything. If he should ask the Freyhellan to leave him alone, it would only prompt a lengthy conversation he really wasn't capable of having. To say or suggest anything else was, at that point, unthinkable.

"I understand how you must be feeling," Galdra said, coming closer. "Everyhar is relying on you, expecting some kind of miracle. What do you think you'll do once you reach Fulminir?"

Pellaz smiled grimly. "I have no idea. Any suggestions?"

"I think you should ask your gods, your dehara, for guidance."

"I do that every day, Galdra. I do it every moment. They are silent on the matter, which is to say my own heart is silent."

"You will have my strength as a resource," Galdra said. "Use it as you will."

"Thank you." Pellaz drew a breath. "Ashmael will lead our troops, and those of all the other tribes who are with us, but I feel in my guts that might isn't the answer. I'm not even sure what we'll find at Fulminir."

"Whatever happens," Galdra said, "it is my intention to be with you." He put his hand over Pell's upon Peridot's nose. Pellaz slid his fingers away and Galdra sighed.

"The potential of the future makes no difference to how I feel," Pellaz said, but he realized they were just words, they didn't mean anything. He wished Galdra would leave, but he was also glad the Freyhellan had found him.

Perhaps sensing this, and realizing he must seize the moment, Galdra put his hands upon Pell's shoulders and pushed him firmly but without roughness to the back of Peridot's stall. The *sedu* remained motionless, as if asleep: a groan echoed deep in his body.

Pellaz felt the wooden wall against his back. He could smell creosote, mixed with the scent of hay. Then somehow, as if he'd blacked out for a moment, he was sharing breath with Galdra. He couldn't remember who initiated it, or when. It was just happening. His fears for the days ahead marched from his mind like a horde of demons. Galdra flicked them away, one by one. His strength was indeed great: it was comforting to know he'd be around when the final moment came. He pulled away from Pellaz and murmured, "Whatever happens, you are capable of facing it and vanquishing it. Know your own strength, Tigron. Know that this moment of doubt is the lone vigil before the battle. You are what you are."

"I will face it because I have to," Pellaz said. "And even if you and a thousand other hara are with me, I feel I must do it alone."

"Tonight, you do not have to be alone," Galdra said.

It would be so easy to give in, Pell thought, to be carried away on a tide of desire and oblivion. If that should happen, would all be lost? Always, the superstitious fear that if he took aruna with the Freyhellan it would banish Cal from his life forever. He was almost angry with himself for feeling that way,

because hadn't Cal made his own feelings known by staying away? It was entirely possible there was another Galdra somewhere, somehar saying to Cal
that he did not have to be alone. *Yet I am stronger than that,* Pellaz thought.

It was the most difficult task for Pellaz to draw away from that warm, giving body, but somehow he managed it. Somehow he was standing some feet
away at the entrance to Peridot's stall, and Galdra was in shadow. Outside, the
rain was still coming down heavily, and everything was shining in the light of
the lamps above the stable door. Pellaz walked toward them. His body felt extremely cold, taken away from the fire.

"Pellaz, don't do this again. Don't walk away."

Pellaz paused at the threshold. He heard Galdra behind him, heard Peridot
move restlessly.

"You don't know what's going to happen," Galdra said. "Neither of us
does. We are on the brink of a big change for our kind. It might change us ir-
revocably. It could mean death."

For you? Pellaz felt as if the threshold of the stables itself was the horizon
for change.

"Will you deny yourself even at this hour?" Galdra said softly.

Perhaps it was not a denial of the self, but a denial of the other. How many
hara must he turn from, hara who cared for him, before he faced the truth?
Galdra was right: there were no certainties, and in the face of that, no blame,
no guilt.

Pellaz waited for the space of three heartbeats. Then he went back into
the stables. He walked past Galdra, making for the wooden ladder that led to
the hayloft. He climbed, unable to feel any sensation in his feet or fingers.
He walked into the hay, stooping a little, for the ceiling was low up there.
Kneeling among the bales, he took off his shirt. Galdra's head appeared at
the top of the ladder. Pellaz didn't say anything. He sat down and took off
the rest of his clothes, clasped his arms around his raised knees.

Galdra laughed softly, in an uncertain way. "Pellaz, I wish you'd say
something."

Pellaz stared at him. Didn't Galdra understand he couldn't and mustn't
speak? His arms were pimpled with cold. His jaw ached because he had
clenched it. Yet his heart was beating strong and fast.

Galdra took off his wolfskin jacket and sat down beside Pellaz. He rubbed
his hands over his face. Pellaz told hold of one of Galdra's hands, pulled him
down into the soft scratchy bed. The smell of hay was so familiar in connection with aruna: it had surrounded Pellaz at Saltrock the first time he'd ever
lain with another har. It was part of Cal's smell. Pellaz spoke to Aruhani in his

mind, *Dehar of life, aruna and death, let this be for him, for Galdra. Let this be sacred and meant. Let it be healing.*

He pushed Galdra onto his back, but Galdra fought him. "No," he said. "It is meant to be another way. Trust me. There is something I have to give."

Like the first time, Pellaz thought. Perhaps Aruhani would not let it happen any other way. Pellaz relaxed and spread himself out like a star. He was beyond being har: he was elemental. His eyes were closed. He slid a hand beneath Galdra's loose shirt, felt the skin, hot and dry. He dreaded and craved the moment of union, then it was done, and they were moving together. Nothing else mattered. He was aware of every atom of Galdra inside him, so deep it hurt. And all the while, he could hear the rain hammering on the stable roof, the chatter as it sluiced down the drain pipes, the thousand different songs it inspired throughout Imbrilim. The experience of aruna was so physical, so here in the present moment, with no languorous visions to sweep him away. He wanted release, needed it quickly, needed this exquisite exchange to be over, or else it must last for eternity. A long time ago, Orien Farnell had taught Pellaz well in the arts of aruna magic. He knew how to control his body to bring a har to searing climax very quickly. He concentrated on controlling the energy; he built it into a shining spire, and then released it over Imbrilim as a fountain of protective force. In that way, what he did with Galdra was grissecon, not aruna, and perhaps that justified it in his mind.

Galdra lay on him heavily, panting, and Pellaz stared up at the ceiling. He could see every strand of every tiny spiderweb up there. He could hear Peridot breathing and the muted noises of other *sedim* and horses in the stalls below.

After some minutes, Galdra rolled off him and lay beside him, one hand pressed against his eyes. Pellaz leaned over him and pulled down his hand. Distress oozed from the Freyhellan like black steam. Pellaz kissed Galdra's face, many times. The cheeks were wet beneath his lips. He had not meant to cause hurt.

"I wanted you to be with me," Galdra said at last. "It would have meant so much. I wanted mutual feeling, not sacrifice."

"I am here," Pellaz said, the first words he had spoken. "Don't ask for what I cannot give. Some things are sacred to me, and the only har with whom I am soume is Cal. If it felt like sacrifice, it's because it was."

"I'm sorry," Galdra said.

"Don't be," Pellaz said. "It wasn't pelki, Galdra. I complied."

"I could feel what you were giving me, but it was distanced. It wasn't your heart or your soul, it was your mind."

"I can give you some of my heart, but not in that way."

"You will lend it to me, maybe, but it will never be mine." Galdra reached out and touched Pell's face. "I will take what I can. I might be throwing myself into the fire, to be sent home lifeless, tied to the mast of a flaming ship, but I will take it."

Pellaz sat up, reached for his clothes. Galdra had not undressed. Naked, Pellaz knew he felt far less vulnerable than the Freyhellan, who he now realized guarded intense need beneath his outer bravado.

"You are leaving now," Galdra said sadly.

Pellaz stood up, fastened his trousers. "I must. I cannot spend the night with you, Galdra. Too many tongues would be quick to spread the news, and believe me, little goes unnoticed in the household of the Tigron. Vaysh knew you were looking for me."

"Why should you care what anyhar thinks?"

Pellaz did not answer. "Where are you staying?"

"In the camp that has been allocated to my hara, beyond the town."

Pellaz grimaced. "Too public. There is an inn called 'The Silver Eye,' on North Ward Street. Take a room there. Disguise yourself somewhat and call yourself Flick Sarestes. I will meet you there tomorrow night at eight."

"So I will be your dirty secret."

"Not dirty, Galdra, and not exactly a secret. I just prefer some things to be private between us. I do not require a greedy audience. I hope you understand."

"And the day after tomorrow, we leave here. And you will travel with your staff."

"That's the way it must be, yes."

"And beyond that?"

"I will be at The Silver Eye tomorrow at eight. Be there or not, as you decide."

Galdra laughed bitterly. "You are adept at this, Pellaz. How did you learn to be so cold?"

"It would take a lifetime to tell you," Pellaz said. "Climb out of your nest, Galdra. Look around at what's happening. I can't succumb to emotion now. This is all I can give. Take it or not. Your choice." He finished dressing, ran his fingers through his hair, shedding strands of hay.

"Did it mean nothing to you?" Galdra said.

"It meant something," Pellaz replied. "I don't yet know what. You wanted this so badly, Galdra. Remember that."

"You are the most beautiful har that ever lived."

"There are many beautiful hara. I am one of them, that's all, as are you."

"And yet you strive to make me see you otherwise. I know what you're trying to do."

Pellaz managed a bleak laugh. "I would not lie here and mull over such thoughts, if I were you. Go back to your hara. Forget about this until tomorrow." He meant to leave, but then some shred of compassion bid him kneel at Galdra's side and kiss his brow. "I will take your essence with me, brother wolf. Part of you will be with me through the night."

"I love you."

"I know."

Pellaz went out into the rain, which had diminished to a fine misty drizzle. He walked back to the house of his son, so slowly because it felt as if his chest were full of heavy stones. The last of the rain soaked his hair and face. When he went back indoors, nohar would notice the tears.

Pellaz was woken early by Vaysh, who came into his bedroom and opened the curtains wide. "The sun is back, and the *sedim* have been busy all night. I'm sure there are more of them than there used to be, but it's difficult to tell because they're flashing in and out of the otherlanes like dragonflies. But best of all, you have a visitor you would not have expected in your wildest dreams."

Pellaz sat up in the bed, clasped his knees in an instinctive gesture of defense. "Who?"

"I'm not going to tell you," Vaysh said. "I want to see your face when you meet him."

"Vaysh, I command you to tell me, otherwise there will be dire repercussions."

Vaysh threw himself down onto the bed, apparently in high spirits, a state he only ever displayed in front of Pellaz. If the Tigron should tell anyhar about this side to Vaysh's character, he would not be believed. Vaysh curled against his side. "It will not be a painful meeting, that's all I'll say." He put one hand flat against Pell's chest. "You smell different. Are you all right?"

Pellaz pulled away from him and got out of bed. "I'm as fine as I can be, under the circumstances. Where am I to meet this surprise visitor?"

"I have arranged a sumptuous breakfast here. Your guests await your presence, downstairs. I was going to ask Abrimel to be present also, but he appears to be missing." Vaysh got up and selected clean clothes for the Tigron from the wardrobe.

"Guests? You didn't mention there was more than one." Pellaz allowed Vaysh to help him dress.

"Oh, it's a delegation." Vaysh pulled Pell's hair from the neck of his shirt. "What's this? Straw? What were you up to last night?"

"It's hay, actually. I was with Peridot for a while, remember? I gave him some fodder."

"I'd better brush it. If you turn up downstairs like this, it will give the wrong impression. The Tigron should not be out feeding animals, even if they are *sedim.*"

"The Tigron grew up feeding animals," Pellaz said lightly. "Don't fuss, Vaysh."

It took longer to wrench himself away from Vaysh's ministrations than he'd have liked, but eventually Pellaz was able to present himself in the dining room downstairs. He asked Vaysh not to be present, and it took no great empathy to sense Vaysh was far from pleased about that. Pellaz, however, wanted to confront whatever lay before him alone.

Three hara were already sitting at the table, being served fragrant coffee by Cleis. The visitors appeared absurdly out of place in the homely environment, but that was no surprise, because they were Kakkahaar, and their natural habitat was the desert. Pellaz recognized only one of them, and he was astounded by the feelings it inspired. At one time, he had scorned the Kakkahaar ways, even though they had helped train him. Now, he experienced the joy of meeting an old friend, somehar who would understand him. He came into the room.

"Tiahaar Lianvis, this is a great, but pleasant surprise."

The Kakkhaar leader stood up. He was dressed in flowing sand-colored robes that draped around his slender body perfectly, like artful dunes. His tawny hair reached nearly to his knees. He bowed. "Pellaz—or is there some title I am expected to greet you by these days?"

Pellaz laughed and went spontaneously to embrace the Kakkahaar. "Don't stand on ceremony. You are partly my maker."

Lianvis remained unyielding in his hold. "We have heard many things about you."

Pellaz drew away. "I expect you have. Have you heard from Ulaume?"

Lianvis's eyes widened almost imperceptibly. "No. He left us years ago."

"I know. I very much want to tell you about him, because it will astonish you. But before that, I suppose I should ask you why you are here. Dare I suppose it is because the Kakkahaar have decided to give me their support?"

"Let us say simply that the Kakkahaar are interested in recent developments," Lianvis said. "We are unconvinced it would ever be in our interests to offer the Gelaming our support."

Pellaz understood this would require delicate negotiations. The Kakkahaar had once been allies of the Varrs, and although they'd slunk back into the desert lands of southern Megalithica after Ponclast's fall, and had paid reluctant lip service to Gelaming authority, they'd since kept to themselves and maintained a low profile. Pellaz wondered if he should have perhaps sought out Lianvis years ago, built some kind of bridge. Pellaz knew the Kakkahaar's dark side and had witnessed some of it. The way he felt now, this genuine joy, was perplexing. "Well, whatever your reasons for being here, I am happy to see you. Please introduce me to your companions."

Lianvis inclined his head. "Of course. This is Tiahaar Rarn and Tiahaar Herien."

The other two Kakkahaar resembled Lianvis greatly, mainly because their attire and hair were similar. Pellaz touched his brow in a gesture of respect. "You are welcome here." He turned to Lianvis. "Please, sit down. We will talk as we eat."

Cleis supervised the serving of breakfast, but once he and his staff had left the room, Lianvis got to the point immediately, "So, the barrier around Gebaddon was broken. Thiede's departure has occasioned unforeseen difficulties for you."

Pellaz shrugged, drank some coffee. "Unforeseen yes. I am unconvinced it is a difficulty, however. Has Ponclast attempted to contact you?"

"Yes. The high cabal of our tribe has discussed it in detail. We have decided against allying with him at this stage."

Pellaz grinned. "What's this? Is a Kakkahaar morality emerging?"

Lianvis smiled thinly. "Is it our opinion that Ponclast is dabbling with forces he can neither comprehend nor command."

"That is true. We have our own thoughts on this matter. Might I ask what yours are?"

"Perhaps if you would share yours . . . ?"

Pellaz smiled. "Please, you are the guest. The Kakkahaar are great adepts. I'm sure your opinions are of high value."

"You don't know anything, do you," Lianvis said flatly.

"I know enough. Will you speak or not?"

Lianvis glanced at his silent companions, who perhaps gave him some unspoken advice. "Very well. We have picked up some distinctly unusual signatures in the ethers of late. They are not from this realm, and their flavor is foul even for our tastes." Here, he gave Pellaz a pointed stare, which the Tigron returned unflinchingly. "If they are working through Ponclast," Lianvis continued, "we can only suppose they are doing so for selfish reasons. They will not be acting for the benefit of erstwhile Varrs. They will have offered tempting bait, which Ponclast has gobbled up, but he will be expendable. It is our belief that all hara are expendable to these forces. Something is occurring over our heads, as it were. I think it might well be nothing more than a dispute over territory, but the outcome for us could be severe."

"We should wonder, perhaps, why they need Ponclast at all."

"Indeed," Lianvis said. "The obvious conclusion is that they lack force in this realm, to some degree. They are empowering the last of the Varrs because they need workers or warriors."

"I will be honest with you," Pellaz said, sensing instinctively it was safe to do so. "We have so far believed that Ponclast summoned these forces. Your words shed new light on the matter. They could, in fact, have summoned him instead."

Lianvis inclined his head once more. "That is our thought. For a time, we believed as you did. We thought that Thiede's departure from this realm weakened the barrier around Gebaddon, which allowed Ponclast to use his abilities and escape. However, I communed recently with our deity, Hubisag, and he filled me with a different knowledge. I saw the dark light beyond creation, its tentacles reaching out. I saw that nohar could summon it. I saw Ponclast as a beacon, a lure, a weak spot. He is the gateway to this realm, because of his inner state."

"You are a casket of jewels, Lianvis," Pellaz said. "Thank you for sharing this information with me. Whatever any of us might think of your ways, tiahaar, I have no doubt they have helped you see the truth of the matter, where we of different nature could not."

"That is obviously so," Lianvis said, smiling with more warmth now. "I wonder whether you have ever regretted declining the education I once offered you. It would be of use to you now."

"I regret nothing of what happened in your pavilions, tiahaar," Pellaz said, "even if, with the light of experience, I understand more of it now."

Lianvis raised his brows, his gaze steady. "Is that so?"

"Yes, for example, I am aware you drugged or hypnotized me in order to take aruna with me before my ascension to Acanthà."

One of Lianvis's companions nearly choked on his food. Lianvis simply laughed out loud. "How long did it take you to guess?"

"It took Cal about a minute. Need I say more?"

"I think it did you good. It was necessary. I had an inkling of your future, even if you didn't, and I can see now you are nothing like the ingenuous idealist I attempted to train."

"Be that as it may, I am glad you are here now." Pellaz made a dismissive gesture with one hand. "We have many things to talk about, but now I would like to tell you about Ulaume. He is chesna with a friend of mine from Saltrock. They live in Shilalama now, in Jaddayoth."

Lianvis cut neatly into a slice of bacon, skewered it with a fork. "You and Ulaume are reconciled?"

"We are friends, yes."

Lianvis ate his portion of bacon slowly, with apparent relish, before speaking. "That is surprising. I chastised him thoroughly for his treatment of you, you know. When he bore a grudge, it was rarely dropped."

"He has changed a great deal," Pellaz said. "But then, it was all so long ago. We have all changed."

One of Lianvis's companions touched the Kakkahaar leader on the arm. "Tiahaar, might I speak?"

Lianvis glanced at him. "Ask what you must, Herien, but be prepared the answer might not be what you seek."

"What do you wish to ask?" Pellaz said.

"Ulaume disappeared from our tribe at a . . . crucial time," Lianvis said. "Herien, you may explain."

Herien appeared agonized. Pellaz had never seen such an expression on a Kakkahaar face before. It occurred to him at once what the question was. "Tiahaar Herien, I believe you must be Lileem's father or hostling. Am I correct?"

Herien put one hand against his mouth. He nodded.

"Hostling," said the other Kakkahaar. "I am Rarn, Lileem's father. Given what you've just said, I expect you know the circumstances surrounding our son's birth."

"I know that you created a Kamagrian between you, yes," Pellaz said. "And I suspect you might have guessed that Ulaume found her in the desert, after your shamans deemed she should be exposed. He took her to safety and brought her up. For some time she lived with him and Flick in Shilalama."

"Since we heard of the existence of Kamagrian, we realized this was what Lileem must have been," Rarn said. He put an arm around Herien's shoulders protectively, because it was clear Herien still could not speak. "We also wondered whether Ulaume might have taken him. I investigated the area where the child had been left and there was no sign of him—*her*." He shook his head. "I'm sorry. That term is strange to me. After Ulaume disappeared, it was fairly simple to come to the right conclusion. Where is Lileem now?"

"I wish I could tell you exactly," Pellaz said. He paused. "We need to talk about this in depth. All I'll say for now is that she is not in this realm. But do not fear, she isn't dead. She's working on our behalf, seeking knowledge of both Kamagrian and Wraeththu, in a place beyond this world. It was her choice to go there, and not even maddened horses could have prevented her from doing so. I have no doubt she will return in the future. Consider yourselves blessed, tiahaara. Lileem is a fine individual, respected by many. I'm sure that once circumstances are resolved here in Megalithica, and we are free to travel, Flick and Ulaume would be more than happy to talk with you about her. I will do all that I can to arrange it, in fact."

"It was so long ago," Herien said in a husky voice, "yet at this moment it feels like yesterday. Thank you, tiahaar."

"Herien and Rarn have had fine sons since," Lianvis said.

"They had a fine one to start with," Pellaz said, gazing at Lileem's parents, "but many mistakes were made in the early days. Do not blame yourself, tiahaara. Lileem had the best childhood a har, or parage, could wish for."

"I always knew it was Ulaume who took him," Herien said. "Sometimes, at night, I thought I heard his voice, telling me all was well with my harling. It was a great comfort." He glanced furtively at Lianvis, whose expression was unreadable. "Even though many thought it was a delusion. Eventually, I began to doubt my own mind."

"Well, now the matter is cleared up," Lianvis said. "If you wish to speak with the Tigron further about it, you must do it some other time. I would now like to discuss more pressing issues, like what the Gelaming propose to do about Ponclast."

Pellaz addressed Herien before responding to Lianvis. "We shall find time to talk, I promise you." He turned to Lianvis. "I can't speak further without the presence of the Hegemony, and other tribal representatives. This will be arranged immediately." He stood up. "If you'll excuse me, I'll instruct my aide to convene a meeting. Please, continue your breakfast. We will meet again shortly."

The Hegemony had a Hegalion building in Imbrilim, and it was there, a couple of hours later, that the meeting took place. Every tribe who was already present on Megalithican soil sent a representative, and Tharmifex, Eyra, Ashmael, and Velaxis were also in attendance. Pellaz waited for everyhar to be seated before he entered the main chamber with Vaysh. The place was packed to capacity, with many hara standing around the edges of the room. Pellaz noticed Galdra sitting on the first tier of seats and a hot flush coursed through his body. The secret of their union, he realized, was delicious, but this was certainly not the time or place to be thinking about it. Their gaze met for the briefest moment.

Lianvis repeated his opinions to the gathering, after which Ashmael Aldebaran was the first to speak. "You say this could be a dispute over territory. Can you expand upon that, tiahaar?"

Lianvis inclined his head. "We farm animals for the resources they can give us. It is the Kakkahaar belief that otherworld entities look upon us, and those like us in other realms, in a similar way."

"That is a disgusting idea!" Ashmael said. "Also, I cannot give it credence."

"We are not aware of it taking place," Lianvis said evenly. "Do you give no credence to the idea of higher life forms than ourselves?"

"Of course I accept that is possible," Ashmael said, "but surely if they were farming us, we'd know it."

"As the horse knows that is born to serve and bear us? As the bullock knows it is bred for the slaughterhouse?"

"Are you suggesting we are food to them?"

"No, feeding, as we do, is a primitive function. Perhaps it is beyond us to comprehend exactly what we provide for these beings."

"Where is your proof?"

Lianvis opened his arms in an expansive gesture. "I am merely offering a theory, based on intense etheric research. There is no doubt that Ponclast has unusual allies."

"He could have summoned or conjured them," Ashmael argued. "That, in my opinion, is more likely, and when he goes, they'll go. I will lead our hara to Fulminir and the *sedim* will help us break through any barrier that has been erected. They've done that in the past, they'll do so again."

Pellaz had still not told anyhar about his ability to commune with Peridot, nor what the *sedu* had told him. He, more than any others present, sensed the possible truth in Lianvis's words. "Tiahaar Lianvis makes sense to me," he said.

Ashmael glanced at him sharply. "How so?"

"Well, what are the *sedim*? Where did they come from and why do they serve us?"

"Thiede made them, or conjured them," Ashmael said. "That is common knowledge."

Pellaz laughed. "You make it sound as easy as modeling a horse from clay and straw! They are not horses, Ash, as you know. They appear to us as horses, because that is perhaps how we can best perceive them. I don't think Thiede summoned them. I think they found *him*."

Ashmael narrowed his eyes. "Why do you think that?"

"I have worked with Peridot intensely, as you do with Zephyr, but he has taken me to another realm, Ash. I have seen a *sedu* in its more natural form. They are higher beings than us, of that I have no doubt. If they choose to work with us, it is for a reason. Perhaps they are our shepherds. And perhaps if a higher power does require something from us as a resource, some other power is now trying to take it from them."

Ashmael uttered a derogatory snort. "Such fancies will not help us at Fulminir. We need to find Ponclast and destroy him. All this nonsense will stop then."

"The Tigron has offered interesting ideas," Tharmifex said. "We shouldn't dismiss them out of hand, Ash."

Velaxis raised his hand to speak and Tharmifex gave him permission to do so. "We should consider that if any of these ideas are based in truth, we are clearly not supposed to be aware of these powers operating above and beyond us. But as Ponclast has been contacted by some agency, perhaps those who are opposed to them could contact us, or we could contact them."

"If there is any truth in it," Ashmael said, "we do not contact any of them! We are not farm animals, and if that is indeed what's taking place, it should be stopped."

"Perhaps it is a symbiotic relationship," Velaxis said, "and therefore cannot be ended or changed."

"And what do you know about it?" Ashmael said coldly. "You are little more than a clerk or an escort for visitors, Vel. It is not your place to speak here."

Velaxis stared at Ashmael with eyes that blazed like silver disks, until Pellaz was sure Ash would burst into flames. "He has a point," Pellaz said, "and it's as valid as any other we've heard."

"What you're all talking about sounds like something out of myths and legends," Ashmael said. "Like the wars of the angels, or something. It's insane. We should deal with the crisis, here on this earth, with our feet on the ground. This is about territory, yes—Ponclast wanting ours."

"And this is why you are not Tigron," Velaxis said acidly. "You have no vision; you are just a fighter, like any common Varr."

"Tiahaar Shiraz!" Tharmifex said, simultaneously signaling at Ashmael for silence. "That is out of order. We have allowed you to speak, do not abuse the privilege."

Velaxis raised his hands. "I apologize. May I suggest we hear what other tribal representatives think of these claims?"

"Indeed," Tharmifex said. "Would anyhar care to contribute?"

Galdra stood up. "The Freyhellans have always believed this is a war that will be fought on astral ground. My personal suggestion is that we should ask Tiahaar Lianvis if the Kakkahaar have any ideas for a possible strategy we could use."

Many other representatives made noises of agreement, most likely because Galdra had spoken. Over time, he had become the spokeshar for just about every tribe other than the Gelaming. *You are just too damn useful,* Pellaz thought.

Tharmifex smiled at Galdra. "Thank you, tiahaar." He turned to Lianvis. "Do you?"

"I have spoken with my colleagues here with me and have also communed with the shamans of my tribe before attending this meeting. The Kakkahaar decision is that we will accompany the Tigron to Fulminir. I will do what I can to divine what action should be taken once I have taken stock of the situation at close hand. Ponclast will be waiting for you to come to him, you already know this. The Kakkahaar, with our *dark magic*"—here, he stared directly at Pellaz in a challenging manner—"should be able to provide a level of protection for your forces. I have communicated with our founder on the matter. He is already working on the problem."

"Velisarius is working on this?" Pellaz asked. He addressed Tharmifex. "The Kakkahaar founder is a recluse. If he is moved to become involved, I'd say our situation is serious, if not dire."

"Velisarius is more aware than most of the way our world functions," Lianvis said. "He believes that each faction involved in this skirmish has an avatar in this realm. We can only suppose that Tigron Pellaz is one of them, and that Ponclast is the other."

"Which makes it between him and me," Pellaz said. "I've felt this for some time."

"Heading for a duel, Pell?" Ashmael drawled. "This is ridiculous. He'll send out his Varrs to confront our forces. He'll use his allies against us. He won't come near any conflict. And neither should you."

"I will not hide miles away from enemy lines, Ash," Pellaz said. "I'm not afraid to ride at your side."

"You are not a warrior," Ashmael said. "Don't get carried away with the whole heroism aspect. Let me deal with the conflict in the tried and trusted way. I saw enough of it when we had to oust Ponclast before."

"Ponclast was ousted mainly by Swift and Seel," Pellaz said. "It was the product of their grissecon that breached Fulminir."

"Then find somehar to take aruna with outside the walls," Ashmael continued. "I'm sure there are many willing candidates. Politeness forbids me from naming those who ogle greedily Cal's empty throne. And that is no secret."

Pellaz felt his face flame. He was powerless to prevent it, and realized his first instinct was to glance at Galdra to gauge his reaction. Fortunately, he stopped himself in time.

"Ashmael!" Tharmifex said. "Enough! You shame us in front of our friends from other tribes."

"I will do whatever it takes," Pellaz said. "Your assumptions are of no interest to me, Ash. I am focused wholly on what is best and right for Wraeththukind."

"Very well," Ashmael said. "I suggest I do as I am inclined to do, and martial our forces from a military perspective. The rest of you devise a magical strategy, and let me know your plans. I presume my hara will have to provide protection for any magical operation."

"We know you will perform perfectly," Pellaz said. "We know you'll do all you can, in any situation. We must remember that Azriel and Aleeme Parasiel are captives of Ponclast. It's possible that will be exploited."

"Possible?" Ashmael said. "I think we can assume that's a given fact."

"That is your territory, Ash," Pellaz said. "You saved the lives of many in Fulminir before. If anyone can get the Parasilians out, it will be you."

Ashmael offered Pellaz a grudging smile. "Thank you."

Tharmifex stood up and addressed the tribal representatives. "Does anyhar else wish to speak?"

Many did, although they made it clear that Galdra har Freyhella spoke for them in most areas. Clearly, the representatives had been having meetings of their own, away from Gelaming eyes. While further discussions took place, little of which added to what had already been said, Ashmael moved his chair closer to the Tigron's. "I am not wrong, Pell," he said. "Guard your back."

"What do you mean?" Pellaz asked in a stiff tone.

"The Hegemony likes the idea of the Aralisian triumvirate. They do not like the idea of absconding Tigrons. I've heard rumors, not least that once this is over, Cal will be stripped of his title."

"They can't do that," Pellaz said. "That's my decision. He is my consort."

"A lot of talk goes on behind your back, Pell. You've proved yourself to be a worthy ruler, in countless ways, but the Hegemony still believe they have the power. You are the figurehead, but brace yourself. I think you might find yourself facing a united front."

Pellaz remembered what Caeru had said to him about opposition in the Hegemony. "What is your opinion of Velaxis Shiraz?" he asked.

"Why?"

"Something Rue once said. Velaxis has heard rumors too, or at least he told Rue he had."

"Velaxis serves nohar on the Hegemony," Ashmael said. "Don't misread

our little spat back there. I admire him greatly, but I have his measure. I sometimes wonder who he does serve."

"That's interesting."

"I know the Hegemony is making plans," Ashmael said. "Or at least some
of them are, but it is extremely clandestine. I don't know what goes on in your
private world, Pell, but be careful. It's not beyond possibility that members of
the Hegemony have already had talks with certain other hara. I trust you know
what I'm speaking about?"

"I hope I don't," Pellaz said. "Would you speak to Velaxis for me, try to
find out more? Rue has tried, but came up with nothing."

"He'll only tell me anything if it is useful for him to do so. Just think on
this: many tribes resent the Gelaming's power. Some might see it of benefit if
one of their own was part of our administration, somehar who could perhaps
make changes from the inside. I'm not saying this is of malign intent—in
their position, we would no doubt do the same. But you should be aware of
any potential for manipulation. Don't let anyhar pull a fait accompli out of the
hat. Understand?"

Pellaz hesitated, then said carefully, "How do you *know*, Ash? Has something been said?"

"Not overtly, but discreet departures from certain Phaonican gatherings
were noticed with—shall we say—relish?"

"Shit."

Ashmael smiled. "Quite. It might be that certain hara are innocent, so don't
jump to conclusions, just be aware."

"Your advice is noted. Thanks."

CHAPTER THIRTY-THREE

Pellaz was relieved to be able to take lunch with Herien and Rarn of the Kakkahaar, to tell them what he knew of Lileem. They went to The Epadocia, a hotel in Imbrilim that was renowned for its cuisine. After they were seated in the elegantly understated dining room, Pellaz told his companions to order whatever they pleased. He was amused to see how true to type they were, with their Kakkahaar love of luxury: they ordered the richest dishes on the menu. It was a pleasure to enlighten these apparently gentle hara, even if they were Kakkahaar and probably not gentle at all. The conversation took his mind off other matters.

"Once we learned about the Kamagrian," Herien said, "I asked Lianvis if we could search for Lileem among them. I knew it would be difficult, because of the Kamagrian's reclusive nature, but wanted to try."

"Lianvis wouldn't allow it," Rarn said. "To be honest with you, tiahaar, part of the reason we're here with Lianvis now is to try and find information about our lost son. It is known Immanion has close links with the Kamagrian. We're delighted our search has been so easy."

"Not that easy," Pellaz said. "Nohar can find her where she is now."

"I'm just relieved to know somehar cared for her," Herien said. "When she was taken from us, it was hideous. We were comforted only by an irrational belief on my part that she would be safe. I can't explain it."

"The Kamagrian call to their own," Pellaz said, "but if it hadn't been for Ulaume, it's doubtful she would have been found in time."

Herien smiled wistfully. "I find it hard to imagine him as a nurturing type."

"I think Lileem helped change him for the better," Pellaz said. "I hope you'll be reunited with her one day."

Rarn ducked his head. "Your kindness will not be forgotten."

As they were drinking coffee at the end of the meal, Lianvis joined them, having taken lunch with members of the Hegemony. He sat down in a flamboyant swirl of robes and hair. "I am a celebrity here. I could get used to it."

Pellaz laughed. "I bet."

"I can see why you stayed with the Gelaming, Pell. What a life you must lead."

"It has its advantages."

Half an hour later, Herien and Rarn excused themselves to use the bathroom, and once they were out of earshot, Lianvis adopted a more serious expression. "There is something I must mention, which I hope is not indelicate."

Pellaz took a sip of his coffee, holding the cup in two hands before his face. "Go ahead. Shock me."

"The discussion concerning the previous destruction of Fulminir. If grissecon is required again, I offer you my services."

Pellaz smiled widely, nodded slowly over his coffee cup. "How generous of you. I will remember it."

"I am not being facetious. Kakkahaar essence will be of use to you."

"I know. You might be right. We'll have to see."

"Please don't let past episodes color your judgment."

"I won't. Perhaps we should spend some time together."

Lianvis raised his eyebrows and said sardonically, "The starry-eyed young har is dead. Long live the Tigron."

Pellaz shrugged. "*You* addressed the subject of aruna before I did. That is what we're talking about, isn't it, continuing that training you once offered me?"

Lianvis looked the closest to flustered it was possible for him to get. "And you are no longer terrified of or repulsed by us?"

"No." Pellaz put down his cup. "It will take some time to reach Fulminir, because we don't have enough *sedim* for everyhar. Also, if the *sedim* are in this realm, they are able to use their energy to protect rather than convey passengers. We will speak further during the journey."

Lianvis narrowed his eyes. "Looking at you, I see Pellaz; listening to you, I hear somehar completely different."

"That's because I am," Pellaz said. He knew it sounded bitter.

Tharmifex had offered an invitation to the Kakkahaar to dine at his residence in Imbrilim that evening, and Pellaz was also invited. He knew he should accept. Whether Ashmael really knew anything about him and Galdra or not, the next day the Gelaming and their allies would begin the journey to Fulminir and Pellaz should have a clear head for it. He was now unnerved by the way he could not get Galdra out of his mind, even while he'd been speaking with Lianvis. Memories of the previous evening had kept flashing through his head. They made him slightly euphoric. The long afternoon, as he showed the Kakkahaar around the Hegemony areas of Imbrilim was a torment, but also exquisite, because of the potential that lay ahead. All day, Pellaz told himself he would not go to The Silver Eye at eight o'clock, even though he knew in his heart he had no intention of staying away. Strangely, what Ashmael had said to him had only fired his inner determination. He wasn't sure why. It also inspired a kind of recklessness.

At six o'clock, having said his good-byes to the Kakkahaar, Pellaz went back to Abrimel's house. Vaysh was worried because Abrimel still hadn't appeared, but Pellaz could barely register his anxiety. "I'm going out tonight," he said.

"I heard Tharmifex had invited you to dinner," Vaysh said. "Ashmael is in conference with the rest of the Hegemony about the final plans for tomorrow. Perhaps you should be there instead."

"They will tell me their decisions," Pellaz said. "I need to relax tonight."

"Rue has sent you a message. I made a transcription. He wants to know how things are going."

"I'll look at it later. I'm going to take a bath. Keep everyhar away."

Vaysh appeared suspicious. "Are you sure you're all right, Pell? You don't seem yourself."

"Of course I'm not all right. I'm going on a hellish journey to hell tomorrow!" He rolled his eyes. "For the Ag's sake, Vaysh, let me be!"

"I'll run your bath."

"Thank you."

Pellaz wandered into the bathroom as Vaysh was finishing up laying out the towels for him. "You know," Vaysh said, "this is going to sound strange, but I keep getting flashes of déjà vu."

"Oh?" Pellaz said, not wishing to inquire further.

"Yes, of Ferelithia, when you met Rue. I wonder why that is?"

Pellaz looked Vaysh in the eye. "I don't know. Perhaps you pay too much attention to gossip."

"Perhaps it's more to do with how well I know you?"

"Perhaps it is. Enjoy Ferelithia, Vaysh, it had its moments."

"And some of them you bitterly regretted. Might be worth remembering that."

"Oh, I will."

"What time will you be back from Tharmifex's?"

"Don't wait up."

Pellaz adopted a cursory disguise, knowing that if he swathed himself too deeply in a cloak and hood, he'd appear more suspicious than if he just scraped up his hair and hid it beneath a wide-brimmed hat. It was doubtful anyhar in The Silver Eye would expect the Tigron to patronize such an establishment. Nohar would recognize him.

When he arrived, the bar was already full. Many of the patrons were Ashmael's warriors: they clearly had no wish to retain clear heads for the morning. The atmosphere was tense and rowdy. Although the warriors swaggered around, enjoying the attention they attracted, Pellaz could tell they were also anxious. Nohar knew what would happen at Fulminir. There were no guarantees the Gelaming had superior force. Pellaz observed groups of hara who would remain in Imbrilim making toasts to those who wouldn't. It was extremely likely that some of them would not return. Everyhar was so intent on their own activities, hardly one of them paid Pellaz attention as he approached the bar and asked which room housed Flick Sarestes.

The pot har barely glanced at him. "You're his visitor, right? First room on the left at the top of the stairs. You taking a drink up?"

"I'll take a flagon of your best wine; red, if you have it."

The pot har looked at him then, and grinned lasciviously. "You leavin' tomorrow?"

"Yeah."

"Best of luck, har. Guess you'll need it. Get in all you can tonight."

"That's my plan."

Pellaz shared a conspiratorial and somewhat bawdy laugh with the pot har: it was blissful to be free of his Tigron mask, to talk like an ordinary har, instead of weaving a complexity of formal words. He took the dripping flagon that was offered to him and went to the stairs, which were situated behind a curtain at the back of the bar. Halfway up the staircase, he stood still for some moments. He couldn't analyze his feelings. At the top of the stairs he knocked on the door and heard Galdra say, "It's open."

The room was lit only by a dim lamp, next to the bed, where Galdra was lying, fully clothed, his long body stretched out.

"Am I late?" Pellaz asked, putting the wine flagon down on a table by the door. He took off his coat and hat, let his hair tumble down, knowing what a spectacle that must make.

"I don't know. I've been here awhile. Took the room late this afternoon."

"You were helpful this morning at the Hegalion," Pellaz said. "Hara look up to you. I think you have more influence over the majority than we do."

"I'm one of them," Galdra said.

"I know that." Pellaz remained by the door, and poured himself a cup of wine. When he tasted it, its consistency was thick in his mouth, like blood. "Want a drink?"

"I already have one," Galdra said. He sounded defensive.

Pellaz came farther into the room and stood at the foot of the bed. "I think a member of the Hegemony has spoken to you, perhaps more than one of them. Am I right?"

"Many hara have spoken to me, including some of your Hegemony. As you said, hara look up to me. Your government sees the uses in that."

"I'm sure they do."

"Are you trying to tell me something?"

"No. I just want you to be aware I know, that's all."

Galdra frowned quizzically. "You're not making sense. What's the matter?"

"I wonder why you haven't asked me what Ashmael Aldebaran meant this morning, when he made those rather inflammatory remarks."

"You've just got here! One foot through the door and you're all spikes and growls. Okay, here's what I think: what Aldebaran said made sense to me. Why should I question it? I imagine that a host of hara would be eager to take Cal's place, if it were an option."

"Are you one of them?"

"I don't want his place, Pell. I'm not that stupid. What I want from you is beyond political jostling and intrigue. I thought you knew that."

"What *do* you want?"

"Your body against mine. Whatever we can enjoy, for however long. It's all on your terms. I've accepted that."

Pellaz sat down on the bed and Galdra reached for one of his hands. "Hey," he murmured. "Forget them all for a while. It's not why you're here."

Pellaz drank the rest of the wine, grimaced, and put the cup on the floor. "You have been with me all day. You're inside me."

"Am I? I thought that was forbidden." Galdra's tone was light.

Pellaz lifted Galdra's hand, kissed it. "No. It's all I've thought about. I shouldn't be here, for several reasons, some of which you don't even know about, but for tonight, I just want you, Galdra. I will be with you in heart and soul, as well as mind. I am so empty. You can fill me. And I need that for what I must face in the weeks ahead."

Galdra squeezed his hand. "Lock the door, Pell. I think you should."

Pellaz nodded. He rose from the bed and went to turn the key. Then he picked up the wine flagon and returned to the bed. Galdra was undressing beside it, his hair startlingly pale against his tanned skin. His body looked so much like Cal's it was uncanny: lean and sculpted and perfect. Pellaz pressed his cheek in the hollow between Galdra's shoulder blades. He curled his arms around that warm body from behind and inhaled deeply. The smell of a har, so beautiful, like soft, sunlit fur. "Take me back," Pellaz said.

Pellaz woke before dawn after only three hours' sleep. He slid from the bed without waking Galdra, his mouth full of the sour taste of the previous night's wine. When he stood up, his head reeled a little. He'd drunk too much and was still affected by it. His body would take a couple of hours to detoxify. As he put on his shirt he gazed at Galdra, who appeared deeply asleep, his thin, finely drawn lips slightly open, his tangled hair spread out about his head. All night, Pellaz had been soume; he had craved to be, which he knew was unlike him. Now, before the sun rose, he should leave, return to Abrimel's house, before Vaysh and the rest of the household got out of bed. Yet he could not leave without kissing those fine lips one more time. As he leaned over the bed, Galdra stirred and opened his eyes.

"It's time," Galdra murmured. "The day is here. It will begin now. Everything."

"I know," Pellaz said. He put his mouth against Galdra's own and Galdra pulled him down beside him, kicking aside the blankets. "Touch me," Galdra said, a whispered message in Pell's head.

Pellaz drew back and gazed into Galdra's eyes as he caressed him intimately. "You are oceanic," Pellaz said. "If I put my ear against you, I would hear the sea."

"I have wanted this all night," Galdra said.

"You should have said so."

Galdra smiled. "No, you needed something. It doesn't matter. Do you have time for this?"

"I don't care whether I have or not. I'm staying a little longer."

Galdra rolled onto his back, pulled Pellaz on top of him. "I will fight for you, Pell, in both senses. I know now I have a chance."

"It should have been you in Ferelithia."

"What?"

"Nothing." Pellaz ran his fingers through Galdra's hair. "I am told this experience can be overwhelming. Essence of Tigron, essence of Thiede."

"I would be disappointed if it wasn't. Let go, Pell. Don't hold back. Give in to it. I can take it."

"There are some mistakes I won't make twice," Pellaz said. "Don't tempt me."

"I'm not sure what you mean."

Pellaz merely smiled. "Relax, Galdra. Open yourself to me."

Vaysh was already up by the time Pellaz reached the house. He had clearly roused the staff, because the bustle of activity could be heard from every room, as the last preparations for leaving were made. Vaysh met Pellaz in the entrance hall, but although Pellaz tensed himself for a barrage of questions or accusations, Vaysh did not ask where he'd been. "Abrimel is still missing," he said. "I've had our hara search Imbrilim. Nohar has seen him since the day before yesterday. I have asked Eyra to commit his Listeners to a search."

"You've been to Eyra already?" Pellaz said. "Vaysh, it's barely even light!"

"Aren't you concerned? Ponclast might have taken him, as he took the Parasilians. Yet nohar seems that bothered. Well, I am."

"Why would Ponclast want Abrimel?" Pellaz said.

Vaysh pursed his lips. "The son of the Tigron should be of prime importance, surely? There's something wrong if he's not."

"Abrimel opted out of family and political life," Pellaz said. "It was his decision. We have never been close. If he's disappeared now, it's because he has no interest in what's going on. Also, he doesn't like being around me."

"We shouldn't leave here until we know where he is."

Pellaz sighed. "You do as you please, but I cannot. If you really want to remain here, Attica can take on your duties as personal aide to me temporarily. You must instruct him."

"I might do that. I could catch you up. My *sedu* can use the otherlanes to do so."

"If that is what you wish."

"I hope my fears are ungrounded, but I feel uneasy." Vaysh paused. "You might as well tell me the truth. The strange mood you've been in: it's the Freyhellan, isn't it?"

"I don't want your judgments."

"I won't give them. It's not a bad choice."

"There's no choice involved," Pellaz said. "It's aruna, that thing we need, remember? It's nothing more than that."

"As long as you're happy about it. I just didn't want there to be another episode like Rue."

"This is not another Rue episode. Give me credit for some sense, Vaysh."

"I'm surprised, that's all, given the way you feel and the rumors that have been circulating, which I presume you've heard. Will you talk to me about it?"

"There's not much to say. Look, I must start preparing myself for the journey. Stay here if you wish and search for Abrimel. I don't have much time."

"I'll ready your bath. Everything is packed and most of your luggage has been delivered to the livery yard. I've left traveling clothes out for you, which are quite ceremonial. You want to look good as you lead our hara out of Imbrilim."

Pellaz touched Vaysh's face. "Thanks. I know it'll all be perfect. You always think of everything."

CHAPTER THIRTY-FOUR

Preparing an army for overland travel is a huge operation. The warriors themselves are the easiest part to manage. What is more complex is the vast infrastructure required to support their needs and the needs of their staff. An army on the move is like a mobile city, and it has to sustain itself.

The wagon train set off long before the warriors and their leaders, moving slowly with an armed guard around them. No herd animals would accompany them, as it had been decided there were more than enough wild and feral cattle, deer, and sheep that could provide meat, although there was a danger that their numbers could be decimated by so vast a company. Hara were appointed to oversee this aspect and to plan hunting parties carefully.

The only members of the Hegemony who would make the journey were the Tigron, Tharmifex, Velaxis, and of course Ashmael, who believed himself to be in charge of everything, and no doubt wished that Tharmifex wasn't involved, as the chancellor of the Hegemony would probably interfere in many of Ashmael's decisions. Eyra would remain in Imbrilim to relay information, although two of his senior Listeners would be part of Ashmael's support staff. The remainder of the Hegemony stayed in Immanion.

Back home in Phaonica, Caeru was sick with nerves, because more than one har had intimated subtly that he might end up being Tigron if things went badly. Not that things would go badly, of course. He shouldn't really worry himself about that.

. Everyhar knew that Cal had gone to Galhea, but further information had been sketchy, seeing as Cobweb and Snake had had to head off into the wilderness. Caeru wished that Cal would simply turn up at Phaonica as if nothing had happened. If it came to the point where he had to become like Cobweb and adopt a different role, he'd go mad. It just wasn't in him. Fond memories of Ferelithia haunted his dreams. He had summoned his Kamagrian friend Katarin to Immanion, who he'd known when she'd been human and who had stood by him during the bad years with Pellaz. She now worked for Opalexian, and no doubt the Kamagrian needed her out in the world, gathering information for them, but Caeru didn't care. He needed her more. He needed a familiar face around him.

Katarin arrived in the evening, dusty with travel, and met Caeru on his terrace. She spoke of Pell's sister, Mima, and how everyone in Shilalama feared for the Tigron. "Lend me a *sedu*," she said. "I should go to Megalithica."

"That is not going to happen," Caeru told her. "I need you, Kate."

"I know. I'm here." Katarin embraced him for some moments, then drew away. "How's the mood in the city?"

"Tense. What can we say to our hara? We don't know anything. I have nightmares of the Varrs killing everyhar in Megalithica and stealing our *sedim*. I have dreamed of them pouring out of the sky to bring ruin to Immanion. It's not beyond possibility."

"You'd have some warning," Katarin said, which didn't help at all.

"We transmit cheerful propaganda about how well things are going in Imbrilim, but for the Ag's sake, these are hara we're trying to bamboozle, not humans. It doesn't work the way it used to for human governments. Hara sense the truth, and it simply breeds more distrust and anxiety."

"Then tell them the truth."

"The Hegemony fears it would induce panic. Hara might flee the city while they can. We wish to avoid that. We want to keep things calm here. More *sedim* arrived the other day. Stable-hara just went to work one morning and found the empty stalls full again. We don't know where they came from. They are mulish. They just stand there looking splendid, full of mystery. Who sent them?" Caeru wrung his hands together. "If they are here, does that mean the ones in Megalithica are in danger? Will we need replacements? What good is that? If the *sedim* know what's going on, why don't they help us properly? Ag, I'm shivering!"

"Sit down," Katarin said. "I'll get your staff to bring us drinks. Also, I'm starving."

"Sorry, I should have ordered you something." Caeru sat down at his table.

"You stay here," Katarin said. "I won't be a moment. Tonight, whatever the future holds, we will get drunk together and not think about it."

"Okay." Caeru smiled shakily and watched her leave the terrace. The evening air was full of the scent of lilies and the tang of the ocean. It reminded him of home. He began to weep.

Whatever intentions Pellaz had had to keep Galdra har Freyhella at a distance during the journey to Fulminir, they came to nothing. The fact was that he found strength in Galdra's steady and serene support. Galdra made no demands; he was easy to be with. He was discreet until it no longer mattered, and even then kept his own counsel.

On the morning that he left Imbrilim, Pellaz went with Attica to the gathering point outside the town where all the highest-ranking hara would meet to begin the march northwest. The atmosphere among the pavilions, which were all in the process of being dismantled, was close and tense. The air smelled of turned earth, because the ground had still not dried out from the recent rain. It smelled of manure and crushed grass. The sky was overcast, the air warm and humid. Few hara were speaking, perhaps because many of them were still affected by whatever last-minute celebrations they'd indulged in the night before. Pellaz wore ceremonial armor that appeared light and insubstantial, as if crafted from mother-of-pearl, but which was in fact very durable. Over it, he wore a long cloak of dark green fabric. His hair was plaited tightly down his back. A warrior held Peridot's bridle as Pellaz swung up into the saddle. All the *sedim* were harnessed. They were warhorses now.

Around the Tigron, leaders of other tribes were also mounting up. The majority of them had been given *sedim,* although the creatures had been given the private instruction by their Gelaming handlers that if a situation looked dire, they must take their passengers to safety via the otherlanes. An abundance of leaderless tribes was not a viable prospect, in the Hegemony's opinion.

Pellaz gathered up the reins and gazed about him. There was Ariaric, Archon of the Maudrah, surrounded by leaders of lesser Jaddayoth tribes: Mojag, Garridan, Natawni, and Gimrah. Lianvis of the Kakkahaar was nearby with Herien and Rarn. Heron har Sulh was next to Ormelte of the Colurastes.

And there was Galdra, like a warrior from myth, wearing wolfskin, his hair in braids, hanging over his chest. For the briefest moment, Pellaz caught a tang of Galdra's scent, imagined the feel of his skin. Then the image shattered as Pellaz laid eyes on a vaguely familiar har mounted on a huge black horse, rather than a *sedu,* and realized it was Spinel of the Irraka, which had been a small-time and rather feckless tribe that Pellaz and Cal had run into many years before. Pellaz hadn't even known the Irraka still existed, never mind that they'd joined the alliance. He caught Spinel's eye and signaled a greeting. Spinel stared back for a moment, as if he'd been punched, then cautiously returned the gesture.

Ashmael rode through the crowd, accompanied by Tharmifex and Velaxis. He brought his *sedu* up alongside Peridot. "Well, Tigron," he said in a clipped voice. "Are you ready to lead your hara?"

"You will allow me to do that?"

"It'll create a good impression leaving Imbrilim. You always look first-rate in a procession."

"Why, thank you, general. You flatter me."

Ashmael grinned savagely and turned his *sedu* away toward his elite guard.

"Are you ready, Pell?" Tharmifex asked.

"Is everyhar else?"

"More or less. We might as well make a start."

Pellaz leaned forward and patted Peridot's well-muscled neck. "Well, old friend. This is it. Lead your brethren with pride."

The *sedu* threw up his head and walked forward. The crowd parted to let him through. Velaxis and Tharmifex rode behind and Ashmael's guard fell in behind them. Before they even reached the end of the pavilions two *sedim* came cantering between them. They bore Terez har Aralis and Raven Jaguar. Pellaz felt his eyes mist and blinked quickly. Emotions were running high today. "You were supposed to stay in Immanion," he called. He didn't need to point out why. Everyhar knew he regarded Terez as his closest heir, despite what other hara might think on the matter.

Terez brought his *sedu* up beside Peridot. "This is where I should be." He reached out and clasped hands with his brother.

"I am glad you're here," Pellaz said, "although it is reckless of you."

"I'm a survivor," Terez said. "You know that." He and Raven joined Tharmifex and Velaxis, riding four abreast.

As they reached the end of the pavilions, the sun broke through the clouds. Every resident of Imbrilim, human and har alike, had gathered alongside the main highway to watch the army leave. The crowd of onlookers went on for miles. Some threw flowers and others held censers of burning incense. Some of them sang. Yet more stood in silence, harlings in their arms. Groups of hienamas from several tribes uttered blessings and called upon dehara light and dark to add their strength to that of those now riding into the unknown.

About a mile from Imbrilim, a force of two hundred or so riders was spotted, approaching at speed from the north. The crowds at the side of the road parted to allow the leader of the new arrivals to reach the Tigron. It was the Kamagrian Tel-an-Kaa, and she had brought others with her.

Pellaz was astonished by her appearance, because he had never seen her in any guise other than the one she habitually employed while seeking out stray Kamagrian around the world, when she generally pretended to be a human female. Then, she was a waiflike gypsy creature, dressed in colorful skirts and adorned with clanking trinkets. Now, she was more like one of Ashmael's warriors, a harder edge to her bearing as well as her clothing of close-fitting leather.

"I haven't brought you much," she said to Pellaz, "but I rounded up as many of our best agents in the area as I could before coming to you. I'm sorry I'm late."

"You're most welcome," Pellaz said, eyeing the rather fearsome-looking collection of parazha behind Tel-an-Kaa. "Does Opalexian know of your . . . *recruitment?*"

Tel-an-Kaa grinned. "I had no time to tell her. I obeyed an impulse. We are ready, tiahaar. It is time Wraeththu appreciated that Kamagrian are not afraid to face whatever dangers lie ahead."

"I can see that," Pellaz said, and leaned from Peridot to embrace Tel-an-Kaa briefly. "We are glad you're here."

"Then, let's ride," she said, and signaled to her parazha to move on. "We'll find a place in the line. I'll speak to you later."

As the tribe leaders left Imbrilim, so their warriors followed, a seemingly endless procession of hara. So great a force. How could Ponclast resist it? He'd made no strikes on Imbrilim recently. He'd made no apparent preparations. Nohar knew what he was thinking, or what his allies were really capable of. There was a clear boundary around Fulminir, and if anyhar crossed it, it invited devastating retaliation from hara who flashed out of the otherlanes. But Swift's forces had been able to survey the area in relative comfort from a reasonable distance. To all intents and purposes, Fulminir went about its daily business as if it were nothing more than a simple Wraeththu settlement. There was no sign of troop training or reinforcements arriving, although hara worked steadily on the walls, throughout the day and night. It was if they were luring the Gelaming to them, attempting to lull them into a false sense of security.

For so great a force, making and striking camp was a lengthy process, but by the time the armies reached the designated resting point that night, the domestic staff who had gone on ahead at dawn had already done most of the work. A vast temporary Imbrilim stood in the wild fields, where feral horses roamed. It was much like the original Imbrilim had been, many years ago: a host of pavilions and floating veils. The flags and banners of the tribes cracked in the evening breeze upon high poles, so that hara could easily find their billets. Woodcutters had been to the forests to gather fuel for cooking fires. Meals were being prepared. *Sedim* and horses churned the fields to mud. It seemed like chaos.

Pellaz retired to his pavilion with Terez and Raven. Before they ate, they were joined by Tharmifex, Velaxis, and Ashmael. Pellaz was aware of an itch inside him, a sense of impatience. It took him a moment to realize what it was: he wanted them all to leave so he could go and find Galdra. It was clear that wasn't going to happen.

Shortly after eleven o'clock, Vaysh arrived. His expression was not joyful. Pellaz didn't want to hear what he was going to say.

Vaysh addressed his opening remarks to Tharmifex, which was telling. "Eyra's Listeners have made a report concerning Abrimel. They picked up otherlane residue, which confirms he left Imbrilim by that means, but no trace of *sedim*. One of Eyra's hara took a *sedu* into the otherlanes. They found a trace signature and from what they could gather, Abrimel left voluntarily. There was no energy fallout of distress. His signature was mixed with that of a being similar to those who have been directing attacks upon our hara."

Tharmifex was silent for a moment, then glanced briefly at Pellaz. "Are you suggesting, tiahaar, that Abrimel has left Imbrilim willingly with an enemy?"

"The evidence suggests it," Vaysh said. "The Listeners were very thorough. They made several checks." He looked at Pellaz. "I'm sorry."

"It can't be so," Tharmifex said. "Abrimel has been glamored. It's the obvious explanation." He frowned. "However, it's strange that nohar picked up any sense of an enemy entering Imbrilim. Security there is extremely tight, and there was a sizable force of *sedim* present. Somehar would have felt or seen something."

"They would," Pellaz said curtly. He put down his plate. "I believe this might be Abrimel's final rebellion against me. I imagine he has a treasury of currency Ponclast would covet, namely whatever he has learned of our plans."

"Can you really say that of your son?" Velaxis said. He appeared more troubled than anyhar else.

"You know that I can," Pellaz said. "I know you are close to him, Velaxis, and I can imagine how you must feel about this, but I think we have to face reality."

"There is no proof," Velaxis said. "I'm sure . . . I'm sure I would have suspected, felt . . . *known* something."

"We'll find out," Ashmael said darkly, and from his tone he could have meant anything by that.

For three days, Pellaz was unable to meet with Galdra, and in fact did not even lay eyes on him. Many hara wanted his time. He spent a poignant half hour riding alongside Spinel, who informed the Tigron that he had been an inspiration to the Irraka. "You made us think," he said. "Now I know why."

"Maybe you just needed time," Pellaz said graciously. "I think that in order to survive you would have changed and grown anyway, but thanks for the compliment."

On the third evening, Galdra turned up without an invitation at the Tigron's pavilion. Tharmifex and Velaxis were there, and in fact seemed to have become permanent fixtures for dinner each night. Both greeted Galdra like a long-lost friend. Pellaz found it was easy, not at all awkward, to integrate Galdra into the gathering. He noticed that his guests left earlier than usual, and the moment the pavilion closed behind them, he was in Galdra's arms, sharing breath as if they were underwater and the Freyhellan was the only source of air.

"I've missed you," Galdra said, right into Pell's mouth. "Ag, how I've missed you! I couldn't stay away any longer."

The walls to the pavilions were thin. Everyhar around the Tigron's abode that night would have been in no doubt that he was taking aruna with somehar, and most of them would have known or guessed who it was.

Ecstasy spent, they lay in each other's arms. Pellaz felt drowsy and contented. The world was a good place. Nothing bad could exist in a universe where this comfortable state abided. They lay side by side, facing each other, and Galdra reached up to take a lock of Pell's hair in his fingers. "You hide it well," he said softly, "but I do *know,* Pell."

"Know what?" Pellaz had no idea what Galdra would say. Already, he knew enough about the Freyhellan to expect anything.

"It should be Cal here, holding you, giving you his strength. I wonder sometimes whether you resent the fact it's me, because you are kept apart from him, unsure of where he is or how he is, or of why he can't come to you."

Pellaz felt his body stiffen involuntarily. The words were like a knife wound. "Don't talk of him here," he said. "Don't."

"You should. You can say anything to me."

Pellaz pulled away from Galdra and sat up. He felt dizzy and had to put his head in his hands. Galdra was silent and motionless behind him, giving him this time. After some moments, Pellaz lowered his hands. "Galdra, Cal is not here simply because he doesn't want to be."

"What do you mean?"

"He went to Galhea. We had news. I thought you might have heard."

"No. The Gelaming are more tight-lipped about your affairs than you realize, at least with outsiders." Galdra sat up also, put his hands on Pell's shoulders. "What have you heard?"

"Not much, but if he can get to Forever, he can get to me. He doesn't want me, Galdra. That's the truth."

"I can't believe that." He kissed Pell's shoulder. "It isn't true."

Pellaz laughed harshly. "It is. I know you love me, and maybe that's because you never knew me before I was Tigron. You love what you see. Cal loves a dream, a dead har. He can't love what lives. He's Tigron of his own life. He can't cope with what I've become. He defers to nohar."

Galdra pulled Pellaz back down to the bed, held him close. He didn't speak, just pressed his lips against Pell's hair.

"There may have to be changes," Pellaz said abruptly. He felt Galdra go utterly still. "After this is all over, there may be changes. Perhaps you understand my meaning?"

Galdra did not respond immediately. "I am here for you in whatever way you want me to be. I think I know what you mean, but I also think we should not speak of it. Too much could happen. I think you might be wrong about Cal."

"But if I'm not? In Immanion, you told me I should let go of my dreams. What if I see them for what they are now—a nightmare? You said we should be together."

Galdra sighed. "I know you more intimately now than I did when I said those words. I have seen things inside you, Pell, things that have made me sad for both of us. We could be together twenty years and if he came for you, you'd still go to him. I know that."

Pellaz uttered an angry, wordless sound. "Too many times I've thrown out a challenge to the universe, to him. Important times in my life. I've asked him to come to me, when it would have meant everything. He never did, not when I blood-bonded with Rue, nor when I met with you in Immanion. He is never there when it would make a difference."

"What if he walked in here now?"

Pellaz shuddered. A chill went through him like a spirit breeze. "Don't say that. He won't."

"But he could, at any time. You should be aware of that."

"If that's the case, then it's not right. I won't play that game anymore. You have made me see this."

Galdra smiled sadly. "I am a blinding light, that's all, and in that light you cannot see the shadows. It does not mean they're gone." He kissed Pell's lips. "Be silent. Be here now. We have said enough."

That night, Pellaz dreamed of Lileem. He met her in a dark place, but sensed vast open space all around him. Lileem came to him out of the darkness and said, "We will meet soon. We will meet when the serpent bites the star and the seal opens. Do not be afraid of what lies beyond. It is safe to step through. I will be with you there. Soon."

Pellaz woke up at once as if somehar had slapped him. Beside him, Galdra slept soundly, uttering gentle snores. Pell could still hear the echo of Lileem's words, as if she had really been there speaking to him. The air in his pavilion was charged.

The message had been very clear: he knew what he had to do.

The day begins very early when an army is on the march. Breakfast is ready by dawn, and even while it is being eaten, the pavilions are coming down around the dampened fires, so the supply wagons, with their guards, can move out ahead of the troops.

Pellaz was woken by the sounds of activity but also by the heavy warmth of Galdra upon him. "I should get back to my hara," Galdra said. "When I'm with you, it's easy to forget why we're here. This idyll, this love, is no part of war."

"Swim in me one more time," Pellaz said. He could feel the pulse of blood in his throat, behind his eyes, singing in his ears.

"You are the primal waters of soume," Galdra murmured, "you are my element."

Pellaz tried to regulate his breathing, distance himself from what was happening. He must take control and be aware, outside and inside at the same time. His consciousness hovered among the folds of the pavilion's ceiling. What he saw below him was one being, a mass of pulsating energy, slowly turning. And in the heart of it was a vortex, like a black hole, drawing into itself all matter. It was shocking, terrifying, for this was where they must go.

Then he was back inside himself, Galdra's breath against his ear. Galdra made the strangest sounds, like the most terrible grief and the most sublime ecstasy.

The sensations in Pell's body were the most bizarre he'd ever experienced. It was as if he were deep underwater, and the walls of enormous ancient caverns were cracking apart all around him. He had a sense of immense forces churning within him. His body was a cosmos and somewhere at its heart stars were born.

"Pellaz," Galdra said, "we cannot do this. Stop. Release me."

"No," Pellaz answered, with his mind. "I control this. There is nothing to fear. We must not stop."

At that moment, the inner tongue of Galdra's ouana-lim shot out like an arrow of fire and made contact with the sixth energy center in Pell's body. The serpent bit the star. The seal opened fully and Pellaz fell through it.

He was on his hands and knees in complete blackness, panting heavily. His whole body felt wet: the experience was totally physical. He heard swift, light footsteps in the darkness, drawing nearer to him.

"Pellaz, call me!" The voice was Lileem's.

"Here!" Pellaz said. He was afraid to move. The surface beneath him felt uncertain, pliable, like a membrane over sinking sand.

He saw Lileem then, her body surrounded by a faint nimbus of light.

"What is this place?" Pellaz asked her.

"We are in the cauldron of creation: yours, to be precise."

"So, I am hallucinating."

"You are not. This is another form of reality, but reality nonetheless."

"How did *you* get here inside *me*?"

"Haven't you guessed? The cauldron is a portal, or can create them. It happened with Terez and me, only different. I am learning about it. Listen, this won't hold for long, because you are inexperienced and events still take their course in your reality. During focused aruna, when the seal to the cauldron opens, opportunistic souls take advantage of it: that is how pearls are created. I have seen it, the myriad of lights beyond your realm, a galaxy of hara reaching for the ultimate. You must learn that this is not the only function of the cauldron. You must learn to control it. Look. I can grant you this perception." She flung out an arm and Pellaz could see beyond her a host of tiny lights, like fireflies. "They are predators. They are circling you. At this moment, you are yaloe, the essence of soume. Do not let them touch you, unless you want a pearl, of course."

"Are they Galdra's aren?"

"Yes. If they touch you, souls will perceive it. They will fight to take possession."

"I need to go," Pellaz said. "Now!" The lights were drawing closer, a fizzing mass of pinprick radiance.

Lileem laughed. "Pellaz, banish your fear. This is your body, your realm. You must learn you have the right and the ability to choose what happens to it."

"Where is Galdra? Is he with us?"

"Your friend thinks he is dreaming. He is wandering the halls of your being waiting to wake up."

"How do we use this? What is its purpose? You have called me for a reason, I know it."

"You can use the cauldron to create more than new hara. You can summon other entities through it. You have little time to gain knowledge of this skill, I know, but it must be done. You must learn to control focused aruna. It is like learning to dream lucidly, to remain aware in the realm of dreams. Do you understand?"

"Yes, I understand it, but how do I put that into practice?"

"When you are next here, call upon a dehar. You are familiar with their pattern. When they obey your summons, command them. Use them as a weapon."

"Will you meet me here again? Will you help me?"

"I'll try. I'll remain alert. You should know that your enemies have no idea you are discovering this information. Higher forces of all factions do not desire for you to know it."

"Even the *sedim* and those they serve?"

"Even them."

"Tell me what you know."

"The Kakkahaar are not wrong," Lileem said. "Listen to them. One day I will return to your realm, but not yet. I too am learning."

"Can the *sedim* be trusted?"

"Yes. They will surprise you. Pellaz . . ." Lileem hunkered down beside him and put a hand on his shoulder. The touch felt real. "Your son who was taken from Rue's body: he lives. Some battles will be fought among the next generation. Do what you can. Repair the tear in your reality that allows your enemy's allies ingress into the earthly realm. Repel them."

"Where is my son?"

"I don't know everything, only some things. The marks in the stone books I read are like fragments. They move and change."

"And my other son—Abrimel. What of him? We believe he has gone to Ponclast."

"I have not looked into that," Lileem said, "but I will do so. Where I am, in the Black Library, there is so much to absorb. It is amazing. I want to show it to you."

"That realm is treacherous," Pellaz said. "I have been there before, to drag you out of it, and we almost didn't make it."

"*Sedim* are not the appropriate medium to reach it," Lileem said. "There are better ways. I cannot explain now. It would take too long. Listen. There is one thing you should know before you leave. Cal still loves you. It is written on every stone that bears a harish mark. It can never be erased."

"Lileem . . ." There was so much Pellaz wanted to ask, but already he could feel the pull of earthly reality upon him. He was faintly aware of his physical body, the feeling of Galdra inside him.

"Go now," Lileem said. "It is time for this congress to end. If you remain here once aruna has peaked, it might be very difficult for you to return to normal consciousness. I don't have full knowledge of this process yet. Think yourself back, Pell. Concentrate on your soume-lam, its feelings. Be flesh once more. Now."

Pellaz closed his eyes and directed his concentration toward his physical body. In an instant, he was back on his bed, his flesh coursing with powerful and paralyzing sensation. The climax of this aruna was like an immense electrical charge, the water of soume conducting the current of ouana. It was not altogether pleasant. Pellaz cried out involuntarily, and yelled so loudly that hara came running.

Vaysh was the first to arrive. He threw aside the door curtain.

Over Galdra's shoulder Pellaz could see his aide's shocked expression. He could not help but laugh out loud as the pulsations in his flesh ebbed away, waves upon a beach, low tide, going back.

Galdra was clearly oblivious to anyhar else being present. "Are you with pearl?" he asked urgently. "You made it happen."

Pellaz gently pushed Galdra away from him. "No, I am not with pearl," he said. "I have discovered something more wonderful."

Vaysh had recovered his composure. "Pellaz!" he said. "Are you insane? It sounded like you were being murdered. Remember who and what you are. You cannot behave like this. It is inappropriate at this time." Other hara had gathered behind him and now he turned on them. "Get out! All of you!"

"Summon Tharmifex and Ashmael," Pellaz said. "Also Velaxis, I suppose. Do it now, Vaysh. I have learned something of great importance."

Vaysh nodded, clearly troubled. "I will." He glanced at Galdra. "You should leave, tiahaar. If they should see you here, like this . . ."

"Let them see," Pellaz said. "I have nothing to hide from them. The Tigron is allowed to take aruna, Vaysh. For the Ag's sake, just go and get the Hegemony."

CHAPTER THIRTY-FIVE

It was not easy to make friends among hara who were naturally suspicious of strangers, made even more difficult because the Teraghasts were acutely aware of Moon and Tyson's heritage. The veiled hostility did not appear to affect Cal, as if other hara's opinions of him simply rolled off his skin like sweat. But then he'd had a lifetime to train himself to ignore the disapproval of others. "They are mostly stupid," he told Tyson and Moon. "Just play up to them, use flattery, bat your eyelashes. It'll work. Trust me."

Such behavior did not come naturally to Moon, and Tyson felt like a fraud if he tried to ingratiate himself with the Teraghasts. Consequently, they spent much time alone. The Teraghasts were happy to give them work to do, such as rebuilding dwellings and workshops, but come break times, Tyson and Moon always sat apart from the other workers. They were escorted to and from the workplace and their accommodation, and were always locked in at night, although their rooms, which were at ground level, did have a small walled courtyard they were allowed to use. Cal was rarely with them during the day, but they didn't know where he went: Ponclast would only see Cal very occasionally. Cal himself was vague concerning his whereabouts. The Teraghasts were close-lipped about their captives, so Cal hadn't been able to find out much about Azriel and Aleeme. He had worked out where they were confined, however. He said that if he asked too many questions, the Teraghasts would guess the truth about his presence in Fulminir, and it would be likely that he and his companions would be put back into more stringent confinement.

This excuse made sense, but Moon was unsure that the rescue of Aleeme and Azriel was the real reason Cal had brought them there. Tyson would not hear a bad word against his hostling, but privately Moon wondered whether Cal believed the outcome of any conflict would leave Ponclast in power. Perhaps Cal simply wanted to be with the winning side when it was all over.

It soon became clear that Cal had been cultivating a friendship with Kyrotates during his absences from his companions, a strategy that seemed eventually to be paying off—but then who could resist Cal on full power for long? Kyrotates was an extremely contained and self-disciplined har, but even so, Moon had caught glimpses of him staring at Cal with the unmistakable expression of intense and smoldering desire. In Moon's opinion, Kyrotates felt confused about it, perhaps wondering where these devastating feelings had come from. Cal in seduction mode was terrifying. He was like a primordial goddess of love: unswervable, inexorable, and merciless, skulls of his victims swinging from his belt. One evening he stretched himself beside the cooking fire they'd built in their courtyard and said, "Kyrotates will soon be cooked to perfection, and I intend to consume him with relish. Then we will have the information we need."

Tyson laughed, but Moon felt slightly disgusted. "Sure he doesn't need longer on slow simmer?" he asked, and could hear the acidity in his own voice.

"Don't want him to burn," Cal said lightly. "Believe me, I know all about this type of cuisine, moonling. I don't have a taste for charcoal."

"But if you don't cook something for long enough," Moon said, inspired, "then it can poison you."

"Yes, the metaphor is fun," Cal said dryly, "but I think we've got more than enough out of it."

"Cobweb thought you'd changed," Moon said, "but he was wrong. It was all just an act. You still use hara as you like."

Cal sat up. "Moon," he said in a low voice, "don't be such a prude. That's very early Cevarro of you! Why are we here? I'm just making light of what is actually an unpleasant circumstance."

Moon went numb with humiliation. He wished Tyson weren't there.

Ponclast took a great deal of pleasure in observing Cal—the other two barely interested him. He could see Cal trying to wind himself around Kyrotates's legs like a demanding cat, and he noted with amusement Kyrotates's inept attempts to stumble away from it. Cal operated on hara with surgical precision: it was a delight to behold. Ponclast dearly wished he could trust Cal—what an asset he'd be—but he was also realistic. If anything, Cal was above and beyond any skirmish between the Teraghasts and the Gelaming. Ponclast knew Cal was not a spy for Immanion, but neither could he be relied upon. At the most crucial moment, he might jump from your lap and be out of the window, to disappear over the rooftops. A cat is a creature unto itself.

Cal still did not know about Abrimel: a morsel Ponclast was keeping in reserve. Abrimel himself had no wish to confront Cal and still thought he should be thrown into a dungeon or killed. Ponclast realized Abrimel was actually terrified of Cal, although he would not admit it. The question was: did he fear Cal's judgment? If that was the case, it would suggest that Abrimel was not wholly free of his Gelaming heritage. And that was a fact to be mindful of.

Ponclast knew that Cal was interested in the fate of the Parasilians, simply because he had not yet asked about them. Aleeme Parasiel had already delivered one pearl for Ponclast, and was currently carrying a second one. His health had deteriorated, but Ponclast did not care. Every time he laid eyes on those hara, he saw Swift's face. He remembered the day that Fulminir had fallen before and Swift's righteous wrath. When he used his will to open the seal in Aleeme's shuddering body he felt like he was beating Swift about the head. He had not yet forced himself upon Azriel: he merely made Azriel watch what happened to Aleeme. Now, he kept the Parasilians apart. Aleeme was dying. When he was dead, Azriel could have him back. Then it would be his turn.

The Hashmallim had made only one further visit to Fulminir. Abraxis had manifested spontaneously in front of Ponclast late one night, this time alone. His towering presence had turned the air in Ponclast's study black. "Let your enemies come to you," he said. "When they arrive, unleash your hara upon them, but selectively."

"This is not a good plan," Ponclast said. "Fulminir is not fully rebuilt, and it will take months if not years for the work to be completed. It is not viable as a fortress. Pellaz har Aralis will bring an army of many thousands. They will have *sedim* to whom walls will mean nothing. There are too few of us. You must give us more assistance."

"You will get what you need," Abraxis said. "The *teraphim* will deal with the *sedim*. That is not your concern. Make one attack, that's all. Small and swift. It will not achieve much, but it will be a warning and it will make them think twice about storming this place. Then you must summon the Tigron. Are you ready to pitch your will and strength against his?"

Ponclast was silent for a moment. "Why am I fighting this war for you?"

Abraxis narrowed his strange smoky blue eyes. "You are fighting a war to reclaim your land and your status among Wraeththukind. We are offering you assistance. Your question puzzles me."

Ponclast was surprised to hear Abraxis admit he was puzzled, not that for one moment he believed it to be true. "Why are you offering us assistance? I think perhaps that we are offering it to you."

"We have mutual interests at stake," Abraxis said. "Let us simply agree we can help each other. If we withdraw our assistance now, the Gelaming will crush you. I hope you are clever enough to know that."

"I do know that," Ponclast said, "but even so some questions I have in my mind are not being answered. The murky areas concern me."

"Let me put my hands upon your new son," Abraxis said. "Take this as a gift."

Ponclast hesitated only a moment, then went to the crib where his and Abrimel's son lay sleeping. He was a perfect harling, so unlike all the others Ponclast had created.

"A beautiful being," Abraxis said, with uncharacteristic warmth. "Have you named him?"

Ponclast was suspicious of this new, strangely sociable aspect of the Hashmal. "Not yet. The name has not come to me."

"Then allow me to name him for you. Understand that this is a rare gift indeed."

Ponclast held the harling close for some moments, then held him out. As he watched the Hashmal's enormous hands close around his son, he felt like he had put a seal over the future, over a single path, eclipsing all other possibilities.

Abraxis's hands began to glow. He lifted the harling high, staring up at him, and the harling laughed. "Son of Hermaphroditus, I name you Geburael, creature of strength and power. May the emanations of the highest spheres penetrate your being." He brought the harling close to his face and kissed him. The newly named Geburael uttered a whimper.

"Give him back," Ponclast said.

The Hashmal did so and when he released the harling from his hands, strings of radiance still hung in the air, from the ends of his fingers to the body of the child. "Affectionately, you will call him Geb, which is also an ancient name for a god of the earth."

The harling pressed himself close against Ponclast, who could feel the tiny heart beating frantically, like a terrified bird's.

"You live at the foot of the mountains," said Abraxis, "and even though I come down from the High Place to you, remember nonetheless from whence I come."

"I don't know of what you speak," Ponclast said.

"You are har, a being of flesh and blood, trapped in a narrow realm. We are not. You could not even comprehend us in our natural state, so you are in no position to question or even ponder our movements."

"What will happen after Pellaz is defeated?"

"You will give him to us, and through him we will eat out the hearts of his associates. Once they are gone, you will ride the spirit paths to Immanion, and the city will offer itself to you. Be merciful or not, as you see fit. Instate your consort on his hostling's throne. Enjoy your realm and forget us."

"You have an interest in my son," Ponclast said. "I find the prospect of forgetting you somewhat unrealistic."

"He is our investment in the future of this realm," Abraxis said. "He will not be taken from you, if that is what you fear. He will carve his own path."

Abraxis drew himself to his full height. "The march has begun. Soon, the time will come for you to capture the hearts of all hara in this realm. You will prove to them who has real power. Be at rest, Ponclast. Walk in your fields. Gaze upon the stars. Be sure they look down upon you."

The air flexed as if squeezed by a divine hand and Ponclast was left alone; the only evidence left behind of the Hashmal's presence was a faint aroma of burnt sugar.

Ponclast kissed his son and walked to the window. He could see out over the fields beyond Fulminir. He could see the stars, hard in a cloudless sky. Geburael reached out his hands to them greedily; a child clutching for pretty, sparkling things.

One evening, Cal did not return to his room at sundown and Tyson and Moon ate in the courtyard alone. "Kyrotates will be little more than bones soon," Tyson said.

Moon rubbed his arms. That night, the air was chill. "The season is beginning to turn," he said. "I can feel the changing time."

"The trees are so heavy," Tyson murmured, "it is like they become too heavy with life at this time."

"That sounds grim," Moon said.

"Perhaps humanity was like that," Tyson continued. "They collapsed under their own weight and died. They went into the earth and we came out of it."

"What's wrong with you?"

Tyson smiled at his dinner plate. "I'm feeling philosophical tonight." He ate the last of his meal, licked his fingers, and put the plate on the ground. He appeared strange, almost drunk. Languorously he undid the tie around his hair, shook it loose, scratched his head with both hands. "Something is coming," he said. "I can feel it."

Moon felt unnerved, as if a crowd of unseen ghosts was shuffling toward them. "Ty?" Involuntarily, he moved closer to the fire.

"If I close my eyes," Tyson said, "it's as if the sky is whirling. It's whirling inside me. I'm not myself. I feel different."

His words had a strange effect upon Moon. He felt disorientated, as if they were back in the City of Ghosts. He experienced the same anxiety about time, as if Tyson would be taken from him at any minute, by the presence of others, particularly the voice of Terez, calling in the night air. But there would be no summoning call. There was no Snake, no Raven, not even an Ember. Just themselves and the night. It was magical. No harsh words had been said. Regret did not discolor the air. They had not even shared breath yet. The same, yet different.

Moon got to his feet. Tyson's head was lowered. Moon could see his neck where his hair parted and fell over his shoulders. He wanted to touch the knuckle of spine there.

Tyson looked up at him and Moon held his gaze for long seconds. Then Tyson stood up. He made a soft sound and rubbed Moon's arms with his hands.

Moon did not think or wait any longer. He curled his arms around Tyson's back and Tyson smiled. "Beauty," he murmured.

"Taste me," Moon said.

They took aruna beneath the sky, their skins made pale by starlight. Moon kept his eyes open the entire time, because then it was impossible not to be aware of exactly what was happening. He found he could move his perception from right inside himself, where he could observe the fluid mechanics of what they did, to outside and above himself, where he could look down and see Tyson upon him. He could feel Tyson's mind inside him, as well as his body. *You see?* He said in mind-touch. *It's not terrifying. You're not losing yourself. We are just together, bigger than we are when we're apart.*

Part of you will stay in me and part of me in you, Tyson said in return. *It is a kind of losing, but not in a bad way.*

It's called giving, not losing, Moon said.

Tyson raised his head and gazed into Moon's eyes. He stopped moving. "For this moment, this is all we are."

Moon's breath came shallow. He too was motionless. Looking into Tyson's eyes, he saw the stars churn deep in the heart of the universe. He could feel energy brewing up, like a storm. A wind had arisen in reality, it lifted strands of Tyson's hair. It made song in the buildings around them. Yet they were so still in mind and body. So still. In the City of Ghosts, late at night, Moon had sometimes heard storms screaming over the water from a great distance, bearing down upon the broken towers of his home. It was like that now. He could feel it coming, even though neither he nor Tyson made a move. Aruna, its own creature, sought its own satisfaction.

Just before the storm broke, and they were lost to the pleasure of ecstasy, Moon realized what was happening. He yelled out and pushed Tyson from him roughly. He rolled away, blind; strong contractions coursing through every muscle of his body, furious and demanding. He felt something open up inside himself and curled into a ball. The pain was searing. For some minutes, nothing made any sense, as if his perceptions had gone into shutdown. The world was incomprehensible, but then he became aware that Tyson was holding him in his arms, saying his name over and over.

"I'm all right," he said. His mouth was full of a foul, bitter taste.

"Why did you . . . ? What did you . . . ?" Tyson shook his head. His pupils in the bright starlight were enormous, as if he'd taken some kind of narcotic.

"I couldn't do it," Moon said. "Not to you, because I know your feelings. You do know what was about to happen, don't you?"

"No. Everything just went completely strange. I did warn you, didn't I? Oh, Moon, does this mean we can't be together? Is that what it means?"

"Tyson," Moon said. "Calm down. We nearly made a pearl, that's all. I stopped it."

"How did you know?"

"I just did. I just felt it. I feel really sick."

"Sit up. I'll get you some water."

Moon managed to haul himself up, although his belly ached abominably. He wondered if he'd damaged himself. He didn't understand what had happened. He'd thought hara had to concentrate really hard to do what they'd done.

Tyson returned with a cup of water, which was tepid, but Moon drank it all gratefully. He wanted to get rid of the taste in his mouth. Tyson had also brought a coat out with him, which he draped over Moon's shoulders. He squatted beside Moon, one hand on the back of Moon's neck. "I feel really odd too. Did I want that to happen, Moon? Is it what I secretly want?"

"I've no idea," Moon said. "It was so good, then it was . . . *that*. I've always thought aruna had a mind of its own; now I know for sure."

"I think this is what it must have been like for Lileem, my Kamagrian friend I told you about. Remember? A bit like that, anyway. When she took aruna or even shared breath with a har, she could step out of this world. I shared breath with her once—she used it as a means to leave this realm. It was amazing. What happened with us just then—it was similar, so beyond our control, like a new world opening up. It was just like what I'd feared."

"We need to talk to somehar."

"Like who? Cal? I don't think so."

"Somehar away from here. Pell. Cobweb. I don't know. I don't want to be here anymore, Ty. I want to be with you, but we have to understand what we've done and why it happened. That won't happen here."

"We can't leave," Tyson said. "What about Azriel and Aleeme? They are the reason we're here."

Moon sighed. "Is it?"

Tyson frowned. "What do you mean?"

"I don't know. I wonder whether Cal can really get them out. It doesn't seem feasible."

"But you said you saw him use some kind of weird power in Galhea. He's had training. He can use the otherlanes."

"But he hasn't," Moon said flatly. "Painful though it might be, we should consider what other motives he might have for being here."

"Why bring us with him, though? If he simply wanted to go to Ponclast, he wouldn't have bothered with us, surely. He needn't have come back to Galhea at all."

"Oh, I don't know," Moon said. "It's all too confusing. Things just don't feel right. It's like we're wasting time." He tried to stand, and winced with pain. "Ty, take a look at me, will you? Something's wrong."

"I'll take you inside," Tyson said. "We need the light."

Moon allowed Tyson to lift him and carry him back into their room, where Tyson laid him on one of the beds. Moon opened his legs a little and even that hurt.

"You're bleeding a bit," Tyson said.

"How bad?"

"Not bad. You must have ripped yourself when you threw me across the yard! By Ag, you have some strength, har! But I should probably give you some healing. Not that I'm a great adept at that."

"Anything will do. What other option do we have?"

Tyson settled beside Moon and put one hand over his soume-lam, the other on the base of his spine. Presently, after a sputtering start, healing energy flowed from him as soothing warmth.

"What if I'm really hurt?" Moon said.

"It'll be okay," Tyson said. "Hush."

Cal returned to them in the morning. He was so preoccupied he didn't react to finding them both in the same bed. Tyson said, "So what's left of Kyrotates?" and laughed, although Cal did not even smile.

"What I discovered isn't good," Cal said. "Aleeme is in great danger."

"Then we must get him out of here as soon as we can," Tyson said, getting out of bed. He began to dress himself.

Cal frowned. "It's too soon. It's not what I planned."

"What did you plan?" Moon asked. He sat up and was relieved to find he didn't hurt so much now. "Should we talk of this here?"

"I have constructed a haze," Cal said. "A little trick to confuse snoopers, but I can't keep it in place for long because then it would arouse suspicion."

"I can't perceive it," Moon said.

"No, I don't expect you can." Cal poured himself a cup of water and drank it. "I wanted to make best use of the confusion when the Gelaming arrive to get the Parasilians out. The only thing I can think of is that I should use the otherlanes to get to Aleeme, but that might be noticed. I still don't know how perceptive Ponclast is—he keeps me in the dark over most things."

"What is wrong with Aleeme?" Tyson asked. "Is he being tortured?"

"In a way," Cal answered. "He is with pearl. Ponclast committed pelki on him and in some abominable way created new life. Aleeme has already borne one pearl, now he carries another. His body is suffering. He has lost all hope. He is dying."

A wave of black passed across Moon's vision. "We have to do something. Do whatever it takes, Cal. Take the risk!"

"Don't state the obvious, moonling," Cal said dryly. "I'm thinking hard." He sighed through his nose. "As I've always believed, the Varrs, or the Teraghasts as we must now call the hara here, are not beyond redemption. Kyrotates is a good sort—very similar to Ithiel, in fact. He is older and wiser than he was—no longer a painted barbarian resentful of everything. He is aware of this, as the majority of first-generation hara have had to become aware of such things. He told me that most of the hara here want only to live their lives in peace. They feel obliged to Ponclast, because his will has kept them alive, and his sacrifice has given them freedom. They all believe his alliance with whatever beings have found him is a sacrifice. I have no doubt that Ponclast loves his hara deeply.

"But anyway, that is hardly relevant to the problem in hand. Kyrotates has mixed feelings about what Ponclast has done to the Parasilians. Like all Teraghasts he reviles Swift's name and feels the Parsics are traitors, but he also believes that the matter should be settled through an honorable fight, not by committing pelki on helpless victims. He has seen Aleeme, and I think the image has stayed with him. He was grateful to relieve himself of it to me."

"Will he help us?" Tyson asked, buttoning up his shirt.

"Don't be ridiculous," Cal said, "of course he won't. He can't. I have asked him to allow me access to Aleeme to give him healing. He wasn't too keen on that idea either. He is loyal to Ponclast, but also afraid of him, and rightly so, in my opinion."

"Then what are you going to do?" Moon asked.

"I might have to get us into Aleeme's room. It is strongly guarded. Then we will have to find Azriel. Aleeme is very sick. I'm not sure how we'll manage this. It will be a dangerous and reckless venture. Oh, shades of Piristil! Where are the good poisoners when you need them?"

"When will we do this?" Tyson asked.

Cal shook his head, as if he wasn't sure. "I think it will have to be when the Gelaming get here. They will be here soon. I wish you two had been trained as I was! It would be much easier if I could distract Ponclast one night and you could use the otherlanes to get to Aleeme and Azriel."

Tyson glanced at Moon, and Moon could tell what he was thinking. "Maybe there is a way," Tyson said.

"Oh?" Cal said.

Tyson screwed up his nose. "No, we can't. It's a mad idea. We don't have enough control."

"What are you talking about?" Cal asked.

"You'd better tell him," Moon said. "Perhaps he can help us."

Cal listened to the story of the previous night's events carefully. He did not interrupt. At the end of it, Tyson laughed uncertainly and said, "So, what do you think of that?"

"I think," Cal said, "that you performed a rather bizarre method of contraception."

"But reality changed," Tyson said, "like it does for Kamagrian and hara."

"Conception is like that," Cal said. "I know, because I experienced it when Terzian and I conceived you. I'm not sure ending it so abruptly was the right thing to do. You must let me examine you, Moon."

"But we didn't want a pearl," Moon said, instinctively drawing up his legs against his chest. "It wasn't intended, and conceptions don't happen any other way, do they?"

"Tell that to your friend Aleeme," Cal said. "You and Ty clearly have intense feelings for one another, and the fact that you've applied a weird kind of tantric discipline to the slow fire of your mutual desire is obviously what opened the seal. I doubt it will happen again. I doubt even more that you can use this phenomenon to access the otherlanes. How I wish you could!" He put a hand on Tyson's shoulder. "I'm glad you two have got over your difficulties. At least *something* good is happening."

"So, we do nothing about Aleeme," Moon said. "We just wait. And then we might be too late."

"I didn't say that. I just need to think about it." Cal sighed. "There is something else . . ."

"What?" Tyson asked.

Cal glanced at Moon. "Your hura-brother Abrimel has allied with Ponclast. It's not exactly widely advertised, but Kyrotates knows."

"He told you a lot," Tyson said.

"He did. He is an anxious har. And I used my wiles on him. I doubt he'll even remember much of what he told me, but I left him happy. It was the least I could do."

"Do the Gelaming know about Abrimel?" Moon asked.

"Kyrotates doesn't know that. I will visit him again, but I'll have to be careful. He's no fool. The next time we meet, I won't be able to question him in the same way. Now the haze is deteriorating. We can speak on this no more. You had better get ready for work. Any chance of breakfast, Ty? I need to eat."

Tyson went out into the courtyard to rebuild the fire, while Cal insisted on examining Moon's body. "There doesn't appear to be a great deal of harm done," he said. "But don't ever do that again, Moon. There are ways you can end aruna when you feel that kind of fire building up. Don't wait until the last minute and tear yourselves apart."

"At the time, it felt as if it was meant to be," Moon said. "It felt so right. Then I just knew what was happening, and I also knew it was something neither of us wanted—not then."

"I told Ty to train you. Clearly, he is not doing a very good job. I can advise you both. We will speak later."

Cal went outside to help Tyson and Moon sat with his chin resting on his knees for some minutes before dressing himself. He thought Cal was missing something. There was more to what had happened the previous night than it appeared. He just wished he knew what it was.

CHAPTER THIRTY-SIX

Pellaz decided that what he did with Galdra was grissecon rather than aruna. It didn't involve love or anticipation, or guilt or heat. Emotions had to be put aside. It was easier that way.

On the evening following his strange discovery of an unmapped inner world, after a long day's ride with his mind in turmoil, Pellaz met again with Tharmifex and Ashmael in his pavilion. He invited nohar else to the meeting, not even Galdra. The pavilion smelled musty to Pellaz, as if a trace of his aruna with Galdra clung to its fabric. He sat on the edge of his bed and couldn't stop thinking of himself lying there with Galdra inside him. Sometimes, when he thought this, Galdra had Cal's face.

Tharmifex and Ashmael were oblivious to Pell's inner wrangling. Perhaps they couldn't see it. Ashmael would never feel like this. His life included a string of conquests: a trail of sad ghosts, blue beside the roadside, who wondered what they'd done wrong. Ashmael went cold on hara very easily. As for Tharmifex, he was a contained individual, who appeared never to have been young, although like all hara he was incapable of looking old. He had a chesnari at home, who other hara rarely saw. Pellaz doubted the word "chesna" could really apply to Tharmifex. If Pellaz should speak his mind now and reveal the

chewed-up contents of his heart, both Tharmifex and Ashmael would look confused; they wouldn't understand a word of what he said. They were, however,
extremely interested in what Pellaz had learned about the cauldron of creation.
So he talked about that, as if it were a real place, and to get there didn't involve
walking a path that was strewn with jewels and sharp stones. Ashmael was especially excited when Pellaz told him Lileem had mentioned his discovery
could, in some way, be used as a weapon.

"It will be similar to what Swift and Seel did the last time we took on
Fulminir," Ashmael said, "except you will have the might of dehara such as
Aruhani and Agave behind you. You must experiment with this phenomenon
intensively. By the time we get to Fulminir, you have to be able to wield this
power properly."

"We must conduct a formal grissecon," Tharmifex said. "I'm sorry, Pell. I
hope that isn't distasteful to you, but we should observe the phenomenon, tune
into it, seek an objective view. I also think that the next time you attempt this
procedure, experienced hara, including Nahir Nuri, should be in attendance."

"Who do you want present?" Pellaz said. His voice sounded like a clear,
cool stream in his own ears, when it should be a squeak or a shriek. He felt
himself being Tigron, this functional thing that had no heart. He wished Rue
were with him.

"Ourselves, obviously," Tharmifex said, "and Velaxis, if you have no objection. Also the Kakkahaar. Perhaps even the Kamagrian, Tel-an-Kaa, because of the parage Lileem's involvement. What do you think?"

Pellaz nodded slowly. "Very well. I would like Vaysh and Terez to be with
us too."

"Of course. What about tomorrow night?"

"I'll tell Galdra."

Tharmifex hesitated. "Pell, I'm sure you know the Hegemony's opinion of
Galdra. Your experiences with him have confirmed our hopes concerning his
potential. I want you to think about the future. I know this might not be the
right time, but events are moving quickly. Galdra is with you. Cal is not. You
and the Freyhellan are achieving wondrous things together. He could be
Tigron."

"Galdra does not seek that position," Pellaz said. "I'm not sure I'd want it
for him either, whatever the circumstances. You are right. Now is not the time
to talk about it."

"At least the matter is out in the open," Tharmifex said. "I hope you'll give
it some consideration."

"I will."

Once Ashmael and Tharmifex had left, Pellaz put his face in his hands and sat that way for half an hour.

The grissecon took place in a woodland glade some miles from camp. Ashmael placed heavy security around the area, so that no curious hara could observe the event. The evening was warm and the presence of the forest very close, as if unseen spirits were drawn to the spot to witness what would happen. Tall ancient oaks stood watchfully over the proceedings.

Tel-an-Kaa had agreed to be present, since Pellaz had explained to her that Lileem was involved. "It does not surprise me," Tel-an-Kaa said, "Lileem was always destined to do something extraordinary. What would you like me to do to help?"

"Simply be present and alert," Pellaz said. "Be open to subtle nuances in the ether. It's possible Lileem might make contact again."

"I'll do what I can. This grissecon business is"—she smiled—"all very new to me."

"I hope it won't discomfort you," Pellaz said. "To be honest, it's new to me too."

"Are you sure you want me there?"

Pellaz sighed deeply. "No. The thought of an audience does not delight me. But it makes sense. I'm sure once we're in the ritual, it'll be different." He hoped.

Of course, Lileem's connection with the proceedings was also of great interest to Herien and Rarn har Kakkahaar. Herien asked if they might attend the grissecon, and Pellaz hadn't the heart to refuse him. At Tharmifex's suggestion, Lianvis would lead the ceremony, no doubt in typically flamboyant Kakkahaar style, with Herien and Rarn acting as his officials.

Just before sundown, everyhar gathered at the designated site, where Lianvis manipulated the energy in the environment to create a temporary Nayati. The witnesses stood around him in a circle, adding their intention to his.

Throughout the day, Pellaz had wondered whether he and Galdra would be able to repeat the experiment in front of observers, especially those who were little more than strangers to him. They would have to adopt the traditional postures of grissecon, which created an experience very different to the relaxed spontaneity of natural aruna. Pellaz knew hara performed these public ceremonies all the time and he'd witnessed quite a lot of them himself, but he still found it difficult to imagine that soon he'd be doing it himself. He didn't really know what Galdra thought about, because he hadn't asked. Galdra had simply agreed to take part because Pellaz wanted him to. But despite his avowals of unconditional love, Pellaz wondered whether Galdra saw the gris-secon, performed in front of high-ranking Gelaming, as a way to stake a legit-imate claim on the Tigron. Now, as Pellaz stood at the edge of the circle, wearing only a light Kakkahaar cloak around his body, he imagined a moment in the future, which he feared would come too quickly. He saw Galdra at his side in the Hegalion, their union signed and sealed. And Cal would not come, because he never did, not when he was needed.

Pellaz was jolted back into the present by the arrival of Tel-an-Kaa at the site. She gave him a smile that was full of kindness and understanding. Her being was geared toward soume far more than hara like Ashmael and Tharmifex could ever even imagine. Pellaz was sure she picked up on some of his confusion, and understood only too well its cause. He wondered how she would feel having to view the intimate procedure of grissecon. The Kamagrian were far more private about aruna than Wraeththu were.

Ten minutes before the opening ceremony was about to begin, Lianvis ap-proached Pellaz and Galdra a Kakkahaar, carrying two small pottery flasks. "Pellaz, you look tense," he said.

"I'm fine," Pellaz said, but he could tell from Lianvis's expression that the Kakkahaar could see right through him.

Lianvis held out the flasks. "This is a Kakkahaar narcotic," he said. "We use it often for grissecon. Drink it and I promise you that you'll forget about the rest of us in seconds!"

Pellaz drank it gratefully, only the desire for oblivion giving him the strength of stomach not to vomit it back up immediately.

Galdra took his share and grimaced. "You make this from ground-up corpses, don't you!" he said, handing his flask back to Lianvis.

"Only human ones," Lianvis answered, deadpan.

Pellaz couldn't help but laugh at the expression on Galdra's face. "He's joking," Pellaz said. Then paused. "You *are* joking, aren't you, Lianvis?"

The Kakkahaar smiled. "Relax; let it do its work."

After only a few minutes, a tide of tranquil well-being coursed through Pell's mind and body. He was hardly conscious of anyhar but Galdra and him-self. Lianvis's potion had smothered all the hot, itchy, and uncomfortable feelings in Pell's heart. All he wanted to do now was go back to the new realm he had discovered. He was no longer remotely self-conscious.

The Kakkahaar uttered the final invocations to create the ritual space, and Lianvis gestured for Pellaz and Galdra to come forward into the center of the circle. Pellaz took off his cloak and handed it to Herien, as did Galdra. Pellaz could feel how chill the night air was, yet it was not uncomfortable. His body was hot. He and Galdra went to the center and sat cross-legged opposite each other. They joined hands and concentrated on connecting their natural energy. The circle of witnesses chanted softly and rhythmically and Pellaz could feel the vibration of it swirling around them, enclosing them in a cone of power. The witnesses were no longer separate individuals, but simply a shield of protection.

Through intention alone, Pellaz made himself soume and Galdra made himself ouana. When they were ready, Pellaz lowered himself into Galdra's lap. Galdra felt icy inside him, burning with a cold fire. He opened the soume energy centers one by one: it was almost effortless. When the sixth opened, Pellaz was filled with the vision of an irislike door spinning open, and he was sucked right through it. This time, he made sure to hook his will around Galdra's essence and drag him with him.

Stay with me! he hissed in Galdra's mind. *Don't wander.*

It was not a place of darkness. Pellaz found himself in a temple of radiance. He realized that Galdra was within him. They were sharing an etheric body.

What is this place? Galdra asked.

I don't know. It's different. It's supposed to be the cauldron of creation. Lileem said I should call upon a dehar, and my instinct would be to call for Aruhani or Agave, as Ash suggested. But this is not a temple to either of them. It's more like Miyacala's.

Then change it.

Or maybe I should call on Miyacala.

They were surrounded by impossibly tall columns of a glittering crystalline substance that pulsed with rings of energy. Ahead was a vague suggestion of a flight of steps, although it was difficult to perceive things properly. Pellaz walked toward the steps and it seemed to take an eternity to reach them, as if they drew away from him as he approached them. He formed the shape of Miyacala's name in his mind and then the steps zoomed toward him, gathered him up, and he was running up them, into another eternity.

You were right, Galdra said.

At the top of the steps was a platform, in the center of which was a tall golden tripod. Steam or incense curled up from the shallow dish it supported. The floor appeared to be constructed of opal tiles. Shuddering drapes framed the platform, hiding whatever lay beyond it from view.

Pellaz stood before the tripod and raised his arms. *I call upon the dehar, Miyacala, master of initiation and of the mysteries. Miyacala, I command you to come to us now! Bring us the light of your knowledge. Astale Miyacala! Extend your hand. Astale!*

An intense white flame spurted up from the golden bowl, then subsided. Once it had died down, Pellaz saw a tall form standing opposite him on the other side of the tripod. His long platinum hair hung around him like a cloak. His eyes were white orbs, but a star blazed upon his forehead. He raised his left hand and a star blazed there also.

Greetings, Miyacala. Pellaz bowed to the dehar respectfully.

Greetings to you, Pellaz har Aralis, and to you also, Galdra har Freyhella. You are welcome in the Nayati of Initiation. You are expected here.

Are you akin to the sedim, *Miyacala?* Now, Pellaz and Galdra spoke with one voice. There was no division between them.

No, the dehara are of Wraeththu. We are yours and you are ours, yet there is no ownership. We are not of the powers beyond. We are your ultimate potential, for you created us.

We have need of your brethren, Aruhani and Agave.

They are aware of this need. They await your word, once you pass beyond this threshold. You need all of us. We are all soume, we are all ouana. We are warriors and mystics. We are seers and kings. We are healers and assassins. Lunil of the blue fire wields the power of the lunar sphere of every realm. Aruhani is the destroyer and the creator. Agave is the flame of many suns. I am the light of knowledge, the truth of all matters, before which hara of unlighted minds would lose their sanity.

Will you grant us initiation, Miyacala?

That is my function in this instance. The dehar reached into one of his sleeves and drew forth a crystal blade that danced with sparks of light. *Come to me. A new inception.*

Miyacala extended his left arm, pulling back the sleeve of his robe, and cut himself with the blade. Pellaz approached the dehar, who was several feet taller than he was. A milky, glowing substance dripped from the wound in Miyacala's arm. To Pellaz, it appeared much like the combined essence of two hara after aruna. He held out his arm. Miyacala took it and drew the blade down the inner forearm. Its touch was incredibly cold, as Galdra's ouana-lim had felt earlier, but it did not hurt. Shockingly red blood sprang from the cut, and splashed down upon the opaline floor. Miyacala took Pell's arm and pressed the wounds together. Pellaz could feel the glacier burn of the dehar's essence pouring into him. He could feel it transforming him.

Then he was rushing through a vortex, bodiless, no more than a ball of energy. Impossible scenes flashed past: cyclopean cities of obsidian stone, impenetrable abysses, endless oceans of liquid metal. Pellaz wanted to cry out in stark terror but had no voice. He knew these sights. He had seen them before, at the time when his first physical body had died and his soul had been sucked through the ethers at Thiede's command.

Don't be afraid.

Galdra's presence.

I am dead.

We are not. Ride it, Pellaz. Make it yours. Follow me.

I will.

Galdra looked deep into the magical myths of his hara and plucked from them an image he liked. Now, they were a winged being, soaring between immense cliffs. Their wings beat monstrously, slowly, with great power. Pellaz had never felt such a sense of freedom and strength. They had no arms, only batlike wings, but long legs they held out behind them, which terminated in birdlike claws rather than feet. They had a tail, like a lion's. They flew toward a golden light, which as they drew nearer illuminated a landscape of marvelous beauty. In some ways it was stark, just barren black rocks and cliffs, but the pure buttery radiance transformed it. There was a huge stepped pyramid ahead of them and they alighted on the platform at its summit.

In the center of the platform was a square opening in the floor, where steps could be seen leading downward. Pellaz and Galdra began to descend them. The walls on either side of them were veined with searing gouts of dark red light. The air was warm and smelled of cloves and frankincense. They had entered the temple of Aruhani.

The dehar awaited them in a garden at the bottom of the steps. Impossibly, it was open to the air, even though it was in the center of the pyramid. Pellaz had never beheld, even in his wildest visualizations, so strange a garden. The plants were of the darkest hues: indigo, black, and crimson. Fleshy flowers, the size of cartwheels, exuded a perfume of jasmine and rot. Thorned vines snaked across the black earth beneath their feet, writhing like serpents.

Aruhani sat cross-legged upon an altar of jet. He was of normal harish size: a beautiful creature with black skin, whose only garment was his abundant braided hair that covered him like a shawl. The soles of his feet were dyed red with ochre. He did not speak, but held Pellaz with a smoking gaze. Pellaz was silenced in the dehar's presence. His power was primal, far more unnerving than Miyacala's. Where Miyacala was thought and knowledge, Aruhani was pure feeling and instinct. He was the harish equivalent of the darkest of the mother goddesses of ancient human cultures. As Pellaz watched, Aruhani uncrossed his legs. Multicolored vapor steamed out of his soume-lam. In this way, he gave birth to his brothers, Lunil and Agave, who took on solid form and stood beside the altar, the dehara of the blue and red fire.

We are with you . . .

Pellaz had no time to commune properly with these incredible beings, for the scene exploded before his eyes, shards of color flying past and through him. In moments, he was back in the real world, shaking against Galdra's chest, sweat pouring off him, his head aching like a cauldron of destruction never mind creation.

Lianvis came forward with Herien, both carrying cloaks, which they draped around the bodies of Pellaz and Galdra. Pellaz lifted his head to thank them, but the words were silenced in his throat.

Beyond the circle of hara, Pellaz saw immense shadowy forms. Fifteen feet high, their arms crossed over their breasts, but carrying weapons of war: dehara. More than four, a myriad. Galdra saw them too, Pellaz could tell. The witnesses stood with closed eyes, perhaps still lost in the last wisps of visualization, perhaps as a mark of respect to those who had conducted the grissecon. It seemed they did not perceive the incredible throng around them.

"We brought them through with us," Galdra said softly.

"Who needs mysterious allies from another realm?" Pellaz said. "Galdra, we can make our own."

CHAPTER THIRTY-SEVEN

Kyrotates came to Ponclast in his broken tower and said, "Tiahaar, a large force approaches us."

It was midafternoon and mellow sunlight gilded all the strangely beautiful ruins of Fulminir. On such a day could any har ride to war?

"Many tribes ride behind the Tigron's banner," Kyrotates said.

Ponclast was in two minds: part of him scorned the Tigron's hubris for thinking he could simply march over to Fulminir and take it, while another feared that Pellaz har Aralis did this because he was confident he was about to enjoy a history-making victory. Pellaz no doubt knew about the shadow assassins, the attack on Galhea, and perhaps even Abrimel by now. Yet still he came, out in the open. In his place, Ponclast would have used *sedim* for a more clandestine approach. Should he send out his assassins now, even before Pellaz reached the fortress? Was that the reaction the Tigron was attempting to provoke? Did he have his own allies? Ponclast was troubled. He wished the Hashmallim were with him. Abraxis had talked of the *teraphim* dealing with the *sedim*, but so far there was only one *teraph* in Fulminir: Golab.

Ponclast summoned Diablo, who now spent most of his time amusing Geburael. The harling was growing swiftly into a strong-minded, demanding individual.

"I want you to observe the Tigron's forces," Ponclast said. "Do it discreetly and do not put yourself in any danger. Report back to me shortly."

He said to Kyrotates, "Bring Calanthe har Aralis to me."

Kyrotates bowed his head, but not before Ponclast noticed a furtive expression cross the har's face.

"I hope he paid well for what you have given him," Ponclast said tartly.

Kyrotates looked him in the eye. "Tiahaar . . ."

"Get out! Bring him here."

Cal came very swiftly, as usual the epitome of reserve and tranquility.

"Your chesnari rides toward us," Ponclast said. "Your thoughts?"

"Be prepared, tiahaar. That is my advice."

"Your thoughts, Cal. Do you intend to fight at Kyrotates's side?"

"My fighting days are over."

Ponclast exhaled through his nose impatiently. "Speak plainly. If you don't, I will be forced to take extreme action. I would imagine that despite your companion Moon Jaguar's Uigenna heritage, Pellaz still regards him as kin. I can think of several ways in which that glad fact might serve me."

Cal appeared to ignore this threat. "You cannot mistrust me completely, because here I am, alone in your presence. You must be aware that if I were representing the Gelaming, now might be a good time to assassinate you."

"You think you could?" Ponclast laughed coldly. "You delude yourself."

"Not anymore," Cal said. "You might be able to use Moon in some way to unsettle Pellaz, but then I wonder whether Pellaz, as he is now, could be affected by such a ploy. I wouldn't count on it."

Ponclast felt he was very near to losing his temper. "I don't want to hear any more of your slippery words, Cal. You are either with us, or you're not. I have just lit a fire beneath that fence you're sitting on. Jump off it before the flames consume you. You must convince me you have something to give and start giving it."

Cal shrugged. "All I can give you is the simple truth: this matter will be settled between you and Pellaz."

"I know that. Give me the advantage. Give me information. You know him more intimately than anyhar. Prove to me he no longer has your loyalty."

"I cannot help either of you with information."

"That is not good enough."

"There's nothing I can do about that. Perhaps Abrimel might be able to offer you more. Why don't you ask him?"

Ponclast was silent for a moment. When this was all over, Kyrotates was in for a nasty shock. "Abrimel will take his hostling's place, on the Tigrina's throne in Immanion," Ponclast said. "I wonder where you will be at that time."

Cal did not respond to that. "Prepare yourself, tiahaar. I told you what I could, and you chose not to heed it. There's nothing else I can do."

"I will take you with me to Immanion," Ponclast said softly. "Let us see how your hara welcome you home. You will be my gift to them."

When the news came about the Gelaming advance, Moon and Tyson were sitting on a rooftop replacing tiles. Naturally, once the information circulated, everyhar around them downed tools and sought out their superiors. Moon noticed groups of hara glancing up at him and Tyson and knew they were being discussed. He was consumed by a raw burst of anger. They were in danger and Cal had put them there. It was likely the Teraghasts would now turn on them, and at the very least incarcerate them.

"What should we do?" Moon said. "Where is Cal? Ty, I'm not happy about any of this."

"Let's just go and ask what to do," Tyson said. "Be cooperative, remember?"

Moon grimaced. "I wonder if that will be any good to us now."

They descended the ladder against the building. Moon followed Tyson to their supervisor, who was surrounded by a group of workers, all talking at once. Tyson adopted his most respectful tone and asked the supervisor what he and Moon should do.

The Teraghast stared at them coldly. "You will be escorted to your quarters," he said. "If the time for conflict has come, pray that it will be of short duration. I doubt if any of us will have time to concern ourselves with bringing you supplies for a while."

Back in their quarters, Moon and Tyson sat out in the courtyard, straining to hear anything they could beyond the wall. There were sounds of great activity, but it was difficult to discern any useful details. Ever since Cal had told them about Aleeme, Moon had been filled with a heavy sense of dread. He couldn't bear to think of his friend suffering alone somewhere within the fortress. Perhaps Aleeme was already dead.

Moon had been too frightened to take aruna with Tyson again, and he sensed Ty felt the same, because it hadn't been mentioned. They slept in each other's arms and were in every other way intimate, but actual aruna was beyond them. Ever since they had been together, Moon had felt strange inside. He was not in pain, nor felt damaged exactly, but it was if a window onto infinity had opened within him. It was a hollow feeling that made him feel unsafe and disconnected from the world. Now, as the day lengthened into evening, Moon leaned against Tyson's chest, trying to find comfort in the contact, and not being too successful. Dusk was coming, soft as a veil over the landscape. What could they do? The idea of rescuing the Parasilians seemed ridiculous now. They would be lucky to escape with their own lives. He closed his eyes and thought about how wonderful it would be to descend into a comfortable darkness and then wake up and find it was all over, just a terrible dream. Then, in the blackness of his mind's eye, he saw a point of light, and a familiar presence brushed up against his consciousness, like the tail of a cat.

Moon drew in his breath sharply.

Tyson murmured, "What is it?"

Moon pulled away from Tyson and sat up. "I think . . ." he said. "Ty, I'm going to try and contact Pellaz."

Tyson frowned. "Is that wise? What if Ponclast senses it?"

"I don't care. What else can we do? I thought I felt Pell, just then, a feathery touch. He is near us now."

"But he doesn't know we're here . . . does he?"

"I don't know. Help me amplify a call."

Tyson twisted his mouth to the side. "I don't think you should. It's too dangerous, and anyway, Pellaz will be totally occupied with other things. I doubt he'll hear you."

"*Please,* Ty!"

"All right. If you insist, but I don't like it."

They sat opposite each other and joined hands. Moon felt a steady pulse of strength pass from Tyson's fingers to his own. He projected a message with all his will: *Pellaz, hear me!*

For some moments, there was nothing, but then came a blast of communication that nearly knocked Moon to the floor.

You are in Fulminir?

Moon felt Tyson's hands grip his own more tightly. He had heard the message also.

Yes.

Why? Were you taken?

We came to help the Parasilians. We are virtually prisoners. A pause. *We came with Cal.*

Moon wasn't sure whether he should have relayed that last piece of information. For some time, there was only silence, and it seemed to Moon as if a desolate wind coursed through his head. Then came another blast of thought.

We are connected for a reason. It makes no sense, yet it does. You are partly in a world I have only recently discovered. Are you taking aruna with somehar?

No. But I did. Something happened.

Show me! Pellaz commanded. *I can sense it. Show me quickly. It's important.*

Show you what?

What happened during aruna. You are still open, Moon.

Moon tried to project a linear narrative of his experience with Tyson, although it was difficult. He felt slightly embarrassed about having to give Pellaz such private information. Once he had shown all he could remember, there were again some moments of silence. Then Pellaz roared in his head once more. *You must go back there. Now. Is that possible? I can meet you there. Guide you. Don't be afraid.*

I don't understand . . . Meet me where?

In the cauldron of creation. In yours.

Moon opened his eyes and found Tyson staring at him. Despite this break in concentration, Pellaz's presence did not diminish.

Pellaz, I am worried, Tyson said, his eyes still open, *will this communication be picked up? We are in danger enough.*

Nohar is watching you, Pellaz replied. *You appear to be far away from all other hara. My impression is that you are unimportant to them. Which is for the best . . . You are important. You don't realize how much. Having you in Fulminir with access to this procedure is priceless. Will you meet me?*

I don't know how, Moon said, still gazing at Tyson. He had never experienced such clear mind-touch before. *I don't know what you mean.*

Take aruna to its farthest point. The seal within you is partially open. I can perceive this. Let your mind go during aruna. Concentrate on the sixth energy center and project yourself through the open seal. Tyson, you must take control and do all in your power to sustain your union. Do not concern yourself with a fear of making pearls. I will be waiting, I promise you. I'll send energy to help you reach for the right state. But hurry!

There was a sense of Pellaz withdrawing slightly, but Moon could tell the communication was far from broken.

Tyson looked as if he'd been beaten about the head, his expression dazed. "What in the Ag's name is this about?" he said. "Is Pellaz serious? He expects us to just . . ." He raised his arms in exasperation. "It's insane!"

"No more insane than what we experienced before," Moon said. "Ty, he knew what I was talking about. He's told us to do it again. We have to."

"More than anything, I want to, but this is crazy. What if it goes wrong?" Tyson shook his head. "Forget I said that. I will accept the consequences, however bad."

"Pellaz said not to worry about pearls," Moon said dryly. He couldn't help feeling slightly insulted by Tyson's reaction, which was ridiculous for he was well aware of Ty's feelings.

"I was thinking of your safety too—*our* safety. We know nothing about this."

"Share breath with me. It's time we learned."

The Gelaming had arrived at their destination and the issue of Ponclast and his otherworldly allies would be settled once and for all. Ashmael's forces had surrounded Fulminir at a distance of a couple of miles. The Parsic troops had joined them. Come sundown, they would slowly close in, the *sedim* alert for otherlanes attackers. At the same time, Pellaz and Galdra would summon the dehara, and Pellaz would seek to draw Ponclast from his lair.

In the center of the Gelaming camp, the *sedim* stood around Pellaz and Galdra in a silent circle, the most potent of guardians. They had come unbidden once Pellaz had entered the site, which was protected and concealed by tall screens of pale silk on wooden frames. It had been the first part of the camp to be constructed: the rest had grown out around it.

Pellaz had asked Galdra to be with him at the temporary Nayati, so that he could make certain preparations for the night to come. He could now access the cauldron at will, and had been experimenting with summoning various dehara there. The grissecon he and Galdra performed every night had somehow sterilized aruna between them: it was functional, utterly in their control, beyond passion or need. They could sustain it for hours, pleasure that was not pleasure. They could hold open the gateway to the inner realms effortlessly.

Pellaz had not expected to come across the presence of Moon in the cauldron, or indeed of anyhar. He realized that his close relationship to Moon had enabled him to discover that hara in the same state might also in some way share the same space. Perhaps there was only one cauldron, and when hara went into it, they could, under the right circumstances, perceive other hara engaged in the same activity. It was astounding. They knew so little and the more they discovered the less they seemed to know. Lileem could access the cauldron alone, presumably because of the way the realm she now inhabited had changed her. She and Pellaz had met three times since their initial encounter.

After he had communicated with Moon, Pellaz directed a message to Galdra. *Can you sustain this for longer?*

Yes.

I'll be as quick as I can.

Pellaz focused his thoughts and called to Lileem. Fortunately, she came to him very quickly, aware that this was a night of importance. They had already made certain plans together for it.

The place where Lileem and Pellaz met appeared as a garden, where all the plants were golden and crystalline serpents shimmered through the undergrowth. Pellaz told Lileem about Moon. *I have asked him to meet me here,* he said. *Was that the right thing to do? Was I rash? Will it harm him?*

I don't know. I'll help you if I can.

Help me perceive him.

I will. I don't know Moon, but I know you. I will feel for energy that is akin to yours. Lileem's image, sitting on the golden grass, appeared almost fluid. She was like liquid crystal. *I feel something . . . do you?*

No. Help him, Lee. Can you bring him closer?

I'll try. Her image disappeared, yet her voice was still in Pell's inner ear. *He is engaged in . . . something. Not just aruna . . . it is strange. He's not looking for you, Pell. He is . . . Wait. It's not Moon: Tyson is not part of it. I know Tyson's essence, because we once shared breath. These are different hara, but one of them is close to you in blood.*

What? Who? Terez? It could be, because of your past intimacy, couldn't it?

No. Trust me, I'd know Terez! But very similar. He draws me. Do you have another brother, Pell?

Yes. Dorado . . . Snake. But how can it be him?

I'll attempt communication . . . wait . . .

Pellaz sat quietly for some moments, taking time to enjoy the peace of the inner realm. He was content to meditate there, away from concerns of the real world. What Moon had relayed to him earlier had troubled him, but he'd pushed it from his mind. Cal was in Fulminir also. Everything was closing in, perhaps spiraling out of control. He did not want to think about it. Perils and difficulties must be faced as they arose. As he calmed himself with this thought, his etheric body experienced a devastating shock. Out of nowhere, a swiftly moving heavy object collided with his being. He was knocked sideways and sensed the link of communication he'd had with Lileem sever abruptly. He also felt Galdra's shudder within him: Galdra was concentrating fully on sustaining their union. The impact had shocked the Freyhellan badly, both in this reality and the earthly realm. Picking himself up, Pellaz saw the form of a har curled up on the ground before him. Moon. He was surrounded by a sparking cloud of aren, which Pellaz quickly brushed away from him, as if it was no more than a haze of gnats.

Moon! he commanded. *Get up!*

Moon appeared senseless, either with shock or terror. Pellaz crouched before him and laid his hands on Moon's body, filling him with calm. Presently Moon lifted his head and gazed about himself.

This is the cauldron, Pellaz told him. *Don't be afraid. You have done very well. I was looking for you, but you came to me by yourself.*

I fell through myself, Moon said. *It was vile. I did what you said, but it was like turning inside out. I could feel this gaping hole inside me and there was nothing beyond it. But I couldn't stop. I had to fall through.*

You are with me now. You're safe. When you leave, I'll show you how to close the seal. But the fact that it was left open by the trauma of what you did means we have made astounding discoveries. Now listen to me. Tonight, I will summon the dehara through the cauldron. You are on the inside of Fulminir. I think you might be able to work with me and manifest them within the walls.

Moon simply stared at his hura, and Pellaz could tell he was not too happy about the idea.

There's no reason to be afraid, Moon. I will be there. You must trust me.

I do . . . Moon's expression was anxious. *But we have to help Aleeme and Azriel. We can't leave them. They're in great danger.*

Hara are ready to bring them out of Fulminir, Moon. You must trust me on that too. Our task is to pull Ponclast's claws, and leave others to deal with everything else.

I'm not sure how much I'll be able to help. I've never done this before.

Pellaz reached out and touched Moon's face. *You are strong, Moon. You are the son I should have had.*

Pellaz . . . Abrimel is in Fulminir. He's with Ponclast.

I know.

Cal found out . . . He took us to Fulminir to try to rescue the Parasilians.

The mere mention of Cal's name affected Pellaz greatly. He became acutely conscious of where he was and what he was doing. *I can't speak of this now, Moon. It's not appropriate.*

Before Moon could respond to this, Lileem's voice shot into the garden like an arrow. *We are coming!*

Who's that? Moon asked. *He's not har, I can tell.*

It is Lileem, she is Kamagrian . . .

I know of her. Tyson knows her.

Yes. Just before you got here, she picked up a trace of another of our family. I think it's Snake. She must be guiding him here.

No! Moon said. *I mean, he mustn't see me here. He'll be . . .*

Hush! Pellaz commanded. *He is har, as you are. You're an adult, Moon. Stop behaving like a harling and he won't treat you like one.*

Even in etheric form, Moon appeared dazed and a little sick. *I feel very strange. This is like a dream . . . or a nightmare, not sure which.*

It's real, Moon. You are privileged, an explorer, an architect of inner space! Moon smiled at that.

At that moment, a pinprick of deep green radiance manifested beside them. It pulsed like a star for several seconds and then expanded with a flash to reveal the forms of Lileem and Snake. In this reality, Snake appeared undamaged, his limbs strong and straight. He was a commanding presence: Pellaz could feel his strength. For a moment he perceived Snake as Dorado, the boy he had once been. They had never been that close as humans. Pellaz was glad that had changed.

Welcome, Snake, Pellaz said. *Who would have thought we'd ever meet like this? The boys we used to be could never have conceived of a life such as this, meeting as shades in a realm of the imagination.*

Snake shook his head. *Pellaz, this is a shock. Your friend has explained some of it to me, but it's almost too incredible to believe. Only the evidence of my senses persuades me this is not a hallucination.* He looked at his son. *It appears your education has progressed in leaps and bounds, Moon. I do wonder, however, how you and Pellaz are here together.*

We are not here together, as you put it, Pellaz said. *Moon is with Tyson, inside Fulminir.*

What? Snake's form began to pulse with angry colors.

I'm safe, Moon said. *Ty and I are helping the Gelaming. We know what we're doing.*

Who are you with, Snake? Pellaz asked. *I presume you are in the process of taking aruna? What are you doing? Making a pearl?*

I am with Cobweb, Snake replied, *but we are not making a pearl. We are healing my physical body. As you have learned things, so have I. This is no idealized vision of me you see before you, brother. This is how I am now.*

Cevarros, said Lileem. *You are one and the same. It's no coincidence all three of you have had these experiences.*

Will you help us tonight? Pellaz asked Snake.

I feel I have the strength to take on Fulminir single-handedly, Snake replied. *So, yes.* He eyed Moon speculatively. *However, I want explanations as soon as possible. Moon in Fulminir?* He shook his head. *The explanations had better be good.*

They are, Pellaz said. *I wish we'd made these discoveries earlier. Terez could have joined us. There is not enough time for him and Raven to learn this technique now.*

Pellaz perceived a flex in Lileem's essence: it had been caused by the mention of Terez. She would not ask about him, but Pellaz guided a private message to her: *He is chesna with a har named Raven, yes. You should know this. It is the har who incepted him.*

Pellaz, Lileem said. *I sense that Moon will leave here shortly. Tyson is losing control. You must tell him what he needs to know.*

Moon's appearance had become insubstantial, a glimmering outline.

Moon, leave your seal open for now, Pellaz said. *It shouldn't harm you for this short time longer. I will contact you very soon, by mind-touch. Be ready to enter this state again.*

Pellaz sensed Moon hesitate.

I am with Tyson and Snake is with Cobweb, Moon said. *Who are you working with, Pellaz?*

Galdra, Pellaz replied. *Galdra har Freyhella.*

CHAPTER THIRTY-EIGHT

Shortly before sundown, the air within Fulminir's walls changed color. It was not something that could be perceived with the physical eye, but more like a miasma of otherness that settled over the ruins. Moon, still sitting with Tyson in the courtyard, was filled with dread. "Something is coming," he said.

"Yes," Tyson agreed. "I can sense great activity, everywhere. I still feel weird, as if all my perceptions are more acute."

"Me too."

Strange noises impinged upon Moon's inner ear; heavy, snorting breath, a rumble like thunder.

"Whatever it is, it's hideous," Moon said.

"I wish Pellaz would get us out of here," Tyson said. "I wonder whether we're capable of doing what he asks of us. He just says, 'Oh, keep aruna going,' as if that's easy. It really isn't. While you were communing with him earlier, it felt like I was holding the entire universe on my back and at the same time had to resist the urge to breathe! Holding back on aruna is like that—you have no idea. The ouana partner is responsible for sustaining the state, and it hurts. It's like suffocating. I have to remain utterly still, yet also charged, so aruna can continue. Do you understand what I mean?"

"Sort of," Moon said. "You make it sound like my part is the easier one."

"I think it is. And Pellaz wants us to manifest dehara while I'm like that, hanging on to sanity and existence with my bare hands? Aruna has peaked, yet it has gone beyond itself, as if reaching for a higher peak. My instinct is to let go, which presumably normally involves creating a pearl."

"But you managed it, Ty, and you've never done it before. That says a lot."

Tyson pulled a wry face. "Yeah, that's true. Weirdly enough, once we'd started I knew exactly what to do and how to be, but I'm not sure how long I can sustain it for. I'm still shaken up from the last time. Moon, this is danger-ous. We're not trained for it. I'm only of Acantha level."

"I know we're not trained," Moon said. "I'm the same caste level as you. But I don't think we have any choice. We have to help, if we can."

Tyson rubbed his face for some moments, then laughed uncertainly. "By Aghama, I know I said that making pearls wasn't the whole focus of intense aruna, but I had no idea it'd be like this. I wish I'd kept quiet. I don't want our union to be simply this: some kind of machine or vehicle. It feels equally wrong. I have a desperate desire to be sentimental and romantic, go back to the ways things used to be between hara. Knowledge isn't always good."

Moon reached out and touched Tyson's arm. "I promise you, we'll have the good things too."

"I hope it's possible, after this."

Moon took Tyson in his arms, but was disturbed by a sound behind him. He looked around and saw Cal standing at the threshold to the yard. Cal appeared tense, slightly distracted.

"Where have you been?" Moon asked.

Cal shook his head. "It doesn't matter. Moon, I need you to come with me now."

Moon pulled away from Tyson. "Where?"

Cal raked a hand through his hair. "It's time to get the Parasilians out of here. Things are about to start happening. I can take one other with me into the otherlanes. It has to be you, Moon."

"Why him?" Tyson snapped.

Cal looked his son in the eye. "Because he is Pell's sori. Because I can con-nect with him in a certain way. I've a feeling I'll need that." He gestured at Moon to get to his feet. "I know Azriel and Aleeme's locations and for the first time Ponclast's guard is down. He's occupied with other things, but I can't do this alone. I need your help."

"I . . . I can't," Moon said. "There's something we have to . . . Cal, we've been in touch with Pellaz. He has a job for us."

A strange expression flickered briefly across Cal's face. "The point of us being here is to help the Parasilians," he said in a flat tone. "Pellaz does not need you. Azriel and Aleeme do."

"Aren't you curious about Pell?" Tyson asked. "He dragged Moon into the cauldron of creation. He made us do this bizarre aruna."

"I'm sure," Cal said dismissively. "Listen, Ponclast has put me into confinement. I've slipped away from my guards, using the otherlanes, but they'll keep a check on me. Also, some of the entities floating around here will pick up on my activities. We don't have much time. Once Aleeme and Azriel are safe, I'll get you out too."

"We can't . . ." Moon said.

"Shut up, Moon. Come to me. Now. I hope this won't take long."

Cal's violet gaze was compelling. He appeared calm on the surface, but it was as if he could explode into violence at any moment. Moon realized he was too frightened to disobey. He got to his feet and went to the doorway, despite a sound of distress from Tyson.

"I'll look after him, Ty," Cal said. "Don't fear. We'll be back before you know it."

Cal put his arms around Moon's body. "Hold tight," he said, "this might be a bumpy ride for you."

It was. When a har travels the otherlanes without the use of a *sedu,* the experience is far from smooth. Strange winds buffeted Moon's body. He sensed mighty, ferocious presences all around him, streaking past, leaving trails of black flame.

Teraphim, Cal told him. *Pay no heed. They are engrossed in preparations to confront their enemies, the* sedim. *We are no more than insects to them.*

There were screams upon the ether, terrible cries of rage. It was as if a great battle were about to start, all around them, but which they could barely perceive. The journey took mere seconds, but it felt like an eternity.

When Cal and Moon squeezed back into earthly reality, they were in a dank cell, where the only light came from an ancient oil lamp on the floor. The glow it gave off was weak, as if the oil was about to run out. There was a close feeling to the air that advised Moon they were far underground.

A har was chained to the wall, in an uncomfortable position that was half sitting, half standing, his arms above his head. Once he noticed Cal and Moon standing before him, the har moved feebly and turned his face against the wall. He had seen them manifest like spirits. He must be terrified.

"Azriel Parasiel," Cal said in a clear ringing tone. "Don't be afraid. We are here to help you. Look at us. Moon's here. You know Moon, remember?"

Moon put a hand over his mouth, swallowed thickly. The air stank of excrement and rot. Now that his eyes were adjusting to the dim light, he could see that Azriel had been left to squat in his own filth. The Parasilian was barely more than a skeleton, covered in rags. Cal went to his side, but Moon hung back. He was extremely reluctant to approach the prisoner, because what he saw before him hardly resembled the Azriel he knew. It was obscene.

"Moon, here!" Cal commanded. "Now. Hurry up."

Moon obeyed, averting his eyes from the pitiful mask of Azriel's wasted face, in which it appeared very little intelligence remained.

"We have to break the chains," Cal said. "I need your energy, Moon. Link with me. Give me your hands. I'll direct the blast."

Azriel whimpered and struggled in his bonds as Moon hunkered down beside Cal. Cal's hands, when Moon took them in his hold, were dry and extremely hot. He felt Cal's mind brush against his own, alien yet strangely familiar, perhaps because of Tyson.

You're familiar too, Cal said in mind-touch, and for a moment Moon experienced a white-hot arrow of emotional pain from him, which Cal crushed at once. He drew energy from Moon's being and melded it with his own, to form a spear of intention, which he directed as a pyrokinetic blast to the bonds around Azriel's wrists. There was a flash of bright orange light, and the air filled with an acrid smell of metal and burning. Azriel slumped to the ground.

"Wait for me," Cal said. He picked Azriel up and, without further words, passed into the otherlanes.

Moon was left alone, stunned. He could hear liquid dripping onto stone somewhere, a thick slow sound. He was surrounded by the fetid stench that seemed to crawl through his hair and slither down his throat. He could not imagine how Azriel had survived this place for so long, but maybe he was mad now, lost forever. Moon felt faint. He was sure his own sanity was beginning to trickle out of him, simply by being there.

Then, with a muffled pop, Cal stepped out of the air beside him. "You ready?"

"Yes, where did you take Az?"

Cal smiled in a cold manner, his eyes were bleak. "To the edge of the Gelaming camp. I delivered him into the hands of a rather startled har. Never mind that. We have to move fast." He grabbed hold of Moon roughly, twisting them into the otherlanes, where nothing was real, where unseen presences snickered like demons and plucked at their clothes, but which still felt far better than Azriel's wretched cell.

Ponclast will feel this, Cal said. *Soon, he will have my room checked. Then you have to leave.*

What about you? What are you going to do?

Cal did not answer. At that moment, he pushed them out of the otherlanes. Moon took a deep breath involuntarily, and immediately wished he hadn't. This time, they were not in a cell, but this did not make it a better place. It was a tower room, with windows that had no glass. Outside, all that could be seen was sky, the first stars appearing in the deepening blue. The immensity of the sky, that glimpse of heaven, contrasted starkly with the contents of the room. There was a mattress on the floor, on which lay a har, or the body of a har. The smell in this place was worse than that of excrement.

As Cal approached the bed, Moon heard a mewling sound. He saw a very young harling crouching among the dirty coverings, and it wept with terror, or perhaps pain. It was emaciated, its head too big for its body.

Moon took a few steps toward the bed. He hardly dared look at what else must lie there. Cal pulled back the filthy sheet and Moon gagged and turned away. "He's dead," he said. "Sweet Ag, he's dead!"

The sight he'd glimpsed would remain with him forever: Aleeme's withered body unrecognizable, covered in dried blood, discolored. A pearl lay between his splayed legs, its covering ruptured. The harling within it was dead and rotting. It looked like its hostling had died delivering it, his soume-lam and lower body were black. Moon had to vomit, he couldn't prevent himself. His stomach convulsed again and again. He wouldn't have been surprised to discover he was bringing up dead flies or metal pins. Nothing about this situation was ordinary.

After some moments, Moon wiped his mouth and straightened up. He felt light-headed, hardly there. Cal was just standing before the bed, staring. He appeared to be in shock, but surely Cal could never be shocked. Then, he leaned down and touched Aleeme's body lightly in several places. "Moon," he said. "Come here."

"No," Moon said hoarsely, shaking his head. "Let's just take the harling and get out of here."

Cal did not look at him. "We can't," he said. "Aleeme is not yet dead."

"He should be . . ." Moon backed to the door, hysteria rising within him. He couldn't bear to think that the body on the bed was still alive. It was obscene. "Get me out, Cal."

The harling's pitiful cries were like needles in Moon's ears. The child was grotesque. Moon seriously feared he was about to go insane. The otherlanes jump had disorientated him, now this. "Get me out! Get me out!"

"Be quiet," Cal said. "I need you. Come here." He turned around, softened his voice. "You can do this. You are Moon Jaguar. You are Snake's son and Pell's sori. You are har Aralis. So am I. Work with me now."

Swallowing with difficulty, Moon took cautious steps forward. Cal put a hand on the head of the harling, which became quiet. He gestured for Moon to sit on one side of Aleeme, while he composed himself cross-legged on Aleeme's other side. The stench was overwhelming. "Cal . . ." Moon was conscious of tears running down his face. This had to be the worst moment of his life.

"Look at me," Cal said softly. "Keep your eyes on my face."

Cal held out his hands and Moon sat down. Cal's eyes appeared enormous, as if they filled the whole world. They were the deep violet of forest flowers. Tentatively, Moon reached out, linked his hands with Cal's. Cal closed his eyes and gripped Moon's fingers firmly. *Submit to me,* he said in mind-touch. *I'll take what I need. Trust me.*

Moon closed his eyes. Cal drew him into a radiant place, a world of light. In that place, Cal's strength was like the beating of an angel's wings. He drew energy from Moon, and it was almost like aruna, so intimate, invading the deepest places of his being. Moon could perceive Cal's very essence, everything that comprised his character, his history. He was like a dehar, neither light nor dark, but both. He embodied ultimate compassion, which he'd learned on his life's bitter journey. His retaliation could be swift and devastating, but his core was love. He had walked every dark abyss, but the experiences had refined him, like a blade that had passed through many fires. Now he drew energy from the deepest heart of his being and plaited it with Moon's. Aleeme's injuries were so great, and he was so near to death that the usual method of energy channeling from the environment would not be strong or immediate enough. It required personal essence, part of Moon's and Cal's own life force. The cost was great, but not to Moon. Cal was gentle with him. He directed their combined force into Aleeme, and Moon could perceive the faintest flicker of life within that ruined frame. It was like the last spark of a dampened fire, but Cal brought the torch of life to it. The tiny flicker became stronger.

Cal pulled them out of the meditation and Moon was shocked at how gray and haggard Cal appeared. He had used a great deal of his strength. "I will take him out, wait here with the harling."

"Don't leave me here. Please!"

"You know I have to. I'll be quick." Cal pulled Aleeme onto his lap and the air folded around him.

Moon stared at the place where Cal had been. He felt numb. He glanced briefly at the bed, felt nausea rise within him once more. Quickly he picked up the harling, which appeared to be sleeping, and went into a corner of the room, where he squatted down, his spine pressed against the wall. He didn't want to look at what was left on the bed. The harling was like a starving bird in his hands, no weight to it.

Cal took longer to return than before. "I can't get you out," he said. "The *teraphim* have put wards in place against me. They are chasing me now."

"Where can we go?" Moon asked, scrambling to his feet.

Cal rubbed his hands over his face. He appeared to be on the verge of collapse. "I hope I have the strength for this, but I have to take you and the harling back to Tyson. The Gelaming are nearly at the walls, and strange creatures are emerging from the otherlanes. Pray that Pellaz comes for you. There's no way I can get out of Fulminir again. I have to keep you safe, put Ponclast's forces off the scent." He held out his arms. "Come here, Moon. Put the harling between us."

Moon did so. Cal was clearly very weak and this otherlane jump might well take the last of his strength. Moon did what he could to help, but the process was unknown to him. All he could offer was the intention of power.

This time, the otherlanes felt crowded, as if throngs of invisible beings were hurtling through them. A huge demonic face loomed up before them and Moon cried out. Then Cal thrust him away, threw him physically back into earthly reality. Moon emerged at a point several feet in the air and fell to the ground with a bone-jarring thump, his arms curled around the harling protectively. He landed virtually at Tyson's feet. Cal did not come through after him. The last thing Moon sensed was a terrible black presence around Cal that enfolded him into itself. The portal sealed with a dull thud. In the final moments, Moon sensed the wards Cal placed about it at lightning speed, the way he hid its presence, and those who lay beyond it, from hostile view. He sacrificed himself for it.

For some minutes, Moon could only sit rocking and weeping, the harling held against him. Tyson said nothing, but enfolded both of them in his embrace. He could perceive how terrible it had been for Moon, because their earlier union still made them close in mind and heart. Then the skies opened above them. It was not rain that came down, and thunder did not roar. The *teraphim* poured through into the realm of earth, shrieking their rage, and even as Tyson and Moon watched in awe and disbelief, the *sedim* reared up to meet them. A war of angels in the sky, etheric blood showering down. It was like the end of the world.

CHAPTER THIRTY-NINE

In the camp of the Gelaming, Ashmael's elite guard had created a protective circle around the ritual space that Pellaz and Galdra would use that night. A circle of *sedim* stood beyond them, as a protective barrier. What had been a clear evening was now occluded by thick unnatural clouds. There was a strange smell to the air, sweet yet foul. Many hara of high rank and caste were in attendance, as well as those who were close to Pellaz: Terez and Raven, Vaysh, Tharmifex, Ashmael, Tel-an-Kaa, and Lianvis of the Kakkahaar. Although they were in the heart of the camp, all was strangely silent, and there was no sense of activity beyond the tall screens that surrounded the circle of flattened grass. Pellaz felt disorientated, unable to comprehend the severity of the task ahead. Hara came to him and wished him luck in grave tones. Implicit in their words was the suspicion that they might mean good-bye. Galdra stood nearby, dressed only in a brightly patterned blanket that Lianvis had given to him. He couldn't keep still, as if he were limbering up for a physical fight. Pellaz ached inside. He felt as if his body were nothing more than a pathway of the otherlanes. Would he ever feel normal again? He had said nothing to Galdra about the information Moon had given him concerning Cal. Fortunately, Galdra had been too disturbed by Moon's arrival to register much of the subsequent conversation that had taken place. Pellaz was aware he wanted

Moon to relay certain information back: he wanted Cal to feel jealous that he was working so intimately with somehar else. But perhaps Cal didn't care. The jumpiness and dizziness Pellaz felt were faintly familiar: it was the way he'd felt when Cal had come to him in Saltrock for their first aruna. It was the excitement of feeling that soon he was going to see somehar he desired very much, the excitement made all the more intense because he was not sure if his feelings were returned.

Galdra came over to him. "Are you ready? You look positively green."

"As ready as I'll ever be." Pellaz stared through the strange light at the silent ranks of Ashmael's guard. He could see the ghostly shimmer of *sedim* behind them. Were there less of them than there had been before?

Lianvis approached, his expression tight. "We will be with you, Pellaz, in whatever way we can."

"I have no idea what will happen," Pellaz said. "I can't even be prepared."

"Perhaps that is the way it's supposed to be," Lianvis said. "I shall be alert for you."

Tharmifex joined the group. "Pellaz, we had better begin. The *sedim* are leaving. Strange influences are about."

Pellaz nodded. He could hear the beat of his heart inside his head, yet his body was numb. As he approached the middle of the circle, he glanced up and saw Peridot standing with raised head beyond the guards. Pellaz sensed that Peridot was also about to leave, and a brief message came to him. *As you fight, so do we. The* teraphim *are upon us. It is our hour of testing.*

Good luck, Pellaz said. He did not know what else to say.

Peridot tossed his head. His outline shimmered for some moments, and then the otherlanes consumed him.

Pellaz took off the cloak he wore and Galdra removed his blanket. It seemed ironic that once their relationship had been comprised of hot guilt and frustrated desire. Now it was this, removed and distant. Could Cal do the things that Galdra did? It was impossible to determine. Galdra was there and Cal wasn't. Perhaps it was no more than that.

For a few moments, before he joined Galdra at the center of the circle, Pellaz closed his eyes and called upon Snake and Moon. It was time for them too to begin work again.

Pellaz and Galdra sat down upon the grass cross-legged and, for some moments before they began, stared into one another's eyes. "If we don't see each other again," Galdra said, "know that I love you."

"We will see each other again," Pellaz said.

At the edge of the circle, the Gelaming guards, warriors of Algoma level, raised their arms, shining swords held in each hand, into which they directed protective energy. Pellaz could almost see with his physical eyes the glowing symbols that the guards projected, ghostly glyphs that hung in the air above him. Galdra was bathed in their light, surrounded by a silver nimbus.

Come to me, Pellaz . . .

For the first few minutes, it was as it used to be: deeply erotic. The crowd around them faded away into indistinct shapes. Then reality began to disintegrate as Galdra's ouana-lim reached for the sixth center. Pellaz sensed once more the great irislike portal that was ready to spin open and suck him through. Was it possible this was the last time he'd inhabit earthly reality? Etheric winds pulled at his body, the moment was so close. Moments before the seal opened, Pellaz heard a cry, followed by another, and another. In his hypersensitive state, he could perceive swift black shadows flitting around the camp, striking out. Ponclast's shadow assassins. Arcs of lifeblood spurted into the evening air. Pellaz tried to cry out, to warn somehar, but it was too late. The portal within him opened and he was taken into it.

The cauldron was in chaos. Pellaz could not recognize it nor was able to mold its appearance through his will. Rushing colors flew past his perception, the suggestion of entities, the rake of adamantine claws across his skin. Galdra's presence was strong. He was giving this procedure everything he could. *Take control, Pell. Remember the abyss. Whatever's happening isn't taking place in here. The cauldron is merely reflecting it.*

Pellaz concentrated hard on ordering his perceptions, imagining clear straight lines. It seemed to help. It was as if the cauldron had become a transparent bubble of black glass hanging within a starless void. Beyond its walls, bizarre entities flickered back and forth, colliding with one another to create strange nebulae of sickly light. Sometimes, dark liquid would splash against the walls, like blood.

The sedim *fight . . .* Galdra said. *I sense other entities approaching, from the ends of the universe, like the end of creation, the horror wind.*

I'll connect with Moon and Snake, Pellaz said. *It's time to invoke the dehara.*

Pellaz extended a tendril of thought, which wormed its way through the skin of the cauldron. He could perceive both Moon and Snake as faint glows in his mind. *When did this become so easy?* Pellaz thought. *I take it for granted now.* Only weeks before, the idea of communicating so precisely with nonlocal minds was no more than a dream. Hara like Cobweb and Snake had been able to achieve it, but not with this degree of accuracy. It was like looking inside your own head, and realizing that in inner space all hara are connected and unified. It was merely a matter of concentration to communicate with them.

Pellaz could sense Moon's hesitancy: he was afraid. Snake was simply raring to go, eager to test himself.

Moon, relax, Pellaz told his sori. *Snake and I will take most of the burden. Simply be open, a channel through which the energy can pass. It will take nothing from you. You are merely a conduit.*

In this state, the summoning required no words of invocation or a physical attempt to raise the energy of the dehara. Pellaz merely formed the images of them in his mind's eye, pulling universal life force from within and beyond the cauldron to shape them; it was as easy as building models from clay.

Aruhani came first, blacker than the void, stamping his elegant feet, his hair writhing around him. Then came Agave with his sword of flame, liquid fire running over his skin. He was followed by Lunil of the blue flame, as cold as Agave was hot, his eyes smoking blue light, and finally Miyacala, surrounded by a white-hot cone of power. All were immense, thunder crackling between them. Beyond them, stretching out into infinity, beyond Pellaz's ability to imagine, were ranks of unnamed dehara, all the permutations of desire and will that had emanated from hara in the earthly realm to take on etheric flesh in the worlds beyond. This was the army Wraeththu had at their disposal to fight what came from the unknown places. It was an army of the imagination, of intention, of courage. It was the soul of harakind.

Pellaz, Snake, and Moon formed a triangle, which was like a prism that would reflect and intensify the energy of the dehara. Pellaz could feel power building up between them. He could almost hear it, the hum of a machine the size of the universe. The dehara raised their voices in song, an earsplitting celestial choir that was the sound of creation itself. But as it could create, so it could destroy.

Whatever entities controlled Ponclast became aware of the dehara's presence. Pellaz could sense it. In his heightened state, he could tell that they'd believed they'd only have the *sedim* to contend with. They were surprised by this new development. Pellaz could sense them drawing nearer to him, sniffing, analyzing his power. He caught fleeting glimpses of them in his mind: hideous beyond imagination, yet also lovely. All that stood between him and them was the fragile bubble of the cauldron. If they chose to, they could reach out and pluck Pellaz from his sanctuary. They could snuff him out like pinching a candle flame. The dehara must manifest more quickly. Pellaz passed this imperative on to his companions. They must project their combined energy soon.

For a brief moment, Pellaz could see into earthly reality. He saw the black shadows of Ponclast's hara snaking throughout the Gelaming camp. He saw hara trying to defend themselves, fight them off. Ashmael had left the grissecon circle, and although his elite guard still provided a protective shield there, he was now leading the allied forces toward Fulminir: troops of every tribe, their banners held high, their voices ululating the battle cries they'd perhaps not sung for decades, since the wars with humanity. They were beautiful and fearless, prepared to die if that meant they could prevent the darkness of Fulminir having power in this land once more. The sky above this scene was like a vision of hell. The clouds were red and black, and immense grotesque shapes rolled through them. There were mighty sounds, like planets splitting in two, the groan of space collapsing, the thunderclap of great forces colliding. Ponclast's hara were stationed on the makeshift battlements of Fulminir. Their position was not good, but there were others among them to whom the flimsy defenses were of no concern. Huge figures, angelic warriors, wielding weapons of fire. Pellaz feared for his hara. Although Ashmael led them with courage, they would be burned like paper by these creatures.

Now! Pellaz screamed into the void. He felt Snake release his energy and at the same time it joined with Pell's and streamed into Moon. The dehara were part of it, spiraling like a braid of fluid force into Moon's body.

Pellaz could see it. He looked down upon Fulminir, into the small courtyard. He saw Moon on Tyson's lap, his head thrown back. At that moment, Moon's eyes and mouth were forced open, and the energy of the dehara poured out of him. The image of his body was lost in preternatural radiance.

In the cauldron Pellaz felt the last of the deharan energy stream through him, disappearing like a wail into earthly reality. He became aware of stillness and then a figure walked toward him: Lileem.

Now, she said. *It is time for us, Pellaz.*

Pellaz looked down upon Fulminir once more and saw, as shadows, unearthly conflict. He saw Ashmael's hara engaged in more traditional forms of combat. But in the heart of Fulminir was an indigo flame. Ponclast.

CHAPTER FORTY

The moment that the *teraphim* had locked in combat with the *sedim,* Ponclast had retreated with Abrimel, Diablo, and Geburael to an area deep underground. He did this not so much to seek shelter, but to isolate himself from outside influences. He did not feel that his hour had come, but was filled simply with a sense of resignation. In order to proceed, certain experiences must be undergone, certain trials faced and overcome.

Abrimel was almost witless with panic and virtually useless, capable only of crouching in a corner with Geburael in his arms. Diablo prowled the perimeter of the underground vault, alert for hostile presences. Ponclast composed himself upon the floor, before a censer of incense. Into it, he threw grains of resin that released a pungent smoke, which burned the throat. He could sense all around him, in this realm and beyond, the strange forces that were attracted to this concentrated sphere of activity upon earth. His allies, the Hashmallim, had come, and other shadowy creatures in their wake, but there were more alien presences too, drawn with curiosity to investigate the tantalizing flavors of conflict and terror. The *sedim* fought alone: their masters had sent no other entities to assist them. They had the advantage in numbers, but the *teraphim*'s power was greater than their own. It seemed to Ponclast that it was only a matter of time before the Hashmallim and the *teraphim* concluded their battles. Hara of flesh and blood were no match for Hashmal weapons. Ponclast's shadow fighters were causing panic and mayhem in the Gelaming camp, obstructing their ability to organize their warriors. A cone of power at the center of the camp protected some kind of magical activity, which was well shielded, but Ponclast sensed that whatever took place there was not a direct attack. He presumed the Tigron was attempting to call upon higher forces to aid him.

"Diablo," he said. "Have our fighters concentrate their efforts on the Tigron."

"The protective shield around Pellaz har Aralis is great," Diablo said. "Many will burn upon it like moths against an open flame."

"Nevertheless, deliver this order. If lives are lost, it will be for the greater good. We must prevent Pellaz from summoning reinforcements."

"I understand," Diablo said. "This will be done." He vanished into the otherlanes.

"Send the Hashmallim!" Abrimel said desperately. "Ponclast, do it. Make them attack the Tigron. No other will reach him."

"The Hashmallim do not obey orders," Ponclast said. "You know this. We cannot expect them to do everything. Our allies will appreciate us having at least some sense of initiative in this conflict."

Abrimel's gaze darted wildly, almost insanely, around the chamber. "You do not know him. He is strong. I can feel it. I can feel him close. Ponclast, you don't know what you're up against."

"Be quiet!" Ponclast said. "Your fear does nothing to help me. Guard that harling and keep your gutless terror to yourself."

"You should have sent our son away from here. This is madness!"

Ponclast did not want to hear any more. He directed an arrow of intention at Abrimel that fuddled his brain, so that he sat motionless and silent, his eyes staring blankly.

In the stillness that followed, Ponclast became aware of gathering hostile energy. It was more than *sedim*. He didn't recognize it, but he could tell it possessed great power. Quickly, he sent out a mind call to Diablo to summon him back. It occurred to him that the order he'd sent to his shadow fighters had been issued too late. He could wait no longer. He must confront Pellaz har Aralis now, perhaps while the Tigron was still weakened from whatever magical task he'd been involved in. But how could he be drawn to this place? The protections around him were great.

"Pellaz, you coward," Ponclast said under his breath, his eyes closed. "Will you not have the courage to confront me, har to har?"

For a moment, there was only silence, but for the sound of breathing, then a clear voice spoke.

"Ponclast, you may call me many things, but coward I am not."

Ponclast opened his eyes and saw a shining figure standing before him. He resisted the urge to scrabble backward. Pellaz had come, unarmed and naked. Was he mad, or simply too confident? Ponclast got to his feet. Now he was confronted with the reality of the Tigron, he felt disorientated. Pellaz must have great power indeed to pass through the wards and cantrips that guarded this place. He must be able to access the otherlanes as Diablo did. But he did not appear about to launch an attack. Ponclast noticed the Tigron glance at Abrimel, although his expression did not change in the slightest. Ponclast raised his arm, his fist gripping a ball of swiftly conjured black flame. He meant to throw it, catch Pellaz off his guard.

"Don't bother with that," Pellaz said.

Ponclast ignored this advice and threw the flame. It burst some inches from the Tigron's body and fell down like flakes of sooty snow.

"You see," Pellaz said. "You can't fight me that way."

"One of us must emerge victorious," Ponclast said. "We are not here to engage in idle conversation." He summoned a different form of energy, which manifested as a forked trident of white radiance. Ponclast released it, but it merely bounced off the Tigron's aura and skidded across the floor like a spear of glass. It shattered against the wall.

Ponclast lowered his arm, unsure of what to do next. The Tigron's proximity affected him greatly, dispersing his concentration. Whatever preparations he'd made, and no matter for how long, he could never have been ready for this. He could see it clearly now. "I will not surrender to you," he said. "There will be no more Gebaddon for me or my hara."

"No," Pellaz agreed. "If you are to survive, your exile must be far from this realm, with no chance of return." Pellaz put his head to one side. "Do you hear the fighting? The dehara, our gods, crush the living essence from your allies, Ponclast. Ironically, they are as much your gods as mine, and perhaps some creations of your own imagination fight alongside them."

Ponclast realized that Abrimel's fears had been justified. The Hashmallim had lied to him or perhaps they too had underestimated Thiede's protégé. Ponclast could tell in every fiber of his being that he could never be equal to Pellaz har Aralis. He was like a living expression of every har's secret dream, radiant and eternal. But if etheric and magical weapons could have no effect, perhaps a more conventional attack was called for. With a furious cry, Ponclast picked up the burning incense and charged at Pellaz, even though the metal bowl burned his hands greatly. He threw the smoldering charcoal in the Tigron's face. The coals, however, simply passed through Pellaz's body.

"Did you really think this was my physical body?" Pellaz said. "You can't harm me, Ponclast. What did your allies tell you? That they had made you strong, my equal? Maybe they have, but you do not have my knowledge. Your hara love you, and now they die for you, but they are only shadows, weak and hopeless."

"What you did to my hara was unspeakable," Ponclast said. The pain in his hands was almost too much to bear; he was afraid he'd lose consciousness, yet lacked the focus to direct healing energy into them.

Pellaz smiled grimly. "You and they should have been prepared for that. You did unspeakable things to others. Every action has a consequence, and you set the rules. Did you expect our mercy? Why should we have given it, when you gave none? That was an unrealistic hope, Ponclast. It still is."

"The Gelaming are liars, warmongers who ride behind a banner of peace!" Ponclast cried. "I know the truth of it. You have no moral high ground, Pellaz. The essence of this conflict is one will to power against another."

"I don't disagree," Pellaz said. "Whatever propaganda Thiede used to put about means little to me. But I like to think our way is more acceptable to the majority than yours. Your indulgences in this citadel all those years ago did not make you greatly popular among the common hara. You despised your own kind, too caught up in the bitterness of the early years, when Wraeththu fought among themselves and with humanity. You didn't move on. We did. There is no place for your ideology in this world now."

Ponclast knew that all he possessed to defend himself was his conviction, his belief in himself and his hara. It had to be enough. "I have no wish to debate this," he said. "Do what you think you can, Tigron, and let us see once and for all whose way is best."

Pellaz laughed. "That is brave talk. Look at your hands. You cannot fight me, in any sense."

"I am prepared to die trying."

Pellaz said nothing to those words. Instead, he threw back his head, closed his eyes, and drew in a deep breath. He looked so vulnerable, yet Ponclast knew now that he was far from that. Pellaz exhaled slowly, and opened his eyes once more. "I would like you to meet a friend of mine," he said.

There was a shimmer of emerald light in the corner of the room, which presently expanded into a luminous oval. It was clearly some kind of other-lane portal, because a figure emerged from it. This was a young har, who to

Ponclast's eyes seemed greatly biased toward soume in his being. The har was dressed simply, in clothes of close-fitting brushed leather. His honey-colored hair hung loose over his breast. He did not resemble a fighter, nor did he emanate any great sense of magical power, but there was something not quite right about him.

"This is Lileem," Pellaz said. "She wishes to share breath with you."

"She?" Ponclast said. Since when had hara, even the ones Varrs had conditioned to be predominantly soume, refer to themselves as she?

"Lileem is Kamagrian," Pellaz said. "You do not know of them, of course. Share breath with her. You will be surprised at the results of combining her essence with yours."

Lileem approached Ponclast, her gaze fixed on his. Ponclast wasn't sure what he saw in her eyes, but for the first time a sense of true fear passed through him. This creature was not Wraeththu, but something else. She was a weapon of the Tigron's.

Ponclast tried to back away from the approaching figure, but somehow he had moved so far across the chamber, his back was pressed against the wall. Lileem opened her mouth and a sparkling vapor curled from her lips. She leapt forward and gripped Ponclast's face between her hands. Her breath was a vortex. Losing consciousness, Ponclast could feel himself being torn from earthly reality, his soul ripped from his flesh.

As if from a long distance away, he heard the Tigron's voice. "Lileem will take you to a place of great interest. You might learn something there. Thiede believed Gebaddon would educate you and indeed it did, but this will be something different."

Ponclast was like nothing more than a scrap of cloth dangling from the strange har's essence. He was helpless. The flight from Gebaddon, the brief time in Fulminir, the attempt to resurrect it, all meant nothing. His allies did nothing to save him. They let him go into darkness. He was an experiment that had failed.

For some moments, Pellaz stood motionless in the underground vault. The harling held in Abrimel's arms was whimpering. Abrimel himself looked mindless. *Am I so heartless,* Pellaz thought, *that I can feel nothing for my own flesh and blood?*

He prepared himself to leave, and it took enormous effort to focus on that simple act. Despite appearances, his confrontation with Ponclast had depleted him greatly. He gazed for some moments at his son, who clearly could not see him. In the aftermath of the conflict, hara could come down here to take

Abrimel into custody. There was nothing else to be done here. Aboveground, the dehara fought with the Hashmallim. Pellaz could perceive now what a strange battle it was, because neither side could actually destroy the other. The dehara were made of thought and emotion, so they could not be unmade, and the Hashmallim were etheric projections whose physical selves resided far from this realm. All the two sides could do was fight for dominance, so that the weaker could slink away. Pellaz perceived that both sides were enjoying the combat. It posed no real risk to them, after all. It was the play of tiger cubs, yet somewhere else the tigers crouched unseen. That was a different matter.

It had all been satisfactorily easy. Lileem had taken Ponclast with her to the realm of the Black Library, which was extremely difficult to escape. Pellaz had no desire to kill his enemy, mainly because ultimately he was not a foe to be feared. If he should somehow rise up, with greater force, and pose a threat in the future, it was because it was meant to be: a further test. *If I am not worthy of facing that,* Pellaz thought, *then I am not worthy of being Tigron.* He knew that beyond this world there were far worse threats than Ponclast. Now, it was simply a case of clearing up. It was time to return to his body and begin that work.

But even as he formed this thought, a ball of black energy manifested in the room. Pellaz observed it, puzzled, for only an instant before it threw itself against him. He was hurled backward. His etheric body slammed through the thick stone wall and landed in a dank corridor outside. He was smothered in a crawling sticky essence that forced its way inside him.

He could not fight you! a voice screamed in his mind. *But I can. I will unmake you, Pellaz har Aralis! Your body will be left without a soul.*

Pellaz knew immediately that this was no idle threat. Whatever invaded his being was strong, and comprised of matter that could affect his etheric form. He fought back, trying to force the blackness away from him, but it was like trying to extricate himself from an immense web. If he pushed parts of it away, it clung to him more firmly in other places. He could feel it squeezing his soul, seeking to crush and dampen forever the flickering flame of it. He could not even escape it by returning to his corporeal form. The blackness anchored him to this place. It was affecting Galdra also. Pellaz became aware of Galdra's being, and knew that his assailant was completely aware of what was occurring. It had reached inside him and taken that knowledge. It would force Galdra to conclude the grissecon, which would mean that Pellaz would have no way to return to his body. He would be snuffed out like a candle flame. Pellaz screamed for Lileem, for Snake, even for Moon, anyhar who could help him now, but none of them could hear him. He screamed for the dehara, but his enemy was a smothering blanket that obstructed his attempts to reach out.

He could feel Galdra's anxiety and terror, the way he was trying to hold on to their union with every shred of will and strength he possessed, but he was losing power. At the climax of grissecon, the most magical and intimate of moments, Pellaz would die.

Pellaz was powerless to resist what was happening. He was too weak. Fighting was pointless. He projected to Galdra a final surge of appreciation and love. They had done what they could.

But then, there was a voice in his mind. *Pellaz, what are you doing? This is an illusion.*

No illusion! cried his enemy.

Pellaz heard soft laughter, so familiar a sound. He opened his eyes and peered through a film of oily blackness. Cal stood over him, beautiful and radiant, an archetypal warrior covered in wounds. *Run, Diablo!* Cal said.

He extended an arm and touched the darkness covering Pellaz's etheric body. At once it convulsed in pain, as a force Pellaz had never encountered before flowed through it. A black shape leapt up from him, transforming as it did so into a weird kind of har with enormous burning eyes. This har hissed at Cal and struck out, although it missed its target. Cal laughed again, his eyes shining with a manic light. He flicked a dart of radiance at Pell's assailant, which passed right through Diablo's shoulder. Dark ichor spurted out. Diablo yelped in pain and then leapt through the wall, presumably back into the chamber beyond.

Cal did not follow. He simply stood where he was, gazing down into Pell's eyes. It took some moments for Pellaz to realize that he was free and not about to die. He stared back at Cal, unable to communicate. He didn't know what he felt.

You should never have doubted me, Cal said. He looked haggard, whether in physical form or not. His clothes were ripped and bloody, his body scored by deep scratches. *I can see,* he said. *I can see what you're doing. He is in you so deep, a hook in your heart.*

Cal . . . please. . . .

Cal shook his head, smiling sadly. As Pellaz watched, his form changed and it was Orien standing there, one finger to his lips. *There are no endings . . .*

At that moment, Galdra let go and Pellaz was sucked back into his body with painful force. He opened his eyes, for a moment unable to feel any physical sensation. He saw the night sky, the stars wheeling like the sparkling motes in the barrel of a kaleidoscope. It felt as if he and Galdra had become one, no division between them. Locked together. Forever. Flesh and blood combined.

Galdra shuddered and spoke aloud. "Pellaz . . . please . . . don't . . ."

It must hurt. It should hurt. *Come deeper,* Pell said in mind-touch. *Pierce muscle and bone. Find my heart. Then we shall see.*

Galdra cried out, a hoarse and ragged scream of agony. The sound spiraled up to the stars. Hara came running. Then there was nothing.

CHAPTER FORTY-ONE

Moon had discovered a dehar who was all his own. At the moment when Pellaz and Snake had projected the mighty force of the dehara into his body, Moon's consciousness had drifted off elsewhere. For some moments, he had hung above the courtyard, looking down. He had seen the veins standing out on Tyson's face and neck, his muscles corded with strain. He had seen his own flesh, no more than a shuddering mass of greenish white radiance, with brighter spots where his eyes and mouth would be. It occurred to him that his corporeal form might be destroyed by the force it channeled, but he could not care about it. *This is what it must feel like to be dead.*

He could see that nebulous outlines were forming from the energy, massive entities, an army of dehara. They strode across the sky toward a boiling mass of black and red clouds, in which dark shapes tumbled and writhed. As Moon watched this, a *sedu* surged past him and rocked the ball of light that comprised his essence. It was like being a harling's plaything, floating upon a choppy sea, drifting far from land.

Heed me, Moon . . .

Moon's dreamy attention became focused. He was in a dark place, where he could perceive no details of his surroundings, and before him stood a young har, whose hair and skin were green. There was a strong scent of apples that reached right into Moon's being. *Who are you?* he asked.

I am Pomonari, the dehar of your childhood memories. I am all that you are, all that you have ever been. I am your strength. Take my hand.

Moon gripped the slim green fingers that Pomonari extended to him. For a moment, he felt like weeping, because he could remember so clearly the way his hostling Silken's hands had felt. Pomonari was partly of Silken too. Moon's memories of his hostling had become vague over the years; now they were brought back in force. He remembered what it had been like to be held, the feeling of utter security he'd experienced in Silken's arms. He remembered his hostling's voice, his wry songs, the smell of his hair.

You are your history, Pomonari said. *You are the book of your life. Come.*

They stepped back into reality, hand in hand. Moon found they had manifested beyond the wall of the courtyard. He could perceive what was happening in the earthly realm and also beyond it. Two scenes of battle were superimposed over each other. The Gelaming had been able to pass through Fulminir's defenses and conventional combat now ensued in the streets and alleyways. Ponclast's otherworld allies were fully occupied with the dehara, although the Teraghast shadow fighters were still intent on flashing in and out of the otherlanes, causing as much mayhem as possible. Moon saw a *sedu* grab hold of a shadow fighter with its teeth and shake him like a dog would shake a rabbit. The har crumpled to the ground, and then a flame-eyed *teraph* pounced upon the *sedu* from behind, its shining hooves digging deep into the flesh of its enemy. The *sedu* roared in pain and anger, turned to confront its foe, and the two of them spiraled upward, striking out and biting. Sparkling ichor spattered down.

Moon and his dehar walked calmly through the chaos, invisible to all. Moon was not aware of time passing particularly, but came to the realization that activity was dying down around him. He saw Ashmael Aldebaran striding over bodies in a wide plaza, lifting them by the hair to see if they were still alive. The ground ran with blood, like rain after a heavy storm. Moon saw Ashmael's *sedu*, Zephyr, leap out of the otherlanes nearby, shaking his mane. Moon knew now that the *sedim* were not as gentle as they appeared. Zephyr was alight with a sense of victory. Ashmael went to him and vaulted onto the *sedu*'s back. He rode over the bodies and entered the citadel itself.

Moon thought maybe he should follow and discover what was left inside. He thought he should try to find out what had happened to Cal, and it seemed merely the intention of this conjured Cal into being. He walked out of an invisible doorway in the air. *What are you doing here, Moon? You're engaged in some kind of grissecon, aren't you?*

Yes. We helped Pellaz summon the dehara.

I know. I saw it. You shouldn't be here now. You are wandering. Go back.

Are you all right? Cal did not appear all right: his clothing was almost ripped to shreds, and his skin beneath was similarly gored. He was covered in blood, but his face was less gray and haggard than when Moon had last seen him.

I'll live. Go back to your flesh, Moon. I will be with you shortly.

This is my dehar, Moon said, lifting the hand that held Pomonari's fingers.

Very nice, Cal said. *Go back, Moon. If you don't, and Tyson ends your union, you'll be lost. Now!*

Moon opened his eyes with a start, as if he'd been jerked awake from a dream. He could feel Tyson's arms around his back, the sweat between them. His whole body was pulsing in the last waves of an orgasm he hadn't been conscious of experiencing. Most bizarre. He was acutely aware of every atom of his body and found the seal within him. For some moments, he entered partially into the cauldron of creation and scoured it of aren. Then he closed the seal. It was as simple as closing his eyes. He felt as if his recent experiences had somehow hauled him up the ladder of caste progression at an alarming rate. He must surely be Algomalid at least.

The soft light of dawn was pushing back the darkness. Birds sang loudly. Tyson uttered a long sigh and gently disengaged himself. "Tell me I'm alive," he said.

Moon got to his feet shakily and the world dipped around him. He didn't feel nauseous, only slightly drunk. "You're alive. We both are."

Tyson stretched himself and staggered from the effort. "That was *hours,*" he said. "How did I do that? Tell me how I did that! I can't even remember it."

"You are the son of Calanthe har Aralis," Moon said. "What did you expect? We met because we were supposed to, as Cal and Pell did. I feel terrible, but also wonderful."

"Imagine I'm holding you full of love and doting glances," Tyson said. "I really can't bear the thought of contact in reality."

Moon laughed and this sound woke Aleeme's harling, who Moon had wrapped in a blanket and laid nearby before commencing his work with Tyson. Now Moon went to crouch beside the harling. It stared at him, silent, but breathing easily. It must be hungry. Moon had never seen such an ugly little creature, but perhaps that was because it was malnourished and emaciated.

Tyson came to stand behind them. "If I'd been Cal, I'd have left that thing where I found it," he said. "It's a freak." He handed Moon a cup of water.

"Hmm." Moon couldn't totally disagree. "But who are we to decide?" He didn't realize how thirsty he was until the water touched his lips. He couldn't stop drinking until the cup was nearly drained, then he gave what was left to the harling. It was so young, yet it gripped the cup and drank like an older har. Moon half expected it to thank him in an adult voice.

Tyson grimaced. "If Aleeme lives, will he really want to see that thing again?"

"I've no idea. It's kin of yours though, Ty. Try to find some compassion inside you."

"After what you told me, I find that difficult," Tyson said. "An innocent wouldn't look like that!"

Moon stood up. "I should find it something to eat."

"There isn't anything."

Moon slumped. "Ag, how long will we stay here? Cal said he'd come for us."

"What's happening outside here? Do you know?"

"I think it's nearly over. I saw Cal and he told me to return to my body. He's all right, Ty. He's injured but not seriously."

"Thank Ag for that!"

At that moment, Moon heard the door inside their room open. He touched Tyson briefly on the arm. "Ssh, somehar's coming."

"I heard," Tyson said softly. "It could be Cal, or it could be a Teraghast coming to finish us off." He moved to one side of the outer doorway and motioned for Moon to do the same on the other side. If an enemy came out, they'd pounce.

But it was no enemy, only Cal, with a couple of Gelaming warriors. His hair was plastered to his head and his clothes were wet: it appeared he'd taken a hasty bath somewhere. His wounds had been washed of blood, but were still visible through his torn shirt. Cal held up a key. "Your captors are helpful," he said. "Left this in the door. And I'd brought muscle with me to break it down too." He gestured at one of the Gelaming. "Take the harling. Take it to the healing pavilions."

"Yes, tiahaar." The warrior lifted the child. "This is a harling?" He appeared disgusted.

"Of sorts," Cal said. "Deal with it, but do not harm it."

"As you wish."

Cal drew Tyson and Moon to him, then winced as they inadvertently pressed against the wounds on his chest. He pushed them back a little. "You were amazing. I'm shocked. Well done."

"Do you know about what we were doing?" Tyson asked.

"More or less. I had to fight off a particularly obstinate Hashmal, but managed to watch most of the show."

Tyson touched Cal's chest. "You're hurt badly."

"Nothing a blast of healing energy won't cure," Cal said. "I just jumped in a water cistern and once the blood was off, the wounds didn't look too bad."

"Do you want us to give you healing?" Moon asked.

"It can wait," Cal replied. "Now it's time to face the worst. Will you be my support? It's most unlike me, but I feel I need it."

"You want to go to the Gelaming camp?" Tyson inquired.

"The nest of vipers, yes," Cal said. "I expect they will be delighted to see me."

A great many Teraghasts had fled into the otherlanes, once it had become apparent the battle was going against them, although many others, predominantly injured hara, had been taken captive by the Gelaming. The camp was in chaos, as healing personnel struggled to cope with many injured hara, of both sides. Cal led Moon and Tyson to the middle of the camp. It was clear that he intended to confront Pellaz immediately.

At the entrance to the grissecon site, Tharmifex Calvel was waiting for them, apparently having been warned of Cal's approach. He blocked their path, arms folded. "Cal, you manifest at the most surprising times."

"Let me past," Cal said. "I have no quarrel with you. Don't make me change my mind."

"We *will* talk," Tharmifex said, "but not here. A great many hara are interested in where you've been and what you've been up to."

Cal drew in his breath. "I will talk to you, tiahaar, but not here, as you suggested. Now, let me through."

Tharmifex's expression became pinched. "If you insist, although you might not like what you see."

Moon felt increasingly uneasy. The grissecon was over. What was there left to see? Presumably, Pellaz was unharmed, because Tharmifex did not appear distressed. Moon and Tyson followed Cal beyond the entrance.

There was a strange close atmosphere inside the wall of silk screens. The dawn light made everything feel surreal. The conflict was over, but something was still going on. Moon felt sick again, the way he'd felt in Aleeme's tower prison. A wide circle had been marked out with salt or chalk on the grass. Around two dozen hara stood in the circle, surrounding whatever remained in the center.

Cal drew in his breath sharply, and a tall har with incredibly long tawny hair straightened up slowly and looked round, straight into Cal's eyes.

"Kakkahaar!" Cal hissed. "Now who would believe that?"

The har glided toward them swiftly and bowed, somewhat insolently. "Tiahaar Calanthe, we meet again. I witnessed some of your activities earlier. Most impressive. Somehar has taught you well. The technique and style seemed almost familiar."

"Tiahaar Lianvis," Cal said, "what pickings are there here for you? You are far from the desert. Are the Gelaming paying you in captives?"

Lianvis laughed. "Now, there's a thought! But no. Somehow I think I'd find resistance to such a demand."

"You could try," Cal said, "if Aldebaran has left any wounded alive after trampling over them on his *sedu*. Where's Pell?"

Lianvis indicated the center of the circle. "There's a slight problem."

"Problem? What? Is he hurt?"

Moon noticed Cal didn't move his gaze from the Kakkahaar's face.

Lianvis cleared his throat and stared at Cal for some moments.

"Well?" Cal said.

Lianvis glanced around quickly, then clearly came to a decision. "We cannot separate them."

"What?"

Lianvis shrugged gracefully. "It is somewhat indelicate, but as far as I can tell there has been no retraction of the inner organs. We cannot pull them apart without risking damage because the Freyhellan is too deep in Pell's body. I cannot communicate with Pellaz. He is unconscious on more than one level."

"How serious is this?" Cal's color had become ashen again.

"We are hoping the condition will subside naturally. Pellaz took on a lot. He required great strength to face Ponclast, who no doubt now believes the Tigron has the power of a dehar. He hasn't. What he projected, coupled with that last attack you helped him with, has effectively closed him down. Galdra har Freyhella is frozen in shock."

Cal nodded, but his expression was distant, as if his mind raced through many thoughts.

"Perhaps," Lianvis said, "you could attempt . . ."

"Yes," Cal said. Without looking at his companions, he marched forward and pushed through the small crowd of hara in the center of the circle. Moon and Tyson exchanged a glance and followed. Moon could feel the Kakkahaar's attention fixed upon him. It was not a comfortable feeling.

The center of the circle was like the scene of a horrible accident, yet without blood. A sour feeling hung in the air, a sense of desolation. Somehar had put blankets over Pellaz's and Galdra's naked bodies; they had not moved from the grissecon posture. Galdra's eyes were open, but unfocused. His breathing was labored and he appeared to be in pain. A har stood behind him, hands on Galdra's shoulders. Moon could hear softly whispered words, but could not catch their meaning. Pellaz was slumped motionless against Galdra's chest, his head turned to the side, so that Moon could see his eyes were closed. Moon could not imagine what Cal must feel to witness this sight. This Galdra, who was only a name to Moon, had taken Cal's place. The Tigrons of Immanion should have performed this grissecon, but it had been Cal's choice not to be with the Gelaming.

Hara stepped aside when they realized who had pushed among them. Cal stared at Pellaz for some moments, then hunkered down beside him. He brushed Pell's hair back with one hand. "Pellaz," he said, and let his hand rest against Pell's head. "Hear me. Let him go."

He did not have to speak those words aloud, and perhaps did so merely to inform or remind the hara present of who and what he was. All was silent as Cal remained crouched at Pell's side. Even the sounds from beyond the circle seemed hushed. Then Pellaz uttered a sound that was half gasp, half cry, and his head jerked up.

Cal withdrew his hand. He stood up and turned to Lianvis. "Lift him," he said, and walked past Tyson and Moon back toward the site entrance.

Lianvis gestured at two hara dressed in similar attire to himself, who must be fellow Kakkahaar. Moon had to watch in ghoulish curiosity as they separated Pellaz and Galdra. He knew he should really look away, but it was too fascinating.

"That," said Tyson, "is unreal! No wonder Pellaz used that har for this grissecon. Did you see . . ."

"Ty, shut up," Moon interrupted. "We should go after Cal."

CHAPTER FORTY-TWO

They found Cal at the healing pavilions asking earnest questions of harried healers about Azriel and Aleeme. Moon wasn't deceived. Behind Cal's focused concern, panic was fluttering like a trapped bird. He didn't feel good at all. He didn't know what had happened to his world. Reality and truth had just reared up and slapped his face. The blow had obviously dislodged some scales from his eyes.

Moon wandered into the crowded pavilions, leaving Tyson to stand by his hostling at the entrance and wonder why Cal was babbling. Moon walked between long rows of beds in the dim light of the tents, where the smell of crushed grass mixed with the stench of blood. Teraghasts and hara of other tribes lay side by side. The Teraghasts in that place were in no condition to attack or try to escape. Most lay motionless. Moon knew he should offer to help, because it was clear everyhar there was worked off his feet, but Moon caught glimpses of the injuries and couldn't bring himself to look closer. Walking through those long tents was like a sickening nightmare, being too scared to look anywhere but straight ahead. Still, he made himself do it.

The healers wouldn't let Moon near Aleeme, who was in a sectioned-off area for critical cases, but he found Azriel lying on a low pallet, staring at the gently swaying ceiling. Moon spoke, but Azriel didn't appear to hear him. The healers had cleaned him up, but he wasn't *there*. Moon hoped that Azriel was deep inside himself and would one day come back. He didn't want to think about the alternatives.

The Gelaming had set up a large canteen tent where food and drink was available for all personnel. Once Moon came out of the healing pavilions, Cal decided they should go and eat. In the aftermath of the conflict, warriors with minor wounds ate breakfast jovially together. Looking at their faces, Moon realized many of them were surprised to find themselves still alive. In the camp around them, tents were already coming down as the tribes made preparations to return home. At some point in the future, there would be a big victory celebration in Immanion, but by that time many hara would be immersed once more in their everyday lives and would tell themselves they hadn't got the time to travel. Relations with the Gelaming would never be the same again, because the Gelaming had proved their point. Moon could sense that some hara were already thinking about that and that it made them uncomfortable.

Cal found them an open-air table near the edge of the crowds and sent Tyson and Moon to fetch trays of food. This required lengthy queuing, and by the time they returned to Cal he had a companion. Moon recognized the long-haired Kakkahaar who had spoken to Cal at the Grissecon site. "This is Lianvis," Cal said, gesturing across the table.

Moon and Tyson sat down, each uttering a muttered greeting. Moon could tell the Kakkahaar was attracting a lot of attention from hara nearby. He must be here simply because he'd been looking for Cal. It struck Moon as odd then that a Tigron of Immanion could wander among ordinary hara, as Cal was doing, and *not* attract attention. Blending in was one of Cal's talents.

"This must be your son," Lianvis said to Cal while looking at Tyson. "You are very much alike."

"And this is Moon," Cal said, "Pell's sori."

"Again the family resemblance is stunning." The Kakkahaar smiled at Moon. "Thank you for all you did last night."

Moon felt embarrassed. He had a feeling this har had seen everything. "How's Pell?" he asked, then regretted it. The question turned to ice in the air, fell heavily, and then shattered over the table. Cal cleared his throat.

"He'll be fine," Lianvis said lightly. "It'll take him a few days to balance himself, but that's only to be expected. It's a small price to pay for victory."

"Victory?" Cal said flatly. "All we did was buy some time."

"Really?" Moon asked. "I thought . . ."

"You're right, Cal," Lianvis said. He began to eat from the plate of food in front of him. "Ponclast's allies overestimated his readiness, and underestimated the Gelaming's, or rather Pell's, resourcefulness. I don't know for sure if this is the last we'll see of the problem. It might be that future skirmishes will take place elsewhere. We might not notice them, or even know they've happened."

"I hope that's the case," Cal said.

Lianvis looked up at him. "Ignorance is bliss, eh? Strange, I wouldn't have thought that would be your philosophy."

Cal shrugged. He'd barely touched his food. "It's becoming so."

Lianvis wiped his mouth fastidiously with a corner of his napkin. "What Pellaz did was simply work," he said in a meaningful tone. "Don't let it get to you."

Cal fixed Lianvis with a stare. "Get me to *him*," he said in a voice that sent a chill down Moon's spine.

"Pellaz?" Lianvis said. "You don't need me for that, surely . . ."

"No," Cal said. "You know who I mean. Where is he?"

Lianvis put his hands against the table and regarded Cal thoughtfully. "I am in two minds whether to tell you. I've heard quite a lot about you since making contact with the Gelaming."

"What do you care? You've done far worse in your time than I ever have, I'm sure."

Lianvis frowned, as if debating why he should care and perhaps surprised because he felt the need to do so. "You and Pellaz mean something," he said at last. "Conflict with Galdra har Freyhella and a possible unpleasant outcome is not how it's supposed to end, either for you or for Wraeththukind in general."

Cal laughed coldly. "I won't kill him. I just want to meet this paragon who everyhar thinks can take my place. Wouldn't you, in my situation?"

Lianvis grinned and began to eat once more. "In your situation, my dear Cal, I most probably *would* kill him, but that's why you are a Tigron and I am not, nor ever could be. Very well, I'll take you to him later."

"I want to meet him too," Tyson said, the first time he had spoken to the Kakkahaar.

Lianvis shook his head in amusement. "Poor Galdra! Perhaps I should consider selling tickets for this event."

Before they left the table, a member of Tharmifex Calvel's staff approached them. He bowed to Cal. "Tiahaar, there will be a meeting of the Hegemony at midday. You are invited to attend." He turned to Lianvis. "You also, tiahaar."

"Tell Tharmifex I'll be there," Cal said. "I'll be with my companions here, so make sure they have places."

The messenger bowed again, assured Cal this would be attended to, and departed.

"You know what I think?" Lianvis said.

"What?" Cal asked.

"Don't visit Galdra har Freyhella before the meeting. If I were in your position, I think I'd simply act my best before the Hegemony. The Freyhellan will have heard you're here by now. He must be . . . *anxious* about it. Anyhar can see he'd lay down his life for Pell in an instant. Show the Hegemony what you're made of—and show Galdra also. He'll be well enough to attend the meeting and in fact I doubt he'd miss it, whatever his condition. It could be the opportunity you need. Two birds brought to earth, lifeless, with one well-aimed missile, don't you think?"

"Thank you, tiahaar," Cal said. "I'll bear that in mind."

"Pellaz won't be at the meeting," Lianvis said. "I can tell you that much. He won't be doing anything of consequence for the next few days. But I think I'll recommend to Tiahaar Calvel that the Tigron is returned to Immanion today. He should be able to take a journey by *sedu* and I think he should be . . . removed from play, don't you?"

Cal narrowed his eyes. "Why this show of devotion to me, Lianvis?"

Lianvis shrugged. "I always liked you, despite what you might have thought. I liked the whiff of danger about you. You see, I have my romantic fancies about you and Pellaz also. In my fond imaginings, you walk off together, into a rosy Almagabran sunset, hand in hand."

Cal laughed. "You are amazing!"

"Don't worry. The Freyhellan's no match for you."

Until the meeting, Cal, Moon, and Tyson walked around the camp, so that Cal could exercise his role as Tigron and speak to whoever mattered, as well as many who didn't. He made no move to go and find Pellaz, which Moon found interesting, although he dared not comment on it. When they came across Ashmael Aldebaran, who had just supervised the removal of Abrimel har Aralis from Fulminir, Ashmael embraced Cal spontaneously. "Not before time," he said. "I'd almost given up on you."

Moon noticed hara observing Ashmael's hearty and clearly sincere greeting. He also noticed Cal didn't let Ashmael go too quickly.

"We have much to discuss," Cal said. "I've been with Thiede."

"*Much* to discuss!" Ashmael agreed. "Will he return to us?"

"Not in the same way as before," Cal said. "I need to speak to the Hegemony about it."

Ashmael nodded, released Cal, and patted his arms. "I'm glad you're back," he said, then grimaced. "So who is the enviable har to tell the Tigrina about his son?"

"Not me," Cal said. "I have another matter to deal with."

"You do," Ashmael said. "Take care of it."

Cal smiled widely in response.

A makeshift Hegalion had been created at the grissecon site. When Moon and his companions arrived there, many hara of high rank were finding places for themselves on the mats that had been laid out as seats in concentric circles. Moon saw Tharmifex, Ashmael, and Velaxis sitting together, along with Swift and Seel har Parasiel, but there was no sign of Galdra har Freyhella. Perhaps he wouldn't attend. The air around the site felt different now, no longer oppressive. Presumably Gelaming Nahir Nuri had cleaned it of residue of the grissecon and its aftermath.

Cal pushed his way through the crowds to take his place next to Tharmifex, as if he'd never been absent from these gatherings. Many hara had their eyes fixed upon him, including Seel har Parasiel, whose expression was grim, to say the least. Ashmael was grinning, although Tharmifex was tight-lipped. Moon knew of the history between Seel and Cal, because Tyson had told him. He wondered what would happen now, but guessed the next hour or so was going to be filled with excruciating moments.

Swift got to his feet immediately and wrapped Cal in a fierce embrace. "I heard what you did for Aleeme and Azriel," he said. "I can't express . . ."

"Hush," Cal said, kissing Swift on the lips—rather pointedly, Moon thought. "They are family. I only did what any of you would have done."

Seel had also got to his feet and now stood with folded arms next to Swift. Cal ducked his head to him. "Seel," he said politely, as if nothing bad had ever happened between them, although the mere politeness of the word could also indicate a lifetime of bad feeling. "I hope Aleeme will be all right."

"We don't know yet," Seel said stiffly. "He'll live, but . . . I suppose I must thank you too."

"I suppose you must," Cal said.

"Ty!" Swift said in a voice that was rather too jovial. He dragged Tyson toward him, effectively placing him between Seel and Cal. "It's good to see you too. Once we get home, we'll have the biggest celebration Galhea has ever known. It'll be the best medicine for Azriel and Aleeme."

From these words, Moon gathered that Swift had not yet seen his son and his chesnari. He felt sick with sorrow for the Parasilians. He expected the healers had kept them away from the pavilions, fabricating some excuse. In their place, he'd want peace and quiet to relay the devastating news of Azriel's and Aleeme's conditions.

Everyhar sat down, and Velaxis came to sit beside Cal, who had now dismissed Seel from his attention. Seel, sitting back by Swift, appeared greatly stunned by the whole business.

Velaxis touched Cal on the arm. "Are you well?"

"Yes, tiahaar," Cal replied.

"You must speak for Abrimel. He has no champions here."

"And I do?" Cal said. He and Velaxis locked gazes and Moon had the strong impression some unspoken dialogue took place.

"We needed the Freyhellan," Velaxis said at last. "It was necessary. You couldn't be here. He was the nearest we could get."

"You were not one of those who suggested he become Tigron, then?" Cal said acidly.

"I never suggested that. I merely reported to certain hara what I had heard."

"As always," Cal said. "The perfect agent."

"You are here now," Velaxis said. "When we return to Immanion, we must talk."

"Oh, we will!"

Something about this conversation unsettled Moon, mainly because he had never heard that Velaxis and Cal were particularly well known to one another. Their exchange had involved an unexpected intimacy. But before Velaxis could say more, Tharmifex got to his feet and raised his arms. Conversation around him died away.

"Tiahaara," Tharmifex said, "our combined efforts have negated the immediate threat against us, and for this we must congratulate ourselves, not just on the skill of our warriors, but the fact that we were able to work together for a common purpose. I hope we have all learned from this. I hope that those of you who suspected Gelaming motives in this alliance appreciate we are not bent on accruing power, only cooperation. Soon, we will all return home, to our friends and families and our everyday work, but I hope that in some ways we remain allied. For in unity, there is strength."

Tharmifex paused for a moment, and the silence around him was absolute. "It would be wrong to assume this is the end of the problem. Whatever grounds impelled Ponclast's otherworldly allies to act as they did still exist. In Gelaming opinion, we should continue to investigate the phenomenon, and every tribe should have Listeners working closely together, to create a network of etheric protection around the globe. The Hegemony does not intend to plant Gelaming agents within every tribe. We will simply provide training in etheric navigation for those tribes who do not have it. This program should begin immediately. I have already been in contact with Eyra Fiumara, who heads the Listeners' Project for the Hegemony, and arrangements will be made at once with those who need his assistance." He gestured toward Lianvis har Kakkahaar. "Now, before opening this meeting to questions, Tiahaar Lianvis will speak to you concerning intelligence gathered by the Kakkahaar during last night's conflict. Tiahaar . . ."

Lianvis got to his feet and fastidiously arranged his robes. "I will be as succinct as possible. We now know that factions beyond this realm compete for resources to be found here. They have hitherto relied upon our ignorance in this matter in order to conduct their operations without resistance. However, it is now clear that we are, or will be, affected by this competition and we can no longer afford to be ignorant. In Kakkahaar opinion, the Tigron, Pellaz har Aralis, is our most useful and potent resource against any threat posed by the struggle between these factions. The mere fact Pellaz was attacked in the otherlanes some time ago is testament to that. Therefore, whatever our feelings for the way Thiede instated the Tigron, he is a resource we must protect. We should also apply ourselves to discovering what this realm provides to those who seek to harvest from it. We should explore the new realms that Pellaz and his kin have opened up to us. As each tribe should have Listeners at work, so they should also have hara engaged upon investigating the inner realms via the cauldron of creation . . ."

At this point, there was a stir at the entrance to the site, and Lianvis fell silent. Moon saw the crowd part to let some latecomers through. It was Galdra har Freyhella and several of his hara. Lianvis remained silent while the Freyhellans came toward the Hegemony. Without speaking, Galdra sat down, his hara around him. He looked only at Lianvis. Moon could see now how similar Galdra was to Cal. His hair was much longer, and he lacked a certain sharpness to his being, but the similarity was unmistakable. Moon glanced at Cal. His skin looked sallow, but his face was expressionless. He stared directly at the Freyhellans.

Once the Freyhellans were settled, Lianvis inclined his head to them. "Much of what I have said, you already know, tiahaara," he said. "There is little more to say."

"Have you spoken of the *sedim*?" Galdra asked.

"No," Lianvis replied. "That sphere of investigation belongs to General Aldebaran and the Hegemony."

"Would you care to speak on that matter?" Tharmifex asked Ashmael.

Ashmael didn't get up. "The *sedim* fought alongside us. We have always known they are more than a useful method of transport. We must conclude they know more about what is going on than we do. As to how we persuade them to communicate with us about that, I don't know. It might be that they can't. I'm simply grateful that they were there with us. They lost several of their number during the conflict. We have received news from Immanion that more *sedim* have appeared there. This might suggest the *sedim* are aware this matter is far from finished. If they see fit to augment their ranks in this realm, well"—he shrugged—"we can only suppose they need reinforcements." He gestured at Lianvis. "Of all hara, the Kakkahaar are renowned for their magical abilities. I admit that when Tiahaar Lianvis first came to us I was skeptical about what he told us. Now, I have seen inexplicable things with my own eyes, and have revised my opinion. I suggest that the Kakkahaar send hara to Immanion to attempt to work with the *sedim*."

Tharmifex looked around the crowd. "Does any tribe have objection to that? I'm sure Tiahaar Lianvis acknowledges that the Kakkahaar have always held a somewhat dark reputation, but I think his hara have more than proved themselves to be part of our alliance. I, for one, am happy to comply with Tiahaar Aldebaran's suggestion. Can we have a show of hands in favor?"

As far as Moon could see, very few hara did not raise their hands.

"There is one other matter," Ashmael said. He looked directly at Cal. "You have something to say to us, Calanthe, I'm sure."

Tharmifex turned to Cal also. "Do you wish to speak now, tiahaar?"

Cal waited some seconds, his hands braced against his knees, before he got to his feet. "Yes, I'll speak," he said.

Tension came into the site like a whiff of acrid smoke. Moon held his breath. He almost couldn't bear to hear what Cal might say.

"As you all know, I have been absent from Pell's side for considerable time. The reason for this is that I have been with Thiede."

Cal waited to let this fact sink in and for the soft ripple of murmurs to die down before continuing. "Thiede cannot return to this realm, simply because if he does, he would be in great danger. He knows, more than any of us, that higher beings are currently in conflict and that part of it involves our own realm. He knows about our genesis, how and why we are here. This knowledge is what has endangered him. He has intimated some of this information to me, and eventually I will reveal what I know to everyhar. Thiede has taught me certain skills he's learned, one of which being how to travel the otherlanes without the use of a *sedu*. It's possible this skill can be learned by other suitably trained hara too. We need to utilize this talent, because it's clear that Ponclast's hara have it, and presumably it could be given to others who are opposed to us. The main purpose of my training was to assist Pellaz last night, which I did. My absence from this realm was unavoidable, but essential." He smiled savagely at Galdra. "I can only extend my gratitude to those who were able to take on part of my role when I was unable to do so. To echo Tiahaar Calvel's words, we have learned it is important for us to work together. I thank you." Galdra did not even flinch. He held Cal's gaze steadily, expressionless. Cal inclined his head to Galdra, then turned back to face the main company. "Now that I can once more fulfill my duties as Tigron, I intend to apply myself to furthering this aim. The Teraghasts must be shown compassion, as should all remaining Uigenna and Varrs on this continent, and other tribes of similar nature farther afield. Tiahaar Calvel spoke of strength in unity, and he is right. But with unity should come tolerance and empathy. We must put aside petty squabbles, stand back, and see our situation from a higher perspective. We are not human; we have been given many privileges. It is time to stop abusing and misusing them, and to fulfill our potential. We are Wraeththu, unique and splendid. I have the greatest faith in my own kind."

Once he'd finished speaking, hara began to applaud him. Moon didn't blame them. Swift har Parasiel stood up and many other hara did also, including Seel, which was rather a surprise. Hara from the more ebullient tribes catcalled and whistled. Cal merely smiled and bowed. His clear musical voice, perfectly pitched, had been that of a great leader. He hadn't said much, but he'd inspired confidence and courage, through intention rather than words. He inspired hope for all that could be, standing before everyhar to display the wounds he'd received in battle. He could reach hara from other tribes far more easily than Pellaz could, simply because he was closer to them in spirit. He spoke with sincerity and nohar present could be under any illusion that he would shrink from helping them or speaking for them, if they wanted him to do so. He was their champion in the Hegemony of Immanion. Moon glanced at Galdra, and saw that the Freyhellan looked utterly defeated, as so he was.

Tyson wrapped an arm around Moon's shoulders. "I want to go home," he said.

"Oh, me too," Moon murmured. "The sooner we get started on the journey, the better."

Unfortunately, this wish was not to be granted, because the meeting continued for some time, as various tribe leaders stood up to say their piece. Moon wished he and Tyson could just slip away, but that was impossible because of where they were sitting. Eventually, however, Tharmifex brought proceedings to a close and hara began to leave the site.

Swift came to Cal's side again. "Where will you go now?" he asked.

"To Immanion," Cal said. "Well, in a day or so. Just a few things I need to finish here . . . meeting hara and so on."

"You know you're welcome in Galhea whenever you want to visit," Swift said.

Cal laughed. "I think we need to give Seel a little more time before planning holidays."

"Nothing is impossible. We've seen that."

"There will be no reunion," Cal said, "but tolerance might one day be possible. And empathy, of course. Can't forget empathy."

Swift smiled and slapped Cal on the arm. "Be well, my friend. Please stay in touch—close touch."

Cal nodded and embraced Swift closely for some moments, watched from a distance by Seel, who was clearly far from happy.

"Well," Cal said to Moon and Tyson, "you should go back to Galhea too. Come to Immanion in a couple of months. I want to talk with you."

"We'll come with you now if you wish," Tyson said.

"No, Cobweb will need you. Who knows what you'll find back home? Some rebuilding will be required, I think."

"We'll go to Imbrilim first," Swift said. "It'll take Cobweb a while to get back to Forever. There are a few things I want to attend to with the Gelaming before returning home. I want you with me, Ty. Your feckless days are over. You are now a Parsic power. Get used to it."

Tyson's shoulders slumped. "If you insist."

Cal laughed. "I hope we all see each other again soon, regardless. I too have unfinished business to attend to."

At that moment, somehar spoke behind him, in a soft, low-pitched voice. "Tiahaar Calanthe . . ."

Moon turned at the same time Cal did, and saw that the voice belonged to Galdra har Freyhella. Up close, he was stunning to look at.

Cal's body visibly stiffened. "Tiahaar," he said. "You are returning to Freygard now?"

"Yes," Galdra said. "I am." He paused. "You spoke well. I'm glad you're back."

"Thank you," Cal said. "I appreciate your words, although under the circumstances, there is little else to be said. You had your moment, tiahaar. Remember it fondly."

Hara had begun to move away from Galdra and Cal, no doubt driven by embarrassment.

"Yes," Galdra said coldly. "I had a moment, as you put it. And you need have no fear that I'll forget it. You are in your place, and I am in mine. I am content with that." With these words, he bowed and then walked away, signaling to his hara to follow him.

"That was cryptic," Tyson said.

Cal stared after Galdra. He said nothing.

CHAPTER FORTY-THREE

>·◄►··Θ·◄►··◄

As Lianvis har Kakkahaar advised, Tharmifex had arranged for Peridot to transport Pellaz back to Immanion almost immediately. After only a few hours, Pellaz had recovered physically, but had still felt dazed, confused, and lethargic. Because of his condition, Tharmifex had traveled beside him, guiding both Peridot and his own *sedu*. Once the *sedim* had broken through into a balmy Almagabran evening, Pellaz had collapsed. It seemed the otherlane jump had used up the last of his energy. The time allowed for his recovery in Megalithica had been too brief. Tharmifex had taken the Tigron directly to the Infirmary.

Now, two days later, Pellaz still lay in an infirmary bed, under strict instructions from Sheeva not to move. He was not badly injured, but his etheric body had taken a battering. To help it recover, his physical body must have total rest for at least a week. Pellaz felt numb, yet at the same time ached with a strange kind of grief that was so passionate it was almost pleasurable. Now that the conflict was over, he half expected Cal to disappear into some other realm again. Why hadn't Cal been to see him immediately? Pellaz knew, because Tharmifex had told him, that Cal had been present at the grissecon site. He knew what Cal had done there. Maybe, because of what he'd seen, Cal had no intention of coming home. Pellaz had sought to punish both Galdra and himself. At the time he'd really wanted Galdra to stop his heart. The moment he'd seen Cal in Fulminir was the moment he'd realized how much he'd betrayed Cal. He had allowed himself to fall in love with somehar else, and surely that was impossible? Cal was his life, his soul mate. The conflicting feelings made no sense. All Pellaz knew was that he hadn't questioned why Galdra hadn't been to see him. Whatever they felt for one another, it was over. It had to be, whether Cal returned to Immanion or not.

Pellaz sighed deeply, staring out of the window at the infirmary gardens. He listened to the sounds his body made, which were loud in his ears; the beat of his heart, the gurglings of his gut, the sigh of his breath. Sheeva had been to see him only half an hour before, and had left him alone to digest some rather startling information.

Pellaz sensed he was being watched and turned his head, a movement that made his eyes ache.

Cal stood at the threshold to the room, head cocked to one side. "Hi. Can I come in?"

Pellaz dared not risk a nod. "Yes."

Cal came to stand at the foot of the bed. "How are you?"

"Flattened. You?"

"Fine. The Parasilians are coming along too. I visited Azriel just before I came here. He could talk sense to me. With Aleeme, it could take a while. Cobweb and Snake came to Fulminir. Snake looks amazing . . ."

"Shut up," Pellaz said. "I couldn't give a damn about any of them at the moment."

Cal pursed his lips. "Just trying to make conversation. What do you want me to say?"

"I don't know. I really don't."

"Hmm." Cal scratched at his hair, leaving it sticking up on his head. Clearly, he hadn't washed it too recently.

"You were never there," Pellaz said. "Never when I needed you. Do you know that? I idolized you, but you had to go mad for no reason whatsoever and kill Orien. You were just too stupid and wrapped up in yourself to investigate sensibly. You could have found me. But no. It was easier to play the mad har. I ended up blood-bonded to Rue because of that. Neither were you here in Immanion before we went to Megalithica. You weren't here and somehar else *was*. You ran out on me. I wanted you so badly. What were you doing?"

"Thiede summoned me," Cal said. "I couldn't refuse. You must have heard that."

"I heard it. Does that mean I believe it? I don't know. I suppose I should have known Thiede would be involved. Even beyond this world, he works to keep us apart."

"That's wrong," Cal said. "It's time for you to see the bigger picture, Pell. It's not always just about you. Thiede knew what was going to happen. He trained me to help deal with it. If he hadn't, Ponclast could be redecorating Phaonica by now."

"Why keep me out of it? Why all the secrecy?"

"You're too public. You had your job to do, mine was different. I could do it because I'm not the face you are. The Hegemony needed you more than they needed me. You must be able to see the sense of that."

Pellaz stared at Cal, unblinking. "Who did you meet for dinner that night, just before Rue was attacked? Who is Thiede's agent? Is it anyhar I know?"

Cal was silent for a moment. "I can't tell you."

"Orien died for a similar silence."

"I know. You'll be told soon, though. Thiede should have more freedom of movement now, at least for a while. He will tell you."

Pellaz briefly closed his eyes. "What were we doing, Cal? What was it all about?"

"Lianvis had it pretty much right."

"You've spoken to him?"

"Extensively over the past couple of days. I don't know if he's changed or I have, but I like him a lot now. He'll be a useful ally."

Pellaz laughed in a choked manner. "Do you intend just to walk back in here and try to take up where you left off?"

"It is my job. The Hegemony can't exactly sack me, not now. They're not stupid. I did my bit in Megalithica. They know that. I made sure they knew. Lianvis backed me. He made it clear he'd be happy to deal with me in a diplomatic sense. I'm his Gelaming of choice, apparently."

"You have secured your boundaries, then?"

"Oh, yes," Cal said. "Count on it. At least, politically. The rest . . ." He shrugged. "That's up to you."

"The Hegemony wanted to replace you, but I expect you know that."

"Yes. Ponclast told me actually. Was that your suggestion?"

"No. I tried to fight against circumstances, but it was pointless. Some things are just meant to be."

Cal nodded distractedly. "We all have our Terzians, I suppose."

"Hardly. This was more of a Panthera. You remember him, surely, your little lapdog? The one who almost took *my* place, until you came here and threw Thiede out into the void. Only, like with Orien, you got away with that too, and now you and Thiede are big friends. How convenient. I wonder what Panthera's doing now?"

Cal rubbed his face with both hands. "This isn't getting us anywhere, Pell."

"Then stop bitching. Are you jealous?"

"Hell yes! You could take aruna with a hundred hara and not one of them would matter. I'd cheer from the fucking sidelines. But this was different, wasn't it?"

Pellaz was silent for a moment. "He's kept away. You know why? Because of you. He'll step out of it now, Cal. That's the way he is. He'd never try to fight you for me, or even beg and plead with me. It's called integrity, or nobility, or something . . ."

"I don't want to know. He sounds far too saintly to be even remotely bearable."

"If you'd been here, it wouldn't have happened, but you weren't. You were saving the world for Thiede. And yet, ultimately, it was me, along with those close to me, who dealt with both Ponclast and his allies. What *was* your job, Cal?"

Cal moved around the bed and sat down beside Pell. "My job? To save our son. To try and negotiate with Ponclast. To be there for you when you needed me. They weren't world-saving things, Pell, but significant, nonetheless. You are the world saver, not me."

"Our son . . . where is he?"

"Safe. I don't know where exactly and I don't want to. It's best for him. This isn't the end, Pell. You do know that, don't you?"

"Abrimel . . ." Pellaz said. He wiped a hand over his face. "I just remembered. I saw Abrimel in Fulminir with a harling. What happened, Cal? Did Ash's hara find them?"

"They found Abrimel," Cal said, "but no harling. Are you sure about that?"

"Yes. Completely. That . . . *thing* you pulled off me must have taken it."

"The charming Diablo. That makes sense. He wasn't found either. Most of the Teraghasts scattered like rats in an opened sewer once the Hasmallim departed. What will you do with Abrimel?"

Pellaz closed his eyes briefly. "I don't know. Let Tharmifex deal with it."

"You've always been such a doting father, haven't you? I take it Rue doesn't know yet."

"He's been here a few times, but I didn't mention Bree. I only just remembered about it."

"You should have tried to be a father to Abrimel, Pell. Maybe you should show mercy now. I've missed out on a lot with Ty. The puffed-up feelings of pride he inspires in me now sometimes feel like illness! It's most odd, but not unpleasant. He is chesna with Moon. What an incestuous family we are!"

"Cal . . ."

"What?"

Pellaz drew in his breath. "I had some very bad news today."

Cal reached for one of Pell's hands, and Pellaz gripped his fingers tightly. He felt, now he'd made contact, he'd never be able to let go. His eyes filled up. He couldn't help himself.

"Hey," Cal said, leaning forward to stroke his face. "How bad can it be? Tell me."

"The grissecon . . . at the end of it . . . I went out of myself. I wasn't in control."

"I saw that. I called you back. Do you remember?"

"Yes." Pellaz locked gazes with Cal. "I wasn't in control. I wasn't aware of it happening. Sheeva, one of the surgeons here, told me a short while ago . . ."

"What? Are you hurt?"

Pellaz felt the tears spill from his eyes. He wouldn't hide them. Perhaps it had always been a mistake to do so. "No . . . Galdra made me with pearl, Cal. Sheeva could tell from the tests he ran on me to make sure my insides were okay."

Cal blanched a little. His eyes widened, but he said nothing.

"I told you it was bad. Apart from the fact that it's the last thing I ever wanted to do, I wonder what kind of creature might have been created. That place where we were: it was not a good place to create life. There was too much dark flotsam floating about. Weird things."

"Have you asked this Sheeva about it? Can't he deal with it?"

"No. I asked him and he said we don't know enough about our physiology. We are not like women. We can't just get rid . . ."

"Oh." Cal twisted his mouth to one side. "One day, you might have an heir who is nonproblematical. What are you going to do?"

"Ask Sheeva to drug me for the duration? I don't know. Send it to Freygard, maybe. Galdra doesn't know."

"Who does?"

"Just Sheeva. And now you."

Cal was silent for some moments. "Well, if you give birth to a monster, most hara would happily believe it was mine. Also, if it resembles its father, it's fortunate you chose a har who looked like me. We've just got back

together. We're blissed out, so much in love. We want to make a public statement about that, don't we? We lost a son—as far as everyhar else is concerned. Seems the obvious solution to me."

"You'd do that?"

"Of course. I don't want the Freyhellan having any claim over you. You
might think he's a saint, but he's still har, and leader of his tribe. Only an idiot
would pass up having that much influence in the Hegemony. If Abrimel's dis-
graced, and our son is kept in hiding, your pearl is the next in line. How loyal
is Sheeva?"

"Loyal enough not to countenance outside interference in Aralisian matters, I'd say."

"Better call him in, then."

"Go and find him."

Cal stood up, but Pellaz reached for his hand to keep him by the bed. "Cal,
I hope we are still in love."

"Course we are. Soul mates. Love that transcends death, space, and time.
Everyhar knows that. We're a legend."

"Galdra *was* my Terzian. I don't want to deceive you about that. He still is."

"I know. But he's not here, and I am. And I will fight for you, Pellaz. I realized that the minute I saw you joined to some har who wasn't me. I was in two
minds about coming back here, but now I know. This har I'm in love with, he's
not the one I took to Saltrock. He's somehar else. Sometimes, he drives me to
distraction, sometimes I could weep for love of him, but I want to get to know
him better, regardless."

"Thank you."

"Don't go away. I'll be right back, loyal Sheeva in tow."

"No, you don't understand. *Thank you.*"

Cal shook Pell's hand a little. "It's okay. Don't go all strange on me. You
look mad. Relax." Cal blew a kiss and went out the door.

"That's all I ever wanted to hear," Pellaz said, aloud to the empty room.

Prisoners in Immanion were confined in the basement of the Hegalion. There
were no proper imprisonment facilities, because the Gelaming had no need of
them. However, Abrimel har Aralis, traitorous son, had to be held somewhere.
The Hegemony had yet to decide his fate.

Velaxis had been the har to tell Caeru about Abrimel. Fortunately, the parage Katarin was still in Immanion. On the evening that Velaxis arrived with
his bad tidings, and Caeru descended into a fit of grief and horror, Katarin

was able to offer her support. For hours, the Tigrina ranted that everyhar was mistaken: Abrimel had been bewitched, brainwashed, manipulated. He would not believe Velaxis's calm repetitions of the facts. Abrimel himself had confessed to joining forces with Ponclast. He had no remorse about it. Eventually, Caeru had ordered Velaxis from his presence, and announced their friendship was over. He spent the rest of the night weeping in Katarin's arms.

The following day, Caeru sent a messenger to summon Velaxis back to his apartment. Velaxis came at once, and made no mention of the previous evening's events.

"I want to see my son," Caeru said. "Can you arrange that?"

"Of course," Velaxis said. "I'll accompany you."

"Thank you," Caeru said.

They rode in a covered carriage to the Hegalion and entered it through a back door, so that nohar saw the Tigrina arrive. Deferential officials, clearly embarrassed by the situation, conducted Caeru and Velaxis to the basement. Here, Abrimel sat on his bed in a small room with no windows. An uneaten meal lay on a table nearby. He looked very ill, his face sunken, his hair matted. Caeru uttered a cry and rushed to embrace him, but Abrimel did not return the gesture.

"Is it true?" Caeru asked.

"Yes," Abrimel said. "I am now a prisoner of war."

"Pell will do something," Caeru insisted. He knelt at Abrimel's feet, his son's limp hands clasped in his own.

"Do what?" Abrimel asked. He looked over Caeru's head at Velaxis. "Do you know what they intend to do?"

"No," Velaxis said. "It hasn't yet been decided. At best, you're looking at some kind of exile, certainly in confinement."

"Will the pious Gelaming stoop to execution?"

Caeru uttered a wail.

"No," Velaxis said, "that is more the style of your erstwhile chesnari."

"Don't call him that!" Caeru said. "He wasn't that."

"He was," Abrimel said. "We had a son." He looked at Velaxis again. "Is Ponclast dead? Nohar will tell me."

"I don't know," Velaxis replied. "Pellaz didn't kill him. He was exiled. That's all I can tell you at this point. You won't be seeing him again."

"What of our child?"

"It was not found in Fulminir."

Abrimel pulled his hands away from Caeru's hold and put them over his face. He did not weep, perhaps because every last tear inside him had already been wept.

Velaxis came to Abrimel's side and put a hand on the top of his head. "I'll do what I can, Bree, I promise. Cal will speak for you. You are not without some support."

Bree lowered his hands. "I don't want *his* support!"

"You're in no position to be fussy about that," Velaxis said. "Whatever your feelings for Cal, you should know he will always champion those who need his assistance. I'll make sure of it."

"I still love you, Bree," Caeru said. "You are still my son. I don't care what you did."

"You're adept at that, I know," Abrimel said callously. "Anyhar can trample over you, and you'll still come back, tail wagging! I wished you dead. I wished you all dead!"

Caeru knew he should feel hurt by those words, but all he heard was the bewildered ranting of a child. He took Abrimel in his arms, and kissed his face.

Abrimel threw back his head and let out a ragged howl. It seemed to go on forever.

Caeru kept hold of him, weeping for both of them. He had lost two sons. It was too cruel.

When they went back out into the sunlight, Velaxis took Caeru's arm. "Let's go for a drink," he said. "Let's go for a walk."

Caeru nodded. "It feels wrong . . . being free. Vel . . . ?"

"Yes?"

"Can't anything be done?"

"He has no remorse, Rue. You have to accept that. Pell treated him with indifference, and this is just the way it's turned out. Nohar could have foreseen this. Nothing can change it. You just have to learn to live with what is."

Caeru shook his head. "I should hate Pell for it, but I can't. Why did Bree go this way, Vel? Why did it happen? It didn't have to."

"It just did," Velaxis said. "He made his choices, that's all."

"Take me to see him every day, for as long as he's here."

"If that's what you want."

They went down to the harbor and watched the ships for a while. The Freyhellan fleet had gone. Immanion was peaceful, and felt strangely empty, now all the tribal delegates had left. Hara went about their business as they'd always done. Nohar recognized the Tigrina, standing upon the quay, throwing stones into the water. A breeze came softly from the south, smelling of flowers, even though the leaves were falling from the trees along the quayside avenue.

"I can smell the future," Caeru said.

Velaxis stood behind the Tigrina and put his arms around him, pressing his hands against Caeru's stomach. "You've lost less than you know," he said.

EPILOGUE

Galhea looked as if it had been abandoned years before. Forever had been ransacked, presumably by Teraghasts who'd returned to finish off any hara remaining in the area, but at least it was still standing.

Cobweb walked with Snake through the house, and in every room a hundred memories assailed him.

"It will be different," Snake said. "But that will not make it less than it was before."

Cobweb stood in the center of the main living room, where all the long windows had shattered, and took Snake in his arms. "Cobweb is dead," he said sorrowfully.

Snake kissed the top of his head: he was so much taller than Cobweb now. "No he isn't. Far from it." He began to undo the braid of Cobweb's hair, pulling it out of confinement so it fell around them in a cloudy mass. They shared breath in the dying light, leaves blowing in from the terrace around their feet.

Swift and Seel came in from the garden; they'd wanted to spend some moments at Ithiel's grave, beneath the cedars by the lake. Swift looked somber, his eyes were wet.

"So," Cobweb said, pulling away from Snake. "Dinner. I'll go and see if Yarrow and Bryony have got the kitchen in any kind of order yet. Swift, scour

this house and the town beyond if necessary for alcohol, preferably sheh. Tonight, we celebrate in the ruins. We shout at the future. You'd better be ready
for it."

Swift smiled a little. "I think I need to be drunk to see beyond the mess and
imagine this as a home again."

"It will be," Cobweb said. "Knock down some walls. Build others. Let's
change things we'd never have changed before."

"I like the idea of a converted attic," Snake said. "With roof lights to look
at the stars. We can sleep there."

"Good idea," Cobweb said. "We've never made use of the attics and they're
huge. We'll make new rooms."

Cobweb went to the kitchens, wishing he was as optimistic as he'd sounded.
In fact, the state of the house depressed him utterly. When he looked at stairs,
in the main hallway, where shards of the fallen chandelier lurked dangerously
amid the rubble, he saw Swift coming down to his feybraiha celebration, so
many years ago, a beautiful young har trembling at the brink of maturity. In the
kitchen, he saw Ithiel, leaning against the frame of the open back door, and the
summer stable yard beyond. When he laid eyes on Yarrow, helping his staff
clean up, Cobweb saw a ghost of past festival preparations, pots bubbling on
the range, the table piled high with food. Bryony was a human girl again and
somewhere upstairs, an interloping har named Cal took aruna with Terzian,
who was hopelessly besotted. Some things in the past it was better to forget.

"Tonight, we all eat together," Cobweb said to Bryony. "All the staff,
everyhar. Do we have enough?"

"Just about," Bryony said. "Yarrow had somehar go out to the fields and
fetch a lamb. It's quite big."

"Good."

Families were returning to the town, coming down from the cloud forests,
and along the old roads that led to the sea. When he went out into the garden,
Cobweb saw the light of fires below the hill. He heard voices singing. And
there were Moon and Tyson riding back from town up the long driveway;
magnificent hara, the flowers of Galhea. Ferany would not visit Forever for
some time, Cobweb thought. But what must be must be. Not everyhar could
have a happy ending. This moved his thoughts to Azriel and Aleeme, who
were still under Gelaming care, too sick to be moved via the otherlanes or
overland. For now, Cobweb had sent Aleeme's harling to Lisia, for if anyhar
could help the wretched child, Lisia was the one. They would have to wait and
find out what Aleeme felt about the whole experience, but Cobweb himself
was uncomfortable with the idea of a child of pelki being reared in his home.

Cobweb waved to Moon and Tyson and went back into the house. Snake was waiting for him. "I watched you there outside," he said. "You needed time alone."

"We are never alone," Cobweb said. "This is something I've learned, and there are no benevolent angels or kindly gods to watch over us. There is something else, and it's watching us through the tall grass."

"We have dehara," Snake said. "We are not defenseless."

"That's true. And we have Lileem. One day . . ."

"A parage I hope very much to meet in person," Snake said. "Tonight, I must dance. I haven't danced for many years."

"We'll dance," Cobweb said. "We'll dance with dehara."

Arm in arm, they rejoined their family. Outside, the fields spread out beneath the moon and the sky went on forever. The world looked just the same.